THE
RESTORER

THE
RESTORER

AMANDA
STEVENS

MIRA®

ISBN-13: 978-1-61793-927-3

THE RESTORER

Copyright © 2011 by Marilyn Medlock Amann

This book is dedicated to
Leanne Amann and Carla Luan
for always going above and beyond.
And to my dad, Melvie Medlock,
for instilling in me a love of ghost stories.

ONE

I was nine when I saw my first ghost.

My father and I were raking leaves in the cemetery where he'd worked for years as the caretaker. It was early autumn, not yet cool enough for a sweater, but on that particular afternoon there was a noticeable bite in the air as the sun dipped toward the horizon. A mild breeze carried the scent of wood smoke and pine needles, and as the wind picked up, a flock of black birds took flight from the treetops and glided like a storm cloud across the pale blue sky.

I put a hand to my eyes as I watched them. When my gaze finally dropped, I saw him in the distance. He stood beneath the drooping branches of a live oak, and the green-gold light that glimmered down through the Spanish moss cast a preternatural glow on the space around him. But he was in shadows, so much so that I wondered for a moment if he was only a mirage.

As the light faded, he became more defined, and I could even make out his features. He was old, even more ancient than my father, with white hair brushing the collar of his suit coat and eyes that seemed to burn with an inner flame.

My father was bent to his work and as the rake moved steadily over the graves, he said under his breath, "Don't look at him."

I turned in surprise. "You see him, too?"

"Yes, I see him. Now get back to work."

"But who is he—"

"I said don't look at him!"

His sharp tone stunned me. I could count on one hand the number of times he'd ever raised his voice to me. That he had done so now, without provocation, made me instantly tear up. The one thing I could never abide was my father's disapproval.

"Amelia."

There was regret in his tone and what I would later come to understand as pity in his blue eyes.

"I'm sorry I spoke so harshly, but it's important that you do as I say. You mustn't look at him," he said in a softer tone. "Any of them."

"Is he a—"

"Yes."

Something cold touched my spine and it was all I could do to keep my gaze trained on the ground.

"Papa," I whispered. I had always called him this. I don't know why I'd latched on to such an old-fashioned moniker, but it suited him. He had always seemed very old to me, even though he was not yet fifty. For as long as I could remember, his face had been heavily lined and weathered, like the cracked mud of a dry creek bed, and his shoulders drooped from years of bending over the graves.

But despite his poor posture, there was great dignity

in his bearing and much kindness in his eyes and in his smile. I loved him with every fiber of my nine-year-old being. He and Mama were my whole world. Or had been, until that moment.

I saw something shift in Papa's face and then his eyes slowly closed in resignation. He laid aside our rakes and placed his hand on my shoulder.

"Let's rest for a spell," he said.

We sat on the ground, our backs to the ghost, as we watched dusk creep in from the Lowcountry. I couldn't stop shivering, even though the waning light was still warm on my face.

"Who is he?" I finally whispered, unable to bear the quiet any longer.

"I don't know."

"Why can't I look at him?" It occurred to me then that I was more afraid of what Papa was about to tell me than I was of the ghost.

"You don't want him to know that you can see him."

"Why not?" When he didn't answer, I picked up a twig and poked it through a dead leaf, spinning it like a pinwheel between my fingers. "Why not, Papa?"

"Because what the dead want more than anything is to be a part of our world again. They're like parasites, drawn to our energy, feeding off our warmth. If they know you can see them, they'll cling to you like blight. You'll never be rid of them. And your life will never again be your own."

I don't know if I completely understood what he told me, but the notion of being haunted forever terrified me.

"Not everyone can see them," he said. "For those of us who can, there are certain precautions we must take in order to protect ourselves and those around us. The first and most important is this—never acknowledge the dead. Don't look at them, don't speak to them, don't let them sense your fear. Even when they touch you."

A chill shimmied over me. "They…touch you?"

"Sometimes they do."

"And you can feel it?"

He drew a breath. "Yes. You can feel it."

I threw away the stick, and pulled up my knees, wrapping my arms tightly around them. Somehow, even at my young age, I was able to remain calm on the outside, but my insides had gone numb with dread.

"The second thing you must remember is this," Papa said. "Never stray too far from hallowed ground."

"What's hallowed ground?"

"The old part of this cemetery is hallowed ground. There are other places, too, where you'll be safe. Natural places. After a while, instinct will lead you to them. You'll know where and when to seek them out."

I tried to digest this puzzling detail, but I really didn't understand the concept of hallowed ground, although I'd always known the old part of the cemetery was special.

Nestled against the side of a hill and protected by the outstretched arms of the live oaks, Rosehill was shady and beautiful, the most serene place I could imagine. It had been closed to the public for years, and sometimes as I wandered alone—and often lonely—through the lush fern beds and long curtains of silvery moss, I pretended the crumbling angels were wood nymphs and fairies and I their ruler, queen of my very own graveyard kingdom.

My father's voice brought me back to the real world. "Rule Number Three," he said. "Keep your distance from those who are haunted. If they seek you out, turn away from them, for they constitute a terrible threat and cannot be trusted."

"Are there any more rules?" I asked, because I didn't know what else I was supposed to say.

"Yes, but we'll talk about the rest later. It's getting late. We should probably head home before your mother starts to worry."

"Can she see them?"

"No. And you mustn't tell her that you can."

"Why not?"

"She doesn't believe in ghosts. She'd think you're imagining things. Or telling stories."

"I would never lie to Mama!"

"I know that. But this has to be our secret. When you're older, you'll understand. For now, just do your best to follow the rules and everything will be fine. Can you do that?"

"Yes, Papa." But even as I promised, it was all I could do to keep from glancing over my shoulder.

The breeze picked up and the chill inside me deepened. Somehow, I managed to keep from turning, but I knew the ghost had drifted closer. Papa knew it, too. I could feel the tension in him as he murmured, "No more talking. Just remember what I told you."

"I will, Papa."

The ghost's frigid breath feathered down the back of my neck and I started to tremble. I couldn't help myself.

"Cold?" my father asked in his normal voice. "Well, it's getting to be that time of year. Summer can't last forever."

I didn't say anything. I couldn't. The ghost's hands were in my hair. He lifted the golden strands, still warm from the sun, and let them sift through his fingers.

Papa got to his feet and pulled me up with him. The ghost skittered away for a moment, then floated back.

"We best be getting on home. Your mother's cooking

up a mess of shrimp tonight." He picked up the rakes and hoisted them to his shoulder.

"And grits?" I asked, though my voice was hardly louder than a whisper.

"I expect so. Come on. Let's cut through the old cemetery. I want to show you the work I've done on some of the gravestones. I know how much you love the angels."

He took my hand and squeezed my fingers in reassurance as we set out across the cemetery, the ghost at our heels.

By the time we reached the old section, Papa had already pulled the key from his pocket. He turned the lock and the heavy iron gate swung silently inward on well-oiled hinges.

We stepped through into that dusky sanctuary and suddenly I wasn't afraid anymore. My newfound courage emboldened me. I pretended to trip and when I bent to tie my shoelaces, I glanced back at the gate. The ghost hovered just outside. It was obvious he was unable to enter, and I couldn't help but give a childish smirk.

When I straightened, Papa glared down at me. "Rule Number Four," he said sternly. "Never, ever tempt fate."

The childhood memory flitted away as the waitress approached with my first course—roasted green-tomato soup, which I'd been told was a house specialty—along with the pecan pie I planned to have for dessert. Six months ago, I'd moved from Columbia to Charleston, making it my home base, but I'd never had dinner at any of the upscale waterfront restaurants. My budget normally didn't allow for fine dining, but tonight was special.

As the waitress topped off my champagne, I caught her curious, sidelong glance, but I didn't let it bother me.

Just because I happened to be alone was no reason to deprive myself of a celebration.

Earlier, I'd taken a leisurely stroll along the Battery, pausing at the very tip of the peninsula to enjoy the sunset. Behind me, the whole city was bathed in crimson; before me, a fractured sky shifted into kaleidoscopic patterns of rose, lavender and gold. A Carolina sunset never failed to move me, but with the approaching twilight everything had turned gray. Mist drifted in from the sea and settled over the treetops like a silver canopy. As I watched the gauzy swirl from a table by the window, my elation faded.

Dusk is a dangerous time for people like me. An in-between time just as the seashore and the edge of a forest are in-between places. The Celts had a name for these landscapes—*caol' ait*. Thin places where the barrier between our world and the next is but a gossamer veil.

Turning from the window, I sipped champagne, determined not to let the encroaching spirit world spoil my celebration. After all, it wasn't every day an unexpected windfall came my way, and for barely lifting a finger.

My work usually consists of many hours of manual labor for modest pay. I'm a cemetery restorer. I travel all over the South, cleaning up forgotten and abandoned graveyards and repairing worn and broken headstones. It's painstaking, sometimes back-breaking work, and a huge cemetery can take years to restore fully, so there is no such thing as instant gratification in my profession. But I love what I do. We Southerners worship our ancestors, and I'm gratified that my efforts in some small way enable people of the present to more fully appreciate those who came before us.

In my spare time, I run a blog called *Digging Graves,* where taphophiles—lovers of cemeteries—and other like-minded folks can exchange photographs, restoration techniques and, yes, even the occasional ghost story. I'd started the blog as a hobby, but over the past few months, my readership had exploded.

It all started with the restoration of an old cemetery in the small, northeast Georgia town of Samara. The freshest grave there was over a hundred years old and some of the earliest dated back to pre–Civil War days.

The cemetery had been badly neglected since the local historical society ran out of money in the sixties. The sunken graves were overgrown, the headstones worn nearly smooth by erosion. Vandals had been busy there, too, and the first order of business was to pick up and cart away nearly four decades of trash.

Rumors of a haunting had persisted for years and some of the townspeople refused to set foot through the gates. It was hard to find and keep good help, even though I knew for a fact there were no ghosts in Samara Cemetery.

I ended up doing most of the work myself, but once the cleanup was completed, the attitude of the locals transformed dramatically. They said it was as if a dark cloud had been lifted from their town, and some went so far as to claim that the restoration had been both physical and spiritual.

A reporter and film crew from a station in Athens were sent out to interview me and when the clip turned up online, someone noticed a reflection in the background that had a vague, humanlike form. It appeared to be floating over the cemetery, ascending heavenward.

There was nothing supernatural about the anomaly, merely a trick of the light, but dozens of paranormal websites ran with it and the YouTube video went viral. That's when people from all over the world started flocking to *Digging Graves,* where I was known as the Graveyard

Queen. The traffic became so heavy that the producers of a ghost hunter television program made an offer to advertise on my site.

Which is how I came to be sipping champagne and savoring a wild mushroom tart at the glamorous Pavilion on the Bay restaurant.

Life was treating me well these days, I thought a little smugly, and then I saw the ghost.

Even worse, he saw me.

TWO

I don't often recognize the faces of the entities I encounter, but at times I have experienced a prickle of déjà vu, as if I might have glimpsed them in passing. I'm fortunate that in all my twenty-seven years, I've never lost anyone truly close to me. I do remember an encounter back in high school with the ghost of a teacher, though. Her name was Miss Compton and she'd been killed in a car crash over a holiday long weekend. When classes resumed the following Tuesday, I'd stayed late to work on a project and I saw her spirit hovering in the dusky hallway near my locker. The manifestation had caught me off guard because in life, Miss Compton had been so demure and unassuming. I hadn't expected her to come back grasping and greedy, hungrily seeking what she could never have again.

Somehow I managed to keep my poise as I grabbed my backpack and closed my locker. She trailed me down the long hallway and through the front door, her chill breath on my neck, her icy hands clutching at my clothes. It was a long time before the air around me warmed and I knew she'd dissolved back into the netherworld. After that I made sure I was safely away from school before twilight, which meant no extracurricular activities. No ball games, no parties, no prom. I couldn't take the chance of running into Miss Compton again. I was too afraid she might somehow latch on to me and then my life would never again be my own.

I turned my attention back to the ghost in the restaurant. I recognized him, too, but I didn't know him personally. I'd seen his picture on the front page of the *Post and Courier* a few weeks ago. His name was Lincoln McCoy, a prominent Charleston businessman who'd slaughtered his wife and children one night and then shot himself in the head rather than surrender to the S.W.A.T. team that had surrounded his house.

The way he appeared to me now was quite ethereal, with no evidence of the wrongs he'd committed on himself or his family. Except for his eyes. They were dark and blazing, yet at the same time icy. As he peered at me across the restaurant, I saw a faint smile touch his ghostly features.

Instead of flinching or glancing away in fright, I stared right back at him. He'd drifted into the restaurant behind an elderly couple who were now waiting to be seated. As his eyes held mine, I pretended to look right through him, even going so far as to wave at an imaginary acquaintance.

The ghost glanced over his shoulder, and at that precise moment, a waitress saw my wave and lifted one finger, indicating she would be with me in a moment. I nodded, smiled and picked up my champagne glass as I turned back to the window. I didn't look at the ghost again, but

I felt his frigid presence a moment later as he glided past my table, still trailing the old couple.

I wondered why he had attached himself to that particular pair and if on some level they were aware of his presence. I wanted to warn them, but I couldn't without giving myself away. And that was what *he* wanted. What he desperately craved. To be acknowledged by the living so that he could feel a part of our world again.

Hands steady, I paid my check and left the restaurant without looking back.

Once outside, I allowed myself to relax as I walked back along White Point Gardens, in no particular hurry to seek the sanctuary of my home. Whatever spirits had managed to slip through the veil at dusk were already among us and as long as I remained vigilant until the sun came up, I needn't cower from the icy drafts and swirling gray forms.

The mist had thickened. The Civil War cannons and statues in the park were invisible from the walkway, the bandstand and live oaks nothing more than vague silhouettes. But I could smell the flowers, that luscious blend of what I had come to think of as the Charleston scent—magnolia, hyacinth and Confederate jasmine.

Somewhere in the darkness, a foghorn sounded and out in the harbor, a lighthouse flashed warnings to the cargo ships traversing the narrow channel between Sullivan's Island and Fort Sumter. As I stopped to watch the light, an uneasy chill crept over me. Someone was behind me in the fog. I could hear the soft yet unmistakable clop of leather soles against the seawall.

The footfalls stopped suddenly and I turned with a breathless shiver. For a long moment, nothing happened and I began to think I might have imagined the sound.

Then he emerged from the veil of mist, sending the blood out of my heart with a painful contraction.

Tall, broad-shouldered and dressed all in black, he might have stepped from the dreamy hinterland of some childhood fable. I could barely make out his features, but I knew instinctively that he was handsome and brooding. The way he carried himself, the almost painful glare of his eyes through the mist, sent icy needles stinging down my spine.

He was no ghost, but dangerous to me nonetheless and so compelling I couldn't tear my gaze away as he moved toward me. And now I could see water droplets glistening in his dark hair and the gleam of a silver chain tucked inside the collar of his dark shirt.

Behind him, translucent and hardly discernible from the mist, were two ghosts, that of a woman and a little girl. They were both looking at me, too, but I kept my gaze trained on the man.

"Amelia Gray?"

"Yes?" Since my blog had become so popular, I was occasionally approached by strangers who recognized me from website photos or from the infamous ghost video. The South, particularly the Charleston area, was home to dozens of avid taphophiles, but I didn't think this man was a fan or a fellow aficionado. His eyes were cold, his manner aloof. He had not sought me out to chitchat about headstones.

"I'm John Devlin, Charleston P.D." As he spoke, he hauled out his wallet and presented his ID and badge, which I obligingly glanced at even though my heart had started to beat an agonizing staccato.

A police detective!

This couldn't be good.

Something terrible must have happened. My parents

were getting on in years. What if one of them had had an accident or taken ill or...

Tamping down an unreasonable panic, I slipped my hands into the pockets of my trench coat. If something had happened to Mama or Papa, someone would have called. This wasn't about them. This was about me.

I waited for an explanation as those lovely apparitions hovered protectively around John Devlin. From what I could see of the woman's features, she'd been stunning, with high cheekbones and proudly flaring nostrils that suggested a Creole heritage. She wore a pretty summer dress that swirled like gossamer around her long, slender legs.

The child looked to have been four or five when she died. Dark curls framed her pale face as she floated at the man's side, reaching out now and then to clutch at his leg or tap on his knee.

He seemed oblivious to their presence, though he was clearly haunted. It showed in his face, in the eyes that were as hooded as they were piercing, and I couldn't help wondering about his relationship to the ghosts.

I kept my eyes focused on his face. He was watching me, too, with an air of suspicion and superiority that could make dealing with the police an unpleasant ordeal, even over something as trivial as a parking ticket.

"What do you want?" I asked, though I hadn't meant for the query to sound so blunt. I'm not a confrontational person. Years of living with ghosts had whittled away my spontaneity, leaving me overly disciplined and reserved.

Devlin moved a step closer and my hands curled into fists inside my coat pockets. A thrill chased across my skull and I wanted to tell him to keep his distance, *don't come any closer*. I said nothing, of course, as I braced myself against the frigid breath of his phantoms.

"A mutual acquaintance suggested I get in touch with you," he said.

"And who would that be?"

"Camille Ashby. She thought you might be able to help me out."

"With what?"

"A police matter."

Now I was more curious than cautious—which made me also foolish.

Dr. Camille Ashby was an administrator at Emerson University, an elite, private college with powerful alumni that included some of the most prominent lawyers, judges and businessmen in South Carolina. Recently, I'd accepted a commission to restore an old cemetery located on university property. One of Dr. Ashby's stipulations was that I not post any pictures on my blog until the restoration was complete.

I understood her concern. The dismal condition of the graveyard wasn't a favorable reflection on a university that espoused the traditions and ethics of the old South. As Benjamin Franklin had put it: *One can tell the morals of a culture by the way they treat their dead.*

Indeed.

What I didn't yet know was why she'd sent John Devlin to find me.

"I understand you've been working in Oak Grove Cemetery," he said.

I suppressed a shudder.

Oak Grove was one of those rare graveyards that evoked uneasiness, that literally made my skin crawl. The only other time I'd experienced a similar sensation was while visiting a small cemetery in Kansas that had been dubbed one of the seven gateways to hell.

I adjusted my collar against the glacial prickles at my nape. "What's this about?"

He ignored my question and asked one of his own. "When was the last time you were there?"

"A few days ago."

"Can you be more specific?"

"Last Friday."

"Five days," he murmured. "You're sure about that?"

"Yes, of course. A big storm blew in that night and it's been raining off and on ever since. I've been waiting for the ground to dry out."

"Camille...Dr. Ashby said you've been photographing the graves." He waited for my nod. "I'd like to take a look at those shots."

Something about his tone, about this whole conversation put me on the defensive. Or maybe it was his ghosts. "Can you tell me why? And I'd also like to know how you found me tonight."

"You mentioned your dinner plans to Dr. Ashby."

"I may have named the restaurant, but I didn't tell her I'd be taking an after-dinner stroll, because I didn't know it myself at the time."

"Call that part a hunch," he said.

A hunch...or had he followed me from the Pavilion?

"Dr. Ashby has my number. Why didn't you just call me?"

"I tried that. No answer."

Well, yes, there was that. I'd turned off my phone for the evening. Still, I didn't like any of this. John Devlin was a haunted man and that made him a dangerous man in my world.

He was also persistent and perhaps intuitive, so the quicker I rid myself of him the better.

"Why don't you give me a call first thing in the morning?" I said in a brisk, dismissive tone. "I'm sure whatever it is can wait until then."

"No, I'm afraid it can't. This has to be done tonight."

I shivered at his foreboding tone. "How ominous-sounding. Well, you've certainly gone to a great deal of trouble to track me down, so I suppose you may as well tell me why."

His gaze swept the darkness behind me and I had to resist the urge to glance over my shoulder. "The rain uncovered a body in one of the old graves at Oak Grove."

It wasn't unheard of for old bones to wash up over time, due to rotting coffins and eroding soil.

"Do you mean skeletal remains?" I asked with some delicacy.

"No, I mean fresh remains. A homicide victim," he replied bluntly. His gaze lit on my face, studying me intently as if gauging my reaction.

A homicide. In the cemetery where I'd been working alone.

"That's why you want my photographs. You're hoping they'll help pinpoint how long the body has been there," I said.

"If we're lucky."

This I understood and was only too happy to cooperate. "I use a digital camera, but I print out most of my shots. I happen to have some enlargements in my briefcase, if you'd care to follow me back to my car." I nodded in the direction from which we'd both come. "I can email you the rest of the images as soon as I get home."

"Thanks. That would be helpful."

I started walking and he fell into step beside me.

"One other thing," he said.

"Yes?"

"I'm sure I don't have to school you on cemetery protocol, but there are certain precautions that have to be taken when dealing with an old graveyard like Oak Grove. We wouldn't want to inadvertently desecrate a burial site. Dr. Ashby mentioned something about unmarked graves."

"As you said, it's an old cemetery. One of the sections is pre–Civil War. Over that much time, it's not unusual for headstones to get moved or go missing altogether."

"How do you locate the graves when that happens?"

"Any number of ways, depending on whether cost is a factor—radar, resistivity, conductivity, magnetometry. Remote sensing methods are preferred because they're noninvasive. As is grave dousing."

"Grave dousing. Is that anything like water witching?" His tone gave away his skepticism.

"Yes, same principle. A Y-shaped rod or sometimes a pendulum is used to divine the location of a grave. It's been roundly debunked in scientific circles, but believe it or not, I've seen it work."

"I'll take your word for it." He paused. "Dr. Ashby said you'd completed the preliminary mapping, so I assume you've already located the graves by one means or another."

"Dr. Ashby is being optimistic. I have a lot more research to do before I'll know where all the bodies are buried, so to speak."

He didn't crack a smile at my feeble pun. "But you must have a general idea."

Something in his voice bothered me and I stopped walking to glance up at him. Earlier, I'd thought his dark good looks had an almost fallen angel quality, but now he appeared merely tough and persistent. "Why do I get the impression you're not just asking for a copy of my map?"

"It would save us a lot of time and potentially some

bad PR if we have an expert consultant on hand during the exhumation. We'll pay you for your time, of course."

"Since you're dealing with an old grave, I suggest you contact the state archaeologist. Her name is Temple Lee. I used to work for her. You'll be in good hands."

"We'd be hard-pressed to get someone down here from Columbia tonight, and as I said, this can't wait until morning. The minute that body was discovered, the clock started ticking. The sooner we get an ID, the greater our chances for a satisfactory resolution. Dr. Ashby seems to think your credentials will pacify the committee."

"The committee?"

"Local preservationists, members of the Historical Society, fat-cat alumni. They've got enough clout to raise a real ruckus if we don't handle this thing according to procedure. You know the cemetery and you know the rules. All you have to do is make sure we don't step on any toes. So to speak." This time, I did see a faint smile.

"And that's it?"

"That's it." He glanced out over the water. "Once the fog lifts, we could get more rain. We need to get this thing done."

This thing done.

What a portentous turn of phrase.

"As I said, we'll pay you."

"It's not that." I didn't like the idea of going out to Oak Grove after dark, but I also didn't see how I could refuse. Civic duty notwithstanding, Camille Ashby currently controlled my purse strings. It was in my best interests to keep her happy. "I'm hardly dressed for the occasion, but I suppose if you think I can be of some help…"

"I do. Let's grab those photos and head on out there." He took my elbow, as if to propel me forward before I could change my mind.

His touch was strangely magnetic. It both attracted and repelled me, and as I pulled away, I found myself dredging up my father's third rule and silently repeating it like a mantra:

Keep your distance from those who are haunted.
Keep your distance from those who are haunted.

"I'd rather drive myself, if you don't mind."

He gave me a sidelong glance as we continued along the walkway. "Whatever you want. It's your call."

We fell silent as we walked back through the mist, the lights from the East Bay mansions softly illuminating the ghost child floating between us. I was careful not to touch her. Careful not to look down as I felt the chilly brush of her hand against my leg.

The woman trailed behind us. It was odd to me that the little girl seemed the more dominant of the two, and I wondered again about their relationship to Devlin.

How long had they haunted him? Did he have a clue they were there? Had he experienced cold spots, electrical surges, inexplicable noises in the middle of the night?

Did he realize that his energy was slowly being drained away?

The subtle radiation of his body heat would be irresistible to the ghosts. Even I wasn't entirely immune.

As we stepped into the haze of a streetlamp, I stole another glance. The illumination seemed to repel the ghosts and as they drifted away, I caught a fleeting glimpse—a remnant, nothing more—of the vital man John Devlin had once been.

He cocked his head, as unmindful of my scrutiny as he was of the entities. I thought at first he was listening to the distant wail of the foghorn, but then I realized the sound that had captured his attention was closer. A car alarm.

"Where are you parked?" he asked.

"Over…there." I pointed in the direction of the alarm.

We hurried across the damp parking lot and as we rounded a row of cars, I glanced anxiously down the line, spotting my silver SUV beneath a security light where I had left it. The back door was ajar and shattered glass sparkled on the wet pavement.

"That's mine!" I started toward it.

He caught my arm. "Hold on…"

Several rows over, a car engine revved.

"Wait here!" he said. "And don't touch anything."

I tracked him as he wove through the glistening cars and only turned away when I'd lost sight of him and the sound of his footsteps faded. Then I walked over to the open back door of my vehicle and peered inside. Thankfully, I'd left my laptop and camera at home, and I had my phone and wallet on me. The only thing that seemed to be missing was my briefcase.

The sound of the engine grew louder and I glanced around just as a black car skidded around the corner. Headlights caught me in the face and for a split second, I froze. Then adrenaline shot through me and I dove between my vehicle and the next as the car sped by me.

Devlin appeared out of the mist just as I picked myself up off the pavement.

"You okay? Did he hit you?" He sounded anxious, but his dark eyes gleamed with the thrill of the hunt.

"No, I'm fine. Just a little shaken up—"

He sprinted away, cutting through the rows of parked cars in a futile effort to head off the culprit before he could get away. I heard the whine of the motor and the squeal of tires as the driver stomped the accelerator and swerved into the street.

My imagination and nerves being somewhat overly

stimulated, I half expected to hear gunshots, but all was silent after the engine noise faded.

Devlin trotted toward me, phone pressed to his ear. He spoke rapidly, listened for a moment, then hung up. "Did you get a look at the driver?" he asked.

"No, sorry. It happened too fast. What about you?"

"Never got close enough. Couldn't make out the tags, either."

"Then you won't be able to track him down, will you? And I'll be stuck with all the damage." I glanced forlornly at my broken window.

He gave me a strange look before turning toward my car. "Can you tell if anything is missing?"

"My briefcase is gone."

"It was in the back?"

"Yes."

"In plain view?"

"Not exactly. It was behind the rear seat. You'd have to peer into the window to notice it."

"Anyone see you put it in there?"

I thought about it for a minute, then shrugged. "It's possible. I spent the afternoon at the university library, so I suppose someone could have seen me toss it in when I left."

"You came straight here?"

"No. I went home to shower and change first."

"Did you take your briefcase inside?"

"I left it in the car. I don't always take it out at home. There's nothing valuable in it. Just work-related stuff."

"Like photos of Oak Grove Cemetery?"

I honestly hadn't made that leap yet.

I suppose my real world instincts had been severely stunted by the solitude of my profession and avocation.

"You don't think this could be connected to the body found in the cemetery, do you?"

He didn't answer. "You say you have other copies of the photographs?"

"Of course. I always store my digital images online. I've had too many hard drive crashes to leave anything to chance." Shock was starting to set in and my disquiet now had very little to do with John Devlin's ghosts. I could no longer see them. It was as if the negative energy surrounding my car had chased them deeper into the shadows. Or maybe they were being pulled back behind the veil. Whatever the reason, I knew they would eventually return. His warmth would lure them back because they couldn't exist for long without him.

I wrapped my arms around my middle and shivered. "What should I do?"

"We'll get you a police report written up and you can file a claim with your insurance company."

"No, I mean…if this is somehow connected to a homicide, then the killer knows who I am. And if he did this to get his hands on those pictures, he'll figure out soon enough that I have copies."

"Then we'd better find him first," said John Devlin.

THREE

Twenty minutes later, Devlin and I walked through the gates at Oak Grove. Even under the best of conditions, the place had an unnerving effect. It was an old grave-yard, dark, lush and gothic. The layout was typical of the nineteenth-century Rural Cemetery movement and at one time, it must have been lovely and pastoral. But now under a shrouded moon, the crumbling statuary took on a ghostly patina, and I imagined a lurking presence, something cold, dank and ancient.

I turned and peered through the darkness, searching for a diaphanous form in the fog, but there were no ghosts in Oak Grove Cemetery. Even the dead didn't want to be here.

"Looking for someone?"

I kept my gaze averted from Devlin. The magnetism he radiated was palpable. It was odd, but I'd felt the pull even more strongly once we passed through the gates. "Excuse me?"

"You keep glancing over your shoulder. Are you looking for someone?"

"Ghosts," I said, then waited for his reaction.

His demeanor gave nothing away as he reached into his jacket pocket and pulled out a small blue tube. "Here."

"What is it?"

"Eucalyptus vapor. I can't promise it'll ward off evil spirits, but it should help with the smell."

I started to tell him that I had no intention of getting so close to the body that I would need to worry about masking the smell, but already I'd caught the trail of something fetid, a malodorous undertone to the earthy fragrances of the ferns and wild hyacinths that blanketed the nearby graves.

"Go on," Devlin said. "Take it."

I rubbed the waxy stick onto my finger, then smeared the balm across my upper lip. The medicated vapor burned my nostrils and tightened my throat. I put a hand to my chest and coughed. "Strong."

"You'll be glad of that in about two minutes." He pocketed the tube without using it. "Ready?"

"Not really, but I suppose there's no turning back, is there?"

"Don't sound so fatalistic. Your part will be over soon enough."

I was counting on that.

He turned without another word and I followed him into the maze of headstones and monuments. The stepping stones that marked the path were slippery with moss and lichen. I trudged along behind him, mindful of my footing. I wasn't properly attired for the cemetery. Already my shoes were caked with mud and I felt the sting of tiny nettles nipping at my bare legs.

The rumble of voices grew louder and I could see

flashlight beams moving along the pathways. The scene was eerie and surreal, reminding me of a time when bodies were buried by moonlight and the glow of the grave digger's lantern.

Up ahead, a small crowd of men in uniforms and civvies had gathered around what I assumed was the unearthed victim. My view was mostly obscured, but I noted the silhouette of the headstone and scanned the surrounding monuments so that I would later be able to pinpoint the location of the grave on my map.

One of the cops shifted and suddenly I caught a glimpse of pale skin and milky eyes. A wave of nausea drenched me with sweat. I retreated down the path on shaky legs. It was one thing hearing about a murder; coming face-to-face with the gruesome aftermath was quite another.

I'd spent most of my life in cemeteries—my graveyard kingdoms. Each a calm, sheltered, self-contained world where the chaos of the city seemed anathema. Tonight, reality had stormed the gates, wreaking havoc.

Drawing in long breaths, I stood there wishing I'd never mentioned my dinner plans to Dr. Ashby because then Devlin wouldn't have been able to find me. I wouldn't have known about the murder. I wouldn't have glanced into those frosted eyes.

But with or without Devlin, I'd been drawn into the violence the moment my briefcase was stolen. On the way here, I'd managed to convince myself the theft had been random. Someone had seen my briefcase through the back window and decided on impulse to take it. Now that I'd glimpsed the body, I feared the worst. If the killer felt threatened by something captured on one of those images, he could be acting purely out of instinct and self-preservation. What if he tried to break into my house to get at my camera and computer? To get at me?

Pulling my raincoat tightly around me, I watched as Devlin joined the circle around the body. Even in my current state of distress, I couldn't help taking an interest in his interactions with his colleagues. He was shown respect, reverence even, but I also sensed an overall air of uneasiness. The other cops kept their distance, which intrigued me. But clearly Devlin was in charge and in his element, and I found it a fascinating dichotomy that he should seem so alive and vital in the presence of a violent death.

Or maybe it was because his ghosts hadn't followed us through the gates.

I turned away, letting my gaze wander through the shadowy necropolis, lingering here and there over broken statuary and vandalized crypts. If most cemeteries offered solace and evoked hours of deep meditation and self-reflection, Oak Grove stirred dark thoughts.

My father had once told me that a place need not be haunted to be evil. I believed him because Papa knew things. Over the course of my childhood, he'd imparted much of that wisdom to me, but he'd also kept things from me. For my own good, I was certain, but those secrets drove a wedge between us where once there had been none. My first ghost sighting had changed us both. If Papa had withdrawn deeper into his own private world, he'd also become even more protective of me. He was my touchstone, my anchor, the one person who understood my isolation.

After that first sighting, I never again saw the old white-haired man, but there had been others. Over the years, legions of beautiful, floating phantoms. Young, old, black, white, they drifted through the veil at dusk, a delicate parade of Southern history that both thrilled and terrified me.

After a while, those unearthly transients simply became a part of my world and I learned to steel myself against the frosty breaths at the back of my neck, the icy fingers that trailed through my hair and down my arms. Papa had been right to train and discipline me, but acceptance of the situation hadn't alleviated my questions. I still didn't understand why he and I could see the ghosts and Mama couldn't.

"It's our cross to bear," he explained one day, keeping his gaze averted as he weeded a grave.

That didn't satisfy me. "Can my real mother see them?"

Papa still didn't look up. "The woman who raised you is your real mother."

"You know what I mean." We never talked about my adoption even though I'd known about it for a long time. I had a lot of questions about that, too, but I'd learned to keep them to myself.

Papa had already started to shut down so I went back to the ghosts. "Why do they want to touch us?"

"I've already told you. They crave our warmth."

"But why?" Absently, I plucked a lone dandelion and blew the seeds into the wind. "Why, Papa?"

"Think of them as vampires," he said with a weary sigh. "Instead of blood, they suck out our warmth, our vitality, sometimes our will to live. And they leave nothing behind but a living, breathing husk."

I seized on the one word that made any sense to me, even though on some level I knew he was speaking metaphorically. "But, Papa, vampires aren't real."

"Maybe not." He rocked back on his heels, his eyes taking on a haunted, faraway glaze that chilled me to the bone. "But I've seen things in my time…unspeakable desecrations…"

My terrified gasp brought him momentarily out of his gloomy reverie and he placed his hand on mine, squeezing my fingers in reassurance. "It's nothing for you to worry about, child. You have nothing to fear, so long as you follow the rules."

But his words had filled me with a formless dread. "Promise?"

He nodded, but turned away quickly, his careworn face shadowed with secrets…

Over the years, I'd followed Papa's rules faithfully. My emotions were well-schooled, always under control, and I suppose that was why I found my response to John Devlin so troubling.

He'd come up behind me in the cemetery and must have said my name, but I was so lost in thought, I didn't hear him. When he placed his hand on my shoulder to get my attention, the hair rose up on my scalp like the aftermath of an electrical jolt. I jerked away from him without thinking.

He looked taken aback by my reaction. "Sorry. I didn't mean to startle you."

"No, it's okay. It's just…"

"This place? Yeah, it's pretty creepy. I would think you're used to that, though."

"Not all cemeteries are creepy," I said. "Most of them are beautiful."

"If you say so." Something in his tone—a cold, brittle undercurrent—made me think of his ghosts. I wondered again who they were and what they'd been to him in life.

He was still peering down at me curiously. For some

reason, his height hadn't been so obvious to me earlier, but now he seemed to tower over me.

"Are you sure you're okay?" he asked.

"I guess I'm still a little jumpy from earlier. And now this." I nodded toward the body on the ground, but I kept my gaze trained on Devlin. I didn't want to stare at the corpse. I didn't want to put a face with a restless, covetous ghost that I might one day see wandering through the veil.

"I lead a dull life," I said without irony. "I don't think I'm cut out for crime scenes."

"There are a lot of things in this world to be afraid of, but a dead body isn't one of them."

Spoken like a man who knew things, I thought with a shiver. His voice was the kind that made one think of dark places. The kind that made the skin ripple along the backbone.

"I'm sure you're right," I murmured, searching the mist behind him, wondering if his ghosts might have slipped through the gates after all. That would explain the unnatural static that seemed to surround him and the sense of foreboding I felt at his nearness.

But no. There was nothing behind him in the dark.

It's this place.

I could feel the negative energy clutching at me like the ivy roots that burrowed into the cracks and crevices of the mausoleums, the kudzu that wound tightly around the tree trunks, slowly strangling the magnificent old live oaks for which the cemetery had been named. I wondered if Devlin felt it, too.

He tilted his head and moonlight washed across his face, softening his gaunt features and giving me yet another teasing glimpse of the man he'd once been. I could see the gleam of mist in his hair and on the tips of his eyelashes. His cheekbones were high and prominent, his thick eyebrows perfectly symmetrical and a fine complement to the strong curve of his nose. His eyes were dark, but I'd not seen them in enough light to tell their true color.

He was handsome, charismatic and intensely focused, and he intrigued me almost as much as he disturbed me. I couldn't stare at him for long without hearing the echo of my father's third rule inside my head:

Keep your distance from those who are haunted.

I drew a breath of moist air and tried to shake off his strange spell. "Have you found out anything about the victim?"

Even to my own ears, my voice sounded tentative and I wondered if he would pick up on my unease. He was probably used to a certain amount of discomfort in his presence. He was a cop, after all. A cop with a very complicated past, I was beginning to suspect.

"We don't know who she is yet, if that's what you're asking."

So the victim was female. "Do you know how she died?"

He paused, his gaze sliding away before he answered. "We won't know conclusively until after the autopsy."

It wasn't so much what he said as what he didn't say. And the way he hadn't been able to meet my eyes. What was he hiding from me? What terrible things had been done to that poor woman?

And then I thought of all the hours I'd spent working alone in this cemetery. What if the killer had happened along at one of those times?

As if reading my mind, Devlin said, "I can tell you this much. She wasn't killed here. Her body was brought to the cemetery for disposal."

Was that meant to comfort me?

"Why here, I wonder?"

He shrugged. "It's a likely spot. This place has been abandoned for years and the ground over the old graves is soft. Makes for easy digging. Cover it up with a few dead leaves and some debris and a casual observer would never even notice the soil had been disturbed."

"But then the rain set in."

His gaze returned to me. "The rain set in and you came along. Even if the dirt hadn't washed away, odds are you would have noticed the fresh digging when you cleaned up the grave."

Call me a coward, but I was glad it hadn't gone down that way. "Who found the body?"

"A couple of students climbed over the wall for a little private party. They spotted the exposed head and torso and reported it to campus police. Dr. Ashby notified Charleston P.D., and then met us at the gate to let us in." There was a slight shift in his voice. "She mentioned that you also have a key."

I nodded. "She gave me one when we signed the contracts."

"You haven't loaned that key out to anyone in the past few days, have you? It hasn't gone missing or anything like that."

"No, of course not." I stared up at him in alarm. "You're not suggesting that the killer used my key to get in, are you?"

"I'm merely asking you the same questions I asked Camille Ashby. It doesn't appear the lock was tampered with, so the logical conclusion is that the killer used a key."

"Maybe he didn't come through the gate. He could have climbed over the fence like those kids."

Devlin glanced around. "Those walls are ten, maybe twelve feet high and overgrown with vines and briars. It would be one thing to climb over with a bottle of Jack or a six-pack. Dragging a body over...not so easy."

"He could have had help."

"Let's hope he didn't," he said, something dark and chilling running beneath his words.

I wondered what was going through his head at that moment. He struck me as a very thorough man, one so meticulous and driven he would leave no stone unturned until he found his answers.

Which brought me back to his ghosts...

Were they bound here because of *him?*

In spite of what my father had told me about the parasitic nature of spirits, I'd come to the conclusion that some did linger because of unfinished business, be it theirs or the unwitting host's. This made them no less dangerous to someone like me. On the contrary, those entities worried me the most because they were often desperate and confused and sometimes very, very angry.

We fell silent and the night grew still. The mist muted the voices of the police personnel as they went about their grim business.

I started to ask Devlin how much longer he would need me, but another officer came up just then and he turned to speak to him in low enough tones that I couldn't hear. I didn't want them to think that I was trying to eavesdrop, so I moved away and went back to my silent lurking.

No one paid me any attention, and after a while, I decided I could probably just leave and no one would notice. The idea tempted me greatly. I wanted nothing more than to be home, safe and sound, in my own private sanctuary, but I resisted the urge. I couldn't just leave after giving Devlin my word. I was a Southern girl raised by a Southern mother. Duty and obligation were as deeply ingrained into my psyche as the need to please.

As Papa had, my mother had instilled in me a certain set of rules by which she expected me to live my life. The more superficial edicts I'd long since discarded—I no longer ironed my bed linens and I didn't always use a tablecloth when I dined alone. But going back on my word…now that was something I would do only under pain of death.

The hair at the back of my neck prickled a warning as the air around me stirred. I knew Devlin had come up behind me again, and I turned before he could touch me.

"The coroner's finished," he said. "They'll be moving the body soon. After that, you can take off. We won't be able to do much out here until daylight."

"Thanks."

"I'll let you know where to send your invoice."

"I'm not worried about that."

"Why not? You earned it tonight. Just one thing, though. When word of this gets out, reporters are going to hammer the university for a statement. If your name is mentioned as a consultant, they'll likely want to get something from you on the record. I'd appreciate it if you wouldn't release any information without first clearing it with me."

"Of course."

I had no intention of talking to the press about the grisly discovery in Oak Grove Cemetery. All I wanted to do was go home, crawl into bed and put this night behind me.

But a tidy ending was not meant to be. Everything in my world was about to change forever.

Including my father's rules.

FOUR

My house on Rutledge Avenue was pure Charleston—a narrow, two-story clapboard with upper and lower verandas and a front garden surrounded by a wrought-iron fence.

More important to me, it was one of those places my father had long ago taught me to seek out. There were no ghosts in this house. It was a sanctuary, a safe haven, the ground beneath hallowed, but I had no idea why. In the six months I'd lived here, I hadn't been able to dig up much of its history, only that the house had been built in 1950 after the original structure had been torn down.

Sometime in the 1990s, the owner had installed central heating and air-conditioning and divided the house into two apartments. Both units had access to a low-ceilinged, dirt-floor basement with brick walls and crumbling mortar—the only part of the original structure that remained—and a quaint backyard garden that smelled like heaven in the late afternoon when the Queen of the Night on the east side of the house started to bloom.

A medical student named Macon Dawes rented the upper level. I didn't know much about Macon. Our paths rarely crossed. He worked a crazy schedule at the hospital and I often heard him coming and going at odd hours.

As I arrived home, I hoped to see a light in one of his windows and his old Civic parked in its usual spot. We were barely on a first-name basis, but tonight of all nights, I would have welcomed his presence. I didn't relish entering an empty house alone, even one protected from the other world. Ghosts couldn't penetrate the walls, but there was nothing to prevent a desperate killer from breaking a window or picking a lock to gain entrance.

But the house was dark and silent, the driveway empty. Palmetto fronds hung heavy and still over the fence as I approached the side gate, door key clutched in my hand. As I stepped through into the garden, a police cruiser pulled to the curb in front of the house and a uniformed officer got out. I didn't allow myself to panic. In fact, I was relieved to see him.

He came through the front gate and we met at the bottom of the porch steps.

"Miss Gray? Amelia Gray?"

"Yes?"

He nodded politely and touched his brim. "Evening, ma'am." He spoke with a thick, country drawl that left me wondering briefly about his background. He was tall, thirtyish and attractive, from what I could see in the dark, but I barely noted his appearance. I was far more interested in whatever new discovery or revelation had brought him to my doorstep.

"Is anything wrong?" I asked, bracing myself.

"No, ma'am. John Devlin asked me to keep an eye on your place tonight."

The use of Devlin's whole name gave it a subtle formality, and I was reminded of the way the other cops had seemed so uneasy around him at the cemetery. What were they afraid of? Or perhaps more aptly...why did Devlin make me so edgy?

The officer's gaze swept over me with more than a passing interest. Whether his curiosity had been triggered by Devlin's request or my own bedraggled appearance, I could only guess. He hauled out his wallet and flashed his ID. After the evening's events, I was annoyed with myself that I hadn't thought to ask for it straightaway.

"I understand you had some trouble earlier," he said.

"Someone broke into my car and stole my briefcase." I nodded toward my parked vehicle, even though the shattered back window wasn't visible from where we stood.

"Rash of that lately. Punks looking for something to hock and nobody ever sees squat." He gave me another long look. "Reckon it could be connected to that cemetery business, though."

He seemed to expect an answer so I shrugged. "I hope not."

"Best keep your eyes peeled, just in case. I'll do drive-bys for the rest of my watch." He fished a card from his pocket and handed it to me. "My number's right there on the back. You see or hear anything out of the ordinary, don't be afraid to holler."

I took the card and thanked him before climbing the steps to my porch. Once inside, I flipped the dead bolt, turned on a light and glanced out the window. The officer had climbed back into his car, but he didn't pull away from the curb. The interior light was on and I could see a cell phone pressed to his ear. I wondered if he was reporting back to Devlin, wondered why the notion of that both relieved and bothered me.

Turning from the window, I faced my empty house.

Light from the wall sconces welcomed me through the arched doorway into a long, narrow hallway. A large parlor furnished with thrift store antiques opened to the right. To the left, a curved staircase led up to a bolted door that separated the first-and second-story apartments.

My office was a converted sunporch all the way at the back of the house, just off the kitchen. In the mornings, a buttery light shone through the long windows and I liked to start my day out there with a cup of tea and my laptop.

Tonight, nothing but darkness lay beyond the windows.

I turned my back on all those shadows as I sat down at the desk, opened my laptop and compressed the Oak Grove folder so that I could send all the images in one email to the address on the card Devlin had given to me earlier.

There.

I sat back and let out a breath. My part in this whole disturbing mess was over. I'd done everything I possibly could to help the police.

But even after I pressed the send button, I still couldn't shake a lingering unease. Unless the killer knew that Devlin was now in possession of those images, he might still consider me a threat. And he couldn't know that I'd sent the images unless he was watching me at that very moment.

I shot a tentative glance over my shoulder.

No one was there, of course. No eyes peering in from the darkness. No face pressed to the glass. Just the faintest hint of condensation creeping over the panes from the air-conditioning.

As I watched, tiny lines appeared in the rime like ghostly etchings, but there was nothing supernatural about the cracks. Nothing more sinister than a cold surface meeting the warmer outside air.

An unpleasant smell clung to my raincoat, and I decided the odor I'd brought home from the cemetery might be facilitating my apprehension.

Rising, I hurried into the bathroom, stripped off all my clothing and stuffed everything into a garbage bag. Then I got into the shower and scrubbed my skin and hair for a good twenty minutes, until every last bit of graveyard grime had been washed down the drain.

Wrapped in a towel, I padded down the hallway to my bedroom and pulled on cotton pajamas and a pair of thick socks, because the wood floor felt cold beneath my feet.

I adjusted the thermostat, then went back to the kitchen to make some tea. Carrying the cup out to the office, I sat down at my desk and once again opened the laptop.

The combination of soothing chamomile and a long shower took the edge off my anxiety and I started to relax and work on a new blog article—"Graveyard Lilacs: The Divine Smell of Death."

The cemetery certainly hadn't smelled so divine tonight, I thought with a grimace.

Unable to gather my thoughts, I gave up and went back to the Oak Grove images.

Using a full-length mirror to reflect light, I'd shot almost every grave in the front section before the rain had set in. Creating a visual prerestoration record of the cemetery was always the first step. Then came the research. The foundation of a successful renewal always lay in the archives. If no directory or map could be found, county death records, church registries and family Bibles had to be meticulously scoured, sometimes for weeks or even months at a time. I kept at it for however long it took, because there was nothing so lonely as an unmarked grave.

Scrolling through the JPEGs, I located the victim's burial site by searching for the monuments and landmarks I'd memorized earlier at the cemetery. I enlarged the image to full screen and zoomed in. Using a magnifier, I went over the grave carefully, scrutinizing every pixel.

Finding no evidence the soil had been disturbed at the time I'd taken the photograph, I concluded the killer had buried the body sometime after I left the cemetery late Friday afternoon and before the storm hit at midnight.

I did notice one interesting detail, however.

Leaning forward, I absently rubbed my thumb against the polished stone I wore on a chain around my neck as I studied the image.

The headstone faced away from the grave. This in and of itself wasn't so unusual. Families sometimes requested this arrangement so that the inscription could be read without treading upon the grave. But whether the headstone placement had anything to do with why the killer had chosen that particular grave to dispose of the body, I had no idea.

Curling one leg underneath me, I moved on to the next shot, which was the face of the headstone. On a yellow legal pad, I jotted down the name, the epitaph, year of birth and death, and made note of the imagery—a weeping willow bough entwined with morning glory vines and a feather floating downward toward the grave.

Then I opened the corresponding document file and scanned through the information I'd collected on the deceased, one Mary Frances Pinckney. She'd died of scarlet fever in 1887 at the age of fourteen.

Nothing unusual there. I went back to my notes and reread the epitaph:

The midnight stars weep upon her silent grave,
Dead but dreaming, this child we could not save.

The verse triggered a moment of melancholia, but there was nothing particularly strange about it. More than likely, the grave had been selected randomly by the killer. Or because it was located away from the walls and gates so that it couldn't be easily spotted by a casual onlooker.

I sat there for the longest time, studying those photographs and worrying about my stolen briefcase. Worrying about my reaction to John Devlin and wondering if somehow my father's rules were being tested in ways I didn't yet understand. But mostly I thought about the dead woman who had been dumped in an old grave at Oak Grove, left there in anonymity, without benefit of ceremony or marker. The callous burial bothered me almost as much as the murder. It spoke to a lack of conscience, a lack of humanity that conjured deep dread.

He was out there, that monster. Stalking the streets, perhaps with the scent of his next victim already burning inside him.

The scent of his next victim...

Absorbed in the images, I'd barely registered the fragrance that had invaded my office.

Now I closed my eyes and drew it in.

Not graveyard lilacs, but jasmine...

So sweet and pervasive, I wondered for a moment if I'd left a window open. The vines were everywhere in the backyard. Sometimes the cloying smell became unbearable at night.

But this scent was different. Deeper, headier, with an undertone of something I didn't want to contemplate.

As I got up to check the windows, I heard the soft tinkle of the wind chimes on the patio.

Strange, because there wasn't a breeze.

Alarmed, I reached back and closed my laptop.

I stood shivering in the dark, gazing past my reflection in the glass to the patio and garden beyond.

Through the fragile layers of mist, I could see the soft glow of moonflowers and gardenias and the starry spill of the jasmine over the pike fence. An old live oak guarded the darkest corner of the garden, and a swing hung like a childhood memory from one of the gnarled branches.

It swayed gently, as if someone had just gotten out of the wooden seat. Back and forth…back and forth…back and forth…

The creak of the rusted chains lifted the hairs on the back of my neck.

Someone was out there walking around in the garden. A shoulder had brushed against the wind chimes. An idle hand had rocked the swing.

I wanted to believe that Macon Dawes had come home from the hospital and was taking a midnight stroll in the garden to unwind. But wouldn't I have heard his old clunker pull into the driveway?

Someone—or something—was out there. I could sense a presence in the darkness, sense eyes on me.

Reaching behind me, I felt along the desk for my cell phone and the card the officer had given to me earlier. Using the lighted display, I punched in the number, realizing a split second before I placed the call that the number I'd entered was Devlin's.

My thumb hovered over the send button. I don't know why I hesitated, some instinct or premonition of what was about to come perhaps. All I knew in that moment was fear. An icy terror of what lay in wait outside my window.

But I still couldn't bring myself to push the button that would summon Devlin back into my life.

And then I saw it. A nebulous, dreamlike form hovering just beyond the fall of pale moonlight.

Devlin's ghost child.

I thought at first I must be seeing things. Prayed that my overwrought imagination had conjured her from my deepest fear.

But she was there.

I felt the cold fire of her eyes through the darkness.

The swing and wind chimes were still now. I heard no sound at all except for the terrified drumming of my heart.

How was it possible? This house was a haven, a hallowed refuge that protected me from ghostly invasions. I was safe here. Or had been—until I met Devlin.

I forced myself to remain at the window, as if casually staring out into the garden. But the moment my gaze strayed from the ghost child, I sensed her annoyance. Her displeasure.

Before I could process this development, she glided from the shadows into a pool of moonlight, and I caught my breath. She was the most beautiful, delicate entity I'd ever laid eyes upon.

Through her wispy aura, her skin looked translucent, her hair a tangle of raven curls. She wore a sweet blue dress with a sprig of jasmine tucked into the waist, and I saw the sparkle of some tiny ring on her finger as she lifted her hand and pointed toward the window where I stood trembling.

There was no mistaking her intent.

She knew I was there.

She knew I could see her.

And she was letting me know that she knew.

Never before had I interacted with a ghost. How could this be happening when I'd followed my father's rules to the letter?

Somehow everything had changed. The rules had been broken and I didn't even know how.

Emotions stormed through me, a mass of swirling confusion. The sensation lasted for only a moment and then the darkness passed.

The ghost lowered her hand, stepped back into the shadows and slowly vanished into the mist.

FIVE

The next morning, I awoke to the half-light of dawn. It was nearly six o'clock, an hour before the alarm would sound, but I switched it off, anyway, then draped an arm over my eyes as the events of last evening came drifting back.

Maybe because I wasn't yet fully alert, everything seemed a bit hazy. The unearthed body in the cemetery. The visit from the ghost child. Even my strange reaction to John Devlin.

I rolled to my side and stared out the window as I contemplated calling my mother later. I knew she'd be worried if she heard about the Oak Grove story on the news, but I was afraid my voice might give too much away if Devlin's name came up, and how could I explain something I didn't even understand myself? He was haunted and, therefore, taboo, so a certain amount of appeal was inherent to the situation. But I wondered if it was more than that. Why else would he unnerve me even without his ghosts?

I'd dreamed about him last night. That rarely happened even with men that I dated. It was nothing graphic or erotic, just a series of strange vignettes that ignited an already unhealthy curiosity.

Of course, if I were wise, I would put Devlin out of my mind entirely. I'd done what he asked and now there was no reason for further contact. And if we did meet again, I would need to engineer an effective defense somehow, because I couldn't chance another visit from his ghost child. What if next time she managed to advance beyond the garden? The thought of such a breach scared me, but even so I couldn't deny that last evening had been stimulating in more ways than one. The encounter with Devlin had shaken things up in my safe little world and given me a lot to mull over as I dressed and brought in the paper.

The Oak Grove story had made the front page of the *Post and Courier.* I skimmed the article as I stood at the kitchen counter sipping a glass of juice. Very few details were given, but as Devlin predicted, in the university's official statement to the press, Camille Ashby had cited me as an "expert consultant" brought in to protect the historical integrity of the cemetery. Not my actual job, but close enough.

Refolding the paper, I set it aside and left the house for my daily walk, heading south on Rutledge Avenue. Two blocks later, I turned east, where the first scorching fingers of sunrise began to creep over the horizon. A mild breeze stirred the palmetto fronds and deepened the scent of the magnolia blossoms that peeked like roosting doves from nests of dark, glossy leaves.

On a morning like this, with the ghosts floating back through the veil, I couldn't imagine a more beautiful place. The Holy City, some called it, because of all the church steeples that dotted the low-rise skyline. Charleston was old South, a state of mind, the luxuriant landscape of lost dreams. Everywhere I looked, everywhere I walked, the past enveloped me.

I'd only lived in the city for the past six months, but I had deep roots here. My mother had been born and raised in Charleston. She'd left her childhood home to marry my father four decades ago, but she remained to this day a Charlestonian through and through. She and her sister, Lynrose, had been raised in a comfortable household in the Historic District. Their parents were teachers, well-read and well-traveled, but it was their sense of tradition and refinement that allowed them to mingle at the fringes of society despite their middle-class upbringing.

By contrast, my father grew up in the mountains of North Carolina. Hill trash to the gentry that lived south of Broad Street. In 1960s segregated Charleston, Papa's Blue Ridge heritage would have placed him only a rung or two above the black men with whom he'd tended garden at St. Michael's, where he'd worked before they married.

Like my maternal grandparents, I was educated and traveled. I'd received an undergraduate degree in anthropology from the University of South Carolina at the age of twenty—what else had I to do but study?—and a graduate degree in archaeology from the University of North Carolina at Chapel Hill. I was a member of the American Institute for the Conservation of Historic and Artistic Works, the Southeast Regional Conservation Association, the Association for Gravestone Studies and the Alliance for Historic Landscape Preservation. I owned my own business, was considered by some to be an expert in my field and, thanks to that viral YouTube video, had become a minor celebrity among Charleston taphophiles and ghost hunters. But for all my accomplishments and fleeting notoriety, there remained a segment of Charleston's dying mansion class that would never accept me because of my father's people.

This bothered me not in the slightest.

I was proud of Papa's heritage, but I did still wonder how he and my mother had managed to meet and fall in love, considering the social chasm that had separated them. Over the years, my queries to both parents had been met with little more than vague details and outright dismissals.

The only clue I'd ever uncovered was in an overheard conversation between my mother and Aunt Lynrose when she'd come to visit us in Trinity, the small town north of Charleston where we lived when my father worked as caretaker for the county cemeteries. Every evening, the two sisters would sit out on the front porch sipping sweet tea from tall, frosted glasses while twilight settled around them as softly as the silk scarves that held back their hair.

Chin propped on the sill, I would sit and listen to them through the open parlor windows, mesmerized by the lyrical quality of their lovely drawls. As I grew older, I learned to pick out the French Huguenot and Gullah influences that made the Charleston accent so distinct. My mother had never completely lost those long midvowels, and to a sheltered child such as I, her exotic speech patterns made her seem glamorous and mysterious.

On one particular evening, as I sat listening through the window, I'd detected a note of sadness in Mama's voice as she and my aunt reminisced.

Aunt Lynrose had reached over and patted Mama's hand. "Things don't always work out the way we planned, but we have to make the most of what we're given. You have a good life, Etta. A lovely home and a hardworking husband who loves you. And don't forget what a blessing Amelia is. After all those terrible miscarriages…"

"A blessing? Sometimes I wonder…"

"Etta." There was a note of censure in my aunt's tone. "Why dwell on something you can't change? Remember what Mama always said. No good can come of living in the past."

"It's not the past I'm worried about," my mother murmured.

Long after they'd moved on to another topic, I remained at the window, frightened and lonely, and not understanding why.

I'd never asked my mother about that conversation. As any good lawyer would advise, a query should never be posed unless one already knew the answer. Or was prepared to deal with the consequences. I wasn't. I preferred to remain in the dark as to why my adoption had not been considered a blessing by my mother.

Turning right on Tradd Street, I left that dark memory and the bells of St. Michael's behind me.

Before me, the city was coming alive. The delectable aromas of coffee and fresh pastries wafted from the bakeries and open-air restaurants that catered to the breakfast crowd.

As I neared the water, the air thickened with brine. Keeping a brisk pace, I retraced last night's steps past the stretch of colorful homes on Rainbow Row and the grand East Bay mansions with their elegant piazzas and jewel-box gardens.

I walked to the very southernmost tip of the peninsula and paused to watch the sunrise. A lone pelican circled overhead and I tracked it for a moment before letting my gaze drop to Fort Sumter, a hazy outline of crumbling walls and Southern history in the middle of Charleston Harbor.

From the corner of my eye, I saw someone step up to the rail and I turned, almost expecting to find John Devlin. The stranger beside me was the same height and build as the detective, and he had the same guarded air. And yet he made me think—not of Devlin—but of his ghosts. This man, too, had the café au lait complexion that suggested a mixed heritage, but his bearing was straight, not regal, his features more handsome than exotic. At least what I could see of them beneath the sunglasses. He wore faded clothes, but he did not strike me as homeless. Nor, for some reason, did I think he was a tourist.

He didn't so much as glance at me as he stared out over the water, seemingly absorbed in the vastness of the harbor.

I grew apprehensive. It was very quiet where we stood, too early for anyone to be about. Whoever had broken into my car and stolen my briefcase was still out there somewhere. The killer of that poor girl whose body had been found in Oak Grove Cemetery had yet to be caught.

Was it just a coincidence that this stranger had appeared on the Battery at the precise time I took my morning walk?

I wanted to move away, but was reluctant to call attention to myself and even more hesitant to turn my back on him.

As if sensing my unease, he waited a moment longer for the sunrise, then turned and slowly walked away, disappearing into the lush foliage of White Point Gardens.

I headed for home, stopping for a bagel and coffee on the way. With each step that brought me closer to my sanctuary, I felt a growing trepidation. A creeping dread that left me wondering...

How had Devlin's ghost child managed to penetrate my defenses? And what would I do if she came back?

When I got home, I went straight to the garden. The moonflowers had withered in the heat as the rising sun slowly awakened the morning glories.

I walked along narrow beds of purple phlox to the spot where I'd seen the little girl's ghost. I don't know what I expected to find. Nothing as earthly or as human as footprints. But something had been left behind.

A tiny garnet ring lay embedded in the soft earth.

I might not have seen it at all had I not been searching so closely for evidence of a ghostly visit.

The ring looked as if it had been buried there for a very long time. Perhaps like the body in Oak Grove, it had been uncovered by the recent rainstorms. I wanted to believe it had been lost by some former occupant of the house, but I couldn't help remembering the sparkle on the little ghost's finger as she pointed to the window where I had stood watching her.

I knelt in the grass, hands on thighs and stared for a long time at that ring.

Had it been left there as a message? A warning?

Could a ghost do that?

I'd felt the spidery crawl of their fingers in my hair, the whisper of their cold breath down my collar, but I'd never found any physical evidence of their presence. And yet there lay a ring in the very spot where one of Devlin's ghosts had vanished back into the mist.

It didn't seem proper to leave it half buried in the dirt, but neither did I want the thing in my house or on my person. Already I had too much of a connection to this entity. The last thing I needed was to issue an unwitting invitation.

After a bit, I got up and went inside to retrieve an antique silver trinket box from my dresser, along with a basket of pebbles and seashells I'd collected from the old part of Rosehill Cemetery, my childhood playground. The artifacts had come from hallowed ground, as had the polished stone I wore on a silver chain around my neck. Whether they held any protective properties of their own, I had no idea. I liked to think that they did.

I went back out to the garden and, using the tip of a spade to carefully tease the ring from the moist ground, I placed it inside the silver box, dug a hole and buried it. Then I fashioned a heart on top of the site with the pebbles.

Working quickly and in deep concentration, I tuned out the sounds from the street along with the soft spit of my next-door neighbor's lawn sprinkler. I only looked up when I heard footsteps on the paving stones, and by then it was too late. John Devlin was already upon me.

I had a feeling he'd been watching me for some time through the wrought-iron gate. Some part of me had sensed him there, I think, but I chose to ignore the warning.

Now as his shadow fell over me, I stared up at him, my pulse reacting erratically.

"What died?" he asked.

SIX

"Nothing died." I spoke in a casual tone that I knew disguised the startled thud of my heart. As did my practiced expression. I never gave any of my feelings away. I couldn't afford to when a nervous tic or the dart of my gaze might betray my awareness to a ghost.

And speaking of ghosts, Devlin was alone. Not surprising with the sun fully over the horizon. His unearthly companions would have drifted back through the veil, waiting for twilight, waiting for an in-between time at an in-between place to reemerge.

"I thought I'd use my unexpected time off to do a little gardening," I told him. "Normally, I would have been at the cemetery by now trying to beat the heat."

"Murder tends to throw a monkey wrench in the best-laid plans," he said, without a trace of irony or a smile. He nodded toward the outline of stones on the ground. "What's the heart for?"

"It's just a decorative symbol. It can mean anything you want. Peace. Love. Harmony." I squinted up at him. It was the first time I'd seen him in daylight, and he looked both younger and older than I'd originally thought him. His face was smooth except for the fine lines around his eyes and mouth, his hair dark and luxurious. He wore it short and styled in a manner that gave him some edge, as did the cut of his trousers and the trim fit of his shirt. He appeared to be a man that took pride in his appearance, and with good reason. He was very attractive, with the kind of brooding intensity that had made women's hearts patter throughout the ages. Mine was no exception.

I placed him somewhere in his early- to mid-thirties, but the shadows under his eyes and the hollow cheekbones aged him by at least a decade, depending on the angle and light. There was something troubling in his eyes. Something that made me think again that here was a man who knew things. Here was a man who had seen many dark things.

But such morbid speculation seemed out of place in a sun-dappled garden perfumed by my neighbor's magnolia trees.

He put out a hand and reluctantly I took it, allowing him to help me to my feet. A thrill raced up my arm, an electric charge that made the world stop for a moment as I caught my breath.

I pulled my hand away, wondering if he had felt it, too. He was either totally unaffected or as much an expert as I in disguising his feelings.

Then he turned his head slightly and I noticed a curious throb at his temple, as if maybe, just maybe he wasn't quite as impassive as he would have me believe.

I thought that over for a moment. Did his reaction make me feel better or worse? It certainly excited me. My heart was still pounding and I drew in some air to try and slow it.

Awkwardly, I dusted my hands on my shorts. "What brings you by so early? You didn't find my briefcase, did you?"

"No, sorry. I want to talk to you about these." He held out copies of the images I'd sent to him the night before. I recognized the top photo as the grave where the victim had been buried. "Did you have a look at these?"

"Yes. I went over that particular photo thoroughly with a magnifier last night. I didn't see any evidence that the grave had been disturbed."

"When did you take these?"

"Last Friday. I'd have to look at the digital fingerprint to give you an exact time, but considering the location of the grave, it was sometime in the afternoon. I finished with that area around three and was just about to move into the older section when the clouds rolled in and I lost the light. I packed up everything and left before four. Does that help with your timeline?"

"It's a start."

He glanced down at the picture and I stared down at his hands. They were strong and graceful, those hands. And warm. I could still feel the heat from his previous touch. It made me start to wonder about other things. If I'd reacted so intensely to the mere grasp of his fingers, what would it be like if he kissed me?

Not that that would ever happen. I couldn't let it happen. Even if Devlin was accommodating.

His eyes were very dark as he regarded me. I was happy he couldn't read my inappropriate thoughts, though I certainly wished I could read his. "You say you didn't see any sign that the grave had been disturbed, but did you notice anything else? Anything unusual or out of place in this or any of the other images?"

"Like what?" I bent to pick up the basket of shells

and stones. A few spilled out and he stooped to retrieve them. Again, I noticed the flash of silver around his neck, a teasing glimpse of a dark medallion that swung out of his shirt collar when he leaned over.

He straightened and the medallion slipped back into place. "You're the expert."

"I haven't had a chance to examine the other images as thoroughly, so I can't say for certain. The only thing somewhat out of the ordinary about that particular grave is the placement of the headstone. The inscription is facing away from the body."

He took another look at the photograph. "How can you tell? It's not like the graves are in neat rows, and the vegetation is so thick, you can barely see some of the headstones."

"Because as I said, I took that picture in the afternoon. I was shooting into the sun. The next image is the face of the headstone and the sun is behind me."

"So?"

"If the inscription was turned inward, toward the grave, the body would be facing west. See?" I took the photograph, careful not to brush his fingers as I demonstrated what I meant. "Almost all the old Southern cemeteries are laid out so that the bodies face east, toward the rising sun. People tend to think the orientation is a Christian tradition, but it actually dates back to the Egyptians."

"Is this east-west situation common knowledge or is it something only someone like you would pick up on?"

"Well, it's certainly not a secret. You could learn everything I just told you from a simple internet search. But I doubt most people would give much thought to the layout of a graveyard, old or new." Absently, I plucked one of the stones from the basket and rubbed it between my thumb and forefinger. "Do you think the killer is someone who has some interest in cemeteries?"

"I'm not ruling out the possibility. Of all the graves to choose from, why that one? What's the significance of an outward-facing headstone?"

I shrugged. "Usually, it's a matter of preference. Or sometimes the layout of the cemetery will dictate head-stone placement, but that's obviously not the case in Oak Grove. Of course, there's also the old superstition that an outward-facing or backward headstone was placed on the grave of a witch, but I doubt that's a consideration, either." I glanced down at the picture. "The person who was buried in this grave was a fourteen-year-old girl who died of scarlet fever in the late nineteenth century. I found nothing unusual about her death in the county records or in the university archives."

"What about the epitaph? Or the designs on the head-stone? What do they mean?"

"The epitaph is fairly standard Victorian verse and the symbols are open to interpretation. You ask five experts, you'll likely get five different answers. And meanings can change from place to place and from year to year. Given the inscription and the age of the deceased, I'd say the severed willow bow symbolizes the sorrow of a broken family and the entwined morning glory vine represents resurrection. Morning glories were also used as a symbol of youth and beauty."

"What about the feather at the bottom of the stone?"

"It suggests the flight of the soul, although it's a little more ambiguous than a dove or a winged effigy."

He glanced up. "What the devil is a winged effigy?"

"Just what it sounds like—a winged face, sometimes a skull. You'll also hear them called soul effigies or death's heads. These types of symbols are much more prevalent in the old New England cemeteries where the puritan stonecutters favored a more morbid and literal repre-sentation—skull and crossbones, bodies in coffins, skel-etons…" I trailed off and glanced at him. "Sorry. I get a little carried away."

"No, it's all good stuff. Keep going." He didn't sound the least bit impatient at my rambling and I appreciated that.

"It wasn't until the turn of the nineteenth century that gravestone art became more ethereal and symbolic and more open to a variety of interpretations, like the ones you see on this headstone."

"So what you're telling me is that the meanings of these symbols are sometimes in the eye of the beholder," he said thoughtfully.

"They can be." I tossed the pebble back into the basket. "Why don't you come inside for a minute? If you really want to learn about gravestone symbology, I have some books you might find helpful."

It probably wasn't a good idea to invite him into my home, but he needed my help and at the moment his ghosts were safely tucked away behind the veil.

I led him into the house by way of the side garden, then through the kitchen and back to my office. The sunlight streaming in through the higher windows was soft and yellow and shimmering with dust.

Choosing a couple of volumes from my collection, I turned to hand them to Devlin. His gaze was riveted to a display of framed photographs on one wall.

He walked over to take a closer look. "Did you take these?"

"Yes." His scrutiny made me oddly nervous. Other than the few I'd posted on *Digging Graves,* no one had ever seen my photographs.

"You double-exposed the film. Interesting the way you superimposed all those old graveyards over cityscapes. There's a definite theme and point of view. Also, a hidden message, I suspect."

I came to stand beside him. "Not really. Like gravestone art, the message is in the eye of the beholder."

He studied the images for a moment longer. "I find them...lonely. Beautiful, but intensely lonely. They make me uneasy." He glanced at me then. "Sorry. I didn't mean that as an insult."

"I didn't take it as one. I'm glad they make you feel."

His gaze lingered, searching. "You like cemeteries, don't you?"

"They're my livelihood," I said with a shrug.

"I'm guessing they're more than that." He turned back to the pictures, frowning. "There's a sense of isolation, but not in the graveyards. In the cities. Within the people. These images are very revealing, I think."

I suppressed a shiver. His observation made me feel exposed and vulnerable. "I wouldn't read too much into them. I like playing around with interesting compositions and different techniques. There's no deep meaning here."

"I disagree," he said. "But perhaps that's a discussion best left for another day."

SEVEN

"**H**ere." I handed him the books. "Why don't you browse through these while I go wash my hands?"

I left him perched on the edge of a corner chaise, thumbing through one of the volumes, while I hurried down the hallway.

In the bathroom, I washed my face and hands, resuscitated my ponytail and pulled on a clean T-shirt. Beyond that, I didn't bother with the mirror. I tend to be a little too hard on myself even though I'm aware of my attractiveness. I'm what people call a quiet pretty. Blond hair, blue eyes, a nice complexion and a generous mouth. I'm thin but my muscles are strong and taut from all those years of working in cemeteries. I enjoy my share of admiring glances, but in no way would I ever be considered exotic or sultry, like the woman who haunted Devlin. Why that mattered to me even a little bit was not something I cared to contemplate.

I couldn't have been gone for more than ten minutes, but when I returned to my office, I found Devlin stretched out on the chaise, sound asleep. One of the books rested on his chest, the other on the floor beside him.

This was an unexpected turn of events.

I walked over to his side and stared down at him. A lock of dark hair fell across his forehead and I resisted the urge to sweep it aside.

Touching him was out of the question. So I said his name instead, but he didn't rouse.

He looked so deeply under, I was a little apprehensive about startling him awake. He was an armed police detective, after all.

I stood in a quandary, wondering if I should just let him sleep. He was probably exhausted and he looked so peaceful. But this was odd. A first for me.

Taking advantage of the situation, I gave him another thorough appraisal. He had a scar beneath his bottom lip that I hadn't noticed before. It was small but indented, as if something very sharp had punctured the skin. A knife, perhaps. The thought of that drew a shiver.

My gaze traveled downward to where the silver medallion nestled in the hollow of his throat. When I leaned in to get a better look at the insignia, another strange thing happened. I grew suddenly breathless. Not the fluttery feel one gets from excitement or fear, but a paralyzing sensation akin to having the wind knocked out of me.

I stumbled back and put a hand to my chest. *Whoa.*

Devlin muttered something in his sleep, and I scurried away even farther, bumping into the desk and dropping, weak-kneed, into my chair. My gaze went back to him as I nervously tucked a strand of hair behind one ear. *What just happened?*

I tried not to overreact, but that pressure in my chest was very uncomfortable. I didn't know what to make of the experience.

Finally as my breathing eased, I decided it was just some weird by-product of nerves or an overstimulated imagination. Forcing my attention away from Devlin, I turned on my laptop to check the responses to last week's blog entry—"Graveyard Detective: Sleuthing for the Dead." A prescient article, as it turned out. Which made me a little apprehensive about my next topic—"Sex in a Cemetery: Graveyard Taboos."

I shot Devlin another look. Still fast asleep.

An hour passed before he finally stirred. He opened his eyes and glanced around in confusion. When he saw me staring at him, he sat up abruptly, swinging his legs over the side of the chaise and scrubbing his face with his hands.

"How long have I been out?"

"An hour, give or take."

"Damn." He glanced at his watch, then ran a hand through his mussed hair. "Sorry. I never do that. I don't know what happened."

I shrugged. "It's a cozy spot with all that sunlight. I always get a little drowsy myself when I sit there."

"It was more than drowsy. I was dead to the world. I haven't slept that hard since…" He paused, frowned, then glanced away.

I wondered what he'd been about to say. "You had a late night. You're probably exhausted."

"It wasn't that. It's this place." He shook his head, as if trying to clear the cobwebs. "It's peaceful here." His gaze met mine and I felt electricity pulse along my nerve endings.

"I haven't felt this rested in years," he said.

Maybe it was my imagination, but he did look different, sitting there in the sunlight. The dark smudges under his eyes had faded and he appeared rested and serene. Rejuvenated, I would almost say.

By contrast, I still felt weak in the knees and though the pressure in my chest had lessened, there was now an unpleasant hollowness in the pit of my stomach and an overall lethargy that was foreign to me. As we sat there staring across the room at one another, I had the sudden notion that Devlin had somehow leeched my energy while he slept.

That was impossible, of course. He wasn't a ghost. At that moment, I'd never seen anyone who looked more alive.

"You okay? You look a little pale," he said.

I swallowed. "Do I?"

"Maybe it's just the light." He picked up the books and stood. "Do you mind if I keep these for a few days? I'll take good care of them."

"No, I don't mind." I rose, too, on shaky legs. "Do you have any idea when I can get back into the cemetery?"

"We're doing another sweep tomorrow afternoon. I'd like you to be there if you can arrange it."

My father's rules raced through my head, then faded. "Wouldn't I be in the way?"

"Just the opposite. You're more familiar with the terrain than any of us. If anything seems out of place, who better to spot it than you?"

"I'm not sure I'm free," I murmured.

"If it's a matter of money—"

"It's not. It's a matter of clearing my schedule."

"One o'clock, if you can make it. It could take a few hours, so you might want to plan accordingly."

I let him out the same way we'd come in, and then I hurried through the house and parted the curtains at one of the front windows to watch him leave.

When he came around the side of the house, his appearance struck me again. Already his gait seemed heavier, and I couldn't help thinking of his ghosts. I imagined them at his side, invisible in the sunlight, one at each arm, bound to him forever.

Whether I could see them or not, Devlin's ghosts were always with him, making him the most dangerous man in Charleston for someone like me.

The rest of the day passed without incident…for the most part.

I took my car in to get the window replaced, and as I waited on the repair, I spent an obscene amount of time obsessing on my latest encounter with Devlin. It reminded me of Papa's analogy about vampires—instead of blood, ghosts suck out our vitality. That was exactly the way it had felt to me earlier, as though my energy had been drained. But there had been no ghost in my office. Only Devlin.

If he had somehow fed on my energy, would it bind me to him the way blood connected a vampire to his victim?

A crazy notion, but under the circumstances, I excused my overzealous imagination. After a while, though, I tired of trying to make sense of the experience and put it out of my mind as I drove into the country to look at a family graveyard on the remains of an old rice plantation. I'd been asked by the new owners of the property to submit a bid for a complete restoration, and walking the burial sites was a welcome distraction.

And since I was so close to Trinity, I thought it would be an opportune time to pay my parents a visit. I hadn't seen my mother in over a month, my father in even longer.

Mama and Aunt Lynrose were sitting on the front

porch of our cozy white bungalow drinking lemonade when I drove up. They came down the front steps, all exclamations and admonishments, and the three of us shared a group hug in the front yard.

As always, they smelled wonderful, their scent a unique blend of the familiar and the exotic—honeysuckle, sandalwood and Estée Lauder White Linen. They were both taller than I, their posture still arrow-straight, their figures as slender as the day they'd graduated from St. Agnes.

"What a nice surprise to find you here," I said, slipping an arm around my aunt's trim waist.

"Serendipitous, one might even say." She reached over and patted my cheek. "Shame I have to come all this way to see my only niece when she lives not more than five minutes from me in Chaa'stun," she drawled.

"Sorry. I've been meaning to get by for a visit. I've just been really busy lately."

"With a new beau, dare I hope?"

"'Fraid not. Between my business and my blog, I don't have time for a social life."

"You have to make the time. You don't want to end up an old maid like your favorite aunt, do you?"

I smiled. "I can think of worse fates."

Her eyes gleamed with affection. "Nevertheless, there's a time for work and a time for play."

"Leave her alone, Lyn."

"Leave her alone? Etta, have you seen your daughter's skin? Brown as a berry and freckles all over the place. What do you put on your face at night?" she wanted to know.

"Whatever's handy."

"Chile." She clucked her tongue in disapproval. "I know a woman on Market Street makes the best face cream in the world. Don't have a clue what she puts in it, but the smell is divine and the formula works like a charm. Next time you come see me, I'll give you a jar."

"Thanks."

"Now let me see those hands."

I held them out for inspection and she sighed. "Always, *always* wear gloves. It's *essential* working outside the way you do. The hands are a terrible betrayer of a woman's age."

I looked down at my callused palms. They did look a little worse for wear.

Mama had disappeared inside the house, but she came back out a moment later with a tall glass of lemonade, which she handed to me as I plopped down on the top step.

"You're staying for supper." I'd always loved the way she said "suppah."

Since it wasn't a question, I merely nodded. "What are we having?"

"Chicken and biscuits. Mashed potatoes and gravy. Collard greens. Sliced tomatoes. Roasted corn. Blackberry cobbler for dessert."

"My mouth is watering already." It seriously was, particularly for the homegrown vegetables.

"I never could fry chicken worth a flip," Lynrose mused as she settled back down in a green metal glider, the gentle sway almost hypnotic in the somnolent heat. "It's an art, you know. I must have tried a hundred different recipes over the years. Buttermilk batter, cornmeal breading, you name it. Finally just gave up. Now when I have a hankering for a drumstick, I get takeout, but it's not the same." She sighed. "Etta got the cooking gene in our family."

"And you got the gift of gab," Mama said.

I smiled as Lynrose flashed me a conspiratorial wink.
She was the only person I knew who could tease out my
somber mother's sly sense of humor. When I was a child,
I loved when she came for visits. Mama always seemed
so carefree with her sister.

The last time I'd seen them together was a month ago
when Mama had driven into Charleston for her birthday.
She'd spent the weekend with Lynrose and the three of
us had gone out to celebrate. We'd had enough wine with
dinner to laugh ourselves silly over some ridiculous play
my aunt had dragged us to. I'd never seen my mother so
giddy. It was a sight to behold. She'd turned sixty that
day, but neither she nor my aunt looked a day over forty.
I'd always thought them the most beautiful women in the
world. I still did.

Now I searched my mother's features, hoping to find a
bit of that same girlish mirth I'd witnessed on her birthday. Instead, I noticed how fragile and gaunt she looked.
How tired she seemed. The dark circles under her eyes
reminded me of John Devlin.

A shiver ran through me and I glanced away.

"Where's Papa?" I asked.

"Rosehill," Mama said. "He still likes to putter around
out there even though the county hired a full-time caretaker last year."

"Did he finish the angels?"

A faint smile touched her lips. "Yes. They are quite
something, aren't they, Lyn? You'll have to go down and
take a look at them before you leave."

"I will."

"Speaking of angels," my aunt said lazily. "Do you
remember Angel Peppercorn? Tall gal with a rather un-
fortunate overbite. I ran into her the other day in a little
tea shop on Church Street. You know the one I mean,

Amelia. Has that cute black-and-yellow awning? Anyway, turns out her son, Jackson, is in the movie business. She says he's a famous director out in Hollywood, but I heard through the grapevine he's in the adult entertainment industry. I can't say I'm surprised. Always was something a little perverted about that boy," she said with malicious glee.

As my aunt prattled on, I began to relax, letting my worries over Mama's health and those dark memories of Oak Grove slip away. We spent a pleasant afternoon gossiping on the front porch, only stirring when Mama rose to start dinner. My aunt and I offered to help, but she would have none of it.

"I don't know which of you is more helpless in the kitchen," she said. "Last thing I need is the both of you underfoot."

After she went inside, I settled back against the post as my aunt launched into a new story. I waited for a lull, then said casually, "Aunt Lynrose, are you acquainted with any Devlins in Charleston?"

"Would that be the South of Broad Devlins?" she asked, naming the most prestigious and historic area of the city.

"I don't think so. The Devlin I met is a cop."

"Probably not one of *the* Devlins then. Unless he's a distant cousin. Plenty of those around, I would imagine, since their roots go all the way back to the seventeenth century. Of course, they're dying out now. Bennett Devlin's only son and daughter-in-law were killed in a boating accident years ago. The grandson came to live with him for a while, but they had a falling-out. I seem to recall hearing that the boy got himself involved in some scandal or other."

My ears perked up. "What kind of scandal?"

"The usual. Fell in with a bad crowd, took the wrong sort of wife." She shrugged. "I've forgotten the particulars."

I tried to recall if I'd seen a wedding ring on Devlin's finger. I was pretty sure I would have noticed something like that.

"You say the Devlin you met is a cop? You're not in some kind of trouble, are you?" my aunt teased.

"Hardly. I'm doing some consulting work for the Charleston Police Department."

"My goodness, that sounds important." She eyed me with unabashed curiosity.

"Actually, that's one of the reasons I drove up this afternoon. I wanted to tell Mama before she heard about it from someone else. A body was found in the cemetery where I've been working. A murder victim."

"Lord have mercy." My aunt pressed a hand to her heart. "Chile, are you all right?"

"Yes, I'm fine. I was never in any danger," I said, conveniently ignoring the stolen briefcase. "My involvement is minor, but my name was mentioned in the *Post and Courier* article this morning. I'm surprised you didn't see it."

"I spent the night here with Etta. I haven't even looked at a paper."

"Anyway, Detective Devlin asked that I be present for the exhumation and I agreed."

"You mean you were there when they dug up the body?" Aunt Lynrose held out her arm. "Look at that. You done gave me chills."

"Sorry."

I caught a movement behind the screen door and wondered how long my mother had been standing there listening to us.

"Mama? You need some help now?"

"You can go find your papa, tell him we're ready to eat."

"Okay."

As I walked across the front yard toward the road, I heard the screen door squeak. Glancing over my shoulder, I saw that Mama had come out on the porch and she and my aunt were speaking in low tones the way they once had when I was little. This time, I was pretty sure they were talking about me.

Instead of driving around the road, I took the shortcut through the woods and went straight back to the old section. The gate was locked, but I knew where Papa had always kept a spare key.

I let myself in, closed the gate behind me, then wandered down a soft incline, along fern-edged pathways and through thick, silvery curtains of Spanish moss to the angels.

There were fifty-seven of them.

Fifty-seven angels adorning fifty-seven tiny graves. The victims of a fire that had ravaged an orphanage in 1907.

The people in the surrounding counties had taken up a collection to buy the first angel, and every year thereafter, a new one had been added, except during the two world wars and the Great Depression.

By the time the final angel had been placed on the remaining grave, some of the earlier statues had fallen victim to weather and vandalism. Papa had been working for years to restore all fifty-seven with nothing more than patience and a set of vintage masonry tools.

When I was little, those angels had been my only companions. There were no other children around where we lived, but I don't think the solitude had much to do with my loneliness. It was inherent, and once the ghosts came along, it was constant.

The sun had already begun its slow glide toward the horizon when I found a patch of warm clover and slid to the ground. Hugging my knees tightly, I waited.

After a few moments, the air stilled in a prelude redolent with summer.

And then it happened.

The sun sank with a gasping flare, a dying day's last breath that gilded the treetops and shot a volley of golden arrows down through the leaves. Light danced off stone so that for one split second, the angels shimmered with life, a fleeting animation that always took my breath away.

As the angels slept under the soft blanket of dusk, I sat waiting for Papa. Finally, I got up and walked back toward the gate. I saw someone standing just outside and I started to call out to him.

Then with a shudder, I realized it wasn't Papa. But I knew him. It was the ghost of the old man I'd seen when I was nine years old. I stood on hallowed ground, so he posed no immediate threat to me, but he terrified me just the same. His presence after all these years seemed menacing, a manifestation of the unrest that had afflicted my ordered little kingdom.

He looked exactly as I remembered him. Tall, gaunt, with long white hair brushing the collar of his suit coat. Glacial eyes and a faintly sinister demeanor.

I felt another presence and glanced over my shoulder.

Papa had come up behind me. His hair was white, too, but he kept it cropped close to his head and his eyes were faded, his demeanor remote but not at all threatening.

He seemed focused on some distant point, but I knew the ghost had caught his attention.

"You see him, too, don't you?" I whispered as my gaze strayed back to the gate.

"Don't look at him!"

His harsh tone startled me, though I didn't outwardly react. "I'm not."

"Here." He took my arm and turned me toward the angels. "Let's sit a spell."

We sank to the ground, our backs to the ghost, just as we had when I was nine. For the longest time, neither of us spoke, but I could sense Papa's tension and what I thought might be fear. I shivered in the gathering darkness and drew up my legs, resting my chin on my knees.

"Papa, who is he? *What* is he?" I finally asked.

He wouldn't look at me, but fixed his gaze instead on the statues. "A harbinger…a messenger. I don't know."

The chill inside me deepened. A harbinger of what? A messenger for whom? "Have you seen him before? I mean…since that day?"

"No."

"Why has he come back? Why now after all these years?"

"Maybe it's a warning," Papa said.

"What kind of warning?"

Slowly, he turned to face me. "You tell me, child. Has something happened?"

And then I knew. Something *had* happened. Something had shifted in this world and the next. Everything had been changing from the moment John Devlin had stepped out of the mist.

My arms tightened around my legs. I couldn't stop shaking.

Papa placed a gentle hand on my shoulder. "What have you done, Amelia?"

Now it was I who couldn't look at him. "I met someone. A police detective named John Devlin. He's haunted by two ghosts, a woman and a little girl. Last night the ghost child came to my garden. Papa, she knew I could see her. She tried to communicate with me. And then this morning, I found a tiny ring in the garden where I saw her disappear."

"What did you do with this ring?"

"I buried it where I found it."

"You have to rid yourself of it," he said, and then his voice took on an edge of something I'd never heard from him before. I couldn't quite put a name to it. "You have to return it from where it came."

I looked at him, startled. "Return it…to the ghost?"

"Take it to the place where the child died. Or to her grave. Just get rid of it. And promise me you will never see this man again."

"I'm not sure it's that simple."

"It is that simple," he insisted. "There are consequences to breaking the rules. You know that."

His stern voice put me on the defensive. "But I didn't break the rules—"

"Keep your distance from those who are haunted," he recited. *"If they seek you out, turn away from them, for they constitute a terrible threat and cannot be trusted."*

I thought of Devlin asleep in my office, draining me of energy. I didn't dare tell Papa about that.

"You must not allow this man into your life," he warned. "You must not tempt fate."

"Papa—"

"Listen to me, Amelia. There are entities you've never seen before. Forces I dare not even speak of. They are colder, stronger, hungrier than any presence you can imagine."

I caught my breath. "What are you talking about? You mean…ghosts?"

"I call them the Others," he said and I had never heard so much dread and despair in a human voice.

The Others. My heart knocked painfully against my chest. "Why can't I see them?"

"Be thankful that you can't, child. And take care you don't let them in. Once that door has opened…it cannot be closed."

I lowered my voice to a whisper. "Have you seen them, Papa?"

He closed his eyes. "Yes," he said. "I've seen them."

EIGHT

The way Papa described the Others—colder, stronger, hungrier than any presence I'd ever known—was terrifying. And yet even on the drive home, a part of me wondered about the timing of such a revelation. Why was he only now telling me about another realm of ghosts that I couldn't see?

Was it because he feared the power of the forbidden, the allure of the taboo? Did he want to spook me so thoroughly I'd keep my distance from Devlin?

It might have worked, too, if Camille Ashby hadn't called the next day.

At least that's what I told myself.

Not only was Camille my current employer, but she was also one of the most well-connected people in Charleston. In addition to her current position at Emerson University, she sat on the board of almost every historical preservation association in the city. A nod from her was a veritable PR gold mine in my field. So when she called and asked to meet at the cemetery, I knew better than to blow her off.

I was nervous about seeing Devlin again—especially after Papa's warning—but I had managed to disabuse myself of the notion that he'd somehow drained my energy while he lay sleeping in my office. Only a ghost could feed on human vitality and Devlin was no apparition. He was a flesh and blood man, handsome and darkly charismatic. The weakness I'd experienced in his presence was nothing more than a physical manifestation of my attraction to him.

And I was attracted to him. I could admit that now, though I would never admit it to Papa. Devlin's secretive eyes and brooding demeanor were powerful libations to a closet romantic like me. In spite of his modern trappings, he had an old-world air about him. An intoxicating fusion of Byron, Brontë and Poe with a modern twist.

And like the fictional creations of the aforementioned, he had a deadly weakness. He was a haunted man.

For obvious reasons, his ghost child had made a strong impression on me, but my thoughts turned now to the woman. I still wasn't certain of her relationship to the little girl. I'd sensed a distance between them, an odd disconnect that seemed to belie a motherly bond. She seemed more guardian than maternal protector.

It was all very mystifying and I had so many questions. Why had the little girl come alone to my garden? If she'd left the ring for me to find, what did it mean? And was Papa right? Should I find a way to return it?

Now that some time had passed since her visit, the thought of a ghostly communication wasn't as frightening as it had been. And that in itself was pretty scary—that I could ponder almost casually her motivation in trying to contact me. Even more disturbing, a part of me wanted to find out what she wanted instead of fortifying my defenses against her.

I supposed like any nightmare, daylight had diluted its power, and as my natural curiosity about her rose to the surface, I had to remind myself yet again of Rules One and Four:

Never acknowledge a ghost's presence and never, ever tempt fate.

If only I had followed those rules. If only I'd heeded my father's warning...

But on that balmy summer afternoon, it was a little too easy to shove aside those early misgivings as I pulled in behind a row of police cruisers and unmarked vehicles parked at the edge of the road.

Oak Grove was well off the beaten track. At one time, a crude trail led up to the gates, but the ruts had long since been obscured by a thick tangle of scrub brush, vines and the thorny yucca that originally had been planted near certain graves to inhibit a spirit's movement around the cemetery. Over time the prickly vegetation had spread outside the walls and now served to thwart would-be trespassers rather than ghosts, though apparently not murderers.

Kicking off my sandals, I reached over the seat for my boots. I never tired of tramping around in old cemeteries, but they were not without hidden dangers. The sunken graves and fallen headstones made perfect sanctuaries for the eastern diamondback. Papa had once told me about finding a den of rattlesnakes in a small graveyard near Trinity. He'd killed twenty-three in one day.

During the cleanup stage of restorations, I routinely came across all manner of snakes, lizards and newts. The run-of-the-mill creepy-crawlies didn't concern me; I paid them little mind. But the poisonous snakes got my attention, as did the spiders. I was on high alert as I waded through the tall weeds toward the gates.

A uniformed officer stood guard at the entrance and I gave him my name. Since I was early for my meeting with Camille and didn't see her around, I asked for Devlin.

"He's expecting me," I told the officer.

"You're the graveyard expert, right? Gate's open. Keep to the paths and stay out of the cordoned-off area."

I nodded. "Do you have any idea where I might find him?"

"No, but it's pretty quiet in there. Give a holler. He's bound to hear you."

Thanking him, I passed through the heavy iron gates and paused just inside to glance around. I didn't see Devlin, or anyone else for that matter, but I had no intention of breaching the solemnity of the cemetery by calling out to him. Papa had taught me early on to treat each graveyard as though I were a guest. Respect the dead, respect the property. Take nothing, leave nothing behind.

I thought about the basket of shells and pebbles I'd collected as a child from the hallowed ground at Rosehill. I'd never told my father about that stash just as I'd kept silent about the episode with Devlin in my office. Papa wasn't the only one who had secrets.

Clouds scuttled over the sun and a welcome breeze wafted across the graves, carrying the distant rumble of conversation somewhere along the wall, where I presumed the police were concentrating their search efforts. As I knelt on one of the mossy stones to tie my boot lace, a female voice drifted down the pathway, followed by the lower cadence of a familiar baritone.

Why the mere sound of his voice should make me so

uneasy, I didn't know. My first inclination was to hurry away before he could see me. Instead, I ignored my instincts and held my ground, and I would later look back on that decision as a turning point in my relationship with Devlin. I would soon realize that was the moment when the door Papa had warned me about opened a little wider.

NINE

I was so caught off guard by Devlin's nearness that it took me a second to recognize Camille Ashby's voice and another moment to realize that I might be listening in on a private conversation. Even then, I didn't make my presence immediately known, but took my time re-tying my lace.

"…must be family or friends, someone who is missing her. Surely one of them will come forward now that the story is front-page news," Camille was saying.

"One would hope."

A pause. "Whoever she is, she can't be associated with Emerson. I think you understand what I'm saying. The last thing we need is some nosy reporter trying to connect this murder to the other one."

"Both bodies were found in the same cemetery," Devlin said. "A certain amount of speculation is to be expected."

A tiny thrill prickled at the base of my spine. Another body had been found in Oak Grove?

The voices were closing in on me. I rose and made some noise on the stepping stones to give them fair warning. Even so, when they rounded the monument that had hidden me from their view, they both stopped cold.

I didn't know why they seemed so shocked to see me or why the sight of them together made me so uncomfortable. I suspected the latter had something to do with the way Camille touched Devlin's arm when she saw me on the path. The familiarity of that gesture struck me most of all because Devlin had always seemed so remote, so untouchable, but apparently not to Camille Ashby.

I pretended not to notice that touch or the glance they exchanged as I mustered up a pleasant greeting. "Oh, hello. I was just looking for you."

"Aren't you early?" Camille's voice sounded tense.

Devlin glanced at his watch. "We said one so you're right on time."

I nodded, unexpectedly pleased by his defense. "I see the search is already underway."

He cast a skyward glance. "It's clouding up. We're trying to beat the rain."

"Then I suppose we should get down to business, as well," Camille said, her tone brusque. "If you don't mind, I'd like a moment with Amelia."

"No problem." Devlin stepped away and took out his phone.

I tried to focus on Camille, but I could feel his gaze lingering on me. It was a little disconcerting to be the target of all that intensity, and I found myself wishing that I'd taken a little more care with my appearance. My ponytail hung limp in the humidity and the only cosmetics I'd bothered with were SPF 30 and a liberal spritz of insect repellent. A more pulled together look, even for the cemetery, might have done wonders for my poise.

Camille, on the other hand, looked cool and collected even in the heat.

"Sorry. I didn't mean to interrupt," I said.

"No, it's fine. I suppose I should thank you for being so prompt. Tardiness is all too pervasive these days and it's a habit that I thoroughly detest." Her brow smoothed and her voice gradually grew warmer. Her accent was beguilingly reminiscent of my mother and aunt's, but the vowels were not as drawn out and the "ah" sound of her "I" was a little more subtle.

She looked different from the times I'd met with her in her office. I'd thought her attractive before, but the Camille Ashby who'd hired me to restore Oak Grove Cemetery had been a woman of indeterminate age and so prim and proper in manner and dress as to be the epitome of good breeding and old money.

In this incarnation she looked younger, fresher and a good deal more approachable in a crisp, white shirt tucked neatly into the waistband of her pressed jeans. Her blond hair, usually brushed into a sleek bob, had curled charmingly in the humidity, and without the filter of glasses, her eyes took on a deep, violet hue.

Devlin was her darker male counterpart—tall, cut and devastatingly masculine. Yesterday, I'd appreciated the superb fit of his shirt and trousers, and now I took note of the expert tailoring of his clothing, the expensive fabric and I realized yet again that he was no ordinary detective. He had a past, a background that I grew more and more curious about each time we met.

I was the odd man out here, neither fashionable nor fine-tuned in my baggy cargos and tank.

"I asked to meet with you here in the cemetery for a couple of reasons," Camille said. "First, I need you present for this search. I don't want there to be a question that the graves have been treated with anything but the utmost dignity and respect during this whole dreadful ordeal. And secondly..." Her gaze swept the cemetery and the crease reappeared between her brows. "To be perfectly frank, I find the amount of work still to be done quite alarming. I expected to see more progress."

"I lost nearly a week to rain before this happened," I reminded her.

"Regardless of rain or other setbacks, we agreed upon a time frame."

"I'm well aware of my deadline, but I can't start the cleanup until the site map is completed, and I can't finish the map until I'm allowed back in here to photograph the old section. Nothing can be removed or cleaned until we have an accurate recording of prerestoration features."

She considered the dilemma for a moment. "What if I could get you some help? Would that make the work go more quickly?"

I tried to remain diplomatic. "Volunteers are always welcome, but they'd have to be properly trained first and that can be time-consuming. I've seen too many instances where well-meaning locals descend upon an old grave-yard with chain saws and axes and start hacking away at centuries-old vegetation without regard to design aes-thetics or symbolic meaning."

"Yes, I suppose that could be a problem," she mused.

"Besides, I don't think there's cause for worry. We're not that far off schedule, and as soon as I'm allowed back in, I'll hire plenty of help. It's a small cemetery. The cleanup will go quickly once everything is in place."

"You're the expert. I'll leave the details to you, but please keep in mind that the work must be completed by the start of the fall semester and not one day later. This year marks Emerson's bicentennial and the committee has decided to nominate Oak Grove for the National Register."

That explained why time was suddenly of the essence after decades of shameful neglect.

Several responses leapt to mind, all of which I prudently kept to myself. Nor did I point out the difficulty of getting a graveyard, even one as old as Oak Grove, listed in the National Register of Historic Places. Camille Ashby would know as well as I the rigid criteria governing cemetery eligibility and how best to get around them.

So I smiled and nodded and assured her once again that barring any further complications, I would bring the project in on time and on budget.

Luckily, the ding of her phone alerted her to an incoming text and she became momentarily distracted as she scanned the message. "Something's come up," she said in a clipped tone and dropped the phone back into her bag. "I have to get back to the office. I'll have someone on my staff contact you for regular progress reports."

"That's fine," I murmured, although I hated nothing more than having someone watch over my shoulder.

She glanced at Devlin, who was still on the phone. "Tell John I'll be in touch. And tell him…I'm counting on him. He'll know what I mean."

I watched her hurry away, annoyed with myself for allowing her to intimidate me. Whatever else I might be lacking, I had the utmost confidence in my professional abilities—even on cemeteries as run-down as Oak Grove. The process of stripping away years of neglect was akin to restoring an old painting. It took patience, skill and almost obsessive dedication.

In the two years since I'd started my business, I'd worked very hard to establish an impeccable reputation. No one could fault my education, but my age and slender portfolio sometimes worked against me, despite the fact that I'd spent the whole of my childhood and adolescence learning about cemetery upkeep from my father.

I considered myself a dedicated artisan, but I was also a businesswoman and I needed Camille Ashby's goodwill and glowing recommendation when the project was completed. So I swallowed my irritation and made a mental note to send her weekly updates, both written and visual, without her having to ask for them.

I had my back to Devlin while I waited for him to conclude his phone conversation, but once again, I knew the moment he stepped up behind me. The hair at my nape rose and I put up a hand to rub away the tingles as I turned to face him.

My father's voice whispered a warning. *Promise me you will never see this man again.*

I took a deep breath and very deliberately closed him out. *Sorry, Papa.*

"Did Camille leave?" Devlin asked.

The use of her first name did not escape me. "Yes. She had to get back to the office. I'm to tell you she'll be in touch and that…she's counting on you. She said you'd know what that meant."

He shrugged, as if the message was of no consequence to him, but a brief flicker of irritation made me even more curious about his relationship with Camille Ashby. They referred to one another by their given names, which seemed to indicate more than a passing acquaintance, as did the overheard conversation and the way she'd touched his arm. She was older than Devlin, but not by much, and age didn't seem to matter for a woman as attractive as Camille.

"Is something wrong?" he asked.

"What? No…sorry. Just daydreaming."

I wondered if he realized the power of his stare. If he had any idea the effect it had on me. Perhaps that should have been another warning—the fact that I couldn't tear my gaze from him. It was as if he had some sort of hold over me, but I couldn't put the blame on him. I was solely responsible for my actions. I hadn't made the trek to the cemetery to see Camille Ashby. She'd just made things convenient for me. I'd come here in pursuit of the forbidden, though I had never done anything remotely reckless in my whole life.

Some of the searchers were moving toward us and I tried to quell my nerves by refocusing my attention on them. "Must be like looking for a needle in a haystack," I murmured. "Won't the rain have washed away any physical evidence like footprints and bloodstains?" All those years of self-discipline normalized my voice even though my heart thumped erratically.

"Not all of it. Something always gets left behind. We just have to keep looking until we find it."

"And if you don't?"

Devlin's gaze met mine again and I felt a deep shudder go through me. "Then we'll have to let her lead us to the killer."

"Her?"

"The victim. The dead have a lot to say if you're willing to listen."

The irony of his statement stunned me. I had a sudden image of the ghost child, tugging on his pants, patting his leg, trying her best to get his attention. What was she trying to tell him? And why wasn't he listening?

She'd come to me, too, but I had good reason to rebuff her. Papa was right. I knew only too well the consequences of breaking the rules. To acknowledge the ghost child was to invite her into my life, offer her the sustenance of my warmth and energy until I became nothing more than a walking, breathing shell. No matter what she wanted from me, I had to protect myself at any cost. To remain safe, I had to distance myself from Devlin and his ghosts.

Yet there I stood, enthralled by his very nearness.

He turned to look out over the cemetery, so lost in concentration for a moment that he seemed to have forgotten my presence. I took the opportunity to study his profile, following the line of his jaw and chin, lingering in that shadowy, sensual place beneath his full bottom lip where that indented scar marred an otherwise flawless profile. For some reason, that one imperfection mesmerized me. The harder I tried to avert my eyes, the stronger I felt its pull.

"I have a confession to make," I said.

I didn't think he'd heard me at first, but then he turned, one brow lifting ever so slightly as he waited for my admission.

"When I first came up, I overheard you and Dr. Ashby talking about another body that was found here."

His expression never changed, but I sensed his wariness, like an animal catching wind of a possible threat. "What about it?"

"When did it happen?"

"Years ago," he said vaguely.

His reluctance to elaborate only whetted my curiosity. He couldn't know it yet, but my persistence could sometimes border on obsession when I set my mind to something.

"Was the killer caught?"

"No."

"Is there any chance the two murders could be connected? I only ask," I hastened to add, "because I'll be spending a lot of time here alone. This is all a little unnerving, to say the least."

His expression was shuttered, his whole demeanor guarded as he stared down at me. "After fifteen years, I'd say a connection is a long shot, but I still wouldn't recommend coming out here alone. Even though it's within the city limits, this place is pretty remote."

"And metropolitan cemeteries, particularly those off the beaten path, can be magnets for the criminal element," I said.

"Yes, exactly. Don't you have someone who works with you? An assistant or something?"

"I'll have plenty of help for the cleanup stage. Until then, I'll be careful."

He looked as if he wanted to say something more, but instead he turned away with a brief nod.

"Can I ask you something?"

"Yes?" That hesitation again. That same veiled wariness.

"I've spent hours and hours researching Oak Grove, and yet this is the first mention I've heard of another murder. How is that possible?"

"Maybe you weren't looking in the right places."

"I doubt that. I always read everything I can get my hands on about each cemetery I restore. Not just county records and church books. I also spend a lot of time scanning newspaper archives."

"What's the point of that?"

"It's hard to explain, but immersing myself in the history gives me a unique perspective. Restoration isn't just about whacking weeds and scrubbing headstones. It's about *restoration*."

"You sound pretty passionate about it."

"I'd find another line of work if I wasn't. Wouldn't you?"

His gaze whisked over me, straying to places that made me grow a little warm. "I suppose I would," he murmured, his voice like cool silk.

"About that body…" I prompted.

He returned to the subject with reluctance. "There's a reason you didn't find anything in the newspapers."

"What reason?"

"There was a concentrated effort by certain parties, including the girl's family, to keep the investigation quiet."

"How did they manage that?"

"In this city, it's all about who you know. Especially among the upper class. People in positions of power and influence tend to close rank." His voice betrayed an old contempt, and I remembered my aunt's remarks about the South of Broad Devlins, a wealthy, aristocratic family who could trace their roots back to the city's founding. If Devlin was a cousin from the wrong side of the tracks, that might explain his scorn.

"At the time of the murder, the police chief, the mayor and the editor of the largest local daily newspaper were all Emerson alumni," he said. "A murder on school property would have done a lot of damage to the school's reputation."

I rubbed the inside of my elbow where a mosquito had vectored in on the one area I'd missed with bug spray. "But why would the victim's family participate in a cover-up?"

"The Delacourts are Charleston royalty. If you're at all familiar with this city's mansion class, you'll know that scandal is to be avoided at any cost. I've pretty much seen it all, and yet I can still be shocked at the lengths those people will go to in order to protect the family name."

"Even hush up a murder?"

"If that murder brings humiliation and disgrace, yes. Afton Delacourt was a seventeen-year-old party girl. A promiscuous thrill-seeker who abused drugs and alcohol and, according to the rumor mill, dabbled in the occult. That's pretty sensational stuff."

Something in his voice, in that careful gaze accelerated my pulse. "What do you mean, she dabbled in the occult? Like Ouija boards?"

"It was a little darker than that."

"Darker…how?"

He didn't answer.

"How exactly did she die?" I pressed.

He spoke quietly. "You don't want the details. Trust me on that."

I thought about the way his gaze had skidded away that first night in the cemetery when I'd asked about the cause of death. I wondered now if his reluctance to divulge certain aspects of the murders—both old and new—was professional discretion or if his upbringing and personality had something to do with the circum-spect way he answered my questions. From what I'd seen, he was something of a throwback to past generations and might well regard his role of protector as extending beyond his duties as a police detective.

Strangely, I wasn't offended by this outdated attitude. I think on some level it fed into an adolescent fantasy that had been nurtured in those lonely years by a steady diet of *Jane Eyre* and Mr. Rochester, of *Buffy* and *Angel*.

Regardless, I was no less determined to get the whole story from him. He seemed to sense this, and to my surprise, continued without further prompting.

"How familiar are you with secret societies on college campuses?"

"Not at all really. I know about Skull and Bones. I also know that those kinds of organizations tend to use a lot of mortuary imagery and that their emblems and symbols sometimes turn up on old headstones."

"The imagery is very deliberate," he said. "Mostly, it's used to create a sense of gravitas and intimidation."

"Mostly?"

His expression didn't outwardly change, but I sensed a subtle tension in his features, an imperceptible tightening of his mouth and jaw. "The society at Emerson was known as the Order of the Coffin and the Claw. It had a long tradition on campus. Legacy pledges went back for generations. Some people think that at the time of her death, Afton Delacourt was involved with a Claw, that he lured her here to the cemetery and murdered her in some sort of initiation ritual."

I felt moisture in the breeze that drifted through the old oak trees. It seemed sinister somehow, like the cold, dank touch of a corpse. "Was he arrested?"

"No one on the outside knew who he was and no one in the Order would give up a fellow Claw. Loyalty is valued, second only to secrecy."

"Is? This group still exists?"

"They were denounced by the university after the murder, but a lot of people believe that rather than disbanding, they went deeper underground and still retain a shadow presence on campus to this day."

I don't know if I'd picked up on something in his voice or if it was an independent thought, but a couple of puzzle pieces suddenly clicked together. "Those people you mentioned earlier...the police chief, the newspaper editor, the mayor...were they Claws?"

"Like I said, membership in the Order is a highly guarded secret."

"But it makes sense, doesn't it? The cover-up wasn't about Emerson's reputation. It was about protecting another Claw." My voice grew animated with my certainty. "Now I'm beginning to understand why you showed up at my house yesterday morning with all those questions about headstone symbolism and imagery. You think whoever committed this recent murder may be somehow connected to this Order."

He never got the chance to respond. Someone called out his name and he turned with a jerk. "I'm over here!"

"We found something!" the officer shouted back. "You'll want to see this!"

"Wait here," he said over his shoulder as he started up the path.

I did wait…for maybe half a minute before I felt compelled to follow him through the muddle of headstones into the older section of the cemetery.

Crossing through the arched divide, I caught a glimpse of a pointed roof straight ahead. The Bedford Mausoleum was the oldest in the cemetery, erected in 1853 to commemorate the passing of Dorothea Prescott Bedford and her descendants. The design was Gothic, topped with a series of crosses. The body of the structure had been carved out of the side of a hillock, which made it unique. Elevated terrain was an anomaly in the Lowcountry and one of the reasons I found Oak Grove so unsettling. The topography was somehow off-kilter.

As I walked deeper into the gloom, the temperature noticeably dropped. Swaying manes of curly moss blocked most of the light, allowing tentacles of ivy to ensnare statues and monuments already blackened with lichen. Where light managed to penetrate, water beads glistened like crystals on giant philodendrons. It was like stepping into the heart of a primordial rain forest.

I'd lost sight of Devlin, but as I came to the end of the overgrown pathway, I heard his voice. He was somewhere to the right of the mausoleum. As I disentangled myself from a wild grapevine, I spotted him. He stood with a group of bedraggled-looking men in sweaty shirts and mud-spattered trousers. They were gathered around a grave marked with a tablet headstone.

Slowly, I walked toward them, expecting Devlin to turn and order me back at any moment. But he said nothing even as I moved up beside him.

I stared down into the mottled light, searching for what had captured their attention.

Then I saw it.

A skeletal hand rising out of the dead leaves like an early spring crocus.

TEN

Within half an hour, they arrived in droves—cops in civvies and uniforms, swatting mosquitoes and mopping sweaty faces as they emerged from the overgrown brush to vie for a peek at the latest discovery. They were professionals, so they kept a respectable distance while the Charleston County coroner, a tiny, redheaded dynamo named Regina Sparks, examined the remains. I'd never met anyone whose name suited her more. Even standing stock-still beside the grave, the woman radiated a kind of manic energy that belied her unruffled demeanor.

I'd retreated to the background where I could observe without being in the way. After a lengthy consultation with some of his cohorts, Devlin came to find me.

"You okay?"

"As okay as one can be under the circumstances." I hesitated, reluctant to give voice to the terrible thoughts rolling around inside my brain. "This can't be a coincidence, can it? What if there are others that haven't been

found yet? What if this is the beginning of something…"
I grappled for the right word. "You know what I mean."

Devlin's expression remained guarded, but I could sense an underlying anxiety that did nothing to relieve my dread. "It's best not to make that kind of leap until we have all the facts. Right now, I'd like to ask you some questions about Oak Grove. I need to know about this place and you're the only one who can help me out."

I nodded, grateful to have something useful to do.

"What's the first thing you do when you take on a job like this?"

The question surprised me a little, but I answered without hesitation. "I walk the whole cemetery. Even before I start to photograph."

"So you've been all over this place. Even back here?"

"I've walked it, yes. But I'd barely begun photographing last Friday when the clouds moved in."

"Did you notice anything out of the ordinary in either section?"

I glanced toward the skeletal remains. "Nothing like that, I assure you."

"I'm talking more along the lines of that outward-facing headstone we discussed yesterday. Are there any more of those in here?"

"Not that I recall."

He frowned. "Wouldn't you remember?"

"Not necessarily. I told you before, an outward-facing headstone is not really that unusual. It only seems so now in context. At the time I walked the cemetery, I would have been preoccupied with Oak Grove's more extraordinary features."

"Such as?"

"Seven slot-and-tab box tombs with the lids still intact. Those are really rare, especially in South Carolina."

"What's a...what you just said?"

"Slot-and-tab box tomb, and it's exactly what it sounds like—a horizontal tomb in the shape of a box. Slots are cut into the lid so that it fits down over vertical head and foot stones. The only other ones I've come across were in northeast Georgia. And, of course, there's the Bedford Mausoleum." I turned and studied the towers and points, barely visible through the lush vegetation. "It's built into a hillside. You just don't see that in the Lowcountry."

"Man-made?"

"The hillside? It would have to be. The whole structure is covered in kudzu so I can't tell much about the construction. Anyway, as I said, those are some of the features that caught my attention. I don't remember any more outward-facing headstones, but there could be others. We'd have to rewalk the cemetery to know for sure."

"That might not be a bad idea," he said.

Regina Sparks came up just then, her round face glistening in the heat. Lifting up her hair, she fanned the back of her neck with her hand. "It's hotter than a two-peckered alley cat up in here. Humidity must be close to a hundred." She sized me up with a friendly smile. "I don't believe we've met. Regina Sparks."

"Amelia Gray."

"She's the cemetery expert I told you about the other night," Devlin said.

Her gaze fastened on him before she turned to me. It seemed she wasn't altogether immune to Devlin's magnetism, either. "The one they call the Graveyard Queen?"

"Yes, but how did you know?" I was both pleased and embarrassed that she knew my nickname.

"My aunt lives in Samara, Georgia. She sent me the video of your interview and the hovering 'ghost,'" she said with air quotes. "That was the biggest news to hit that place in forty years. She couldn't stop talking about it."

"Small world," I murmured.

"No kidding. Wait'll she hears about this. You don't have a headstone rubbing or something you could sign for her, do you?"

"Uh, no, sorry. And I don't recommend rubbings, anyway. The process can actually be damaging to head-stones."

"Really? Well, that's too bad. She would have gotten a kick out of something like that."

"Do you mind?" Devlin cut in. "If it's not too much trouble, I'd like to hear your initial assessment."

"Of Amelia?" Regina gave me a wink. "Lovely girl, handled herself well on camera."

"I'm talking about the remains," he said drily.

"Oh, him. Dead as a doornail."

Regina's wisecracks were probably a little hard for someone like Devlin to take. He was all business and I'd yet to see anything more than a hint of a smile. But those who were haunted often had a grim demeanor. One could hardly blame them.

She pushed back her bangs, giving herself an odd plumed appearance that I doubted was the look she'd been aiming for. "I don't exactly have a lot to work with here. I can't even say for certain we're looking at an in-trusive burial. The hand looks pretty damn clean. No muscle or ligament, just bone. Whoever that poor bastard was, he's been here for years."

"She," I said, garnering simultaneous eyebrow lifts. "If the bones are from the original burial, the remains are most likely female."

"You don't say." Regina swatted a mosquito, leaving a

bloody smear on her arm. Absently, she wiped her hand on her jeans. "I'm mighty curious as to how you came to that conclusion. The inscription on the tombstone is illegible."

"If you look at the top of the stone, you can just make out a floral motif…a rose, which is almost always used to symbolize the feminine. Whether the rose is a bud, flower or somewhere in between indicates the age of the deceased. A bud, a child under twelve. A partial bloom, a teenager and so on. A full bloom and a bud are sometimes used together to represent a dual burial of mother and child. I only saw one rose in full bloom on this stone."

Regina turned to Devlin. "I guess they don't call her the Graveyard Queen for nothing."

"Evidently not." His eyes in the shade looked almost black. "Anything else you can tell us?"

"Yes, and it's a bit of a coincidence, considering our previous conversation. If you look closely, you can also make out the outline of a winged effigy. Not a death's head, but a cherub, which is more common to the mid-nineteenth century."

"Now you've lost me," Regina said, scratching the bug bite.

I gave her the top-line version. "A skull—a death's head—was used to represent the grimmer aspects of death like mortality and penance, but the evolution of cherubs and the like symbolized a more hopeful outlook—the soul in flight and the ascension to heaven."

"The soul in flight," Devlin said thoughtfully. "Like the feather on the other headstone?"

There it was. A connection between the body found last night and the skeletal remains discovered less than an hour ago. Neither of us said anything, but I knew our minds had gone to the same dark place.

Regina's gaze hopped back and forth. "Well?"

Devlin gave her a rundown of our previous conversation.

She heard him out with a pensive scowl. "I've never given much thought to what they put on tombstones, but wouldn't anything to do with wings and feathers—all that soul in flight stuff—be pretty common in a Christian cemetery?"

"It's not uncommon," I agreed. "Especially in a graveyard as old as Oak Grove. Different eras evoke different imagery, but certain symbols never go away. They just evolve."

Regina turned back to Devlin. "You really think there's something to this?"

"I'm taking a wait-and-see approach. It's too early to consider the symbols anything more than an interesting observation."

"Interesting is right." She glanced at me. "You got anything else for us?"

"Just this. If the bones are from the original burial, you'll need to notify the Office of the State Archaeologist. Remains over a hundred years old fall under her jurisdiction. Her name is Temple Lee. I can make the call for you if you like."

Regina shrugged. "Couldn't hurt. We'll need Shaw for the exhumation and I'll have to line up an entomologist to help us determine PMI."

"What's PMI?"

"Postmortem interval. The amount of time passed since death."

"I thought Shaw was still in Haiti," Devlin said.

Regina snagged a phone from her back pocket. "One way to find out." She walked away to make the call, leaving me alone once again with Devlin.

"Would she be referring to Ethan Shaw?"

He looked surprised. "Yes. He's the forensic anthropologist we normally use in these kinds of cases. I take it you know him?"

"I met him once, very briefly, through his father."

"The ghost hunter?"

"Rupert Shaw is more than a ghost hunter. He runs one of the most respected institutes for parapsychology studies in the state."

"Hardly an overwhelming endorsement," Devlin said. "Don't tell me you believe in all that mumbo jumbo."

"I try to keep an open mind. Do you know Dr. Shaw?"

"Our paths have crossed."

Something in his voice caught my attention. "Crossed professionally?"

"Look, I'm probably not the best person to ask about Rupert Shaw. I think he's at best a kook and at worst a fraud. Though I can't say I'm surprised he's been able to make a name for himself in this city. Charlestonians have always had a high regard for the eccentric."

"But not you."

A shadow flicked across his face. "I don't place much stock in anything I can't see with my own two eyes."

Something told me I should let the matter drop, but apparently I wasn't too keen on listening to warnings these days, internal or otherwise. "What about emotions? Fear, loneliness, grief. Or even love. Just because you can't see something doesn't mean it's not real."

He froze, and I saw something waver in his eyes, a darkness that made me tremble before he shook off whatever cloud had passed over him.

"Just a friendly word of advice about Rupert Shaw. I don't know what kind of dealings you've had with the man, but I'd be careful of any future associations."

"I appreciate your concern, but unless you can offer something more concrete than your disdain for his profession, I see no need to alter my opinion or my relationship with Dr. Shaw. He's been nothing but kind to me."

"Have it your way," he muttered.

I thought that was the end of the subject, but then he took my arm and ushered me deeper into the shadows, where we wouldn't be overheard. We were standing so close I could smell the graveyard on his clothing. Not the putrid odor of death, but the sensual earthiness of a lush, secret garden.

It wasn't fair, I thought. The cemetery was supposed to be my domain, so how come I was the one short of breath here? How come I was the one with tingling flesh where his fingers circled my arm?

As if sensing my discomfort, he dropped his hand. "You asked earlier about an arrest in the Afton Delacourt murder. No one was ever formally charged, but Rupert Shaw was brought in for questioning."

"On what grounds?"

"He used to be a professor at Emerson University. He taught classes in ancient burial practices, primitive funeral rites, that sort of thing. After Afton's murder, some of his students came forward to say that they'd attended séances with him at his home and in a mausoleum here at this cemetery. They said he had a theory about death that he was obsessed with proving."

"Which was?"

"According to him, when someone dies, a door or gate opens, which allows an observer a glimpse into the other side. The slower the death, the longer the door stays open, so that one might even be able to pass through and come back out."

Papa's voice darted through my head. *Once that door has opened...it cannot be closed.*

Alarmed, I stared up at him. "What does that theory have to do with Afton Delacourt?"

His expression didn't waver. "She was tortured in such a way that her death was a long time coming."

"That's horrible, but it hardly proves—"

"Her body was found in the mausoleum where Shaw allegedly held his séances."

I had no response to that. My mouth had suddenly gone dry.

"I'm not saying he's guilty of anything," Devlin added. "Just be careful. Don't get too involved with him or that shady institute of his."

It had been less than forty-eight hours since I'd first set eyes on John Devlin, and yet neither of us seemed to think twice about his meddlesome interest in my personal affairs.

"How do you know so much about this?" I asked uneasily. "You said the investigation was kept quiet back then and you're too young to have been on the police force."

"My wife was one of Rupert Shaw's students," he said quietly. And with that, he turned and walked away.

ELEVEN

A million questions swirled in my head—about Devlin's wife, about his ghosts—but I kept them to myself as I watched him walk back over to Regina Sparks. Perhaps I wasn't yet ready for those answers. Maybe I still harbored some notion that if he remained a stranger, I could keep my distance from him.

Nothing could have been further from the truth, of course, because despite everything, our destinies were already intertwined. We just didn't know it.

With some effort, I turned my thoughts to other things as I walked back to my car. I didn't know what to make of the information I'd learned about Afton Delacourt, but I was beginning to fear the worst. I didn't see how the discovery of three bodies in the same cemetery could be unrelated, no matter the gap in time. However, if the skeletal remains turned out to be original to the grave, then I could more readily buy two bodies—Afton's and the recent murder victim—being coincidental. As Devlin had pointed out, fifteen years between discoveries was a lot of time and an abandoned cemetery wasn't an uncommon dumping ground.

The only certainty I'd gleaned from any of Devlin's revelations was his disregard for Rupert Shaw. As far as I was concerned, his assessment couldn't have been further off the mark.

I'd met Dr. Shaw shortly after my arrival in Charleston. Someone had sent him the Samara video and he'd contacted me through my blog. We'd kept in touch via email and the occasional dinner ever since. It was through one of his research associates that I'd found the house on Rutledge Avenue. For that reason alone, I was inclined to have a favorable opinion of him, regardless of what Devlin thought.

Emerging from the tall weeds onto the road, I hustled over to my SUV to retrieve my phone. It was lodged between the seat and console, where it must have slipped from my pocket earlier as I pulled on my boots.

Temple wasn't in her office, so I left a brief voicemail explaining the situation and asked her to call me back as soon as she got the message.

As I closed the car door, I noticed a man leaning against the vehicle parked in front of mine. In spite of the overcast sky, he wore sunglasses and held his head in such a way that I couldn't see his face straight on. But I recognized him at once. He was the man I'd seen on the Battery the day before.

And now here he was at Oak Grove.

I glanced up the road, where a uniformed officer stood talking on the radio outside his cruiser. The occasional burst of static from the transmission assured me that he was close enough to hear me scream, should I feel the need.

The newcomer lifted his head slightly as I walked to the front of the SUV. "Amelia Gray?"

A warning bell sounded. "How do you know my name?"

"I read about you in the paper," he said. "I'm Tom Gerrity." Instead of shaking my hand, he folded his arms and crossed his feet at the ankles as he leaned back against the vehicle. He appeared to be very much at ease. I couldn't say the same for myself.

"Have we met?"

"No, but I've seen you around."

"Like on the Battery yesterday morning?"

A smile flashed. "I'm flattered you remember."

I shot another look at the cop. He was still on the phone. Still within screaming distance.

I could feel Gerrity's gaze on me. It was disconcerting not being able to look into his eyes. The part of his face that I could see was very attractive. He was even more handsome than Devlin, but he didn't possess Devlin's dangerous allure, so therefore, he posed no threat to the rules.

Fate had a very strange sense of humor, I decided. The first man in forever that had ignited my carnal spark and he had to be haunted.

But I couldn't worry about that now. Tom Gerrity had been following me and I needed to find out why.

"What do you want, Mr. Gerrity?"

"Direct and to the point," he said. "I like that. What I want, Miss Gray, is a conduit into the police department."

I stared at him with open suspicion. "A conduit? Are you a reporter? Do you expect me to leak information to you about the investigation? Because that's not going to happen."

"I'm not a reporter. And I'm not after information. I want you to give John Devlin a message for me."

I nodded in the direction of the gates. "He's still inside the cemetery. You can tell him yourself."

"There's a guard at the gates. I'd never be allowed through."

"But if you have information—"

"Doesn't matter. I'm persona non grata with the Charleston P.D. these days."

I shooed away a fly buzzing around my face. "Why is that?"

"Let's just say, cops and P.I.'s don't mix. Devlin won't see me and he'd never take my call. I need you to be my go-between."

"And why would I do that?"

"Because I know who the victim is."

The revelation caught me off guard and I gaped at him.

"Her name was Hannah Fischer," he said. "Her mother asked me to find her."

"Find her? Was she missing?"

During this whole time, he had remained in the same pose. Arms folded, ankles crossed, head tilted. I wondered how he could remain so static.

"Last Thursday, the day before that big storm, Mrs. Fischer found Hannah in her room packing. The girl looked as if she hadn't slept or bathed in days. It was obvious she'd been hiding out from someone, but she wouldn't say who. She didn't want to put her mother in any danger. She asked for enough money to disappear, insisting that was the only way either of them would be safe. Mrs. Fischer gave her all the money she had on hand and the keys to her car. Hannah fled and I've been looking for her ever since. Until a couple of days ago, the trail had gone stone cold."

"How can you be so sure it's her? The newspaper account didn't give a description."

He lifted a shoulder. "Call it a hunch, an instinct. My grandmother would tell you it's a gift. All I can say is that I'm never wrong about these things. *Never.* That's why they call me the Prophet."

Gooseflesh popped at my nape. "Do you know who killed Hannah Fischer?"

"That's something you'll have to figure out."

"You don't mean me literally, I hope."

"Hannah Fischer's body was left in that grave for a reason. Find the reason, find the killer."

"I'm not a detective."

"But you know cemeteries. And that just might be the key."

Not a very comforting thought.

The jarring sound of my ringtone startled me so badly I jumped. Reluctantly, I took my eyes off Gerrity to check the display. It was Temple returning my call.

"I have to take this," I said. "Is there anything else you want me to tell Devlin?"

"The last time anyone saw Hannah alive, she had on a white sundress with red and yellow flowers. You can tell him that."

I put the phone to my ear and walked around to the back of my car so that Gerrity wouldn't overhear what I had to tell Temple.

"Thanks for calling me back so soon," I told her.

"Sounds like you have a real mess on your hands."

"All I can tell you for certain is that a pre–Civil War grave is about to be disturbed for an exhumation. I thought you'd want to be here for that."

"I do, but…hold on a second." She said something unintelligible and I heard excited voices in the background.

"Where are you?" I asked.

"Your neck of the woods, on one of the islands. We're excavating a possible burial mound out here. Just turned up some pretty interesting artifacts so I won't be able to get to the cemetery today."

"Tomorrow?"

"I'll do my best. Who do I contact to coordinate?"

"John Devlin at Charleston P.D., but they're also calling in a forensic anthropologist named Ethan Shaw."

"I know Ethan. I'll give him a ring as soon as we hang up. In the meantime, why don't you buy me dinner tonight and tell me what you've been up to? Besides getting yourself involved in a murder investigation."

We agreed on a time and place and hung up. When I walked back around to the front of my car, Tom Gerrity had vanished.

I checked the road in both directions, didn't see him, and started back to the cemetery. I was halfway to the gates when I had the strangest sensation of being watched.

Glancing over my shoulder, I almost expected to find Gerrity on the path behind me, but no one was there. I saw no movement at all except for the swirl of foxtail grass seeds near the woods. I admired the snow-globe effect for a moment, then continued on.

A dozen steps later, I experienced the sensation again.

My senses on high alert, I monitored my surroundings with sidelong glances. Off to the right, a flash of movement in my periphery quickened my pulse.

Deliberately casual, I turned and saw something just beyond the tree line. A dark form slinking out of the woods.

The silhouette had been moving away from me, but the moment my gaze reached it, the shadowy head came up and slowly rotated in my direction.

The air went very still and I sensed hesitation, like an animal sizing up its prey. Then the weeds parted violently, as though an invisible scythe cut a path straight toward me.

Whatever it was, it came at me like a freight train, preceded by an unnatural chill the like of which I'd never felt before. I stood there breathless and immobile, bound by a nightmarish paralysis.

A blizzard of cotton fluff swirled in the air as an icy gust swept back my hair. It was getting closer. So close I could feel a preternatural dampness against my skin, but still I couldn't move.

Then my heart jerked, sending a spurt of adrenaline through my bloodstream. I spun around to the path and ran.

I heard nothing behind me. No pounding footsteps. No snapping twigs. But I knew it was back there, knew that I couldn't outpace it for long, that...*thing,* that dark entity.

Still, I kept going.

A moment later, I emerged from the weeds and saw Devlin. He was alone and coming toward me, and I reacted purely on instinct. I ran straight into his arms. I had some momentum going, but he caught me with ease and without noticeable reluctance.

He was so warm, so strong, so...human. And he felt so good. I didn't move away as I should have, but sank even deeper into the embrace.

"What's wrong?"

Too breathless to speak, I could only shiver.

His arms tightened around me and now I felt a bit of that protectiveness I'd sensed in him earlier. He lent me the comfort of his chest for a moment longer before he stepped back and held me at arm's length, searching my face.

"Tell me what happened."

Fear and shock made me speak without thinking. "I saw something at the edge of the woods."

"What was it? An animal?"

"No…a shadow." An entity. A ghost. One of the Others.

He stared down at me, perplexed but trying to make sense of my babbling. "You saw someone's shadow?"

Not some*one*. Some*thing*.

"I didn't get a good look at it. When it came after me, I just turned and ran."

His hands gripped my arms. "Came after you? Someone chased you?"

"Yes. At least…yes."

"But you didn't see a face."

"No. I didn't see a face."

His gaze swept the woods behind me. "It was probably just some kid from the university trying to scare you. I'll go have a look."

"Devlin?"

I'm not even sure what I meant to say to him, but the words fled as I glanced over his shoulder where a luminous shimmer had appeared.

A moment later, his ghosts floated through the veil into the falling twilight.

Devlin found nothing in the woods. I wasn't surprised. The thing I'd glimpsed at the tree line didn't have enough substance to leave even a footprint, but somehow it had force. I'd never felt anything like it.

But at the moment, I had something else to worry about. We were standing by my car and Devlin's ghosts were with him. The chill of their presence consumed me. It was all I could do not to shiver and give myself away.

The child remained at his side, cheek resting against his leg, but the woman had glided forward this time. Her boldness alarmed me. The icy fire of her eyes frightened me. I didn't look at her full on, of course, but I could still see her. She had been a beautiful woman. Exotic and sultry. Even in death, her essence was powerful. Palpable.

Devlin peered down at me. "Are you sure you're all right?" He touched my arm and a bolt of lightning shot through me. The air all around us became electric and my every nerve ending tingled from the charge.

Drawn by the surge of energy, the woman drifted to my side. She placed her hand on my arm, mimicking Devlin. The heat of the day still lingered on my skin, and she slid her fingers up my arm, savoring the warmth, as she floated around me. I could feel her hands in my hair, her breath in my ear. Her lips against my neck. Her touch was like the coldest of whispers, and it came to me that she wasn't just drawn to my warmth. She was taunting me.

She stood behind me, Devlin in front of me. A more chilling ménage à trois I couldn't imagine. It took every ounce of my strength to ignore those ghostly caresses. Devlin had said something to me, but I didn't hear a word of it.

I stared at him now, making him the focus of my concentration. His expression never changed. He was completely unaware of the dynamics that played out all around us.

"I almost forgot to tell you," I said, my voice only slightly breathless. "I saw someone earlier. A private detective named Tom Gerrity."

Everything shifted. The ghost's hands stilled in my

hair as Devlin's expression grew rigid. She drifted back to his side, and then she and the child melted into the background, as if his sudden tension had repelled them.

"What did he want?" His words came out cold and clipped. I had to suppress another shudder.

"He asked me to give you a message."

"What message?"

Quickly, I told him everything I could recall of my conversation with the P.I. Devlin said nothing, but I could tell the very mention of Gerrity's name had upset him.

"He said he needed a go-between because he's persona non grata with the police department," I said. "What did he do?"

A muscle worked in Devlin's jaw. "He used to be a cop. A case went bad and another cop died because of him."

I had a feeling there was a lot more to the story, but I wouldn't hear it from Devlin. Which was just as well. It was time the night ended for us. I needed to get away from him and his ghosts. Away from Oak Grove and that thing that had come out of the woods. A lot had happened and I wanted to be home, safe and sound, in my own little sanctuary to try and make sense of it.

But as I drove away, I found myself missing Devlin's touch. Cold and bereft, I summoned Papa's rules and chanted them to myself.

TWELVE

Temple and I had agreed to meet at Rapture that night, a fusion cuisine restaurant housed in a beautiful old building on Meeting Street that had once been a rectory. Whether the building or the ground beneath was hallowed, I had no idea, but it was one of the few places in Charleston—despite its many churches—where I felt safe and at peace. And I needed that tonight more than ever.

After leaving the cemetery, I'd gone home to shower and change, and had tried not to think about that thing that had come out of the woods. Or of Devlin and his ghosts. I wanted to believe my imagination had played some role in the events of the day, but hours later, I was still shaken.

Even as a child, I'd never experienced the kind of terror I'd felt on the path. My father had instilled in me a fear of ghosts, but he had also given me a way to protect myself from them. Now I wasn't so sure those rules would be enough. Whatever had surfaced from the woods was like nothing I had seen before.

They are colder, stronger, hungrier than any presence you can imagine.

Papa's warning made me shudder with dread and I wondered how it all tied together—Devlin's ghosts, the reappearance of the old man's entity and now that shadow creature. And at the center of it all, my burgeoning attraction for a haunted man. It should have been a simple matter to keep my distance from Devlin, but even when we were apart, I felt his pull.

Finding a parking place a few blocks from the restaurant, I hurried along the still-bustling streets, keeping watch over my shoulder. It wasn't just otherworldly dangers I had to worry about tonight. As long as a killer was on the loose, I wasn't about to let down my guard.

The breeze died away and my hair bristled a warning as the barometric pressure dropped, trapping the city in a heavy, waiting stillness. That eerie calm before the storm.

Temple was waiting in the bar area when I arrived and I was nonplussed to discover she'd invited Ethan Shaw to join us. Not that I minded his company. He'd inherited enough of his father's charm and charisma to be an interesting dinner companion. But where Rupert had the fading looks of an aging film star, Ethan was more the boy-next-door type.

Once we were seated, I quickly discovered that he and Temple knew one another from their undergraduate studies at Emerson. I was dying to find out more about Afton Delacourt's murder and the rumors that involved the Order of the Coffin and the Claw, but since Rupert had apparently been implicated in the slaying, I thought it best to wait until Temple and I were alone. After debriefing them on the Oak Grove discovery, I quietly sipped my Cabernet Sauvignon and let the two of them catch up.

My chair was situated so that I had a view of the garden through the arched window by our table. Just beyond the fountain, a ghost hovered in deep shadow.

From what I could see, he'd been a young man when he died—high school age, I assumed, because he wore a maroon letterman's jacket with a gold *W* on the breast and sleeve. He had a beefy build with a thick neck and broad, bullish features.

He stood with feet apart, arms in an aggressive, simian position away from his body. Ghosts of the young, particularly those of children, always touched me, but this one was different. There was something about him—apart from being dead—that I found extremely unpleasant. Frightful even. No matter what they'd done in life, the aura that surrounded most ghosts was misty and ethereal, but I saw no grace or beauty in this manifestation. He was surrounded by darkness, contorted by hostility and wrath, and I didn't like looking at him.

Casually, I picked up my wineglass and turned away from the window, wondering if he had a host somewhere inside the restaurant.

Temple had deftly maneuvered the conversation around to her favorite subject—her work. She looked lovely tonight in a white cotton tunic and jeans. The beaded neckline gave the simple shirt a bohemian flair that suited her.

"Two years and I still haven't found a suitable replacement for Amelia," she lamented to Ethan. "She was my detail person. A real pain-in-the-ass stickler. We moved a cemetery once and everything had to be replicated right down to the placement of each seashell. Drove me crazy back then, but now I only wish I had two of her."

"Flatterer," I accused.

"No, it's true. You just don't find that kind of work ethic these days."

"I guess I was raised right."

"I guess you were." She smiled.

"Dad told me you were awarded the Oak Grove contract. Congratulations." Ethan saluted me with his wineglass.

"Thank you, but how did Dr. Shaw know about the contract? I understood the whole operation was to be kept under wraps until the unveiling."

"He sits on the committee that gave final approval."

"I see. Well, I appreciate his faith in me, but unless I can make significant progress fairly quickly, I'm not sure how much longer my services will be needed."

"The delays aren't your fault," he said. "The committee will understand that."

"The committee, maybe. I'm not so sure about Dr. Ashby."

"Camille Ashby?" Temple gave a derisive snort.

I stared across the table. "How do you know Dr. Ashby?"

"Camille was at Emerson with us," Ethan explained.

"She and I were roommates for a time." Delicately, Temple blotted her ruby lips on her napkin. "We were quite close until she tried to kill me."

"She...*what?*" I stared at her in amazement.

"It's true." She shrugged, as though an accusation of attempted murder was an everyday occurrence. "I woke up one night to find her standing over me with a pair of scissors. It was pretty apparent she didn't have arts and crafts on her mind."

"That's crazy. Why would she try to kill you?" I'd never known Temple to exaggerate, let alone outright fabricate, but this accusation was a little far-fetched. I couldn't imagine anyone less likely to attack another person with a pair of scissors than Camille Ashby, if for no other reason than abhorrence for the mess it would make.

"I'm afraid it's one of those unseemly little tales," Temple said, her eyes glittering in the candlelight. "Shall I tell it?"

"By all means," Ethan said and shot me a grin.

"Well. It happened during our junior year," she began with a flourish. "We'd had some classes together the year before so we were already acquainted, but then outside circumstances conspired to throw us into the same arena. We found we had a lot in common—both into freedom of expression and experimentation, socially as well as sexually."

"I like this story already," Ethan said, with some enthusiasm.

"To cut to the chase, Camille wasn't as liberated as she led me to believe. She was competitive, jealous and quite the vindictive little bitch. She took our fling seriously—"

"Wait, back up. Fling, you say?" Ethan gave her a pained look. "Why must you gloss over the most interesting details?"

"You have an imagination, use it," Temple advised. "Anyway, when Camille caught me with a guy one night, things got ugly. She smashed my computer, ripped up all my clothes. Told the most vicious lies about me. I tried to salvage our friendship, but after the incident with the scissors, I got the hell out. I haven't seen her in years, but with her issues, I can't imagine she's changed much."

"She's still wound pretty tightly," Ethan agreed.

Temple picked up her glass. "It has to be exhausting

spending most of your life pretending to be something you're not. Given enough time, secrets have a way of becoming terrible burdens."

I thought of my father's secrets, *my* secrets, and felt a momentary depression.

"Why would she have to keep her sexual orientation a secret?" I asked rather naively. "I can't imagine anyone caring about her personal life."

"Don't kid yourself, Pollyanna. Emerson may be a liberal arts college, but the board and much of the alumni are still very conservative. And her family's even worse, especially her father. The old man's head would probably explode if she came out. Not that that would be a bad thing," Temple added, her voice tainted with venom.

Earlier when I'd seen Camille and Devlin together at the cemetery, I'd been quick to jump to the wrong conclusion about a romantic relationship, and it wasn't to my credit now that mostly what I felt was relief.

I thought of his hand on my arm, the ghost's taunting caresses, and shivered. The episode at the cemetery had upset me in so many ways for so many reasons. Devlin could not have been more off-limits to me if he had been a ghost himself. And yet I couldn't stop thinking about him.

The table fell silent as our first course arrived— she-crab soup for Ethan and Temple, beet and arugula salad for me. When the waiter stepped away, I saw the ghost again.

His frozen gaze locked with mine, giving me a terrible chill. But unlike my behavior with Devlin, I was in perfect control...until I heard the shatter of glass.

For a terrifying moment, I thought he'd caused the window to break. Then I realized the sound had come from our table. Temple's glass had cracked and smashed against her soup bowl. I stared in shock at the crimson dripping between her fingers.

"Temple, your hand!"

"No, it's okay. Just wine. See?" She dabbed it with her napkin. "I don't know what happened. The glass just... disintegrated."

Ethan had jumped up from his seat and rushed around to her chair. "Are you sure? Let me take a look."

"I'm not cut," she insisted, pushing back her chair. "I'll just go clean myself up. You two eat."

Before she'd stood, the waitstaff had arrived to mop up the spill and sweep away the broken glass, all done so discreetly that only those seated nearby were aware of anything amiss.

Another glass was brought to the table, more wine was poured, and I chanced another glance out the window. It had started to mist. I watched the candles sputter out on the tables and wondered where the ghost had gone.

A man from a nearby table rose and approached Ethan. I assumed he was a colleague so I paid little attention to their conversation until I heard my name. I looked up with a start.

"Sorry. I was a million miles away."

"I was just wondering if you'd met Daniel," Ethan said. "He's one of South Carolina's most distinguished historians."

"Dependant on whom you ask, of course." His smile was a little wistful, a little self-deprecating. "Daniel Meakin."

"Amelia Gray."

"If there's anything you need to know about Charleston, Daniel is your man," Ethan said.

"I'll remember that."

He turned to Meakin. "Amelia is something of a historian herself. She's a cemetery restorer."

"Ah. Now, there's an intriguing profession." Meakin stood with his right hand clasped over his left, a self-conscious gesture that made him look as though he was trying to control some nervous tic. "I love graveyards. We can learn so much from the dead."

Exactly what Devlin had said earlier, but in an entirely different context.

"You'll be happy to hear that Amelia has been hired by the committee to restore Oak Grove." Ethan gave me a contrite glance. "Sorry. I'm letting the cat out of the bag, but in light of what's happened, I don't think it matters anymore."

A shadow flitted across Meakin's birdlike features. "Dreadful business. I can't fathom…"

"Yes, terrible," Ethan agreed. They exchanged a glance.

"Had you been working long in the cemetery when they found the body?" Meakin asked.

"A few days. I'd just started photographing."

He shook his head. "Such a shame. I certainly hope you'll be able to resume the restoration once things get back to normal. Whatever that means," he added with an ironic smile. "Oak Grove has been a thorn in Emerson's side for years. I can't imagine why it's been allowed to linger for so long in such a dismal state. A matter of funding, I suppose."

"It's not unusual. Cemetery upkeep is expensive and there are other priorities. Once the gates are locked on abandoned graveyards, people tend to forget they exist."

"But now you're here to bring it all back to life." He beamed down at me, his small, white teeth gleaming in the candlelight. "Oak Grove is actually two separate cemeteries, you know. The older area especially has a number of important historical features, including at least a couple of markers carved by the Bighams," he said, naming a famous family of stonecutters.

"I'm particularly fascinated by the Bedford Mausoleum," I told him. "But I haven't been able to dig up much history on it."

"Ah, yes, the Bedford," he murmured, and exchanged another glance with Ethan. "I would love to discuss it further, but I can see poor Ethan's eyes are glazing over."

"Another time, then."

"It would be my pleasure. My office is located in the humanities building, second floor. Stop by anytime."

"Thank you. I may take you up on that."

"I hope you will. In the meantime…enjoy your dinner." He backed away from the table, turned and almost smacked into Temple.

"Daniel."

"Temple."

They spoke for a moment and then Temple took her seat at the table and shuddered. "Weirdo."

"Daniel? He's not so bad," Ethan said. "But he does tend to suffer from tunnel vision."

"He gives me the creeps. I don't trust anyone whose skin is that pale. Unless they're dead, of course." Temple shook out her fresh napkin. "He tried to commit suicide, you know."

"What? No. He's not the type." Ethan scowled at her. "What on earth gave you that idea?"

"I saw him come out of the biology lab one day. He was still adjusting his cuff—have you noticed how he always wears long sleeves even in summer? Anyway, I saw the scar." She smoothed the napkin over her lap. "I suppose I shouldn't speak so harshly about the poor fellow. We're all a bit strange when it comes right down to it. You, me, Camille, Daniel. Maybe there was something in the water at Emerson."

"You may be onto something," Ethan said, eyes twinkling. "Amelia seems to be the only normal one at the table."

Whatever that means.

"Speaking of strange," Temple said. "Isn't that John Devlin?"

My smile disappeared and I whirled in my seat. "Where?"

"Don't be so obvious," Temple scolded. "Over there. In the corner."

He was seated alone at an out-of-the-way table that would have allowed anyone else to fade into the woodwork. But not Devlin. Even across the crowded restaurant, his magnetism was conspicuous.

My eyes lingered for only a moment before I turned back to Temple. "How do you know Devlin? No, don't tell me. You had a torrid affair with him at Emerson." I was only half joking.

"Don't I wish," she said with a knowing smile. "If he was at Emerson, we moved in different circles. I didn't recognize the name when you mentioned it earlier, but now that I see his face, I remember him. We met a few years ago here in Charleston. I'd come down to examine some human artifacts that were found at a construction site, and Devlin and his partner were in charge of the investigation. He was young and had just made detective. The older cops teased him about his first homicide being nothing more than a few teeth and some vertebrae. It was all just good-natured ribbing. Then a young woman showed up—Devlin's wife, I later learned—and the atmosphere changed. I can't explain it. It was like she cast some sort of spell over us. We were all enthralled and she lapped up the attention like a kitten with a bowl of fresh cream."

I found myself leaning forward in anticipation. It was all I could do not to glance back at Devlin. Silently, I urged Temple to continue, but I needn't have bothered. This was Temple, after all.

"Devlin went to talk to her—how she even knew where to find him, I have no idea—and the whole time they stood there, I couldn't stop staring at them." Temple's fingers tangled in the gold chain around her neck. "They were quite literally the most stunning couple I'd ever laid eyes on. And even though they were in the middle of a heated argument, there was something so primal and hungry about the way he stared down at her... the way their bodies unconsciously strained toward one another as if nothing—not time, not distance, not even death—could ever keep them apart."

My breath quickened and I could feel the slow burn of a flush creeping up my neck. I fought temptation, lost and glanced over my shoulder.

Devlin stared back at me.

THIRTEEN

"Her name was Mariama," Ethan said quietly.

Temple and I glanced at each other. Her brows rose slightly as she turned back to Ethan. "What an unusual name. And I noticed you used the past tense."

He nodded, but didn't clarify. "My father knew her family and he brought her to Emerson. Very bright young woman, but she had a hard time merging her personal beliefs with the science."

"What were her personal beliefs?" Temple asked.

"What you get when you mix superstition and religion. Part Methodist, part witchcraft with a smidgen of voodoo. Her people were Gullah descended," he said. "Atlantic Creoles."

"That explains the gorgeous complexion and hair," Temple murmured.

I knew a little about the Gullah history in the Sea Islands and the strong connection to the Rice Coast during the slave years. Until a few decades ago, some of the sects in South Carolina and Georgia had remained so isolated from society that certain words, names, even songs in their language could be traced directly back to Sierra Leone. Their belief in *joso*—witchcraft—could also be traced back to their African roots.

"Interesting that she would hook up with a police detective," Temple said. "That must have been quite a culture clash."

"Especially when you factor in *his* background. He's from the same old Charleston that produced Camille Ashby. People with their pedigree don't take lesbian lovers or Creole wives. But John never put much stock in tradition. He was already the black sheep long before Mariama came along."

"Do tell." Temple propped her chin on her hand and leaned in.

"Don't look so eager," Ethan said. "It's not nearly as decadent as your story."

"Pity."

Ethan grinned. "John gave up a position in the family law firm to join the police force. It may not sound like that big a deal, but his decision went against an age-old legacy and a lifetime of expectations. I doubt he and his grandfather have spoken two words since the day he graduated from the academy."

Temple sat back in her chair. "How do you know so much about him? Is he a personal friend of yours?"

"He is, as a matter of fact." Ethan smiled at her over the rim of his glass. "And, anyway, this is Charleston, darling. Everyone knows everyone."

I said nothing to any of this. I thought it a little disrespectful to be discussing Devlin's personal life in such intimate detail. His table was far enough away and there was so much chatter in the restaurant that I knew he couldn't hear us, but I was uncomfortable with the discussion just the same. Temple and Ethan apparently had no such compunction. They were like a pair of chattering magpies.

"So what happened to his wife?" Temple asked.

Ethan's eyes clouded. "It was a horrible accident. Her car went through a guardrail and plunged into a river. She was trapped inside the vehicle and drowned."

An image of Devlin's ghosts rose before me.

"Was she alone?" I heard myself ask.

"No, sadly, their four-year-old daughter was with her. Their deaths very nearly destroyed John. He took six months' leave from the department and just disappeared. No one knew where he went, but rumors eventually surfaced that he'd been checked into some sort of private sanitarium."

"Can't believe everything you hear," Temple said. "But it does give a juicy twist to the story."

Their voices faded as the air grew electric. I wanted to believe it was my imagination, but I knew better. Devlin's ghosts were nearby. I couldn't see them, but I could sense their presence. Maybe they were out in the garden with the other ghost, waiting for their hosts to cross whatever divide kept them apart.

They might be waiting for me, too, if I wasn't careful.

Pushing back my chair, I rose. "Would you excuse me? Little girls' room."

I made my way through the crowded restaurant without glancing in Devlin's direction. Inside the bathroom, I splashed cold water on my face and then studied my reflection in the mirror.

This fascination with Devlin could go no further. I'd put myself in a dangerous position because of my attraction, but it wasn't too late. I could still put a stop to this. I could hole up in my sanctuary until he and his ghosts just went away. All it took was a little common sense and a great deal of willpower. Normally, I had both.

Patting my face dry, I straightened my spine and exited the bathroom.

Devlin waited for me in the narrow alcove outside. To get back to my table, I would have to go past him.

I hesitated, then started forward.

He leaned a shoulder against the wall, folded his arms and watched me with the darkest eyes I'd ever looked into. Sorcerer's eyes, I thought. Numinous and mesmerizing.

It occurred to me in that moment that no matter what I did, Devlin and I were already irrevocably bound by circumstances. If the clues to the killer were hidden within the gravestone imagery, I might be the only person who could interpret them. He needed me and that knowledge thrilled me far more than it should have.

There wasn't much room in the narrow passage, and when someone jostled me, I found myself pressed up against him. In that brief moment of contact, I caught the scent of cologne on his skin, a whiff of whiskey on his breath. And something else, too. A faint whisper of musk that belonged only to Devlin.

Our faces were close, our lips only inches apart. For a moment, I thought he might kiss me, and I wondered how I would respond. Even the thought of it made me breathless, and I closed my eyes, imagining the pressure of his mouth against mine. I felt his hand on the back of my neck, the tease of his thumb across my lips and a deep shudder ripped through me. When I opened my eyes, he hadn't moved. I had conjured it all, and I didn't know whether the emotion storming through me now was relief or bitter regret.

Shaken, I backed away from him, away from my fantasy. Those magnetic eyes followed me. I had the strangest feeling that no matter where I went or what I did, Devlin's gaze would always be on me.

"I thought you barely knew Ethan Shaw," he said.

His cool tone, coming on the heels of my overheated imagination, caught me off guard. "What?"

"You only met him briefly through his father. Isn't that what you said?"

"Yes…"

"And yet here you are together."

The disapproving note in his voice released me from his spell and I frowned up at him. "Is there some reason I shouldn't have dinner with Ethan Shaw? And not that it matters, but Temple is the one who invited him. It seems the two of them are old friends."

"Good to know. Maybe we can avoid a turf war over the remains," he said.

"Maybe we can."

What a strange encounter. What an awkward conversation. If I didn't know better, I would almost think he sounded jealous. But then that would mean—

I cut off the half-formed thought. I couldn't allow myself to go there. Not after today. Not after everything my father had warned me about had come to pass. A door had been opened and something terrible had come through. I had to stay away from Devlin and his ghosts. I couldn't let that door swing open any wider.

And yet in the face of all that, his attraction was so powerful and mesmeric, I couldn't tear myself away.

Music from the restaurant drifted through the arched doorway where we stood. The beat was dark and heavy and something primitive stirred within me. Something I had never felt before.

I looked up into Devlin's face, searching. He had no

idea the battle that raged inside me. He had no idea the havoc he had wreaked on my peace of mind.

His dark eyes drew me in and I shivered before somehow mustering the strength to break free. "I should get back."

He moved aside to allow me to pass, but I stood motionless, trapped now by my own weakness.

Temple came up to us then and placed her hand on my arm. "There you are. We were beginning to think you'd deserted us." She studied my face curiously, then turned to Devlin and put out her hand. "Temple Lee. We met years ago, but I'm certain you don't remember." Her tone implied that of course he would remember. She was Temple Lee.

Devlin smiled noncommittally, making me think he couldn't place her, and I don't know why that amused me. "Nice to see you again. I got your message earlier," he said. "A time for the exhumation hasn't been set yet, but I'll let you know."

"Thanks." She looped her arm through mine. "We should get back. Poor Ethan will think we've both left him."

I said nothing, merely nodded. In a way, it was a relief to let Temple take charge.

"I couldn't help noticing that you're dining alone," she said to Devlin. "Would you care to join us?"

My heart skipped a beat as I gazed up at him, hoping he would decline. An evening of trying to make small talk in his company without giving anything away was more than I could bear at the moment.

"Thank you, but not tonight," he said. "I wouldn't be very good company. I have a lot on my mind."

And then his gaze dropped, swept over me, and I felt as if I'd just been given a very intimate appraisal. Everything inside me stilled, then trembled and Temple's earlier words came rushing back to me.

There was something so primal and hungry about the way he stared down at her...the way their bodies unconsciously strained toward one another as if nothing—not time, not distance, not even death—could ever keep them apart.

After Ethan left, Temple and I stood outside the restaurant talking. It was still drizzling, but neither of us minded the damp weather. We leaned against the wall, faces upturned to the sky.

"I love the smell of rain," she said with a sigh. "So crisp and clean, and yet there's always an undercurrent of flowers here. For my money, this is the most gorgeous city in the South. If New Orleans is midnight, Charleston is twilight. All soft and misty and sweet-smelling."

"You're such a romantic," I teased.

"Only in moments of weakness. Or when I have too much wine."

"Temple...can I ask you something?"

"Hmm..." she said dreamily.

"Were you at Emerson when Afton Delacourt was murdered?"

Her eyes slowly opened. "How do you know about Afton Delacourt?"

"Her body was found in Oak Grove, right?"

"Who told you that? Who's been talking to you about Afton Delacourt?"

The hard edge in her voice took me by surprise. "I've been doing a lot of research in preparation for the restoration, remember?"

She looked unconvinced. "What is it you want to know?"

"I heard that Rupert Shaw was questioned by the police. Do you think there's any chance he was involved?"

"Of course not. That whole situation was created by someone who had a grudge against Dr. Shaw. They deliberately set out to ruin his reputation and very nearly succeeded. He was asked to leave Emerson, you know."

"That must have been a difficult time for him and Ethan."

"It was a difficult time for all of us. Everyone on campus was on edge. We thought there could be a murderer in our midst." She glanced at her watch and scowled.

"Did you know anyone who belonged to the Order of the Coffin and the Claw?"

"What is this, an inquisition? Why all these questions about something that happened a hundred years ago?"

"It was fifteen years ago and now two more bodies have been discovered in the same cemetery. I might buy two as a coincidence, but three is a pattern."

"Jesus, Amelia. Are you trying to give me nightmares? Can we talk about something more pleasant before I have to go crawl into bed all by my lonesome?"

"What would you rather talk about?"

"Oh, I don't know. Detective Devlin, maybe?"

My pulse jumped at the very mention of his name. "What about him?"

She gave me a crafty glance. "Don't act all innocent. I saw the way he looked at you. And the way you looked at him. What's going on between you two?"

"Nothing. I barely know the man."

"Maybe you should remedy that situation. You could do worse, you know. A lot worse. A man like that could do a woman like you a world of good."

"What's that supposed to mean?"

"You spend far too much time in the company of the dead."

"Look who's talking."

She shrugged. "Yes, but at least I know how to have a little fun. You, on the other hand, always play it safe. Step out of your cemeteries for a moment and loosen up. Live a little dangerously now and then."

"You think Devlin is dangerous?"

"Don't you?"

"I don't know anything about him."

"Not true. We found out all sorts of fascinating things about him tonight. He comes from money. He's estranged from his family. He married an exotic woman who died tragically and he may or may not have spent time in a mental institution." Her eyes danced in the light from the street. "I'd say that qualifies John Devlin as a dangerous man. Deliciously dangerous, in fact. Remember, I've seen him in action."

"You mean that incident with his wife?"

"That was something to behold, Amelia. I've never considered myself a voyeur, but it was like getting a peek of what he might be like in the bedroom—at least Mariama's bedroom. Dominant, explosive…completely out of control."

My pulse quickened in spite of myself. "I'm not sure that sounds altogether appealing."

"Maybe not after all the milquetoasts you've dated."

I shrugged, refusing to be offended. "I like the quiet type."

"No, you like the safe type, but it's time you broaden your horizon."

I tried to remain indifferent, but I couldn't deny that Temple had planted some rather titillating images in my mind.

She lolled her head against the wall. "Mariama. Even her name gives me shivers. I can still see Devlin looming over her, so dark and angry, and that lustful defiance of her response." Temple's eyes closed on a sigh. "There was a breeze that day. It blew her skirt back and molded the flimsy fabric to her body so that you could see the outline of her thighs and her—"

"I get the picture!" I suddenly wondered where Devlin was at that moment. Was he home alone or had he other plans for the evening?

"Can you imagine all that pent-up intensity after years of celibacy?"

I glanced at Temple. "What makes you think he's been celibate? I doubt very seriously he's remained alone since his wife died."

"Don't be a spoilsport. Let me enjoy my fan-wanking."

"Your what?"

"Let me arrange the story to meet my own personal needs."

"Be my guest then. Just please leave me out of it."

"Don't worry. You're not my type. Too white-bread and staid. Although…" Her voice turned silky and sly. "I've always sensed some spice beneath all that vanilla. In the right hands—"

"Please stop."

"You're right. Just ignore me. It's the wine making me a fool for love. Or lust. I'll drop the whole subject, but you have to promise me something."

"Doubtful. Unlike you, I'm stone-cold sober."

But she was serious. A worry line formed between her brows and she placed her hand on my arm. "Be careful with Devlin. Flirt with him, sleep with him, do whatever with him, but…be careful."

"What do you mean?"

"There's something about him…I'm not sure I can explain it. I've known men like him before. Controlled and guarded on the surface, but under the right conditions… with the right woman…" She trailed off and glanced at me. "Do you know what I'm saying?"

"Not really."

"A woman like Mariama would know how to push his buttons. She would do everything in her power to make him lose control, because that's how she got off. That's what gave her power. But with you…"

"What about me?"

"You said it yourself. You like the safe guys. And Devlin is anything but safe. He's not the man for you."

"A minute ago, you said he was just what I needed."

"As a brief fling, yes. As a lifetime companion, no way. I see you with someone like Ethan."

"Ethan? Where did that come from?"

"I'm just using him as an example. You need a man who will—"

"Don't say take care of me. That's the last thing I want."

"Someone who'll always put your interests above his own," she insisted. "That man is not John Devlin."

"How do you know that?"

She smiled. "I may be a switch hitter, but I know men. Trust me on this one. It'll save you a lot of heartache down the road."

FOURTEEN

When I got home that night, I went straight back to the office, grabbed my laptop and settled down on the chaise for some online sleuthing. Research was an important aspect of my job, and given enough time, I could usually uncover anything I needed. But tonight, even after the most persistent digging, I found nothing on Afton Delacourt, either before or after her death. Apparently, Devlin had been right about the media blackout. It was as if her whole life had been expunged after the murder.

Rupert Shaw was a different matter. A Google search yielded a wealth of links, most of them in conjunction with his work at the Charleston Institute for Parapsychology Studies. For the most part, the articles I scanned portrayed him in a favorable light—a scholarly, if somewhat eccentric gentleman who had an obvious affinity for the paranormal. Not out of line with my own perception of the man.

I did glean one new morsel from a video interview I found on a local ghost hunter website. The questions to

Dr. Shaw ran the gamut from haunted houses to near-death experiences, but the part that caught my attention was a little off-the-cuff chat at the end.

The interviewer had complimented Dr. Shaw on a ring he wore on his right pinkie. I'd noticed the ring myself the first time we met. It was silver and onyx, with an ornate symbol embedded into the stone. Dr. Shaw had mentioned at the time that it was a family heirloom, but he told the interviewer the ring had been a gift from a colleague. It was entirely possible we were talking about two different rings, but I didn't think so. Nor did I consider it anything more than a curious tidbit.

Moving on…

Like Yale's infamous Skull and Bones Society, the Order of the Coffin and the Claw had been established in the early nineteenth century and counted among its membership some of South Carolina's power elite. In 1986, the all-male policy had been amended and every year thereafter, two women from the junior class had been tapped for membership.

I found references to obscure symbols, numerology, secret retreats, and clandestine initiation ceremonies, but no mention of Afton Delacourt's murder and only a passing reference to the organization's demise.

Next, I searched the name Hannah Fischer and came up with at least a dozen hits, but only one of them led me to a woman in the Charleston vicinity and she'd recently celebrated her ninety-ninth birthday.

Earlier, when I brought up Tom Gerrity's name to Devlin, I'd gotten the distinct impression there was bad blood between the two. But I was so anxious to get away from the cemetery I hadn't pursued the matter. Now I wished I'd gotten more answers from him.

I glanced down at the screen, my fingers posed over the keys. One last search remained.

Mariama Devlin.

Even entering her name made me feel guilty and a little frightened, because no matter how I tried to justify my interest, I was prying into Devlin's personal affairs. I was no better than Ethan and Temple, who had greedily and gleefully dissected bits of Devlin's life over dinner like vultures picking at a carcass.

But my distaste for the task did nothing to thwart me.

The first link took me to a newspaper article about the accident, and the account matched Ethan's. The car had crashed through a guardrail on a rural bridge and plunged into a river. The only thing that Ethan had failed to mention was the frantic 911 call that Mariama had placed mere moments before her death, as the car took on water. Even then, she must have realized the rescuers would never arrive in time. Trapped by her seat belt, she couldn't free herself or her four-year-old daughter.

My head fell back against the seat as I closed my eyes. With very little effort, I could conjure the whole chilling scene. The bone-jarring thud of the initial collision. The muddy river washing over the windshield. The sickening tilt of the car as it sank.

Inside, Mariama tearing at the seat belt, frantically tracking the rising water as she tried to calm her terrified child.

Then darkness as the car settled to the bottom.

Don't leave me here...Mommy, please...

The cries were so real I opened my eyes and glanced around.

I was all alone with a pounding heartbeat.

Pressing a hand to my chest, I drew a shuddering breath. How many times had that scene played out in

Devlin's nightmares? How many times had he awakened
to his daughter's devastating pleas?

No wonder he'd needed time away to deal with his
grief. The weight of all that guilt, those endless what-ifs
must have been an unbearable agony.

Even if he couldn't see them, his ghosts had kept that
torment fresh. For as long as he was haunted, his wounds
would never heal.

I took a moment to collect my thoughts, and then continued to read.

The accident had occurred in a remote area of Beaufort County near a town called Hammond. Mariama and
her daughter had been on their way to visit family when
the tragedy occurred.

Two photographs accompanied the article, one a close-
up of the broken guardrail, the second a wider shot of the
onlookers who had gathered on the river bank to wait for
the rescue divers to surface.

I didn't study the faces in that crowd because I didn't
want to find Devlin's. I didn't want to see his eyes in that
terrible moment.

Backing out of the article, I clicked the next link,
which took me to the obituaries. There were no photographs here, but I already knew what they looked like—
Mariama and four-year-old Anyika.

Anyika.

Somehow that name didn't fit the ghost child I'd seen
at Devlin's side and in my backyard.

I started to say the name aloud, then thought better of
it.

Rule Number Four—never, ever tempt fate.

Quickly, I shut down the computer and set it aside. I'd
had enough research for one night.

Rolling to my side, I laid a cheek on my folded hands

and closed my eyes. So many thoughts and images strobed through my head. So many unanswered questions…

I kept seeing Mariama and Anyika trapped in that car, gasping for breath as the water closed over their heads…

I imagined what it must have been like for Devlin when he first heard the news…how he would have rushed to the scene praying for the best but fearing the worst. And then that long ride home, knowing the house would be empty when he got there. Knowing that he would never again hold his daughter in his arms…

I pictured Afton Delacourt's ravaged body in the mausoleum where Rupert Shaw had supposedly conducted séances, and I pondered his theory that at the time of death, a door opened, allowing someone to cross to the other side and back. What if someone had crossed over at the time of Hannah Fischer's death? What if that person had brought something back through the veil with them? Something dark and fetid and cold like the thing that hovered at the edge of the woods…

I thought about Temple's claim that Camille Ashby had come at her with scissors and her assumption that Daniel Meakin had tried to commit suicide because of a scar she'd glimpsed on his wrist. And then later, outside the restaurant, her hesitation to talk about Afton's murder and the Order of the Coffin and the Claw. Was it possible that she was somehow associated with that society? Was Ethan?

On and on the questions swirled as an endless reel of faces paraded through my head. Camille Ashby. Ethan and Rupert Shaw. Temple. Tom Gerrity. Daniel Meakin. The brutalized bodies of Afton Delacourt and Hannah Fischer. The ethereal visages of Mariama and Anyika.

And Devlin. Always back to Devlin.

Finally, I grew drowsy, but it seemed too much effort to get up and move into the bedroom.

Outside, a soft breeze ruffled the palmetto leaves, a comforting murmur as my muscles began to twitch.

For the longest time, I swam in that soft, misty void of half sleep before I gave myself up to exhaustion. And then all those chaotic thoughts transitioned into my dreams, creating strange, disjointed vignettes as I slept.

I was back in Oak Grove Cemetery, hovering on the bottom step of the Bedford Mausoleum. Temple was there, too. She stood at the very top, peering into a half-open doorway.

"What are you doing?" I asked her.

She wore the same white tunic she'd had on at dinner, but now the trim was far more exotic. I could see the flash of garnets worked into some intricate pattern at her neckline.

"I've never been a voyeur, but I can't stop looking at them," she said.

"At who?"

Her smile was sly and suggestive. "Come see for yourself. It'll do you a world of good."

Slowly, I climbed the steps and joined her at the doorway. The room inside was gauzy and candlelit. Like looking through a veil.

And then I saw them…

Devlin and Mariama…

There was something so beautiful about the glow of their contrasting skin tones in the candlelight, something so darkly erotic about the sway of Mariama's long hair against her naked back, the outline of her full breasts cupped in Devlin's hands, the way their bodies moved as if to some primal rhythm.

As we stood there watching, Mariama glanced over

her shoulder, eyes hooded, lips slyly curled, a temptress's invitation that aroused and unnerved.

"We shouldn't be here," I said, backing away.

"Don't be so vanilla. You know you like watching him."

Mariama's taunting laughter followed me down the steps.

I felt a chill at my back and turned to glance over my shoulder. Something dark flashed at the corner of my eye and I whirled to run, but the ghost child blocked my path.

The scent of jasmine filled my nostrils as she lifted a hand and beckoned for me to follow. I tried to summon my father's rules, but I couldn't remember them. Nor could I resist her silent command.

She led me away from the mausoleum, into an area of the cemetery where I'd never been before. Off to the side, I noticed a gathering of people around a headstone. They all turned when they heard me and I recognized their faces—Camille, Temple, Ethan, Daniel Meakin. Even Dr. Shaw. With an enigmatic smile, he stepped aside to make room for me in their circle.

Moving up beside them, I stared down at the ground, searching for what had captured their attention.

I saw nothing but an empty grave.

Then I felt pressure on my back and suddenly I was falling, falling into that dark, fathomless pit.

My grave...

Gasping, I bolted upright on the chaise.

It took a moment to orient myself, another to calm my racing pulse.

The office had grown cold while I slept. I'd turned down the air when I got home from dinner because the house had been hot and stuffy. I hadn't thought to adjust the thermostat before I fell asleep, and now the room was so chilly the windows had fogged over.

I reached for the afghan draped over the foot of the chaise, then went completely still, my hand suspended in midair as I sniffed. The scent of jasmine floated across the room, so faint and delicate it might have been a remnant from my dream.

But I knew it was real. She was here.

Drawing the spread over me, I lay shivering in the dark. I couldn't see the garden through the frosted windows, but I knew she was out there.

Light from the kitchen filtered into my office, illuminating the beads of condensation that ran down the glass.

I caught my breath, waiting...

A pattern emerged in the frost, as though an invisible finger traced it from the other side.

A heart.

Like the one I'd formed in the garden with pebbles and seashells.

The image was there one moment, gone the next, melting into rivulets of condensation as the jasmine scent faded.

She, too, had vanished back into the mist, but I knew she'd be back. She wouldn't leave me alone until I figured out what she wanted.

FIFTEEN

Sometime during the night, the drizzle turned into a downpour. The exhumation had to be delayed until the weather cleared and the ground had time to dry out so that the loose dirt could be sifted through a screen.

Since I couldn't work outside, I spent the rest of the morning at Emerson. A number of unmarked graves near the north wall had yet to be identified, and ironically, I couldn't locate graves for two names that had turned up in an old family Bible I'd come across.

Creating a site map for a cemetery as old as Oak Grove was always a challenge, not unlike putting together a jigsaw puzzle. Missing markers, lost records, illegible headstones, overgrown graves—time wreaked havoc on the dead as well as the living.

I was so engrossed in the task at hand that the scrabbling sound didn't register at first.

Then my head came up and I sat very still, wondering if a mouse might have chewed its way into one of the file boxes.

Located in the basement of the Emerson library, the archives room was a crowded space of shadowy alcoves and dim corridors that traced through rows and rows of packed shelving.

Normally, I didn't mind the gloom of closed-in places, but with the unidentified sound came a slight panicky sensation of isolation. I was all alone down there. The desk where I worked faced the wide staircase that led up to the first floor. I hadn't seen anyone come down since I'd been sitting there.

It was nothing, I told myself. The place was old and creepy, filled with the sounds and smells of the past. No different from the dozens of other basement archives where I'd spent many a contented hour immersed in the lives of the long dead.

Shrugging it off, I went back to my work.

The sound came again—fierce scratching followed by a loud thud.

One of the boxes must have fallen to the floor. Not the work of a mouse, I was quite certain.

Fear tapped along my spine as I tilted my head, listening.

A shadow appeared at the end of one of the corridors, and I gasped before I realized it was a person instead of that frightening silhouette I'd encountered on the path at Oak Grove.

"Hello?" I called out.

"Hello!" came back the surprised rejoinder. "I had no idea anyone else was down here. Have you been sitting there long?"

"A couple of hours." I peered into the gloom. "I didn't see you come down the stairs."

"I used the back stairwell. I guess that's how we missed one another." He came toward me then, but I didn't recognize his face or his voice until he was almost upon me. "Ms. Gray, isn't it? Daniel Meakin. We met at Rapture."

"Yes, of course. Nice to see you again, Mr. Meakin."

"Daniel, please."

I inclined my head. "Amelia."

He glanced down at the files and record books strewn across the desk. "More Oak Grove research?"

"Yes." I explained about the graves without names and the names without graves.

"Quite a grave dilemma, isn't it?"

I smiled. "Indeed."

"They don't match up then?"

"Unfortunately, no. But you may be able to help me out. I understand there used to be a church next to Oak Grove."

"Yes, in fact, the old section of the graveyard was owned by that church. When the building was destroyed, city officials took advantage of what was then a remote location to open a new, more parklike cemetery right up against the old churchyard. In time, people forgot about the boundary and both sites became known as Oak Grove."

"Do you know if any of the registries were lost or destroyed when the church came down?"

"It's certainly possible. A lot of the old records were burned during and after the Civil War. Perhaps some of them have been misplaced or misfiled in here." He glanced around with a frown. "Like Oak Grove, the archives have been shamefully neglected for years. The system is in dire need of a complete reorganization."

"I won't argue with that. I've spent an inordinate amount of time down here poking around in all these old boxes."

"My favorite pastime," he said with a smile.

"Mine, as well."

"You don't mind the solitude?" he asked. "So many people find this place depressing."

"I've never minded being by myself." Loneliness was an old friend. "I just wish I could find what I need."

"You know, I believe I have some books in my office that reference Oak Grove. I'll have a look when I get back and see if I can find anything that might be useful to you."

"Thank you. I'd appreciate that."

The whole time we spoke, he'd been holding his left wrist awkwardly at his side, reminding me of Temple's speculation about his scar and a possible suicide attempt.

As if reading my thoughts, he began to edge back into the shadows. "I should let you get back to work."

"Just one more thing before you go…"

He waited obligingly.

"The other night at dinner, Temple and Ethan mentioned that you'd attended Emerson with them as undergrads. You have a long history with the university, it seems."

"Too long, I sometimes think." That deprecating smile again.

"During my research, I ran across a reference to a secret society on campus. It was called the Order of the Coffin and the Claw. Do you know anything about it?"

He didn't look too keen on answering. His eyes flickered with indecision. "I know a bit about it, but I don't think that information will help solve your grave problem."

"No, I know. But cemetery art includes a lot of symbols and imagery from secret societies. I thought I might have run across something from this organization in Oak Grove."

"I can't tell you anything about the symbols. They're secret for a reason. What I can tell you is that the Order of the twentieth century became a very different organization from the one founded in the 1800s. The evolution, to my way of thinking, was not always successful."

"I read somewhere that the bylaws were amended in the eighties to include women."

"One of the more enlightened phases. Though 'enlightenment' is a bit of a misnomer when describing an organization that is, by its very nature, exclusionary."

"I take it you don't have much regard for these kinds of societies."

He shrugged. "I have a problem with elitism in general. I'm more a storm-the-Bastille type."

His self-assessment gave me an inward chuckle. I could barely imagine Daniel Meakin with a pocketknife, let alone brandishing sword and musket.

"The exclusivity of a secret society's membership is for one reason and one reason only," he said. "To empower and protect the status quo. At any cost."

"What do you mean, at any cost?"

"Exactly that."

"Do you think the Order had something to do with Afton Delacourt's murder?"

The question seemed to make him very nervous. He glanced over his shoulder toward the stairs. "That's still a very tender subject in certain quarters. I think it might be best to let that poor girl rest in peace."

"But now that there's been another murder, questions are bound to arise," I said.

"Those questions are a matter for the police, surely."

"Of course, but—"

"I'm sorry. You really must excuse me. I'm late for an appointment…"

He couldn't get away from me fast enough.

His rapid retreat reminded me of the way Temple had shut down my questions about Afton Delacourt's murder. Fifteen years after the fact and apparently the blackout was still in place.

I watched Meakin disappear down one of the corridors and it was only then I realized we were not alone. I had no idea how long Camille Ashby had been in the basement or why she hadn't made her presence known. She stood in the shadows beneath the stairwell, well within earshot of our conversation. I caught only a glimpse of her before she stepped back, and a second later, I heard a door click.

After that, I didn't care to spend any more time alone in the archives. The basement was too isolated from the rest of the building. I packed up everything and left for an early lunch.

As it turned out, I never made it back to Emerson that day. By midafternoon, when the rain finally stopped, I found myself on the Coastal Highway heading toward Beaufort County.

Ever since leaving the archives room, I'd battled a morbid compulsion—I desperately wanted to see the place where Mariama and Anyika had died.

The impulse wasn't at all logical, but then, neither was the heart that had been traced in the frost on my window or the dark figure that had come out of the woods at Oak Grove. I was a young woman who saw ghosts. Nothing in my life had been logical since I was nine years old.

Perhaps I should have gone home first and dug up the garnet ring from my backyard the way Papa had told me to, but I didn't. Keeping a connection to the ghost child certainly wasn't logical, but now that I knew who she was, I couldn't bring myself to throw the ring into the river where she'd drowned. That seemed too cold, an affront to both her and Devlin.

Once I left US 17, the route became trickier, and if not for the SUV's navigation system, I could have easily become lost in the tangle of two-lane blacktops and back roads that crisscrossed the rural area. However, I'd programmed the course carefully before leaving Charleston and the efficient, computerized voice led me straight to my destination.

Pulling to the side of the road, I got out and walked up the slight embankment to the bridge.

The whole time I was there, I saw only one other car, and as the driver passed by, he rolled down his window to ask if I needed help. I thanked him and waved him on, then resumed my contemplation of the river.

The water level rose to only a few feet beneath the bridge. If the river had been full when Mariama's car crashed through the guardrail, the impact might have been cushioned, though the outcome would have probably been the same.

What had made her lose control that day? I wondered. The lanes were narrow, so maybe she'd swerved to miss an oncoming car or perhaps an animal had darted in front of her. If the bridge had been slippery, the car might have gone into a skid and hydroplaned right through the railing.

It was all useless speculation. No one would ever really know what happened.

The sky was gray, the air heavy with moisture and the scent of brine from the tidal creeks. Everything around me was silent and still.

I stood there for the longest time, but I never felt their presence.

Finally, I walked back to my car, reset the navigator and drove across the bridge without looking back.

My next stop was Chedathy Cemetery, located a few miles northeast of Hammond, down a single-lane gravel road that tunneled through thick rows of leaning live oaks.

I'd learned from the obituaries where Mariama and Anyika were buried, but I didn't understand my obsessive need to visit their graves any more than I could make sense of my compulsion to see that bridge. I only knew that I wouldn't rest until I did both.

A rusted metal arch marked the cemetery entrance, but the shoulder was too narrow to pull over. I drove around to the back and parked at the edge of a ditch filled with black-green water.

The graves here were old and decorated in Gullah tradition: clocks set to the time of death, battered lamps to light the way to the afterlife, broken pottery—pitchers, bowls, cups, tureens—to break the chain of death. Whole sections of the cemetery were covered in white sand to protect against the *bakulu,* restless spirits that lingered in our world to interfere with the living.

I was in the land of superstition, the land of the Lowcountry Boo Hag. A woman—according to Papa's old tales—practiced in the ways of sorcery and witchcraft. When night fell the hag would leave her body and roam unbridled over the countryside, draining life force through the breath of her victims. She couldn't be seen, but she could be felt. Her touch was warm, Papa said, and had the texture of raw meat.

"She's not a ghost then," I'd pointed out with what I

considered perfect logic. "Their touch is cold and damp. It makes me think of being trapped in a tomb."

"Shush," Papa warned. "Don't let your mother hear you talk about such things."

I'd clammed up like the obedient daughter I was, but it bothered me that I couldn't share this part of my life with Mama. After an encounter with a ghost, I'd longed more than anything to feel her warm arms around me, holding me close, keeping me safe from the dangers that floated by our windows at dusk.

If my first ghostly sighting had changed my relationship with Papa, his rules had created a chasm between my mother and me. We could never have the kind of bond I wanted because I kept things from her.

Papa kept things from her, too, and his secrets had become a heavy burden for both of us.

Mariama and Anyika's graves were in the newer section of the cemetery, near the entrance. They'd been laid to rest side by side beneath the gnarled branches of an ancient live oak.

Mariama's grave was decorated similarly to the others, but Anyika's tiny burial site had very little adornment. A simple headstone and a few scattered sand dollars and whelks.

But what struck me the most was the date of birth on the marker. Today would have been her birthday.

I knelt and with gentle hands cleared away the dead leaves from the grave, exposing a heart that someone had fashioned from cockleshells.

Slowly, I traced the outline with my fingertip, seeing in my mind's eye the heart forming on my frosted window.

I heard the crunch of gravel out on the road as a car approached. I waited for it to pass by, but it pulled to a stop and a second later, a car door slammed.

Rising, I walked quickly away. I couldn't explain it, but I didn't want to be found at those graves. Since I didn't have time to make it all the way back to the car, I stepped behind a tree and hoped no one would come my way.

Huddled behind the massive trunk, I watched as the visitor came through the arched entrance, walking with shoulders forward and head slightly bowed. I knew him instantly.

It was Devlin.

SIXTEEN

As soon as he was inside the gate, his head came up and he paused to scan the cemetery, as if sensing my presence.

More likely, his years as a cop had made him wary of isolated places. Whatever the case, I jerked back and pressed myself up against the bark. When I didn't hear footsteps coming toward me, I chanced another glance.

He had moved over to stand between Mariama and Anyika's graves. He was turned away from me so that I couldn't see his expression, and I was thankful for that. I hated myself for spying on him in such a private moment, but I couldn't look away. Or maybe I just didn't want to. Maybe I'd convinced myself that because of my connection to the ghost child—to him—I had a right to be there.

He gazed down at Mariama's headstone for the longest time, then knelt and placed something on Anyika's grave.

The cemetery was very quiet. I fancied I could hear his voice.

After a moment, he rose and strode from the cemetery. Out on the road, I heard his car door slam.

I waited until the sound of the engine faded before I emerged from my hiding place. It was to my shame—and later, my bitter regret—that I didn't leave the cemetery right then and there, but instead walked back to the graves to see what Devlin had left.

In the center of the cockleshell heart, he'd placed a miniature antique doll, hand-painted with a dusky complexion and adorned with lace parasol, silk bustle and buckle-up shoes. She was the most exquisite thing I'd ever seen.

The offering stirred something deep inside me. Tears stung behind my lids and I tried to blink them away.

Then, as soft as the whispering trees, I heard a voice. A name...

"Shani..."

For a moment, I thought I must have imagined it, but then I glanced up and saw that I was no longer alone. An old woman and a girl of about ten stood beneath the drooping tree branches, watching me.

Awkwardly, I stood. "Hello—"

The woman put up her hand and I fell silent.

She wore a faded red skirt that flapped about her ankles and a green shirt buttoned all the way up her throat. Her hair was gray and wiry and she wore it in a loose bun at her nape.

The girl was the epitome of youth, all arms and legs in cutoffs and a lemon-colored blouse that set off her beautiful skin tone. A mane of wild curls framed an angelic face made all the more stunning by a pair of light green eyes.

The study in contrasts couldn't have been more striking, and yet there was no less beauty and elegance in the weathered face than in the child's.

They were both barefoot, but the twigs and pinecones littered over the ground didn't seem to faze them as they walked toward the graves.

The woman paused between the headstones, mumbling something I couldn't understand. Then she took a packet from her pocket, poured something into her palm and blew. I saw a tiny blue flash before the breeze carried the shimmering particles away.

Her eyes came back to me, taking my measure in silence.

"I'm...Amelia," I finally said, because I could no longer bear the quiet.

The girl skipped over and looped her arm through the woman's. "I'm Rhapsody. And this is my grandmother."

"Rhapsody. What a lovely name," I said.

"It means excessively enthusiastic. A state of exalted bliss." She preened like a peacock, then leaned down to scratch the back of her knee. "Did you come for Shani's birthday?"

"Who's Shani?"

She pointed to the tiny grave.

"Why do you call her Shani? It says Anyika on the headstone."

"Shani's her basket name."

I remembered reading about the Gullah tradition of dual naming. Every child was given a formal name at birth, along with a more intimate moniker used within the family circle, a secret name assigned to them when they were still small enough to fit inside a rice basket.

Rhapsody twirled a dark curl around one finger. "My basket name is Sia on account of I'm a firstborn girl."

"What does Shani mean?"

She made a symbol with her fingers. "My heart."

My knees went weak as a numbing chill went through me and I thought again of that heart traced on my window. Shani had wanted me to know who she was. She'd used her basket name to connect us, bind us...

It was daylight, hours before the veil would thin. But at that moment, I could feel the child's presence as strongly as though she stood at my side.

Unaware of the emotions storming through me, Rhapsody nattered on about other basket names in the family.

Her grandmother pinched her arm.

"Ouch! What the heck!"

She shook her finger in the girl's face. "Hush, gal. I swat dat b'hin' luk e' wuz a muskituh."

Rhapsody held her tongue, but her jutted lip spoke volumes.

"And don' gimme dat longmout', edduh!"

"Yes, ma'am."

To me, the woman said with an imperious note, "Oonuh! Come'yuh."

"I'm sorry?"

Rhapsody, already recovered from her sulking spell, came over and took my hand.

"Granny wants you to come with us."

"Come with you...where?" I wasn't at all sure I liked that notion.

"To her house." She nodded toward the gravel road. "It's just down yonder."

Her grandmother said something else, very rapidly, but I didn't understand a word of it.

Rhapsody obligingly translated. "She says if you want to know about Shani you better come with us. I'd listen to her if I were you," she added with a sidelong glance.

"Granny says without her help, Shani won't ever leave you alone."

The invitation had suddenly become irresistible.

We walked down the gravel road together. Or rather, Rhapsody danced along between us, her movements so light and airy, she almost appeared to float.

All the while she chattered nonstop about her father, who was on some sort of extended trip to Africa. About their house in Atlanta, which was like a million times larger than Granny's old place. They had their own pool and Rhapsody could have friends over whenever she wanted. Granny didn't even have television, much less cable or the internet. If Rhapsody wanted to chat with her friends, she had to walk all the way into Hammond and use the library computer.

Despite her grumbling, she seemed happy and I sensed a deep affection between her and her grandmother, Essie.

At the end of the road was a tiny community of clapboard houses surrounded by piles of tires, abandoned cars and a hodgepodge of rusted appliances. The structures were all single-story and lifted above ground on wooden pilings.

As we walked past the first place, I saw a girl of about fourteen staring at us from the shade of a sagging porch. When Rhapsody waved, the older girl got up and hurried inside the house.

"That's Tay-Tay," Rhapsody explained. "She doesn't like for me to look at her."

"Why not?"

"She's afraid of me."

"Why would she be afraid of you?"

"Granny's a root doctor and I'm the only girl left in my family," she said mysteriously.

Essie muttered something under her breath—an admonition, I suspected—which Rhapsody blithely ignored.

"Tay-Tay claims I put something in her Pepsi to make her hair fall out, but I didn't. Could of if I wanted to, though." She tossed back her own glorious mane with all the hauteur a ten-year-old girl could muster. Which, in Rhapsody's case, was quite a lot.

"Some li'l gal gwine tuh bed widout'uh suppuh tuh'night," Essie warned.

"Sorry, Granny," Rhapsody said contritely, but she shot me a cagey grin as she kicked a rock toward Tay-Tay's house.

As we passed by the next house, a tethered mutt in the front yard let out a bloodcurdling yowl. Essie lifted her hand and the dog fell silent, much as I'd done back at the cemetery.

"That's Granny's house over there." Rhapsody pointed to a tiny white cottage at the end of the road. It was easily the prettiest in the neighborhood, with a well-tended garden and fresh laundry flapping on the clothesline.

They led me up a set of concrete steps, across the porch with its plank flooring and blue ceiling—the sky color a Gullah tradition to keep away wasps and ghosts—and into a narrow hall that smelled of sage and lemon verbena. I noticed three things at once: a mirror that hung backward on the wall, a straw broom just inside the doorway and an arrangement of angel-wing seashells laid out across a small bench.

Essie bustled off to the kitchen, leaving Rhapsody to show me around the cozy parlor where every inch of table space was decorated with the most gorgeous sweetgrass baskets I'd ever seen. When I complimented them, Rhapsody said with an indifferent shrug, "Those old things?

Granny makes them all the time." She couldn't have been less impressed.

She waved a hand toward a wall of fading portraits. "Those people are my kin, but don't ask me their names. They passed a long time ago. Granny says we Goodwines have a habit of dying young. Except for her, I reckon. We're probably cursed or something."

Her granny, she told me, was in fact her great-grandmother. Her father and Mariama had been first cousins, but were more like brother and sister on account of they'd both been raised by Essie.

"What did you mean when you said your grandmother is a root doctor?"

"She's a witch," Rhapsody said with that same crafty smile I'd seen earlier. "And since I'm the only girl left in the family, I get to be her helper. That's why I'm here for the summer. So I can start learning how to cast."

"Sia! Tie yo' mout', gal!"

Essie had come up so quietly that Rhapsody and I both jumped and spun toward the door. She carried a tray with a pitcher of sweet tea, three glasses and a plate of sesame-seed cookies. Before either of us could offer to help, she turned and disappeared down the tiny hallway. A moment later, I heard the screech of the screen door.

Rhapsody and I followed her outside to the front porch where she settled herself in an ancient cane rocker and poured us each a glass of tea, taking a moment to swat Rhapsody's hand when she reached for a cookie.

Essie offered me the plate and I took one because I had a feeling it would be a terrible insult if I refused. Besides, I liked benne wafers and they were said to bring good luck.

I sat down on the top step while Rhapsody perched precariously on the flimsy railing. I could taste honey and lemon and the barest hint of orange in the tea. Like my mother's, it was sweet and delicious.

While Rhapsody and I nibbled on the wafers and sipped our drinks, Essie watched the sky. The sun had finally come out, and as the breeze died down, the heat index soared. I held the cold glass against my face and wondered how to broach the subject of Shani.

After a bit, I began to feel a little woozy in the syrupy heat. I leaned over to place my empty glass on the tray Essie had set beside her chair, and when I straightened, the porch started to spin. I gasped and clutched the newel post for support.

Rhapsody hopped down from the railing and came to squat in front of me, peering into my face. "What's wrong?"

"I feel dizzy…"

She put a hand to my forehead. "She don't look so good, Granny. Maybe you should give her a dose of Life Everlastin'."

Suddenly, I felt an urgent need to get away from there. I tried to rise, but the porch spun faster.

Rhapsody placed her hands on my shoulders and pressed me back against the floorboards.

SEVENTEEN

I swam up through a pounding headache.

It was only with a great deal of effort that I managed to open my eyes. Blurry faces peered down at me.

"She's coming to," someone said. I thought it was Rhapsody.

I tried to get up, but instead sank deeper into whatever softness had cushioned my fall.

"Are you sure she's seen her, Granny?"

"She see huh all right."

I recognized Essie's voice and strangely, I could now understand her just fine. Whether she'd altered her manner of speaking or I was becoming accustomed to her Gullah-influenced words, I didn't know.

"Can you cure her?"

"No, chile. No root can fix dis gal. She ent hexed. She ben on tuddah side. She crossed t'rue dat veil and back, and now her spirit don' know weh it b'long."

"Is that why she can see Shani?"

"I reckon it is."

There was a long silence during which I had the impression of movement, like someone waving a hand back and forth in front of my face. I smelled something sweet, something acrid, then nothing at all.

"What's wrong, Granny. What do you see?"

Another pause. Another strange scent.

"Somebody uh-comin' for dis gal. Somebody with a soul black as midnight. Somebody dat walk with the dead."

I tried to ask her what she meant by that, but I couldn't speak. My tongue felt too thick and I couldn't make my lips work.

My eyes closed and the voices faded.

When I roused the second time, I was fully alert, with only the faint throb of a headache to remind me that I'd been unwell.

I knew instantly where I was—in Essie's house, lying on a bed in a room that had once been Mariama's.

Propping myself on elbows, I glanced around.

The space was cramped with only a mahogany wardrobe in one corner, the iron bedstead in another. I lay atop a handmade quilt in a pattern that had probably been handed down from the Underground Railroad years.

I could see daylight outside the single window, but the sun that shone through the glass had the soft-focus filter of late afternoon. I got up, found my boots and carried them with me through the quiet house.

Essie was on the front porch piecing quilt blocks while Rhapsody played kick ball with some kids in the road. She was smaller and younger than the others, but I had a feeling she could more than hold her own.

Essie glanced up and gave me a once-over before going back to her work.

"Bettuh?"

"Yes, thank you. I don't know what happened."

"Sun hot down yuh for town gals."

"No, it wasn't that. I work out in the heat all the time. What was in that tea?"

"Nutt'n' bad in dat tea. I mek it muhself."

I wasn't sure that was much comfort.

"Somethin' else be drainin' you," she said with a knowing look.

I thought instantly of Devlin.

"Essie, can we talk about Shani now?"

Her hands were steady as she pulled the needle through the fabric. "Dat baby can't git no rest."

"Why not?"

"She dont want tuh leave huh daddy. She can't pass on 'til he let huh go."

I felt a pang deep inside as I gazed down at her.

I remembered the first time I'd seen Devlin's ghosts— the way Shani had barely left his side.

"I don't think he knows she's here," I said softly.

"He know." Essie's gray head lifted as she placed a hand over her heart. "In yuh, he know."

I closed my eyes. "What does she want from me?"

"Fo' you tuh tell him."

"I can't do that."

Essie's troubled gaze met mine. "Mebbe not yet you can't, but dat day uh-comin'. Din he haffuh mek his choice."

"What choice?"

"'Tween the livin' and the dead."

I turned and stared out over the yard, where Rhapsody and her friends were still playing ball. It was a remarkably normal sight.

Essie rose from her chair and taking both my hands in hers, pressed something into my palm.

I stared down at the tiny cloth pouch tied with a blue ribbon. "What is it?"

"Put it underneet yo' pillow at night. Keep dem bad spirits away." She pulled a packet of what looked to be dried herbs from her apron pocket and placed it in my other hand. "Life Everlastin'. Cures wut ails you."

"Thank you."

She made a shooing motion with her hand. "Now go. Somebody at home be worryin'."

There was no one to worry, but I didn't argue. I sat down on the top step and pulled on my boots. When I stood, Essie cast a worried glance at the sky.

"Mek haste, gal. Sundown uh-comin'."

EIGHTEEN

Rhapsody and her friends walked me to the cemetery, but they would go no farther than the entrance. I moved alone through the modest headstones, pausing at Mariama's and Shani's graves to glance back. Rhapsody stood on the side of the road, staring after me. Something in her anxious expression reminded me of the conversation I'd overheard between her and Essie.

Somebody uh-comin' for dis gal. Somebody with a soul black as midnight. Somebody dat walk with the dead.

A chill settled over me, followed by a sinking sensation.

Then I scoffed at myself for taking her words so literally. I was making too much of the whole thing. Essie might have the ability to cure certain ailments with her roots and berries and her Life Everlasting, but that didn't mean she had the gift of second sight.

Nevertheless, I picked up my pace, anxious to be well away from the graveyard before dusk. The sun still hovered at treetop level, spangling down through the oak leaves like long streamers of glitter. I had plenty of time, but already I could feel the budding prickles of unease that always accompanied twilight.

Pressing the remote to unlock the car doors, I scrambled down a small embankment and jumped the ditch to the road. But as I approached the SUV, my steps slowed and I swore under my breath.

The front tire on the driver's side was completely flat. Not an uncommon occurrence on the back roads I traveled, which was why I always took care to keep my spare aired up and my jack working properly.

Tamping down my impatience and just a tinge of panic, I hauled around the necessary equipment and set to work, the light at my back.

The lug nuts were always the hardest part for me. Each one took extra effort to loosen. By the time I finally got the car jacked up and the tire off, the sun had dipped below the treetops.

Somewhere in the woods behind me, a loon wailed, the eerie sound running a cold finger up my spine.

Feeling exposed and vulnerable with my back to the trees, I positioned the spare onto the wheel studs, fumbling the lug nuts in my haste. Then I lowered the jack. Tightened the lugs. Glanced over my shoulder.

All clear.

But I heard the loon again, a tremolo this time, which Papa always said indicated agitation or fear.

Throwing everything into the back of the SUV, I climbed behind the wheel and left the same way I'd come in.

The trees on either side of the gravel road grew inward, creating an impenetrable tent dripping with Spanish moss. My headlights came on automatically, and now and then I saw the gleam of wary eyes from the underbrush, the scurry of some small creature along the ditches.

As much as I wanted to be away from the cemetery, away from Essie's warning, I took it slow over the bumpy road. But once I reached the highway, I stomped on the accelerator. With every mile, the sun sank lower, flaming out as it slid toward the marshes, leaving a comet's tail of gilded crimson just above the treetops.

I'd gone less than five miles when I heard a telltale thump.

No!

No, no, no. No!

This could *not* be happening. Not another flat. Not here. Not now.

Fighting back panic, I tried to assess the situation.

I could keep driving, get as far down the road as I possibly could before the tire came completely off the rim. Or I could turn around and try to make it to Hammond, which was probably seven or eight miles the other way.

From the sound of the flapping rubber, I doubted I'd get very far in either direction.

Hobbling to the shoulder, I parked and checked my phone for a signal. A solitary bar flashed in and out.

I got out, climbed onto the hood and then scrambled up to the roof where I turned in a slow circle, my eyes glued to the signal.

The light was fading fast. All around me, utter stillness. The hush of twilight. That end-of-day moment when the ghosts came out.

There!

Another bar!

Quickly, I placed a call to my roadside service and managed to ramble off the directions before the signal faded. Whether a tow truck would be forthcoming, I had no idea.

I kept turning, hoping for a stronger signal. As I finished a second rotation, I saw a flicker of movement just beyond a row of trees.

The hair bristled at the back of my neck, but I didn't outwardly react. Instead, I made another circle, surveilling the woods from the corner of my eye.

I saw it there, hiding in the gloom.

Whatever it was, it had followed me all the way to Beaufort County. And now it hunkered among the trees, watching me.

I didn't move, didn't even dare breathe.

It wasn't like any apparition I'd ever encountered. There was no aura, no ethereal lightness. This thing was dark and dank, with no more substance than a shadow. But I could feel its presence. The evil that emanated from the woods was palpable.

Now the hairs on my arms rose, as well. I tried to take my time climbing down from the roof, but my feet slipped and I ended up on my butt, sliding down the windshield, bouncing off the hood and landing on my hands and knees in the dirt. Gravel and glass cut into my flesh, but I paid little mind to the sting. I leapt to my feet, jumped into the car, slammed and locked the door.

As if that would keep the thing out.

I reached into my pocket for my phone, found Essie's amulet and clutched it in my hand.

A foul chill oozed through the closed windows, turning my stomach, making my heart pound even harder.

I saw a flash at the passenger window. There one moment, gone the next.

Pulling the mirror toward me, I watched the rear,

almost expecting to find something peering in at me, but I saw nothing.

No...there *was* something...

About two hundred yards back, a car had pulled to the shoulder.

I experienced a momentary elation before I realized that I hadn't heard the engine or seen the lights.

Very odd. And creepy.

My eyes fastened on the mirror, I tried to detect movement.

Nothing.

But at least a car was real, the driver a flesh-and-blood person.

Climbing over the seat, I grabbed the tire iron I'd used earlier and then returned to my place behind the wheel. My gaze went again to the mirror and I wondered if I should go back there and ask for help.

I waited.

An eternity passed before I finally spotted a faint glimmer on the horizon that gradually morphed into twin pinpoints of light.

Whoever was in the car behind me must have seen the headlights, too, because I heard the engine start up. The next thing I knew, the vehicle was flying up the shoulder so fast I thought the driver meant to ram me.

I caught my breath and braced for a collision, but at the last moment, he veered onto the road and shot around me, still without lights. I could make out nothing more than a dark color and the boxy shape of a late-model sedan.

As the other car approached, I got out and stood shivering at the edge of the road. Terrified the driver might fail to stop, I dashed into the middle of the highway, screaming at the top of my lungs and waving my arms like a madwoman.

The vehicle slowed, stopped and a door opened. I heard the crunch of shoes on gravel and then miraculously, my name.

"Amelia?"

My knees went weak with relief.

NINETEEN

Devlin came around the car and I saw his ghosts then. I wasn't surprised they were with him. It was full-on dusk and we were out in the middle of nowhere, far away from hallowed ground.

I hadn't seen him since our encounter at Rapture, and all the things that I'd learned about him since that night flashed through my head. He was, in fact, one of *the* Devlins and was estranged from his grandfather because he'd pursued the wrong profession and married an unsuitable woman. That told me a lot about him, about the man he'd once been before tragedy and grief had made him so guarded.

It was strange, but the more I knew about him, the more remote he seemed to me. Which was probably a good thing, considering. Too many things had happened since he'd entered my life. His ghost child had appeared in my garden, his dead wife had taunted me at the grave-yard, the old man's entity had returned, perhaps as a warning, and a door had been opened, unleashing a cold, terrifying presence that now trailed me.

It was also a good thing I'd tempered my impulse when I first saw him tonight. I'd wanted to launch myself into his arms the way I had at Oak Grove, but his ghosts held me back. Already I could feel their consuming chill as Devlin walked toward me.

"What happened?" His gaze was narrowed as he focused on my face.

"Flat tire. Thank God you came along when you did. You have no idea how glad I am to see you." I was proud of myself for the right amount of relief and nothing more in my voice.

He glanced around. "What are you doing way out here?"

Was that suspicion I heard in *his* voice?

"I came to look at a cemetery." Not a lie, though I purposefully let him assume an untruth. "What about you?"

"Personal business." His voice was as flat as my tire. "Do you have a spare?"

"It's on the car. This is my second flat, lucky me. I must have picked up a couple of nails somewhere."

Maybe it was my imagination, but the angles of his face seemed harsher than usual, the circles under his eyes even darker. Then I remembered his trip to the cemetery and the date on that tiny headstone.

I glanced away because I couldn't bear to look at him. Couldn't bear to think about Essie's prediction. I had a hard time envisioning a scenario where I would ever be able to tell him about his daughter's ghost.

"Two flats, huh?"

"Yes. I called my roadside service, but the signal kept fading in and out. I'm not sure the operator even heard the directions. If you hadn't come along when you did…" This time a tremble in my voice betrayed me.

He turned to peer down at me. "What?"

"It was probably nothing. A car was parked a little way up the shoulder. I never heard the engine or saw the lights. It was just…there. Then the moment your car appeared, the driver took off. I actually thought he was going to hit me for a moment."

"This part of the county is rural and poor. A lot of drugs, a lot of crime around here."

"You think I stumbled across a drug deal."

"Wouldn't surprise me." He glanced at the tire iron I still clutched in my hand. "Do you have a jack to go with that?"

"Yes, of course."

"Then let's get this tire off. I know a guy in Hammond who owns a garage. Maybe we can persuade him to stay open long enough to fix both flats."

"Thank you."

He knelt to loosen the lug nuts. "No problem. It's not like I was going to leave you stranded out here."

"I know but…" My gaze swept the edge of the woods and I shuddered. "You really have no idea how glad I am to see you."

The mechanic in Hammond was subject to persuasion, but not without a price. Sixty dollars and two patched tires later, I finally drove across the Ravenel Bridge into Charleston.

Devlin followed me all the way back home and waited at the curb in front of my house until I was inside. I hurried down the hall turning on lights, and then stepped out on the veranda to wave him on. If I had been a bit more socially adept, I would have invited him in for a drink or a cup of coffee. It probably wasn't a good night for him to be alone. But years of caution and solitude still governed my behavior so I stood there and watched him drive off.

And, to be truthful, I was a little afraid to be alone with Devlin in my house. It wasn't just the odd instance of my waning energy while he slept that made me uneasy. Something Temple had said the night before kept coming back to me. *"There's something about him...I'm not sure I can explain it. I've known men like him before. Controlled and guarded on the surface, but under the right conditions...with the right woman..."*

What worried me the most? I wondered. That Devlin would lose control with me...or that he wouldn't?

That was crazy. I had so many more important things to worry about.

Locking the front door, I went straight to the bathroom, showered and got ready for bed. I was so exhausted from the evening's ordeal that I wanted nothing more than a long night's sleep.

But I couldn't shut down my brain. The moment my head hit the pillow, my thoughts ran rampant.

I hadn't told Devlin what I'd seen at the edge of the woods—on either occasion—because I didn't know how to explain it. What would I say? *Because of my connection to you and your ghosts, something dark has come through the veil and I don't know if my father's rules can protect me?*

There was another darkness that frightened me, too— the black sedan that had sped away the moment headlights appeared on the horizon. I really wanted to believe I'd chanced upon some illegal activity that would explain the driver's peculiar behavior, but already doubt had started to gnaw a hole in that theory.

The vehicle that had nearly run me down in the parking lot the night my briefcase was stolen had also been a black sedan.

I'd tried to convince myself the killer would have no reason to target me once I'd sent those photographs to Devlin, but now I worried…

What if I'd seen something I didn't even know I saw?

What if there was something in those images—a hidden symbol—that only I could interpret?

What if I really was the key to solving Hannah Fischer's murder?

Outside, the wind picked up. I could hear the rustle of limbs against the house, the faraway tinkle of the wind chimes in the garden. I lay there shivering even though the night was balmy and warm.

Easing my hand from beneath the cover, I reached for Essie's amulet on the nightstand. The pouch had a fusty odor I hadn't noticed earlier. I started to toss it on the end table, but slipped it underneath my pillow instead.

Keep dem bad spirits away.

I hoped she was right.

My eyes fluttered closed and my muscles finally began to relax.

Floating down into a deep slumber, I was oblivious to the creak of my garden gate, the howl of my next-door neighbor's dog and the eyes that gleamed with madness peering in through my bedroom window as I slept.

TWENTY

The Charleston Institute for Parapsychology Studies was located on a dead-end street just inside the Historic District. It had once been a run-down neighborhood of sagging antebellums, but a flurry of redevelopment had spit-shined the grand old dames into a semblance of their former luster.

With the facelifts had come a rather pretentious promenade of trendy new businesses—art galleries, design houses and antique shops—all entering into an unlikely waltz with the tattoo parlors and the adult video stores that had dominated the area for the past twenty years.

The CIPS building was the fairest belle of them all, a three-layered confection of white columns and lovely piazzas with off-street parking in the rear. I located a space in the shade and cracked the windows to allow for airflow.

As I walked back to the side entrance, my gaze was drawn by the flicker of a hand-shaped neon sign on the house across the street, where some enterprising palmist named Madam Know-It-All had set up shop. The irony of her proximity to the loftier Charleston Institute for Parapsychology Studies gave me the best laugh I'd had in days.

I'd been to the Institute before, so I knew the drill. Ringing the front bell, I waited for the lock to disengage, then passed through from the muggy midmorning heat into the cool, shabby elegance of crystal chandeliers and brocade wallpaper. Somewhere in the house, a grandfather clock chimed, enhancing the sensation of having stepped back in time.

No hoop skirts for the young woman who came out to greet me, but she was quintessentially Southern— golden hair, golden skin, friendly smile. She'd added a bit of mystery to her appearance by rimming her blue eyes with kohl and adorning herself in silver rings and chains dangling with exotic charms.

She was new since the last time I'd been there, but she recognized my name. Escorting me down the hall to a set of pocket doors, she slid them open to announce me, then waved me in.

Unlike the rest of the house, Rupert Shaw's office was sparsely furnished with a mishmash of seedy castaways and a noisy window AC unit that kept the temperature somewhere between warm and frigid, depending on where one sat.

What the room lacked in style, it made up for in substance. A view of a cozy back garden, a huge marble fireplace and books—hundreds and hundreds crammed into wooden shelves, stacked on the floor, spread out over every square inch of desk space. Old leather-bound volumes reeking of mildew and knowledge of the ages sat alongside dog-eared paperback novels.

It was a room I would have felt very comfortable in if I could have adjusted the air-conditioning.

Dr. Shaw rose when I came in and walked over to kiss both my cheeks before motioning me to the empty leather chair across from his desk. He wore his usual tattered attire of flannel trousers, houndstooth vest and a light blue shirt that complemented his eyes and an impressive helmet of white hair. He was taller than Ethan, with a lankier build and a graceful carriage that suggested, despite his threadbare garb, a lifetime of affluence.

As I sat down across from him, I was reminded of the first time we'd met. Someone had sent him the Samara video, and he'd contacted me through my blog, persuading me to come by for a tour of the Institute. Afterward, he and his research assistant had taken me out to dinner. She was a grad student who'd recently accepted a teaching assignment overseas and needed to sublet her apartment on Rutledge Avenue. Since I was looking to move to Charleston and had yet to find suitable accommodations, I'd asked if I could take a look at her place. The moment I set foot in the door, I knew it was where I needed to be. A week later, I was moved in, and when the assistant decided not to return at the end of her term, I boxed up all her personal belongings, stored them in the basement and signed my own lease. I'd lived there in perfect harmony ever since...until Devlin's ghost child appeared in my garden.

But that wasn't the purpose of my visit.

After we'd exchanged pleasantries, Dr. Shaw steepled his fingers beneath his chin and gave me a curious scrutiny. "So what can I do for you today? Your phone call sounded a little mysterious."

"I'm hoping you can provide a plausible explanation... or any kind of explanation...for what I've been seeing lately..." I trailed off, uncertain of how I wanted to proceed. I wouldn't tell him about the ghosts. Until my conversation with Essie, I'd never talked about the sightings to anyone but Papa. Though not a specific rule, silence and secrecy had always been implied.

But the new entity I'd been seeing was a different matter. I'd never witnessed anything like it and I didn't know how to protect myself from it.

I settled back in my chair, willing myself to relax. Opening up about a paranormal event, even to someone like Dr. Shaw, wasn't so easy. It made me feel exposed and subject to ridicule.

"You know I've been working in Oak Grove Cemetery, right? In fact, Ethan told me you're on the committee that awarded me the contract. I'd like to thank you for that."

He made a dismissive motion with one finger. "Your work speaks for itself."

"Still, I'm grateful for the vote of confidence."

He inclined his head and waited patiently for me to get to the point of my visit.

"I'm sure you've also heard about the murder victim that was uncovered in one of the graves. It's been in the papers and on the news..."

Still he said nothing. I wondered if he was thinking, as I was, about another homicide victim discovered in that same cemetery fifteen years ago. He'd been questioned by the police in Afton Delacourt's murder and, according to Temple, had been dismissed from Emerson because of certain rumors connected to that crime.

Even knowing all that, I wasn't apprehensive about being alone with him, perhaps because our friendship preceded my knowledge of the murder. I'd had time to form an opinion before it could be tainted by past events, and so my initial impression of a refined, somewhat eccentric gentlemanly scholar hadn't changed. I simply couldn't imagine Rupert Shaw involved in murder, let alone a slaying as brutal as Devlin had implied.

His blue eyes continued to regard me thoughtfully.

With an effort, I reined in my scattered thoughts and focused. "Two days ago, I saw something at Oak Grove I can't explain. I was walking alone on the path to the gates just before dusk when I caught a glimpse of something out of the corner of my eye. It was like a silhouette or a shadow hovering at the edge of the woods. When I stopped to look at it, the thing came at me with such speed and power that I know it couldn't have been human. It never touched me, but I felt this awful chill, this fetid dankness. Fetid isn't even the right word because that implies an odor. There was no smell. And yet I had the definite impression of something foul, something…putrid." I paused to observe his expression. "Yesterday, I saw it again. I was about five miles out from a cemetery in Beaufort County when I had a flat tire. I spotted that… thing, that silhouette…in the trees and again at my car window. It was there one moment, gone the next."

"On both occasions, you say it was almost twilight and you saw this dark shape at the edge of woods?"

I nodded. An in-between place at an in-between time.

"And each time, you caught it out of the corner of your eye?"

"Is that important?"

"It could be." He swiveled his chair and stared out into the garden. "I wonder if you might have experienced what some people refer to as a shadow being. A shapeless mass that can morph into human form."

"You mean like…a ghost?"

"No. This is a different type of entity. Almost anyone who has ever witnessed a ghostly apparition describes the appearance as misty or vaporish, but distinctly humanlike, with discernible clothing and features. Shadow beings are…well, shadowlike and are often accompanied by a malevolent sensation that leads some researchers to speculate they may be demonic in nature."

"Demonic?" An icy fear quilled my nerve-endings. What kind of door had I opened?

Dr. Shaw reached for a volume on his desk and leafed through the pages. "Here." He handed me the book. "Did your entity look anything like this?"

I stared down at the rendering of a dark creature with a human form and red glowing eyes. "I don't know about the eyes…" I studied it for a moment longer. "I guess it was kind of like that…"

"But in hindsight, you're unable to give an accurate description because you didn't get a very good look at it."

"No, I guess not…" I sensed he was leading up to something. "What are you thinking?"

"I can give you a couple of possible explanations."

"Besides a demonic entity? I'm all ears."

"The shadow being you saw could have been a physical representation of an egregore."

"I don't have a clue what that is."

"An egregore is the product of collective thought, sometimes created by events in which extreme physical or emotional stress has taken place."

Like murder? I wondered.

"It can best be described as the psychic entity of a group. A thoughtform created when people consciously come together for a common purpose. Some mystical fraternities and organizations have learned how to create egregores through the use of ceremony and ritual. The danger being, of course, that the egregore can become more powerful than the sum of its parts."

"This is real?" I'd never heard of such a thing.

He shrugged. "I personally have never seen one, but as I said, it's a possible explanation."

"You said there was another."

"There are those who believe that shadow beings can only be summoned through black magic."

I thought instantly of Essie's amulet that I carried in my pocket.

Dr. Shaw sat forward and folded his arms on the desk. "Sadly for me, I don't believe any of these theories account for what you saw."

"You don't? Then how do you explain it?"

He waved a hand. "Optical illusion."

I stared at him in surprise. "Meaning, I didn't actually see anything?"

"Are you familiar with the term *pareidolia?* It's a condition in which the brain interprets random patterns of light and shadow as more familiar forms—like the human shape. This incorrect interpretation usually occurs with images seen in the peripheral areas of the vision and in low light conditions. Dusk, for example."

I frowned. "So you think I imagined these silhouettes?"

"No, each time you saw something very real. Just not what you perceived."

I sat back in my chair. "I have to say, I'm a little surprised by that explanation coming from you."

His smile seemed weary. "It pains me to offer it. But in all the hundreds, perhaps thousands of psychic and paranormal cases I've studied over the years, only a handful remain without scientific or logical explanation."

I wondered what he would think of all the ghosts I'd seen over the years.

Pulling Essie's amulet from my pocket, I slid it across the desk. "Have you ever seen one of these?"

He picked up the tiny pouch, turned it over in his hand, then lifted it to his nose and sniffed. "Dirt and cinnamon," he muttered. "In West Africa they call them *sebeh* or gris-gris. They're used as protection against evil spirits. Where did you get it?"

"From a woman who claims to be a root doctor. I met her in Chedathy Cemetery down in Beaufort County."

He looked up. "Before or after you saw the shadow being?"

"Before. I had a really strange episode at her house. I think she put something in my tea." I pulled out the packet of herbs and handed it to him, as well. "She called this stuff Life Everlasting."

"Been around forever. The leaves are harvested from a plant in the daisy family. It may have intoxicating properties when smoked, so it's now illegal in South Carolina." He lifted the packet to his nose and inhaled deeply. "Said to cure the common cold. Basically harmless."

"Harmless? I passed out."

"Not from this, you didn't. I've had the tea myself to no ill effects. In fact, I found it quite invigorating. Rather like a B_{12} shot."

"Then she must have put something else in my tea. Or maybe it was the cookies…except she and her granddaughter ate from the same batch and drank from the same pitcher. So I don't know what happened, but it was very surreal. Like a dream. I heard her say some truly bizarre things about me."

He glanced up, his eyes keenly alert. "What things?"

"She said I've been to the other side and now my spirit doesn't know where it belongs."

"Interesting." He fingered the gris-gris thoughtfully. "Have you ever had a near-death experience?"

"No."

"Not even as a child?"

"Not that I know of."

"What else did she say?"

"She said someone is coming for me. Someone with a dark soul who walks with the dead. Then she gave me the amulet to put under my pillow to keep bad spirits away."

He passed the amulet back to me and I returned it to my pocket.

"It's certainly possible she slipped you a mild hallucinogenic as you suspect. It's also possible you experienced a phenomenon known as hypnagogia—waking sleep. Interestingly enough, this may also account for your shadow beings. A person can be alert and aware of their surroundings, but also in a dreamlike state where the subconscious transmits certain stimuli that can be interpreted as moving shadows or even strange voices. This condition is often accompanied by some very dark feelings—dread and paranoia—and has been used to explain a number of paranormal experiences, including ghosts and alien abductions."

I gave him a rueful smile as I stuffed the packet of Life Everlasting back into my bag and stood. "There you go again with your logical explanations."

"Believe me, I would like nothing more than to be proven wrong." He rose to see me out. "Those cases that remain without satisfactory explanation are what keep me plodding along day after day, year after year. Parapsychology can be a very frustrating, often lonely field of study."

When he took my hand at the door, I noticed once again the onyx ring on his pinkie. "I'm still fascinated by your ring," I said. "The symbol is so unusual and yet I feel as if I've seen it somewhere before. Maybe on a headstone."

"It's possible, I suppose. I don't know the origin. It caught my eye at a flea market one day and I've been wearing it ever since."

At a flea market.

I shook my head slightly at this latest account. "Thank you again for your help."

"If you experience any more of these events, call me at once. There's always a chance I could be wrong and you really are being visited by a demonic manifestation," he said hopefully.

TWENTY-ONE

I took an unfamiliar route home from the Institute and got caught in a logjam near Old City Market. A nightmare for motorists, the place was a tourist's paradise of indoor and outdoor stalls where one could barter for every Lowcountry souvenir imaginable, from T-shirts to sweetgrass baskets to cornrows.

Wedged between a bicycle taxi and a rusted Toyota, I crept along Church Street, letting my gaze wander to the churchyard at St. Philip's, home to some of the oldest and most ornate wrought-iron gates in the city, as well as the twice-exhumed body of John C. Calhoun. The gravestones here were in excellent condition, the upkeep impeccable, but what I found most fascinating about St. Philip's was the unusual layout: it had two separate cemeteries, dubbed "Friendly" and "Stranger," for those parishioners born in Charleston and those who were not.

The churchyard was said to be haunted by a young woman grieving for her stillborn baby. A number of sightings had been reported over the years by tourists and locals alike, and allegedly her ghostly image had been captured on film by at least one professional photographer. But in all my visits to St. Philip's, I'd never caught so much as a glimpse of her.

The bicycle taxi slowed to a crawl while his excited passengers snapped pictures with their cell phones. I grew increasingly impatient, wanting to be home where I could spend the rest of the day alone with Google.

Egregores, shadow beings, pareidolia—Dr. Shaw had served up some exotic food for thought and I needed to do some research.

I still wasn't convinced of his optical illusion and waking dream theories, because I knew better than anyone that logic sometimes had to be taken with a grain of salt. But his explanations were certainly more palatable than the notion of some dark entity coming for me.

All of this rolled around in my head as I sat drumming my fingers on the steering wheel, waiting to make the next turn. As we inched our way down the street, I happened to look out my side window at the very moment Devlin was getting out of his car at a small seafood place with a shaded porch and tropical landscaping.

Until a few days ago, I'd never set eyes on the man and now I saw him everywhere. It was at once a strange, exhilarating and unsettling phenomenon.

All my life I'd been trained not to react to stimuli and not to act on impulse. So it was quite out of character for me to make an illegal turn, circle the block and pull into the restaurant parking lot with a fanfare of sputtering gravel.

Devlin had already been seated on the porch by this time and he glanced up from his menu as I approached his table.

"I hope you don't mind," I said with all the ease and

confidence of an adolescent confronting her first crush. "I saw you pull up outside and I wondered if I might have a quick word with you."

"Have a seat." His expression was completely neutral. I couldn't tell if he was annoyed, pleased or just plain old indifferent to the intrusion.

The waitress came over to ask if I wanted to see a menu. "Oh, just iced tea for me, thanks."

Devlin lifted a brow. "You're not eating?"

"I'm not about to intrude on your meal. I thought we could chat while you wait for your food."

"Suit yourself." He turned to rattle off his order—a basket of shrimp, hush puppies and a Palmetto Amber.

While he talked to the waitress, I took the opportunity to study his profile. The nose, the chin, the jawline…that shadowy space beneath his bottom lip. All becoming so familiar to me now. I had even grown accustomed to his scar, and now the deep indention seemed less of an imperfection and more like an intriguing secret.

His white shirt looked stark against his tan, and it made me think of the dream I'd had of him and how I'd admired the contrast of his skin tone against Mariama's.

I wondered what he thought when he looked at me. Could he see past my reserve, past my sensible-girl trappings? Did he sense the stirring of a dark passion that was as foreign to me as it was forbidden?

He had said something while I indulged in a little fantasy and I blushed. "I'm sorry. My mind wandered."

"You do seem a little preoccupied." He searched my face. "What's wrong?"

I may have grown accustomed to his scar, but the smooth timbre of his lowered voice still had a disconcerting effect on me.

"I just wanted to thank you again for coming to my rescue last night."

"You don't have to keep thanking me. You would have done the same for me."

"Yes, I know. But if you hadn't come along when you did, I might have been stranded out there for hours." The images that flashed through my head stripped away my pretended lightness and I shivered in the late-afternoon heat. "Anything could have happened."

"The tow truck would have arrived eventually."

"Maybe. But by then it could have been too late."

The low-hanging ceiling fan ruffled his dark hair as he gazed across the table at me. His expression never changed, but I saw a flicker of something I couldn't discern in his eyes. "You're talking about that car?"

"Yes. The black sedan that was parked behind me and took off like a shot when the driver spotted your headlights. It was also a black sedan that nearly ran me down the night my briefcase was stolen."

"Do you know how many black sedans there are in South Carolina?"

"Hundreds, thousands…" I shrugged. "I still think it's odd."

He started to respond, but paused when the waitress brought over our drinks. I watched as he poured the beer into a frosted mug. My gaze lit on his hands. So graceful. So steady.

We were seated near the railing, where a row of crape myrtles blocked the traffic. The breeze tousled the flower clusters, unleashing a shower of pink petals that rained down on our table and onto my lap. As I bent my head to sweep them aside, Devlin reached across the table to pick a blossom from my hair.

I froze at his touch. My breath caught. I didn't look up.

And then it was over.

He leaned back in his chair, cradling his beer, apparently oblivious to the firestorm he'd ignited.

"You were saying?" He spoke casually, but there was a flare in his eyes, a molten gleam, that belied his apathy, and I saw him exhale carefully, as if trying to fortify his guard.

I didn't quite know what to make of all that, but the notion that he might have to work to keep himself under control with me was thrilling. A little frightening, too, but mostly thrilling.

I swallowed. "We were talking about that black sedan." Absently, I circled the straw in my glass, trying to recoup my previous thoughts. "I'm starting to wonder if I might have seen something at the cemetery that I don't even know I saw. Or maybe there's something in one of the Oak Grove images we haven't found yet." I paused, sensing darkness in the breeze now, a harbinger of a distant storm cloud. "What if Tom Gerrity was right? What if my knowledge of cemeteries is the key to finding the killer?"

Devlin had been in the process of lifting the mug to his mouth, but now he set it down with a thud. His gaze hardened and I suddenly remembered what he'd told me about the private detective. A case had gone bad and another cop had been killed because of Gerrity.

No wonder the mention of the man's name seemed to set him off.

"The minute you start taking Tom Gerrity's word for anything is the minute you ask for trouble," he said.

"Was he right about Hannah Fischer?"

Devlin glanced away, eyes glinting with anger.

"He was, wasn't he?" I pressed.

"Yes, he was right. Mrs. Fischer ID'd the body this morning." He looked as if it pained him greatly to admit it.

"Poor woman. It must have been so hard for her. I can't even imagine the horror of seeing your child dead…" I froze.

The anger in Devlin's eyes vanished, replaced by the dull gleam of something too tragic to contemplate, something too sad to look at. The fleeing vitality made his face go flat and stiff, like a cardboard cutout. I thought if we sat there long enough, every last drop of life in him might drain away.

Already, the circles under his eyes had darkened, the hollows beneath his cheekbones deepened. He looked ghostlike himself now. Pale, gaunt, lifeless.

I glanced away, shaken.

It took a moment for both of us to recover a semblance of normalcy.

"Mrs. Fischer came by the station and gave a statement," he finally said, his voice strained.

I nodded. "Were you able to talk to her?"

"Yes." He picked up his beer, his eyes meeting mine over the rim. With some effort, I managed not to look away.

"Did she corroborate Gerrity's story?"

"For the most part. She did hire him to find Hannah. According to Mrs. Fischer, she'd suspected for some time that her daughter was in an abusive relationship. One of many, apparently, that began with her father."

"Then whoever she was seeing is a suspect, right? Did she tell you who that is?"

"She didn't know his name. Hannah never brought him home, never even talked about him. She knew her mother would 'try to save her,' is how she put it."

"Well, that's not much to go on, is it?"

"It's enough. I've managed to track him down through some of Hannah's friends. He has an airtight alibi."

"How airtight?"

"He was in jail during our time frame. The guy's a creep and I don't doubt Hannah was scared enough to try and run away from him. But he couldn't have killed her."

"So we're back to square one. And since the rest of Gerrity's story panned out," I said slowly, "don't you have to give credence to what he said about me?"

Devlin sighed. "I don't want to drag you into this any more than you already are. Besides, Gerrity's just guessing about the cemetery. He's not clairvoyant. He wasn't even a particularly insightful cop."

"He would disagree with that assessment. In fact, he told me his grandmother thinks he has a gift. That's why he's called the Prophet—"

Devlin's hand shot out, trapping mine against the table and rendering me speechless with shock as he leaned across the table. "Did he tell you to say that to me?"

There was nothing empty about his expression now. His eyes glittered murderously, animating his whole face in a way I'd never seen before.

"What? No. Not specifically. I just assumed everything he told me was part of the message."

"You didn't say anything about it the other night at Oak Grove."

"It slipped my mind." I pulled my hand from his. "What's the big deal? It's just a nickname, right?"

"It's a nickname, but it's not *his* nickname. He used it because he knew it would get to me."

"Get to you how?"

"It's not important." But he appeared to have quite a

struggle corralling his emotions. This was yet another side of him I hadn't seen. The out-of-control side.

I shivered.

"You sound so angry when you talk about him. What did he do, exactly?"

"That's between him and me." His dark eyes surveyed the traffic. "I'm done with this subject. Anything else you care to talk about?"

"Yes. Can we go back to Hannah for a minute? I know you have limitations on what you can tell me, but if the killer drives a black sedan, I could be in a lot of trouble. There are some things I'd like to know."

"Such as?"

"How did she die?"

Only a slight hesitation as he contemplated how much to tell me. "Exsanguination. Do you know what that means?"

"She bled to death, basically."

"Basically, yes."

"How?"

"I'm not going to give you specifics. That's something you don't need to know." When I started to protest, he lowered his voice. "That's something you don't *want* to know."

I felt a tremor of dread. "What was the cause of death in the Delacourt case?"

"I don't know."

"But you said she died in such a way that the end was a long time coming."

"That's what I heard. I wasn't a cop back then. I relied on rumors just like everybody else."

"But you're a cop now. Can't you look in the file and find out?"

"That file is sealed. No one can touch it without a court order."

"Is that normal?

"It happens in cases where a minor is involved."

"Do you think that's why this file is sealed, or is it because someone in power doesn't want it released? You said there was a concentrated effort to keep the investigation quiet by some pretty important people. The society you told me about—the Order of the Coffin and the Claw—if they were responsible for Afton's death, then the members who were involved might now be in those positions of power. It's like a circle. A never-ending cover-up."

"That's why groups like the Order are so effective. The members have to protect each other. If one falls, they all fall."

"Then how would you ever be able to prove anything? They've stacked the deck."

He glanced around, his manner suddenly uneasy. "We're getting ahead of ourselves, anyway. We don't know that anyone in the Order did anything wrong. There were a lot of rumors flying around back then, including some pretty disturbing talk about Rupert Shaw."

"About Dr. Shaw…" I brushed another petal off the table. "Let me just say that I still don't think he did anything wrong. I can't imagine him having anything to do with that girl's murder. I just can't. But…" I glanced up. "There is something that's been…not bothering me, but puzzling me."

"I'm listening."

"He has this ring. Very unusual and ornate. Silver and onyx, I think, with some sort of emblem on the stone. I don't know what the symbol is, but it looks familiar to me. I think I've seen it somewhere before. Anyway…

what's really strange is that he keeps changing his story about where he got it. The first time I noticed the ring, he said it was a family heirloom. Then he told someone else it had been a gift from a colleague. This morning he told me he bought it at a flea market. I feel silly even bringing this up because I'm sure it's nothing. But in the interest of full disclosure, I needed to get it off my chest."

"Anything else you want to get off your chest?" He said it so smoothly I almost didn't notice the steel in his voice.

"Uh, no. That's it."

Deliberately he slid his glass aside and folded his arms on the table. "What about your visit with Essie? In the interest of *full disclosure,* why didn't you tell me you saw her yesterday?"

All the air swooshed from my lungs. For a moment, I could only gape at him in awkward silence. Then I rushed into an embarrassed justification. "It wasn't planned. I didn't go down there to see her. I didn't even know about her. We met in the cemetery…" I trailed off at the look on his face. "I'm sorry. I should have told you."

His eyes were very dark, very cold, very unforgiving. "The next time you have a question about my private life, I suggest you ask me directly instead of going behind my back."

TWENTY-TWO

Devlin's anger hit me hard. I'd never handled disapproval well nor had I learned to let criticism roll off my back. Sometimes I wondered if being adopted had something to do with my almost obsessive need to please. Or maybe I overcompensated because of my father's rules and my mother's melancholy.

Whatever the reason, I knew that if I went home, I'd spend the whole day in a mood, so late that afternoon I called Temple and asked her to meet me for drinks.

We chose a place with a waterfront view, and by the time I arrived, she was already seated on the patio watching the sailboats put in.

"There you are," she said as I sat down across from her.

"Am I late?"

"No, I'm early." She picked up her drink, some potent-looking concoction in a tall, frosted glass, and sipped. "After ten days of babysitting undergrads, I needed this more than you. Although…" She cocked her head. "You do look a little flushed."

"It's summertime in the Deep South. What do you expect?"

"Hmm, yes, except you're not exactly sweating."

"We glow down here, remember?"

She didn't take her eyes off me as she motioned for the waiter.

"What?" I asked.

She shrugged. "Something's different about you. I can't quite put my finger on it." She waited until I'd given the waiter my order, then leaned in. "Are you sleeping with Devlin?"

"I hardly know him! And after today," I said a bit glumly, "the possibility of that is even more remote than the last time we talked."

"What happened?"

"Something stupid." I rubbed a hand across my forehead. "I'm almost too embarrassed to tell you."

She propped an elbow on the table, drink in hand, and waited.

"I drove down to Beaufort County yesterday to visit his wife and daughter's graves." I glanced up to view her reaction.

She arched a brow. "And why did you do that?"

"I don't know. Curiosity, I guess. While I was there, I met Mariama's grandmother—who is a root doctor, by the way—and a young girl named Rhapsody, Mariama's second cousin. Anyway, one of them must have told Devlin I'd been there, and now he's angry that I pried into his personal life and I'm completely mortified."

"If that's the worst thing you've ever done to a man, then you obviously have never been in love," Temple said with a shrug. "But I still don't understand why you went to visit those graves. What did you hope to accomplish?"

"Nothing. I just wanted to see where they were buried."

"And so now Devlin's upset with you." She contemplated the matter for a moment. "What are you going to do about it?"

"Wait for it to blow over, I guess."

"The fatalistic approach. I'm not a fan."

I sighed. "What would you do then?"

"Try my damnedest to make him forget about Mariama—at least for a night. But that's me. And for you, I'm afraid that might be a tall order."

Her gentle ribbing went right over my head. "I don't want him to forget Mariama. Why would I want that?" I thought of my encounter with Mariama's ghost and shuddered.

Temple gave me a look over the rim of her glass. "I said for a night."

The waiter brought over my drink and I used the opportunity to change the subject. "How did you get here so fast, anyway? You must have already been in town."

"I was. We wrapped up early and now I don't have a thing to do for the next couple of days but hang out by the pool and soak up some sun. Well, except for a report to file and a mountain of papers to grade." She did look relaxed and quite exotic in a mustard-colored peasant blouse with embroidered flowers. In comparison, my skinny jeans and tank seemed a little too coed. A little too vanilla.

"When are you going back to Columbia?"

"Not until I take a look at your skeleton. And speaking of Devlin, he called. He's rescheduled the exhumation for tomorrow."

"Yes, I know. Ethan Shaw left a message on my voice-mail earlier."

"You're planning on being there then?"

Was that a note of disapproval I heard in her tone? Or was I being a little too sensitive after Devlin's censure? "I don't see why not. I've been involved from the very beginning. Which is another reason I wanted to see you today. I've been trying to research Afton Delacourt's murder, but I can't find anything about it online or in the newspaper archives."

Her relaxed mood faded as she sat back in her chair and gazed out over the water. A breeze tickled the dark curls at her nape and the palmetto fronds that hung over the railing. "Why are you so obsessed with that murder?"

"I wouldn't call it obsessed," I said a bit defensively. "But I am interested. Two, possibly three murder victims have been found in the cemetery where I spend a lot of time alone. I think my concern is understandable."

"Maybe. But we both know what's really going on here, don't we? You're overcompensating. Something exciting has come into your careful little world and you've latched on with both hands."

"That's not it!" But I wondered if my vehemence was due in part to her hitting a little too close to home. "And, anyway, I thought you said I needed some excitement."

"I hardly meant involving yourself in a murder investigation."

I stared at her across the table. "Why does it bother you so much to talk about Afton Delacourt?"

"I'm not bothered. It happened a long time ago and I don't see the point of dredging up ancient history."

"What kind of archaeologist are you?"

Her smile was ironic and she seemed to unwind a little. "Good point. I know this sounds odd, but it feels...intrusive somehow. Like maybe we should leave that poor girl alone."

"It's strange that you should say that. Daniel Meakin made almost exactly the same comment the other day."

"Meakin?" She couldn't have been more dismissive. "Where did you see him?"

"In the archives room at the university."

"Figures. I suspect he spends most of his time down there. He's like a mole."

"I saw Camille down there, too, that day. I think she was spying on us."

"That sounds like Camille. She's always had a tendency to stick her nose in where it doesn't belong. I used to hate the way she'd go through my things when I wasn't around."

"Did you really have a fling with her or were you just teasing Ethan the other night?"

"Camille and I definitely had our moments. But there's darkness in that woman. It drives her to do impulsive, hurtful things. Just like the darkness in Meakin drove him to attempt suicide."

"You really think he tried to kill himself?"

She flicked at an invisible speck from her blouse. "Let me put it this way. The scar I saw on his wrist wasn't exactly a scratch. It was thick, raised, raw and ugly. The kind you get from a deep gash. I don't blame him for trying to keep that thing covered."

"Did you know him very well when you were at Emerson?"

"Not really. We had a few classes together, but we didn't socialize." She was growing impatient again. "Why all the questions about Daniel Meakin? I thought you wanted to talk about Afton."

"I do. Whatever you can tell me."

She shrugged. "I guess the thing that stands out most in my memory about that time is how scared we all were when the body was discovered."

"We?"

"My little group of friends. Everyone I knew had partied in that cemetery at one time or another. It was a rite of passage at Emerson. To hear that a girl had been killed there was very upsetting."

"Did you know Afton?"

"Only by reputation. She was a rich, spoiled party girl who, until she was murdered, led a fairly charmed life."

I wasn't altogether certain the irony was intentional. It was hard to tell with Temple. "Where did you meet her? She wasn't a student at Emerson, was she?"

"Every hotshot on campus dated her. Or so they claimed."

"Was there much talk after the murder about her involvement with a member of the Order of the Coffin and the Claw?"

"Some."

"Did you know any of the Claws?"

"I may have, but I wouldn't have known it."

"No one ever let anything slip?"

"About the Claws? Never."

"But Emerson is such a small campus. You must have had your suspicions."

"There was always speculation. Among the girls I knew, it would have been considered quite a coup to sleep with a Claw and then out him. Or her."

"Did you ever hear any rumors about occult activity?"

"Nobody paid any attention to that stuff."

I perked up. "So there was talk."

"All those secret initiations, midnight orgies, Dionysian rituals—nothing more than a bunch of frat boys' wet dreams."

"You never went to any of them?"

She frowned. "Why do I get the feeling you're leading up to something?"

I hesitated as the waiter brought her a fresh drink. "It did occur to me that you might have some inside knowledge about the Claws."

"I already told you I didn't."

"I know, but the other night at dinner, you mentioned that you and Camille were roommates for a time when you were juniors. You said you were thrown together by circumstances. And I read recently that the Order's bylaws were changed to include women. Two from every junior class. So I just thought—"

"That I'm a Claw?" She gave a low chuckle. "Now that would be an unexpected twist, wouldn't it? Especially if I'd dated Afton."

That stopped me cold. An involvement with Afton Delacourt had never even occurred to me.

"Before you ask, no," she said flatly.

"I wasn't going to ask. And I don't think your being a Claw is so far-fetched. I imagine you were just what they looked for in a recruit—smart, ambitious, attractive."

"And poor. I was at Emerson on a full scholarship. Big black mark against me." She stirred her drink. "Not that it mattered. I was never much of a joiner or a follower and I detest ceremony and ritual. Probably why I'm a lapsed Catholic."

Not exactly an outright denial, I noted.

"Speaking of ceremony and ritual, have you ever heard of something called an egregore?"

"An egre-who?"

"An egregore. A thoughtform. A physical manifesta-

tion of collective thought. Some secret societies create
them through ceremony and ritual."

She narrowed her eyes. "Where are you getting all
this stuff?"

"I saw Rupert Shaw today."

"Aha! Now it's all starting to make sense."

"What is?"

"You. These questions."

I shrugged.

"Look, I've known Rupert for years. He was a favorite professor of mine at Emerson and I consider him one
of the last true Southern gentlemen. But let's face it. His
knapsack's been short a few biscuits for years."

"He seems perfectly fine to me."

She smiled. "That's one of his talents. He's so sweet
and down-to-earth and *reasonable* that you don't realize
you're buying into his crap until you find yourself glancing over your shoulder for the bogeyman."

I didn't need Rupert Shaw to make me watch out for
bogeymen.

"He's been unstable for a long time," she said. "I'm
sure that's why he was asked to leave Emerson."

"I thought you said he was fired because of unfounded
rumors."

"The rumors may have been unfounded and I do believe somebody deliberately set out to ruin his reputation,
but none of that stuff would have had legs if not for his
previous behavior."

"By previous behavior, you mean the séances he conducted with some of his students?"

"It wasn't just the séances." She glanced away, her
expression troubled. "He had an obsessive interest in
death. I always wondered if it had something to do with
his wife passing. She was sick for a long time. Years, I

think. Maybe the agony of watching her suffer and the guilt of waiting for her to die unhinged him somehow. I don't know. As I said, he was one of my favorite professors, but I'm not surprised he's taken up permanent residence in Crazy Town. Aka, his ridiculous institute."

"I've spent a lot of time with Dr. Shaw and except for an occasional memory lapse he seems perfectly lucid and very in the moment," I said. "*Unhinged* I don't get from him at all."

"That's just it. Even someone truly sick can hold it together for a while." Her smile turned hard. "Then one night you wake up and find them coming at you with a pair of scissors."

That night I tucked Essie's amulet underneath my pillow again. I had no idea if the pouch contained anything more than dirt and cinnamon—a root doctor's placebo—but I felt better having it nearby.

Propping myself against the headboard, I opened my laptop and started a search. As I skimmed through article after article on shadow beings and egregores, I realized that something Temple said earlier had been bothering me all night. That seemed typical of our conversations. The impact sometimes didn't hit me until much later.

"She was sick for a long time. Years, I think. Maybe the agony of watching her suffer and the guilt of waiting for her to die unhinged him somehow."

I hadn't made the connection before, but now I realized why I felt so uneasy about Temple's speculation. It went back to Dr. Shaw's theory about death—and back to my father's warning about the Others. When someone died, a door opened that would allow an observer a glimpse into the other side. The slower the death, the longer the door would stay open, so that one might even be able to pass through and come back out.

Was it possible Dr. Shaw had tried to open a door to the other side by murdering Afton Delacourt? Had he been that desperate to make contact with his dead wife?

I tried to shove such a nasty, baseless thought from my mind, but already an insidious seed had been sown and I felt the chill of something dark creeping over me.

Listen to me, Amelia. There are entities you've never seen before. Forces I dare not even speak of. They are colder, stronger, hungrier than any presence you can imagine.

Sitting up, I scoured every nook and cranny of my bedroom. I was alone, of course, with nothing but the nighttime sounds of my apartment to keep me company. Settling floorboards. A noisy air vent. My neighbor walking around upstairs.

My gaze lifted to the ceiling.

Macon Dawes was hardly ever home, so it surprised me to hear him up there now. In a way, I felt better knowing another warm body was so nearby.

Slipping out of bed, I padded over to the window to glance out. The garden wall blocked my view of the driveway, but it also gave me privacy from the street and from my next-door neighbor's windows. I didn't always bother with the blinds. Now I pulled them tightly closed before I got back into bed.

As I settled under the covers, my thoughts returned to Dr. Shaw.

I remembered how his voice had sharpened when he asked if I'd had a near-death experience. I could see in my mind the way his eyes had gleamed with…curiosity? Obsession?

The very thing that Temple had accused me of.

See how easy it is to distort someone's intentions?

I was getting myself all worked up over nothing more than hearsay. Dr. Shaw was a harmless introvert with an interesting profession. The same could be said about me.

Time to move on.

I needed to cleanse my brain with more agreeable thoughts before trying to fall asleep. And for once, I would not dwell on Devlin.

Digging Graves was always a pleasant diversion, although now my blog had also become a lucrative business endeavor. Writing steady and interesting content was both challenging and time-consuming, but on most evenings, I had nothing better to do, anyway.

I'd yet to moderate the comments from my latest entry—"Poisoned by His Wife and Dr. Cream: Unusual Epitaphs"—and now as I sifted through the responses, I began to relax. I was in my element here, sharing my passion and my experiences with taphophiles and online acquaintances from all over the world. In cyberspace, I didn't have to look over my shoulder for ghosts.

Halfway down the page, an anonymous post caught my eye—not because the poster hadn't used a screen name. That was common enough. But because I recognized the epitaph:

The midnight stars weep upon her silent grave,
Dead but dreaming, this child we could not save.

It was the headstone inscription on the grave where Hannah Fischer's body had been buried.

How odd. And more than a little disturbing.

I glanced up from the screen to search my room once again. Still alone. But now the house was completely quiet. The air wasn't running at the moment and the footsteps above were silent. Macon Dawes had finally settled in for the night.

I went back to the epitaph.

The comment had been published several hours earlier, well after the last time I'd logged on. I wanted to believe it was just some random posting, one of those bizarre coincidences, but that was asking too much.

Who else would know about that epitaph?

Devlin, of course.

And the killer…

Grabbing the phone from the nightstand, I scrolled to Devlin's number in the directory, then hit Send before I could change my mind. The call went straight to voice-mail and I left a quick message.

The moment I hung up, I regretted the impulse. What if the post *was* just a strange coincidence?

And what could Devlin do about it tonight, anyway? Anyone with even a basic knowledge of the internet knew how to use a proxy server. And anyone who had some-thing to hide—like murder—would undoubtedly access a public computer at the library or an office store.

Besides, a number of people could have seen that epi-taph. Regina Sparks. Camille Ashby. All the cops and crime scene techs that had been at the cemetery the night of the exhumation and on the day of the search.

I thought of Tom Gerrity's contention that my knowl-edge of cemeteries could be the key. Was the epitaph a message?

While I waited for Devlin to return my call, I opened the Oak Grove image folder and began a meticulous search through the hundreds of photographs I'd taken on the day after Hannah Fischer's mother had last seen her alive. It was tedious work made even more difficult because I had no idea what I was looking for.

Thirty minutes later, I still hadn't found it.

And Devlin had not returned my call.

I glanced at the clock. Eleven twenty-two. Still early. He might be tied up on another case. Charleston was a small city with an understaffed police force and an alarming murder rate. A homicide detective would always be on call.

Opening the Oak Grove document folder, I started reading through my notes.

Eleven fifty-five. Still no Devlin. Still no clues.

I got up and padded into the kitchen for a glass of water. As I stood drinking at the sink, my gaze strayed to the clock over the stove. So strange that Devlin hadn't called me back.

I wandered out to my darkened office, a room I'd been avoiding since the heart had appeared on the window. The night was clear and still. Moonlight shining down through the tree branches cast an opaline glow on the garden. I thought about the ring I'd buried there and the doll Devlin had left on his daughter's tiny grave. How long had he searched for such an exquisite offering?

At the farthest corner of the garden something stirred. My heart quickened as I stepped back from the window.

It wasn't her. It wasn't anything. Just a random pattern of shadow and light. A pareidolia.

I went back to bed and resumed my search. A little after one, the phone finally rang and I snatched it up. "Hello?"

"Amelia?" The way he said my name sounded very proper. Very Southern. Very controlled.

I slid down under the covers with a shiver. "Yes."

I heard something in the background then—a soft, feminine query followed by Devlin's muffled reply.

Then he was back on the phone. "Sorry. Are you still there?"

My heart had started to beat a very painful tattoo against my chest. He wasn't alone. He had a woman with him. "Yes, I'm here."

"What's wrong? You didn't leave much of a message."

"I know…" I trailed off, my fingers clutching the cover. This was so awkward. "I thought I'd found something, but…I may have overreacted. It's nothing that can't wait until morning."

"Are you sure—"

"Yes, quite sure. I'll talk to you tomorrow."

I couldn't hang up fast enough. A part of me thought he might call back, but no. The silence from the phone was deafening.

Falling back against the pillow, I closed my eyes. How funny that I should be so upset by this. I hardly knew Devlin. He was nothing to me. Could *be* nothing to me.

And yet I couldn't stop thinking about that soft voice in the background.

I couldn't stop thinking about Essie's assertion that one day soon, he would have to make a choice.

TWENTY-THREE

I didn't see or speak to Devlin again until the next day at the exhumation and we only had time then for a quick word. I explained about the epitaph posting on my blog and he agreed it was a curious development, though hardly a smoking gun.

"I doubt it's enough to warrant a court order to access the ISP's logs, and I'm willing to bet the poster used an anonymizer service, anyway. That information can't be subpoenaed because they don't store it. Or so they claim."

"That's what I thought, too."

"I'd like to go over the Oak Grove images with you again, though. I think you could be right. You may have captured something in one of those shots that we just haven't found yet. We need to spend some time with them."

"Sure. Whenever you want." He seemed to be over his anger with me, and I was happy about that, although a part of me had to wonder if his improved state of mind had something to do with the company he'd kept the previous evening.

He was more casually attired today than I'd ever seen him—jeans, a cotton shirt rolled up to the elbows and a lightweight jacket that he'd removed in the heat to reveal a belt holster and sidearm.

Carefully, I averted my gaze from the weapon, but I was transfixed by it just the same. It tied in so well with the persona Temple had painted of him as a dangerous man.

"I'll also see about getting the patrols in your neighborhood beefed up."

"So you do think the killer posted that epitaph," I said in alarm.

His eyes were hooded, as though he was trying very hard to disguise whatever concern he might have. "I think it's always better to be safe than sorry."

Hardly a comforting platitude under the circumstances.

A small crowd had started to gather and Devlin went off then to speak to one of the other detectives. I moved into the shade and watched as Ethan laid out a grid pattern over the grave. Then he and Temple set to work with trowels, easing away dirt from the skeleton, while his assistant manned the screen and Regina Sparks shot stills.

At one point, she came over to stand beside me, her red bangs plastered to her forehead in the heat, the underarms of her T-shirt stained with sweat. "Another hot one."

"Sweltering."

"Not a good day to be digging up human remains."

"Is there a good day for that?"

She grinned. "I've seen just about every imaginable thing that can be done to a body—and some things you don't want to imagine—but this business still creeps me out."

"An exhumation? That surprises me."

"I know." She fiddled with her camera as we talked. "It's weird, but if the body is fresh—like the other night—I don't mind as much. But digging someone up who was planted there by loved ones...prayed over, grieved over... that just seems wrong."

"So you'd rather deal with a murder victim than a body that was formally interred?"

"Told you it was weird." She gave me a sidelong glance. "You seem pretty cool about all this. Have you ever been to one before?"

"Yes. When I worked for the state archaeologist's office, we moved a whole cemetery once."

"How many bodies?"

"Dozens. One of the caskets was cast iron and shaped like an Egyptian sarcophagus. It was perfectly preserved and weighed a ton. I'd never seen anything like it."

"Did you open it up?"

"No, not a good idea. Back in the nineteenth century, embalmers experimented with a lot of interesting fluids, including arsenic."

"Now that would make for a nice batch of coffin liquor, wouldn't it?" she said, referring to the viscous black liquid sometimes found in burial containers.

It was a little surreal standing there in the shade conversing so casually about something so gruesome, but I supposed it was a fitting enough topic, considering. My gaze went back to Ethan and Temple. They were backlit by the sun so that from where I stood, they were mere silhouettes, a pair of grim reapers with trowels and sunglasses.

The skull was already exposed and facing me, the

stare of those empty eye sockets chilling even in broad daylight.

All around the grave, cops spoke in hushed tones or watched the excavation in silence. I heard someone laugh and turned to glance over my shoulder. No one was there. It was the oddest sensation.

"Devlin sure seems to be keeping an eye on you," Regina remarked.

"What?" I turned in surprise.

She nodded in his direction. "He's always looking over here."

It took some willpower not to glance at him. "How can you tell? He's wearing sunglasses."

"Oh, I can tell. I can always tell." She cocked her head as she regarded me. "You wouldn't be the first to succumb to his charm, you know. Devlin's one of those men that makes us women overly aware of our biological clocks. It's the pheromones, I suspect."

"Have you worked with him a long time?" I tried to ask casually.

"Long enough to know that it'll take a far stronger woman than I to crack that shell."

"Did you know his wife?"

She eyed me curiously. "I met her once. That was enough."

"Why do you say that?"

"Hard to explain. It was the way she would look at you...like she knew things about you even if she'd just met you. Strange woman. Beautiful...but strange."

I thought of Mariama's ghostly hands in my hair, the touch of her frigid lips against my neck, and shivered. What did she know about me?

I was brimming with questions, but I didn't want to seem too obvious, so I let the matter drop. After a bit,

Regina wandered off and I turned my attention back to
the digging. I'd worked for Temple long enough to know
what she would be looking for as evidence of formal
burial preparation: bits of coffin lining and fabric clinging to the bone, tacks or pins that had held clothing in
place, and in graves as old as this one, copper pennies
that had been placed over the eyes.

Ethan would be looking for more grisly evidence—
soft or mummified tissue, muscle, ligament, insect inclu-
sions, the color of the bones and the odor of decay.

I didn't smell anything from where I stood. On such
a hot day, I was pretty grateful for that.

By late afternoon, a partially intact skeleton had been
recovered, along with teeth, bits of clothing and some
jewelry. Everything went into the body bag to be trans-
ported to Ethan's lab.

Once the remains had been carted away, the crowd
began to disperse. Temple and I stayed behind to take
stock of the damage to the grave. Then she, too, left and
I found myself alone as I opened my bag and removed
the tools of my trade.

Using a soft-bristled brush and a wooden scraper, I
cleared away as much of the moss and lichen as I could
from the marker without damaging the fragile stone.
Then, positioning a mirror to reflect light, I adjusted
the angle until I could just make out the imagery and the
epitaph:

How soon fades this gentle rose,
Freed from earthly woes,
She lies in eternal repose.

I read it once, then again more slowly. With each word,
I felt something sinister pressing down on me.

Hands trembling in haste and excitement, I took out my phone, logged on to the internet and opened my blog, scrolling quickly through the comments.

There it was, published a few minutes after the first epitaph had been posted. I searched through all the other anonymous comments, then logged off and put away my phone.

I read the lines a third time, the tickle of gooseflesh lifting the hair on my neck.

The inscription on a grimy headstone could stay hidden for decades, but if viewed in a proper light from a certain angle, the markings would sometimes pop through the layers of crud. It could be quite eerie, in fact.

But who would know to do that?

Someone with an interest in graveyards. A cemetery restorer like me. A taphophile like those who posted to my blog. An archaeologist, perhaps.

Or a desperate man looking for a door to the other side.

All those thoughts raced through my head in the space of a heartbeat.

As I stood watching, the light shifted and the epitaph disappeared.

TWENTY-FOUR

I found Devlin at the Bedford Mausoleum. His back was to me and he seemed so lost in thought that I didn't think he was aware of my approach. But then he spun around quickly and if I hadn't been so adept at concealing shock and fear, I might have jumped.

"It's just me," I said lamely.

"Force of habit." His gaze went past me as if making sure no one else tried to sneak up on him.

I wondered if his job made him so wary, or if on some level he sensed his ghosts. Did he ever feel the frost of their breath? The tug of their wintry hands? The bite of a ghostly kiss?

My gaze raked over him as he turned back to the mausoleum, and as I studied his profile, my thoughts turned to that soft voice I'd heard in the background last night. I wondered who she was, what she looked like and how well Devlin knew her.

Had she measured up to Mariama?

I was a little ashamed of my petty jealousy. Two homicide victims had been discovered within these cemetery walls and I had just witnessed the exhumation of what might well turn out to be a third. Devlin's private life should be the least of my worries.

"I've found something," I told him, and he turned with a lifted brow.

"What is it?"

"The inscription on the headstone of the grave we just dug up." I tucked back a strand of hair that had fallen loose from my ponytail. "After everyone left, I took it upon myself to check the epitaph."

"But the markings on that headstone are illegible," he said. "We talked about it the other day with Regina Sparks. How did you manage to read the epitaph?"

"I used a mirror to reflect light. Full-length works best, of course, but I didn't have one with me today so I had to make do with something smaller. It's all about the angle. Directing the light diagonally across the face of a gravestone casts shadows in the indentions and makes it easier to read the inscriptions."

"That's pretty clever."

"Yes, but it's not my cleverness. It's a trick of the trade. My father taught me how a long time ago. It saves a lot of wear and tear on the stones. You never even have to touch them…" I stopped. "Sorry. I'm rambling again."

Nine out of ten men would have agreed and asked that I just get to the point. Not Devlin. He merely said, "Go on," and then proceeded to hang on my every word as if I were the most fascinating creature he'd ever encountered. Of course, we both knew that wasn't true.

"Anyway," I said in conclusion, "the epitaph from that headstone was published in a comment on my blog just like the other one." I recited the inscription from memory.

He waved aside a fly. "When?"

"When was it published to the blog? A little while after the first one. I thought I recognized the verse so I used my phone to verify the posting."

"Anonymous again?"

"Yes. But I'm certain it was the same poster."

I set down my bag and closed the distance between us, coming to stand beside him at the bottom of the mausoleum steps. He waited in silence, watching me intently until I was the one who had to look away. After as much time as we'd spent together, I should have been over my reticence around him, but I thought it a good thing that I wasn't. I could never allow myself to forget about his ghosts or discount my father's warning about him. I couldn't lose sight of the fact that Devlin was a terrible threat to both my physical and mental well-being.

And yet even now I could feel his pull. Even now my eyes lingered on his lips, wondering yet again what it would be like to kiss him. I'd never felt anything like this before. Everyone always said that in the movies, but for me it was true. Temple was right—I'd always sought out only those men who didn't threaten the rules or my peace of mind. I'd lived in my own little world, cocooned from reality and sustained by fantasy, until the night John Devlin had stepped out of the mist.

His gaze on me flickered and I wondered if something of my feelings had shown on my face. Quickly, I turned away.

"What else can you tell me about the inscription?" he said.

"It's not so much the inscription itself that we should be concerned about. As I said, the lettering can only be read under certain conditions. The angle of the light has to be just right. The thing is…who else would know that?"

He gave me a shrewd glance, comprehending my meaning precisely. "What about the archives? Would epitaphs be included in the written records?"

"Sometimes they are, along with a description and dimensions of the headstone. But again, one would have to know where to look. And in this case, so many of the records from the original cemetery are missing. But I suppose it's possible that someone could have stumbled across one of the old church books. I've been looking for one in particular in the archives room, but the system there is a mess. Completely disorganized."

"Who would have access to those records?"

"Students. Faculty. And someone like me who has special permission, of course."

He eyed me thoughtfully. "You've spent some time down there, I take it."

"Yes, quite a lot."

"Have you ever seen anyone else down there?"

"Sure. People come and go all the time. The last person I saw was Daniel Meakin, the historian. No, wait. I take that back. Camille Ashby was the last person I saw down there." I explained to him about having seen Camille underneath the stairwell right after my conversation with Meakin.

"I had the strangest feeling she was spying on us, but I can't imagine why. She and Meakin are colleagues. Do you know him?"

"I know who he is," Devlin said as he turned his attention back to the mausoleum. "What can you tell me about this place?"

"The mausoleum? Not a lot. I haven't been able to find much information about it. I do know that it's the oldest in the cemetery, built in 1853 by the Bedford family, who donated land to Emerson University. The architecture is

Gothic. Beautifully doom and gloom. Mourning became something of an art form in the Victorian South, though nothing compared to their English cousins, of course."

"Have you been inside?"

"I've taken a peek through the door. It's in terrible shape. Graffiti and trash all over the place. Dust, cobwebs, you name it. The vaults were vandalized years ago and the remains are long gone."

He turned at that. "Someone took the bodies?"

I shrugged. "What can you do? Grave robbery is an age-old profession. In cemeteries like Oak Grove, armed guards used to patrol at night to prevent medical students from stealing fresh bodies to use as cadavers. Body-brokering is still a big business."

"Pleasant thought." Devlin placed his foot on the bottom step. "How do you go about restoring a place in this kind of shape?"

"Scrub away the graffiti, haul off the trash, reseal the vaults. It's a lot of hard work. Manual labor, actually." I stared down at the calluses on my hands. "And the sad thing is, without the bodies, the restoration is never going to be truly complete." I lifted my gaze to Devlin, a troubling suspicion starting to take root. "Is this where Afton Delacourt's body was found?"

"Yes."

"Why didn't you tell me that before?"

"I didn't know it then. Since I can't access the file, I had to track down the detective who was in charge of the investigation."

"He's still on the force?"

"Retired five years ago. He has a place on Lake Marion in Calhoun County. I finally managed to get an address through a sister who still works for the city. He didn't want to see me at first…until I told him about Hannah Fischer."

"What did he say?" I asked anxiously. "Did he give you any leads?"

Devlin expertly evaded my novice questions, along with my probing stare. "We're treading on tricky ground here. I shouldn't be telling you anything about this case. Things are moving fast…" Absently, he rubbed a thumb across his chin.

"What do you mean?"

He shrugged, a strangely expressive gesture that seemed to convey everything and nothing at all. "People in high places are starting to pull strings."

"A cover-up?"

"Let's just say there's interest at the highest levels. The thing is…we need a break in this case and we need it quickly, before the investigation gets booted upstairs. For whatever reason, this cemetery is being used to dispose of the bodies. As much as I hate to admit it, Gerrity could be right. If the killer is leaving clues in headstone symbols or in those epitaphs, you may be the only one who can unravel his motive. I've already dragged you into this. I won't involve you any further unless you know exactly what we're dealing with."

All of a sudden, my heart was pumping ice water into my veins. "What *are* we dealing with? What did that detective tell you about Afton Delacourt's murder?"

"How she died, for one thing. In explicit detail." His voice was quiet, but inflected with something I couldn't quite decipher.

I caught my breath at the look on his face. "How did she die?"

"Exsanguination."

Something bleak and cold rose inside me. Dread, fear

and maybe just a tinge of excitement. "Just like Hannah Fischer."

"Yes. Just like Hannah Fischer…"

The way he trailed off made me think there was something more. My fingers itched to take his arm and turn him toward me so that I could look into his eyes, study his expression. But, of course, touching him was not a good idea. Though I certainly wanted to.

"What else did he tell you?" I asked.

"There were ligature marks on Afton Delacourt's body. The way he described them sounded like the ones we found on Hannah Fischer."

"Ligature marks? They were both tied up?"

He hesitated. Whatever it was, he didn't want to tell me.

"It's all right. I want to know," I told him.

His eyes pinned me for the longest time, until I shivered as though an icy wind had swept over me. "They were strung up by their feet with leg irons," he said.

The blunt description took a moment to process. Then I stared at him in revulsion. "Strung up…*like meat?*"

"Strung up and bled out," he said grimly.

A wave of nausea washed through me. I felt hot and cold all over. Sweat trickled down my back, but I couldn't stop shivering. I had the most awful, bloody images in my head. Dripping carcasses, strung up on hooks in packing houses.

I tried to blink away the vision, along with the spots that swam before my eyes. "What kind of monster would do something like that?"

Devlin's voice was level, his face expressionless, but I saw something in his eyes that scared me. "My guess is, he's a hunter."

TWENTY-FIVE

I couldn't say anything to that. The chill that slid over me was more pervasive than a ghost's touch.

Devlin watched with sympathy as I struggled for control. "Are you okay?"

I nodded, glanced up at the sky and tried to focus on a small cloud shot through with sunlight. It was luminous and ethereal and reminded me of one of the dancing angels at Rosehill.

Drawing another shaky breath, I nodded again, as much to reassure myself as Devlin. "I'm fine."

But, of course, I wasn't fine. How could I be fine when I might already be in the sights of this sadistic madman?

I thought about those epitaphs posted to my blog—messages or a warning?

I thought about that black sedan—coincidence, or was I being stalked?

"What are you thinking?" Devlin asked.

"About being hunted."

He stared down at me for the longest moment. I

thought he might offer me a bit of comfort by taking my hand or patting my shoulder or—what I really wanted— pulling me into his arms. He did none of those things, but there was a feral gleam in his eyes that sent a little shiver through me. That told me the hunter was about to become the hunted.

Maybe comfort wasn't what I wanted after all.

"You don't have to be involved in this, you know. You can walk away right now, go home and put it all behind you," Devlin said. "You have no obligation here."

"And if I did see something that day? If my knowledge of cemeteries really is the key? You said yourself, you need a break in the case before it's covered up."

"That's not exactly what I said."

I shrugged. "Close enough. I can read between the lines."

"So it would seem."

"Can I ask you something?"

"Yes. But there's not a lot more I can tell you."

"You said yesterday that if I had a question about your personal life, I should ask. I'm asking."

I could sense his wariness, but he nodded. "What's the question?"

"It's about those students that came forward after Afton's death. The ones who talked about Dr. Shaw's séances and his theory on death."

"What about them?"

I paused, wondering how best to go about this. I decided to be blunt. "Was your wife one of them?"

"She wasn't my wife then. But to answer your question, she did attend one of Shaw's séances. She was too scared to go back."

"What happened?"

"She was repulsed by what Shaw was trying to do.

According to her beliefs, a person's power isn't diminished with death. A bad or sudden passing can result in an angry spirit wielding that power to interfere with the lives of the living. Even enslave them, in some cases. The prospect of bringing back the dead terrified her."

I could hardly comprehend the tragic irony of that statement.

"She was a very superstitious woman," Devlin said. "She wore amulets to bring good luck, painted all the doors and windows in the house blue to ward off evil spirits. I thought it charming...at first..."

I pictured the amulet underneath my pillow, felt the coolness of the stone I wore around my neck. And I wondered what Devlin would say to the rules I'd followed all my life.

I thought it charming...at first...

"I'm going inside," he announced abruptly.

"Inside the mausoleum? There can't be any evidence after all this time." Then I realized that his intent might have nothing to do with Afton Delacourt's murder and everything to do with his wife. "Should I wait out here?"

"Only if you're too spooked to go in."

"I'm not at all spooked. I've been in lots of mausoleums. I've never been bothered by any of them, and even if I were, I'd be hard-pressed to avoid them in my line of work."

"That's a very sensible outlook. Sometimes you surprise me."

"I do?"

He hesitated. "Don't take this the wrong way, but those photos in your office were very revealing," he said. "I wager you feel safer in your cemeteries than you do in the city, in the company of people."

"Not an unreasonable assessment," I admitted.

He nodded. "It seems you've created your own world behind these walls, and yet at times you can be stunningly practical."

Yes, a practical woman who consulted with directors of parapsychology institutes about shadow beings and egregores. Who followed her father's rules to the letter so that the ghosts floating through the veil at twilight wouldn't latch on to her and drain away her life force.

"Speaking of practical," I said, as I followed him up the steps, "rattlesnakes tend to like these kinds of places. Take care sticking your hand in a vault."

"I'll keep that in mind." He pushed open the dilapidated door and stepped inside.

Late-afternoon sunlight slanted in through the broken windows, illuminating the thick cobweb drapes that hung from the ceiling and in every corner. There was a smell, too, something earthy and ancient.

I paused just inside and glanced around. Nothing slithered away. No telltale sound of a rattle. That was a relief.

Vines and briars crept in through the windows and moss carpeted the brick floor. Layers of dust covered everything. I wondered if anyone had been inside since Afton Delacourt's body had been recovered fifteen years ago.

"Where was she found?" My voice sounded harsh and intrusive in the utter stillness of the mausoleum.

"On the floor. About here, I'd say." By contrast, Devlin's voice was silky smooth.

I glanced down at the floor. The bloodstains had long since disappeared with the crumbled brick and mortar.

"Who found her?" I asked, shooing away a fly that buzzed around my head.

"There was a groundskeeper back then. He didn't do much in the way of upkeep, obviously. His job was to chase away trespassers, mainly kids climbing over the wall to party. He spotted the body in here. The door was open, sunlight shining through…"

Just like now, I thought.

"Was he a suspect?"

"He was questioned, but he was an old guy. He died of a heart attack within weeks of finding the body."

"Shock or coincidence?"

"A little of both, I would guess."

I moved to the back wall where the vaults were better preserved. Using my hand to sweep away some of the grime, I read the vertical row of names—Dorothea Prescott Bedford, Mary Bedford Abbott, Alice Bedford Rhames, Eliza Bedford Thorpe—slowly lowering myself until I squatted before the bottom vault that had once housed the remains of Dorothea's youngest daughter, Virginia Bedford, who had died only weeks before her mother.

The day breaks…
The shadows flee…
The shackles open…
And now blessed sleep.

Above the inscription was a symbol of a broken chain hanging from a disembodied hand. A broken chain, a broken family.

I went back and reread the last two lines of the epitaph:

The shackles open…
And now blessed sleep.

There was another symbol at the bottom of the plaque. I had to press my head almost to the floor to see it. Three poppies tied together with a ribbon, the symbol of eternal sleep.

Once again I returned to the verse, absently swatting a fly from my face. It landed at the corner of the plaque and slipped through a crack in the vault door. I watched in disgust as another followed suit. Then another and another...

I scooted back, slapping at my hair.

Devlin saw me and came to my side. "Are you okay?"

"I hate flies."

"What?"

"Don't you see them? There must be dozens."

He knelt beside me and I pointed toward the plaque where several had alighted. One by one they disappeared through the crevice.

"Where are they coming from?" I asked, still shooing them away from my hair.

"The better question is, where are they going?" Devlin muttered, reaching inside his pocket for a penknife. He inserted the blade at the edge of the vault and pried open the door. Then he lowered himself all the way to the floor to peer into the chamber.

"Do you see anything? There can't be a body in there." I was almost afraid to hear his answer.

"No body, but I think I see something farther back. I need a flashlight."

"I have one in my bag." I scrambled to my feet. "Hang on. I'll go get it."

Outside the sun was low, splashing crimson through the trees and across the monuments. I could smell marsh and pine and honeysuckle in the air, and the scent that lingered over every cemetery—the gentle perfume of mortality.

It was quiet outside, though I fancied I could hear

voices in the distance. Cops milling around outside the walls perhaps, chatting about what they'd seen, reflecting on the grim business of murder.

I ran down the steps and as I bent to grab my backpack, I could have sworn I felt someone's gaze on me. Slowly, I straightened and turned. Nothing there. Just the yawning doorway of the mausoleum.

Clutching the straps of my bag, I hurried back inside, back to Devlin.

He was halfway inside the chamber. I could see nothing of his body past his knees.

"What are you doing?" I asked in alarm.

He backed out, brushing dust from his shirt. A cobweb clung to his eyelashes and I reached up to remove it. I must have startled him because he caught my hand reflexively, an automatic response to a sudden move.

"Sorry. You have a…" I motioned with my finger. "On your eyelash."

He swept the strand aside, his gaze inscrutable in the grayish light. "Did you find a flashlight?"

"Oh, right here." That incident rattled me a little and I felt clumsy as I fumbled through my bag, searching for one of two flashlights I always kept handy.

He turned on the light, tested the strength of the beam on the wall, then flattened himself on the floor and shined the light back into the chamber.

I lowered myself, as well, and peered into the opening.

"Do you see it?" Devlin asked.

I squinted. "What?"

"All the way back." There was a note of—not excitement exactly—but tension in his voice.

I wiggled forward on my stomach. "What am I supposed to see?"

"Some of the bricks are missing from the back wall. When I shine the light through the hole, there's nothing but empty space."

"Meaning…"

"That's where the flies are going. There must be a tunnel or a chamber behind that wall."

Now my own excitement started to mount. "I've heard about tunnel systems underneath old graveyards. Some of them were used by the Underground Railroad to hide fleeing slaves. Do you realize what this could mean? A discovery like this could be exactly what Camille Ashby needs to get Oak Grove entered into the National Register."

"I'd hold off on the celebration," he said drily. "It could be nothing more than a big hole in the wall. But there's only one way to find out."

He slithered headfirst into the vault, shoulders disappearing, then torso, then legs and feet, while I rummaged in my bag for the spare flashlight.

"Can you see anything?"

His voice came back muffled. "There's a room or chamber about twenty feet down." He backed out of the vault, his dark hair nearly white with cobwebs. But this time I knew better than to brush them away. "The opening is pretty narrow. I couldn't get my shoulders all the way through, but I think the hole must be about ceiling-high in the chamber."

"I'm smaller. Maybe I can get a better view."

He looked skeptical. "I don't know if that's a good idea. It's close in there. Kind of creepy when you think about where you are."

"To you maybe. I'm not just a cemetery restorer—I'm also an archaeologist. We live for this sort of thing."

He lifted a brow and waved a hand toward the opening. "Be my guest then…"

I checked my flashlight, took one last look at Devlin and crawled willingly—enthusiastically even—into a burial vault.

The crumbling mortar cut into my hands as I inched forward, making me wish that I'd taken my aunt Lynrose's advice about gloves.

Pulling myself up to the opening, I shined the light into a sea of shimmering white. I'd never seen so many cobwebs. I wondered how long they'd been there.

Balancing on one hand, I lifted myself up and poked my head and the other hand through the hole so that I could angle the light downward, sweeping it back and forth across brick-and-mortar walls and, in the corner, even thicker shrouds of cobwebs.

"You see anything?" Devlin called from behind me.

As I turned to reply over my shoulder, I caught the spark of something metallic out of the corner of my eye.

I tried to swing the light in that direction, but I'd put too much weight on the wall. As the mortar disintegrated, the bricks loosened and I fell against them with a hard clip to the chin.

The shock knocked the flashlight out of my hand and I heard the glass shatter against the hard floor of the chamber.

"What was that?" Devlin asked in alarm.

Before I could respond, the bricks below me gave way and I went tumbling after the flashlight.

TWENTY-SIX

Was I dead?

I lay sprawled in complete darkness, dazed, breathless, the taste of blood in my mouth.

"Amelia!"

Devlin's voice penetrated the fog. With an effort, I sat up, rubbing the back of my head, gingerly testing my arms and legs.

"Amelia, can you hear me?"

"Yes. Yes! I'm down here!" I said excitedly and quite unnecessarily. "I can't see anything. It's pitch-black."

"Are you all right? Are you hurt?"

I shook my head, clearing away cobwebs. And other cobwebs.

"I think I'm okay." I got up slowly, aware now of the sting in my palms and my knees, the bruised ache along my right hip bone. A sharp pain at the base of my skull. And still that metallic taste of blood in my mouth where I bit my tongue.

I felt in my pocket for my cell phone. That would have

provided a little light, but I'd left it in my bag. Wobbling forward in the dark, I touched the wall. It was cold and damp, a little slimy. I drew back my hand in disgust.

As my mind cleared and my senses regrouped, panic set in. What was this place? And how the devil was I going to get out?

I lifted my head and stared up into Devlin's flashlight beam. It flicked over me, raked the space around me, then came back to me.

"Are you sure you're okay?" he called down.

"Yes. Nothing's broken, apparently." I took a breath to steady my nerves. The air smelled musty, like a dank cellar. "Can you get me out of here?"

"Yes. But you'll have to hold tight while I call for help. Just hang on, okay?"

The light momentarily vanished.

"Wait!"

Devlin reappeared over the edge of the vault. "I have to make a call. Get some people out here…"

"I know. It's just…"

"I'll drop my flashlight down to you. Be ready to catch it."

I moved into place.

"On three. One…two…three…"

The light fell toward me, beam straight up. I caught it, fumbled it, then finally had the metal case in my grip.

"I'll be right back," Devlin called down. "Just hang tight."

He was gone an eternity.

But now that I had the flashlight and the relief that I'd managed to escape serious injury, some of my excitement returned. Turning, I brandished the beam across the space, taking stock of my surroundings. More brick walls. More brick floors. Cobwebs glistening like cotton candy from every corner.

On the wall facing the opening, large symbols had been painted on the brick. I saw an anchor, a compass, a broken wheel. All common gravestone symbols.

Below the images was another opening, just large enough for a person to crawl through. I wondered if it led to a tunnel and eventually to freedom.

As I angled the light through the hole, something skittered across the floor and disappeared over the edge of the bricks.

I jumped back, breathing hard.

A rat. Just a rat.

Scurrying away from the opening, I moved the light back over the symbols. God only knew how old they were or how long it had been since anyone else had seen them.

It was an exciting find, but the place was starting to get to me. There was something about that hole—apart from the rat—that worried me. If it led to freedom, it could also lead someone here to this chamber. To me. I felt like a sitting duck.

I'd been backing steadily away from the opening, crisscrossing the light over the rest of the space, but now I froze as my legs bumped into something that clanged as it scraped against the floor. Whirling, I splashed the light over the object, and then let out a breath of relief. Someone had set a folding metal chair in the center of the room.

An odd place for it, I thought. And it made me think that maybe it hadn't been so long after all since someone else had been down there.

What would one see from that seat?

I stepped behind the chair and played the light along the facing wall. Nothing there.

Slowly, I moved the beam up the wall and over the ceiling. The chamber was supported by old wooden beams, and as the light penetrated the gloom, I once again saw the gleam of something metallic.

I steadied the light on the ceiling until I realized what I was looking at. A series of chains and pulleys had been suspended from a ceiling joist. Bolted to the ends of the chains were leg irons.

The shackles open... And now blessed sleep.

"Devlin?"

No answer.

"John!"

I heard a scrambling sound, then his voice. "What is it?"

"Can you see this?" I moved the light up and down the chains, then angled the beam over the pulley.

"Not from here, I can't. What is it?"

I drew a breath. "Chains with shackles hanging from the ceiling. A pulley. Some other kind of device."

He said something then that I couldn't understand.

I stared and stared at those chains. "This is where he brought them, isn't it?" I hated the tremor in my voice, but it would have taken someone far stronger than I not to react. "This is where he did it."

Devlin must have sensed I was very close to the edge. Who wouldn't be? He said in a soothing tone, "He's not there now. No one's down there with you. You're safe."

I could process nothing beyond the frantic drumming of my heart. "I need to get out of here."

"We'll have you out in no time. Take a deep breath and try to relax. You're an archaeologist, remember? You live for this stuff."

"Not anymore I don't."

"Stay calm. Everything's going to be fine."

I did as he advised and drew a deep breath. "Just… don't leave me, okay?"

"I'm not going anywhere," he said. "You're my eyes right now. Tell me what else you see."

I knew he was trying to distract me and I appreciated the effort enough to play along. "The floors and walls are brick. The support beams are wooden." I turned in a slow circle. "There's an opening in the wall facing you. I think it leads to a tunnel." Another way out, another way in. I shuddered. "Someone has painted symbols on one of the walls."

"What kind of symbols?"

"Gravestone art. I think they may have been used in the same way that quilt patterns and song lyrics were used in the Underground Railroad days. A broken wheel by land, an anchor by sea…"

"What else?"

"You wouldn't believe how thick some of the cobwebs are." I aimed the light toward an area I had yet to explore. "They're like cotton gauze in the corners, but they've been cleared away in the center of the chamber."

The beam probed through the fibers, into the darkest recesses of the room. I felt something on my arm and extended it in front of me. A spider as big and thick as a fist inched its way up my shoulder.

I was so startled and my nerves already so fragile that I screamed as I flung it away. Stumbling back, I tripped over the chair and lost my footing. The flashlight banged against the brick floor and went out.

I held my breath as the cold darkness settled over me. Then a loud thud sounded behind me and I whirled.

"Amelia?" Devlin called softly.

He was in the chamber with me. He'd just dropped

twenty feet into total blackness when he heard my scream.

Whoa.

"I'm here." Maybe it was my imagination, but I could have sworn I felt warmth emanating from his body, pulling me like a magnet. Arms outstretched, I moved toward him. When we made contact, he put his hands on my shoulders and brought his face down to mine.

"Are you all right? What happened?"

"I saw a spider on my arm and panicked." Already I was reacting to his nearness. "Did I happen to mention that I have a mild case of arachnophobia?"

"And yet you thought it a good idea to crawl through a bunch of spiderwebs?"

"I normally have it under control," I said. "But the hairy ones always make me lose it."

"That's good to know."

"Anyway, thank you for leaping to my rescue. I can't believe you did that."

He was silent for a moment. "When you screamed…"

The slight hesitation in his voice quickened my pulse. He'd thought I was in danger and had come immediately to my aid, without regard to life or limb. That was…powerful.

It was also his job, but I chose not to look at it that way. My first assessment was more in keeping with my romantic views.

"I dropped my flashlight," I said, because I needed to say something and I couldn't share what was really on my mind at that moment.

"Did it break?"

"I don't think so. I heard it roll over that way." Which was not at all helpful since he couldn't see where I pointed.

I heard the sound of striking flint and then a flame danced between us. His face looked pale and a little ghoulish in the flickering light. I'd never seen a more beautiful sight.

He peered at me through the shadows. "Are you sure you're okay?"

"Yes, I'm fine. I completely overreacted. It was stupid."

"Not so stupid. Not in this place." He glanced around. "Where did you drop the flashlight?"

"Over there."

"I see it." He bent to pick it up, then held the lighter out to me. "Here, hold this."

I obliged, lifting the flame high enough so that he could see to unscrew the glass, tighten the bulb and then put the housing back together. A battery adjustment, a couple of taps against his palm and the light sputtered on.

Releasing the thumbwheel, I let the flame die and handed the lighter back to Devlin. It was ornate and heavy and looked quite old, from what I could see of it. "I didn't know anyone used these anymore."

"It belonged to my father. I've carried it around for years."

"For good luck?"

"It's just a keepsake," he said. "Nothing more."

But as he pocketed the lighter, I was reminded of the amulets he said Mariama had worn to bring good luck and the stone from Rosehill that hung from my neck. We all had our gris-gris, our placebos. Even Devlin, whether he would admit it or not.

He held the flashlight shoulder-high, sweeping the beam up and out as he surveyed our temporary prison. I followed the light as it played over the symbols on the walls, the cobwebbed corners and finally up and down the chains.

Devlin walked over and stood staring up at the ceiling where the pulley was secured to a wooden beam. He tracked the ropes with the light until he found the end wrapped around a metal spike that had been hammered into the brick wall. The shackles were bolted to the chains, which in turn were secured to some sort of device that could be raised and lowered with the pulley.

Devlin released the rope. The chains dropped and I jumped as the metal yoke crashed against the brick floor.

Terrible images flashed in my head as Devlin lifted the device with the pulley and tied it back into place. Then he walked over to examine the floor beneath the chains. The bricks looked darker from where I stood. I felt queasy as I watched him squat and touch his finger to the surface. Then he rose and resumed his search.

The silence stretched on forever.

"What do you suppose he used the chair for?" I finally asked. "Do you think he sat there and…watched them?"

"That or he had an audience," Devlin said, so matter-of-factly that my blood turned to ice.

He moved the beam back over the walls and I rotated with him. The cobwebs were so thick in places, the strands so tightly articulated that the light couldn't penetrate.

Devlin swore and I saw his hand jerk. I thought at first he'd seen another giant spider…or worse, the killer. But the light was trained upon the wall, almost all the way to the ceiling. Through a gossamer cocoon, I saw it, too.

A human skeleton shackled to the wall in the darkest corner.

TWENTY-SEVEN

The skeleton was bound at the wrists, not strung up by the ankles as Devlin had described earlier. I had a feeling that was important, but I was too shaken at the moment to try to make sense of it.

There wasn't much else to see through the webs. Bits of clothing. Tufts of hair clinging to the skull.

"It's been down here for years, by the looks of it." Devlin shifted the light from side to side, trying to get a better look. "I'm surprised it's held together so well. Maybe there's more ligament and tissue than what we can see from here." He sniffed the air. "But no smell." He took out his phone and checked the display. "No signal, either. We'll need to get a forensics team down here. And get Shaw back out." He was speaking quietly, but his voice echoed eerily in the chamber.

I had remained silent for a very long time because I didn't trust myself to speak. If I opened my mouth, I was very much afraid I might start screaming.

Devlin ran the flashlight back and forth across the

chamber. "What I want to know is where all those flies went."

I hadn't even thought about that. Now I looked at him aghast. "You don't think there's another body down here somewhere, do you? Or someone still alive? Someone..." *Someone who is taking a long time to die.*

A week ago, I would not have been able to imagine such an atrocity. Now I felt a creeping certainty as I stared at that hole in the brick wall, that dark, menacing gateway.

"I'll have to go in there and find out," Devlin said, and I thought I detected a note of dread in his voice.

"Right now?" I didn't even want to contemplate what lay beyond that gaping rift.

"If there's even a remote chance someone else is down here, yeah. Right now."

"But...shouldn't we at least wait for backup? You said help would be here soon."

"It may not be soon enough. Sometimes even a minute makes all the difference." The quiet way he spoke made me think of his wife and daughter trapped in that sinking car. "I've got to find out what's in there." His voice was hard, resolved. No talking him out of it.

"Then I'm going, too," I said, though in truth, I was operating more out of fear than altruism. I didn't want to stay behind in that chamber of horrors. I'd take my chances with whatever lay beyond that wall. With Devlin.

I thought he might argue and I was fully prepared to stand my ground, but then his gaze lifted to those chains and he nodded. "I think that might be for the best."

Shining the light into the aperture, he crawled through and I went in after him.

On the other side, the space opened up enough to stand upright. The walls here were also brick and slick with slime. When Devlin aimed the flashlight straight ahead, I could see nothing but endless tunnel.

The space was so narrow we had to move forward in a single file. When I glanced over my shoulder, the darkness behind me was complete.

"I've been thinking about the timing of all this," I said softly, as I moved along the passageway behind him. "Hannah's mother said the last time she saw her alive was last Thursday. If her body was buried sometime after I left the cemetery at four on Friday and when the storm hit at midnight, then she could have been down here while I was up there photographing headstones. I could have walked right over where he had her hanging. If only I'd heard something…seen something, I could have called the police—"

Devlin glanced over his shoulder, his face grim and shadowed. "Don't do that. There was nothing you could have done."

"I know, but it's a hard thing to think about."

"There are a lot of hard things in this world," he said. "You don't need to beat yourself up over something that's out of your control."

I wondered if he'd managed to take his own advice, or if he still played those terrible what-if games in the middle of the night, when sleep would not come and his ghosts would not leave.

We fell silent as we trudged along the tunnel. It seemed to me that we were descending, but I couldn't be certain. The claustrophobic confinement and the utter darkness behind us were a bit disorienting.

And everywhere, more cobwebs. I couldn't imagine how many spiders it had taken to spin them over the years.

"I can feel them in my hair," I said with a shudder.

"What?"

"Spiders. They're everywhere. Must be thousands. Millions…"

"Don't think about it."

"I can't help it. You know why I'm arachnophobic? I was bitten by a black widow when I was ten."

"I was bitten by a copperhead when I was twelve."

"Okay, you win." I ran fingers through my hair, trying to shake loose the unwelcome visitors.

"I didn't realize it was a competition," Devlin said. "Should we compare scars?"

I appreciated his attempt—feeble though it was— to lighten the mood. "Where were you when you were bitten?"

"My grandfather has a cabin in the mountains. We used to go up there for a week every summer when I was a kid. I had an old bike I kept around to take out on the trails. The snake was lying across the path late one afternoon. I didn't see it in time and ran over it. The body coiled in the spokes and when I tried to nudge it loose with my toe, the thing struck. Nailed me on the shin right through my jeans."

"Was it bad?"

"Not as bad as you might think. My grandfather kept antivenin in the cabin. He gave me an injection and some antibiotics for the infection."

I started to ask if his grandfather was a doctor, but then I remembered Ethan had said that Devlin came from a long line of lawyers. He was, in fact, the black sheep of the family, because he hadn't followed the traditional path.

"You didn't have to go to the hospital?"

"No. A little suffering builds character, according to my grandfather. I was pretty sick for a couple of days, but that was about it. Your black widow was probably a lot worse."

"Not that it's a competition."

"Right. Where did it get you?"

"My hand. I moved an old headstone and disturbed her home and her babies. My fault entirely."

"You've spent a lot of time in graveyards, haven't you?"

"It's my job."

"Even when you were a kid?"

"More or less. My father was a cemetery caretaker. He had several that he looked after, but my favorite was the one by our house. Rosehill. Have you ever heard of it? It's surrounded by dozens and dozens of rosebushes. Some of them are over a hundred years old. They climb up in the trees and hang down from the limbs. In the summer, the scent is like heaven. I loved playing there when I was a little girl."

"You played in a graveyard?"

"Why not? It was quiet and beautiful. A perfect little kingdom."

"You are a very strange woman."

"I thought I was practical."

"Strange, stunning and practical."

My heart quickened. I loved his description even though it seemed so out of character for him. It made me think of Rhapsody for some reason. Strange, stunning and practical. A girl who could play kick ball and cast spells.

The steady beam of the flashlight revealed nothing ahead but more brick walls and more darkness.

We'd only been walking for a few minutes, but already we seemed a long way from the opening through which we'd crawled. I wondered if help had arrived yet. Devlin must have told them I was trapped in the chamber, but how would they know to look for us in here? We were far enough away by now that I doubted they would even hear us if we called out.

Devlin stopped so abruptly I almost plowed into his back.

"What is it?"

"Another opening." He slanted the beam toward the bottom of the wall to our right. Some of the bricks had been removed to make a hole large enough to crawl through.

He knelt in front of it and shined the light through.

"Is it another tunnel?" My query bounced off the walls and came back to me.

"Looks like it." He paused, still probing the darkness. "I smell mildew and rot. This place is old."

"What do you suppose it was originally used for?" I stood in the dark, hugging my arms around my middle. The air was damp and dank. Like the touch of a ghost. "These tunnels must have taken years to dig."

"Maybe there was an old plantation house here before the cemetery was built. This could be part of a cellar system. They sometimes put the slave quarters underground."

Slave quarters. Perhaps that explained the pall that lay over Oak Grove.

My gaze lifted. It must be twilight up there now.

"Wouldn't this place flood when the water's up?" I asked.

"Probably why there's mildew and slime all over the place."

I glanced around nervously. "How do you suppose he found it?"

"Old records, deeds. Or maybe he stumbled upon it by accident like we did."

"We keep saying *he*."

"Most predatory killers are male." Devlin straightened.

I nodded toward the opening. "Are we going in there?"

"No. I think we should stay in the original tunnel. We can always double back. Let's just keep going."

We started walking again.

"This place reminds me of a recurring dream I had as a child," I said, falling into step behind him. I tried not to project beyond the strength of the flashlight beam. "It was terrifying. So traumatic you would think I'd been lost in a tunnel or a cave in real life, but there was nothing like that where I grew up."

"Maybe the tunnel represented a different kind of trauma."

"Maybe. At one end, I could see a faint glimmer of light and on the other end, nothing but darkness. I would always start out walking toward the light, but then something would compel me to turn and I would go toward the darkness, only to be tugged back around to the light. This would happen over and over again. A few steps in one direction, turn, a few steps in the other direction. It was the most awful tug-of-war you can imagine."

"Were you alone?"

"Yes. Except…once in a while I could hear a woman's voice. She spoke in whispers. I could never quite make out what she said, but I always listened and listened, hoping that she would tell me where I was supposed to go, but she never did. And if I stopped for too long, the hands would come out of the walls."

"Hands?"

I shuddered. "Dozens of them. Pale and grasping. I

knew that if they managed to grab me, they would pull me down into some dark place far more terrifying than what awaited me at either end of the tunnel. So I would start walking again. A few steps toward the light. Turn. A few steps toward the darkness."

"You never made it to the end?"

"Never. I'd wake up with the most dreadful feeling of being lost and not having a clue where I was or where I was meant to be."

"Sounds like a near-death experience," Devlin said. "Not that I believe in any of that stuff, but the way you described your dream is a lot like the way I've heard people talk about an NDE. Except for the hands," he added. "That's new."

"The hands were the scariest part."

He waved the flashlight over the walls. "See? No hands."

"Thanks." I tripped over the corner of a loose brick and righted myself with a palm to his back. Quickly, I pulled away. "Have you ever had a recurring nightmare?"

"Yes." He paused. "And then I wake up and remember that it's real."

The silence stretched on and on.

TWENTY-EIGHT

We were well into the tunnel by this time. Too late to turn back. I could feel a chill at my back and imagined a ghost behind me, creeping through the shadows, coveting my energy, leeching my warmth.

I whirled, my heart in my throat. "Did you hear something?"

"No." Devlin turned and swung the light down the tunnel.

I caught the gleam of beady eyes and then the scurry of tiny feet. Just a rat.

We pressed forward. I was breathing a little easier now, knowing the sounds I'd heard from behind me were nothing more than the scratch of rodent claws on brick. And oddly, telling Devlin about my dream had lightened my mood, unchained me from a childhood terror that had dogged me for years. It had also made him my confidant. I'd never told anyone about that nightmare. What this said about my feelings for him, I was a little too scared to consider.

We had been keeping a steady pace, but now I slowed, my head turning to the side as a new sound invaded the silence. I paused, took a step forward, then glanced over my shoulder.

"Something's back there."

Devlin barely broke stride. "Another rat."

"No, not a rat. Listen."

Nothing but silence.

Then it came again, a sort of furtive shuffle. The hair sprang up at my nape.

"There! Did you hear it?"

Devlin whirled, the light beam piercing the darkness. "Stay calm."

"I am calm," I said over the thunder of my heartbeat. "What do you think it is?"

"I can't tell."

It wasn't a ghost. This was something very real, something solid and alive.

Devlin transferred the flashlight to his left hand, and with his right, drew his gun from the holster. Again and again, he swept the beam across the darkness.

"Get in front of me," he said and handed me the flashlight.

"He's back there, isn't he?" I whispered.

"Just keep moving."

We walked in complete silence now. Once the sound faded, my nerves settled and I noticed we were ascending. And just when I hoped that meant the end would soon be in sight, we came to a dead end.

There was nothing in front of us but a solid brick wall.

The thought of turning around and going back toward that sound, back to that chamber of horrors was too much. I was emotionally drained. Spent. I felt like dropping to the floor and bursting into tears.

"Over there," Devlin said, and pressed my hand holding the flashlight down and to the left.

Another opening. Another way out.

He took the flashlight and shined it into the hole.

"Is it a way out?" I asked nervously.

"I think so. Come on." He went first and waited for me on the other side.

We were in some sort of circular chamber maybe five feet wide in diameter. Metal steps had been bolted into the wall and I felt a surge of elation until I realized those stairs led up to nothing. There was no opening at the top. Just total darkness.

"I think we're in an old well or cistern," Devlin said. His voice had a metallic sound as it ricocheted off the round walls.

"How do we get out?"

"There must be a lid or something over the top." He slanted the beam upward for a moment, then handed me the flashlight and his gun.

"Do you know how to use a weapon?"

"No, not really."

"The safety's off. If anything comes through that hole, point at it and squeeze the trigger. Don't think, just do it."

I nodded.

"Keep the light," he said. "Don't watch me, watch that hole."

"Okay."

He tested his weight on the ladder, his footsteps clanging as he went up. Within seconds, he was twenty feet above me. I heard the click of the lighter and a grunt or two from Devlin as he tried to dislodge the cover, but I resisted the temptation to glance up.

"Is it bolted down?"

"It's a door. I see hinges and a handle, but something solid has been placed on top of it outside. I can move it, but I can't open it more than a crack."

My eyes were still glued to the opening as I clutched the weapon in one hand and the flashlight in the other. For a moment I could have sworn—

There it was! That stealthy shuffle, as though someone was inching his way along the tunnel, skulking through the darkness so as not to give away his position.

"He's coming," I whispered.

My voice carried all the way to the top. The stairs clanged as Devlin quickly descended. He took the gun and the flashlight and swept the beam up the ladder.

"Get to the top. I've managed to pry the door open a few inches. See if you can squeeze through."

"What about you?"

"Just go. I'll be right behind you."

But as I started up the ladder, I glanced over my shoulder and saw the light disappear through the hole.

"Devlin?"

No answer.

I was torn between going up and coming back down. The torturous indecision was like my nightmare all over again. I was still hanging there a moment later when Devlin crawled back though the opening.

He didn't say a word, just waited at the bottom until I'd climbed to the top and then he followed me up.

I shimmied through the opening, scraping elbows and knees against the rough brick, and then once through, I used all my strength to heave a boulder aside and open the door.

Devlin crawled up out of the well and we both turned to survey our surroundings. We were somewhere in the woods outside the cemetery gates.

It was not yet dark. The horizon still glowed in the west. To the east, the moon rose over the treetops. A breeze whispered through the leaves and I could smell jasmine in the twilight.

Devlin took my hand and we walked through the cooling air as his ghosts slipped through the veil behind us.

TWENTY-NINE

By the time I left the cemetery, the place was swarming with cops. Crime scene techs had descended upon the chamber and a small army of policemen was combing through the tunnels. I assumed Devlin would be occupied for hours so I was completely shocked when he showed up at my door later that night.

I'd been home long enough to shower and fix myself a light dinner, though I couldn't bring myself to do much more than pick at the salad. What had been seen in that chamber could not be unseen, and I had a bad feeling it would be days, if not weeks, before I managed a full night's sleep.

Devlin had brought a laptop with him so that we could go through the Oak Grove images together. I assumed he'd come to the same conclusion I had earlier—Hannah Fischer had been in that chamber either dead or alive while I'd been aboveground photographing headstones. The theft of my briefcase solidified my suspicion that the killer believed I'd captured something incriminating in one or more of those shots.

But how had he known those pictures were in my briefcase…unless he'd seen them?

On the day the body had been discovered, I'd spent the afternoon at Emerson, both upstairs in the main library and in the basement archives area. The briefcase had been left unattended for long periods of time while I combed through boxes of records and scrolled through the database. If the case had been open, anyone passing by could have glimpsed the pictures. Which would mean that at some point during the day, I had been in proximity to the killer. We might have brushed shoulders or exchanged pleasantries. The thought of that now in the aftermath of our discovery—with the purpose of those chains and pulleys so gruesomely apparent—made me ill.

Before Devlin arrived, I'd put together a chart of everything we knew about the burial site of each victim, starting with Hannah Fischer.

Along with a floral design, the headstone had been engraved with a floating feather and this poetic epitaph:

The midnight stars weep upon her silent grave,
Dead but dreaming, this child we could not save.

The headstone on the grave where the unidentified remains had been excavated contained a single full-blown rose, a winged soul effigy and the inscription:

How soon fades this gentle rose,
Freed from earthly woes,
She lies in eternal repose.

Since Afton Delacourt's body had been left on the floor of the mausoleum rather than buried, I had no headstone art or epitaph with which to compare, but I thought

the art and inscription on the vault that had led us to the
hidden chamber might be significant clues. The broken
chain deviated from the soul-in-flight motif on the two
headstones, but the verse intrigued me:

The day breaks...
The shadows flee...
The shackles open...
And now blessed sleep.

As I looked down through my chart, underlining
"feather," "soul effigy," "broken chain" and "shackles,"
I felt a stirring of excitement. Maybe Tom Gerrity was
right. The answer was there, staring me right in the face,
if only I could interpret the killer's message.

How much time did we have, I wondered, before he
claimed his next victim?

"What is it?" Devlin asked.

His voice startled me in the quiet. I'd almost forgotten he was there, which also surprised me. "I was just
sitting here going over all the epitaphs and symbols and
thinking that Tom Gerrity was right. There is a message
in all of this, but I don't know how to read it." I paused.
"Have you found anything?"

"No, unfortunately." He sounded as frustrated as I felt.

"You know what's still bothering me? How the killer
knew about those tunnels."

"Like I said earlier, old records, deeds. By accident."
He glanced up. "I'll tell you what's bothering me. The
way the skeleton was shackled."

"Because it breaks the pattern?"

"Yes, exactly."

"When will you hear from Ethan?"

"Soon. He'll make it a priority. At least now he can

compare any anomalies or details he finds in this skeleton with the remains we exhumed from the grave."

We both fell silent for a moment as we concentrated
on the Oak Grove images.

Then I thought of something else I wanted to tell him.
"Remember I mentioned earlier about seeing Daniel
Meakin in the archives room at Emerson? I asked him
that day about the possibility of a missing register from
an old church that was once connected to Oak Grove. He
said a lot of records were destroyed during and after the
Civil War, but he also mentioned that some of them might
have merely been misplaced because everything is such
a mess down there. And he's right about that. Someone
could have easily removed any record or book that cited
those tunnels and no one would have missed them."

"Did he mention anything other than a church in connection to that property?"

"No. And we talked about it, too. He did tell me that
he has some old books in his office that reference Oak
Grove. He was going to look up some information for
me, but I haven't seen him since that day."

Devlin nodded. "I'll go talk to him."

"I think that's a good idea. If anyone would know
whether something had been there before the church, it
would be him." I hesitated as something else occurred
to me. "This probably has nothing to do with anything,
but Temple told me that Meakin once tried to commit
suicide."

Devlin glanced up.

"I know it's just gossip, but apparently she saw a nasty-
looking scar on his wrist. And he does tend to favor his
left hand. You'll see what I mean when you talk to him.
He holds it at an odd angle as if he's constantly bothered

by that scar or overly aware of what he tried to do to himself."

"He's always been a little strange," Devlin said.

I cocked my head in surprise. "You know him? When you said you knew of him, I assumed you were familiar with his work."

"He was a few years ahead of me in school."

"What school? Emerson? *You* went to Emerson?"

He frowned at the accusatory note in my tone. "Is that a problem?"

"No…it's not a problem, but why didn't you mention it before?"

He shrugged. "I don't talk about my personal life unless it's relevant."

I stared down at my chart, wondering if he would consider my next question relevant or just plain nosy. "Did you meet your wife at Emerson?" I almost said "Mariama," but caught myself because Devlin had never once called her by name. Another odd thing.

He hesitated. "Yes."

"Did you know Dr. Shaw?"

"Everyone on campus knew Shaw. He was an enigmatic presence, to say the least."

"Did you ever go to one of his séances?"

"I can't think of a bigger waste of time."

So much scorn from someone so haunted.

"Did you know any of the Claws?"

He closed his laptop. "You sure have a lot of questions tonight."

"Sorry."

"I'd say you've taken to detective work like a duck to water."

I wasn't sure he meant that as a compliment, but I decided to take it as such. "In some ways, it's not so differ-

ent from my job. And I like mysteries. Which is why I'm
so intrigued with the Order of the Coffin and the Claw.
Have you noticed that no one wants to talk about them?"

He made a noncommittal sound I couldn't interpret.

I gave him a surreptitious appraisal out of the corner
of my eye. "You said earlier that people in high places
were starting to pull some strings. Do you think that has
something to do with the Order? They have generations
of influence behind them and apparently no one wants
to take them on. Are they closing rank to protect one of
their own?"

Devlin scrubbed a hand down his face, looking bone-
deep weary when only moments ago he'd seemed relaxed.
"I don't know. I've seen signs of manipulation, but I don't
know where it's coming from."

"They can't cover it up, can they?"

"No. Not after what we found today. But they can
control it by bringing in their own investigators."

"But it's your case."

"You're right. And I don't intend to give it up without
a fight."

The look in his eyes scared me a little. "What can they
do to you if you don't cooperate?"

"Nothing," he said. "They can't touch me."

With Devlin's confident assertion still ringing in my
ears, I rose and went into the kitchen to make tea. I took
my time boiling the water and setting out cups because I
wanted a chance to think back over our discussion. I felt
that I'd learned some important things about Devlin. The
revelation that he'd attended Emerson was of particular
interest, and I still found it curious that he hadn't mentioned it on the many occasions we'd discussed Afton

Delacourt's murder. But maybe he really was just that discreet about his personal life.

I carried the tea out to the office only to find Devlin stretched out on the chaise, fast asleep.

Sitting down behind my desk, I returned to the images, but the longer I sifted through the now-familiar symbols and epitaphs, the less enthusiasm I had for the task. I was beginning to feel a little off—weakness in my knees, an uncomfortable hollowness in my stomach. The same symptoms I'd experienced the last time Devlin had fallen asleep in my office.

I told myself I wouldn't go to him this time. I would just let him sleep, and when he woke up, we would resume talking about the case or he would leave. And that would be that.

I wouldn't go to him.

But, of course, I did go to him because I couldn't stay away. I stood over him, bracing myself for the jolt, for that breathless pressure in my chest, and when it came, it still took me by storm. My legs buckled and I sat down heavily on the chaise beside him.

Devlin's eyes flew open. He stared at me intently, but I had the strange notion that he wasn't really seeing me. That he might not even be fully awake yet.

Something fleeted across his face, an unbearable sadness that came and went so fast I wasn't even sure that I'd seen it. But I was reminded of what he'd told me that afternoon about his nightmares.

And then I wake up and remember that it's real.

He sat up and glanced around. "What happened?"

"Nothing happened. We were going through the Oak Grove images and you fell asleep."

He sat back against the chaise and rubbed a hand over his eyes. "What is it about this place?" he muttered.

"It's not this place. It's you," I told him. "You've had a long day. We both have. I feel a little drained myself."

He frowned at that. "How long was I out?"

"A half hour. Forty-five minutes, maybe." It occurred to me then that he might be wondering why I was sitting beside him. Quickly, I grabbed the afghan from the back of the chaise. "I thought you might be cold."

As I pulled the cover over him, his hand closed on mine. I knew that I should pull away from him. The ebb and flow of energy between us made me light-headed, but I didn't move.

"I feel like I've been asleep for hours." His head rested against the back of the chaise, but his eyes were still on me. We spent a few moments of uneasy silence and I did contemplate getting up and returning to my desk. But his hand was still on mine. I couldn't extract myself without some awkwardness.

"Who are you named after?" he asked unexpectedly.

I looked at him in surprise. "No one that I know of."

"There's no story behind your name?"

"Should there be?"

"I thought it might be a family name. It suits you, though. It's a little old-fashioned."

I bristled at that. "There's nothing old-fashioned about the name or me."

His eyes glinted. "I didn't mean it as an insult. I'm old-fashioned, too. It's how we're brought up down here. Saddled with tradition, yoked with expectations. And all those damn rules."

"I know about rules," I said. "You have no idea."

His hand slid away from my wrist and he entwined his fingers with mine. I couldn't have been more shocked and I wondered if he could feel the way I trembled.

"I shouldn't be here," he said on a sigh. He held up

our linked hands and studied them, as if trying to divine some elusive message in the way our fingers were entangled.

"Why not?" I knew why he shouldn't be here, but I was dying to hear his take. "I'm not so old-fashioned that I can't be alone with a man in my own home."

"I don't mean that. I mean…I shouldn't be here. With you." He put a subtle emphasis on the pronoun. "You scare me."

"I do?"

He grew very still. "Sometimes you make me forget."

My heart was pounding so hard, I thought it might burst from my chest. "Is that bad?"

"I don't know. I've held on for so long…I'm not sure I'm ready to let go."

"Then you shouldn't."

He said my name then. Just that. *Amelia.* But in the slow, proper drawl of the Charleston aristocrat, stringing out the syllables with an elegant, imperious cadence that was tinged with decadence, indulgence and the kind of secrets that can only fester in the deepest shadows of the South.

He cupped my face and drew me toward him, staring for the longest time into my eyes. I thought that he meant to kiss me and my eyes closed in anticipation. Instead, he moved his thumb slowly back and forth across my bottom lip, exactly the way I had imagined in the restaurant. It wasn't a kiss, hardly even a caress, but no one had ever done anything so sensuous to me in my life. It was as if he'd read my mind that night, discerned my innermost thoughts and desires.

He pulled me down against him, wrapped his arms around me and we lay there in silence until he drifted back off. I could feel the steady thud of his heart beneath my hand. It grew stronger as he slept and I grew weaker.

Still, I didn't move.

I stayed in Devlin's arms until the scent of jasmine became unbearable in my office.

Then I got up and went over to the window to look for her. Shani was in the swing, moving slowly back and forth, her long hair swaying in the breeze.

She hadn't come alone this time. Mariama stood at the very edge of the shadows, her taunting gaze not on her daughter, but on me.

I heard Devlin leave just before dawn. I'd gone to bed fully dressed and now I slipped from beneath the covers and hurried to the front window to see him off. As he opened the front gate and stepped onto the sidewalk, Mariama and Shani appeared in the gray light. They floated on either side of him as he crossed the street to his car.

Halfway across, Mariama's ghost turned to glance over her shoulder. I pulled back from the window, but she knew I was there. And like Shani's ghost, she wanted me to know she knew.

I didn't look out the window again, but I knew when Devlin drove away. The more distance he put between us, the stronger I felt, and it seemed clear to me now that this house, this hallowed sanctuary, could protect me from ghosts, but it could not protect me from Devlin.

THIRTY

I left the house later that morning freshly showered, dressed and with a renewed sense of purpose. My first stop of the day was the Charleston Institute for Parapsychology Studies, and as I headed around to the side entrance, I wondered if I might be just as well served across the street at Madam Know-It-All's. My last visit with Dr. Shaw had left me with more questions than answers.

The same blonde with the same silver adornments greeted me at the front door and ushered me down the hall to Dr. Shaw's office, then discreetly slid the pocket doors closed behind me.

The sunlight pouring in through the garden windows dazzled me so that I had to blink and readjust my focus. Dr. Shaw wasn't at his desk, but stood at the far end of the room, in deep shadows, paging through a thick, leather-bound tome. No sooner had I noticed him than he carelessly tossed the book aside, plucked another from the shelf and riffled almost frantically through the leaves.

His appearance stunned me. I'd always found a certain absentminded charm in his threadbare attire, but now he looked unkempt, his shirt and trousers so rumpled I thought he must have slept in them. And that gorgeous dome of white hair—the one area of his toilette that seemed to command careful attention—looked dull and lifeless.

I stood quietly for a moment, not certain he even knew I was about. I cleared my throat, shifted my feet, but nothing budged his attention from his task—shuffling through the pages of yet another book. He was obviously looking for something and it was just as obvious that the nugget he sought remained frustratingly elusive.

"You can stop fidgeting," he said without looking up. "I know you're there."

"Have I come at a bad time? I did call first."

"No, it's fine. I'm having a rather exasperating morning, I'm afraid."

"Anything I can do to help? I'm a pretty good researcher."

He looked up, smiled faintly, then discarded yet another volume. "It would be hard to enlist your help when I don't even know what it is I'm looking for."

"I'm familiar with that feeling."

He walked toward me then and when the light from the window hit him, I realized that my initial impression of him had been superficial. The wrinkled clothing and uncombed hair were the least of it. He didn't look well. His skin had an unpleasant yellowish tinge, his eyes watery and bloodshot. I wondered if he'd been to sleep at all since the last time I'd seen him.

His usual elegance was absent, too, as he sat down heavily behind his desk. When he waved me to a chair, I saw a slight tremor in his hand that I hadn't noticed before.

"What brings you by so early? Dare I hope you've gotten a better look at your shadow man?" His smile was almost pained, as if he found it a struggle to summon even a hint of his usual geniality.

"No, actually, I'm here for another reason. Another... event."

The light now fell upon him harshly, revealing skin pulled so tightly over bone that I might have been conversing with a corpse. Then he shifted in his chair and the illusion thankfully vanished.

I cleared my throat, wondering if I'd made a mistake in coming here. He was obviously upset and preoccupied, but I couldn't just get up and leave without an explanation.

Those glassy eyes were still on me, waiting for me to proceed.

Again I cleared my throat. "I'm wondering if it's possible for one human being to unconsciously siphon the energy of another. I'm not talking about emotional energy. I mean physical energy."

"I'm not sure the two can be separated," he said. "After all, emotional well-being can severely impact physical health, can it not? And vice versa."

"Yes, of course."

"But I think I know what you're asking, and the answer is...maybe. You're familiar with the concept of a psychic vampire?"

"I've heard of it."

"There are two schools of thought regarding the psy-vamp. One—there is a paranormal entity within such a person that feeds off the psychic energy of others. And two—social parasitism. People with various personality disorders or those individuals who find themselves in an emotionally or spiritually weakened state can influence others to the point of leaving them feeling physically exhausted and emotionally drained or even severely depressed."

I thought of what Ethan had said about Devlin's emotional state after the accident and the rumors that he had been checked into some sort of sanitarium. If he was emotionally and physically depleted from grief and from his ghosts, might his subconscious search for a way to replenish?

"How do you stop it?" I asked.

"The simplest, most effective way is to simply avoid this individual altogether. Cut them out of your life." He slashed the air with his hand.

"If that's not possible...?"

"You can try confronting them, though I'm not sure how much good that would do. As it happens..." He stared across the desk at me, his eyes so bloodshot they almost appeared to glow red when sunlight hit them. "I find myself in a similar situation."

"You have a psychic vampire?" I asked in surprise.

"Worse. It isn't my energy that's being siphoned—it's my life's work."

"Someone is stealing from you?"

He made a helpless gesture. "Years of notes, research...leeched so slowly that I didn't notice until it was too late. Now they have everything they need."

I drew a quick breath, alarmed by the note of fear in his voice. "What do you mean?"

He took a long time answering. "I'm very much afraid the killer of that young woman is someone who is in our midst. Someone who is subtle, cunning and unassuming. Someone we would never suspect..."

My hand fluttered to my throat, where my pulse had

begun to throb almost painfully. "Are you saying you know who the killer is?"

He seemed to catch himself then and gave a negligible wave with his ring hand. The spark of that silver emblem drew my eyes again. I'd seen it before. I knew I had…but where?

"It's a hypothesis only," he said. "I know nothing more than what I've read in the paper."

I wasn't sure I believed him. "You haven't talked to Ethan about your hypothesis? Or about the theft of your papers?"

"Ethan? No, I haven't spoken to my son about any of this," he said with an odd hitch in his voice. Then he swiveled his chair to stare broodingly out the garden window.

I let myself out in silence.

Devlin had left me a voicemail. I was to meet him at Oak Grove so that we could walk the cemetery together. On my way, I stopped by the Emerson library for a quick check of the archives.

As I hurried across the landscaped campus, I kept glancing over my shoulder, keenly aware of Dr. Shaw's cryptic warning that the killer could be someone in our midst, someone we would least suspect. Even the echo of my footsteps on the stone staircase that led down to the archives seemed ominous and foreboding.

I'd spent enough time in the basement to know exactly where the Oak Grove files and records were stored. Dr. Shaw's assertion that his own papers were being stolen made me wonder again about that church book I'd been searching for.

As I knelt and ran my finger along some of the labels

on the boxes, a shadow fell over me. I was so startled,
I rocked back on my heels and nearly lost my balance.

"Are you all right?" Daniel Meakin asked in concern.
"I didn't mean to frighten you. I thought you would have
heard my footsteps."

I'd heard nothing.

He knelt beside me, and as he put his left hand on one
of the boxes to brace himself, his sleeve rode up over his
wrist bone and I saw the scar. But it wasn't just *a* scar. It
was a series of ridges that crisscrossed over one another.
There had not been one suicide attempt. There had been
many.

Quickly, I averted my gaze. The light was so hazy in
the basement I hoped he hadn't noticed the slight parting
of my lips, the wide-eyed horror of my gaze.

After a moment, he shifted his position, dropped his
hand and the scars were once again hidden by his sleeve.

"Are you still searching for names to go with those
unmarked graves?" he asked.

"Yes. I keep hoping I'll run across more records or
that missing church book will turn up."

"I understand," he said. "I must have looked through
these boxes dozens of times, but I still come down here
with the hope of uncovering an elusive piece of information or some unexpected revelation. It's like a treasure
hunt."

"It's addictive," I said.

He beamed. "Yes, exactly." He turned back to the
boxes, his gaze moving over them. "It's a coincidence
to find you down here this morning. I was just coming
to look through some of the Oak Grove records myself."

"Really? Why?"

"I was contacted by a police detective this morning.
He has some historical questions about the cemetery, it

seems. He wouldn't say much, only that he'd like to stop by later this afternoon, but he dropped one hint that has me intrigued. He asked if there had been any other buildings on the property, other than the old church, before the cemetery was put in."

"Were there?"

"No...none that I'm aware of."

I sensed his hesitance. "You would know, wouldn't you? You said you'd been through everything down here a number of times."

"Yes, but the records are incomplete. As I mentioned the other day, a lot of the old papers were destroyed during and after the war."

"Can you tell me anything about the property that might not be common knowledge?"

"Nothing concrete. But I've always assumed that Emerson was built on the site of the old Bedford plantation house. The original home burned down in the late eighteenth century and I was certain the house had been rebuilt over the old site. But now that Detective Devlin has posed the question about Oak Grove, I'm wondering if that might have been the site of the original plantation house."

"Wouldn't there be some mention of it in the county deed books?"

"Not if they were deliberately removed."

I glanced up. "Why would someone do that?"

He glanced nervously over his shoulder. "To protect whatever it is that Detective Devlin has uncovered in the cemetery."

My heart skipped a beat. "You're talking about someone scrubbing county records, church registers, the university archives..."

"If one has enough money or influence, one can make anything disappear," he said softly.

"That's a very interesting observation," I said.

He shot another furtive look over his shoulder and leaned in a bit. "After our talk the other day, I've done some research on the Order of the Coffin and the Claw. There was talk about a connection to Oak Grove long before Afton Delacourt's murder."

"You think someone in that organization destroyed the records?"

"A collective someone, perhaps. I don't know. This is all purely speculation on my part, but…I did find something I thought you might be interested in."

"Yes?"

"You wanted to know if you might have run across some of their symbols on old headstones. This is the only one I've ever been able to link to the Order." He produced a paper from his pocket and smoothed out the wrinkles as he placed it on the floor in front of me.

The emblem was a snake coiled around a talon.

I stared down at the drawing for the longest time, afraid to glance up because I knew my expression would give me away.

The symbol was a replica of the one on Dr. Shaw's ring. Only now I knew where I'd seen it before.

On the medallion Devlin wore around his neck.

THIRTY-ONE

The revelation left me shaken. Devlin was a member of the Order of the Coffin and the Claw, the secret society that had been implicated in Afton Delacourt's murder.

Not that I believed for a moment he'd been personally involved.

But a memory was stirred of that overheard conversation between Devlin and Camille Ashby. She'd been adamant that the discovery of Hannah Fischer's body in Oak Grove not be linked to Emerson or to the first murder. Had she expected Devlin to cover up whatever connection to the university he might find because he was a Claw?

Only the crème de la crème of Emerson students were extended membership, those from privileged backgrounds like Devlin. While he was at Emerson, the Order would have had every reason to believe he would one day become a mover and shaker in his family's powerful law firm. Undoubtedly he'd been a legacy pledge with a long Devlin tradition in the society behind him. No wonder he said they couldn't touch him. He was one of them.

I didn't have a chance to confront him when I arrived at Oak Grove. There were too many people around. Above and belowground, the cemetery teemed with cops. Devlin himself spent most of the morning in the tunnels. I walked the cemetery alone, searching for signs of fresh digging, disturbed graves, clues hidden within imagery and epitaphs. Like Dr. Shaw, I had no idea what I was looking for, but I had a feeling I would know it if I saw it. At least I hoped so.

By noon, I was a hot mess. The sun was brutal overhead and I still felt a bit weak from my encounter with Devlin the night before. I had on my usual cemetery attire of boots, tank and cargoes. The large pockets in the pants provided convenient storage for my tools, but they were hardly the most flattering fit. My hair was plastered to my head, and I wore no makeup or sunscreen—a foolish lapse because already I could feel the sting of sunburn on my cheeks.

Devlin, on the other hand, looked fresh and well put together—suspiciously revitalized—as he emerged from the web-laden tunnels. As he headed toward me, Ethan Shaw approached from a different angle, and their paths converged directly in front of me. Unlike Devlin, Ethan looked a little worse for wear after his foray belowground. He walked up brushing dust and cobwebs from his sleeves.

The two men couldn't have looked more different: Devlin with his black hair, piercing eyes and brooding demeanor and Ethan, a sun-streaked brunette with an easy smile and gold-flecked hazel eyes.

Night and day, I thought, and for some reason the analogy made me uneasy.

"I'm getting ready to head back to the lab," Ethan said. "But if you have a minute, I'd like to talk to you about the remains we exhumed from the grave yesterday."

The conversation was a little awkward for me. I didn't know whether I should back away and let them have privacy or stay and hear what Ethan had to say.

Neither of them seemed too concerned about my listening in so I decided to stay put.

"She's a female Caucasian, early twenties," Ethan was saying. "Somewhere around five feet nine inches tall and a hundred and twenty pounds. Give or take."

"PMI?" Devlin asked.

"Five to ten years. I'm saying closer to ten."

Devlin frowned. "She was in the ground for a long time."

"Normally, that would make identification a lot more difficult, but we've got plenty of dental work to go on and extensive premortem injuries."

"How premortem?"

"Months. Cracked ribs and clavicle, fractured vertebrae, pelvis and right femur. My guess is she was in a severe accident, probably a car crash. She was on the mend, but I would imagine she suffered from chronic pain and was facing months, if not years, of physical therapy."

"That narrows the field considerably," Devlin said.

"We've already put her in the system. Should be just a matter of time."

Devlin's phone rang and I watched him walk off as I made the calculations in my head. Afton Delacourt had been murdered fifteen years ago. The remains dug up yesterday had been in the ground from five to ten years. Hannah Fischer had been dead only a matter of days. I wondered if another pattern was emerging or if we'd yet to find all the bodies.

"Are you all right?" Ethan asked and I shook myself out of my reverie.

"I'm just tired."

He gave me a careful appraisal. "You look a little flushed. Are you sure you're not overdoing it out here?"

"No. I'm fine. Why?"

"I heard you and Devlin were the ones who discovered the hidden room and tunnels. And the skeleton," he added grimly. "That couldn't have been easy on the nerves."

"It was a little traumatic," I admitted.

"Did you get any sleep at all last night?"

I thought about Devlin, slumbering so peacefully in my office while I lay fully clothed in bed, staring at the ceiling and fretting.

"Not much."

"And here you are back out here today. I see at least half a dozen cops standing around who could be walking this cemetery."

"I know the terrain and I know what I'm looking for, sort of."

He shrugged. "Okay. But if you need a break, take it. John pushes himself hard, but that doesn't mean you have to."

I glanced over my shoulder. Devlin had disappeared down one of the walkways and was out of earshot. "You've known him a long time?"

"Yes. He can seem a little taciturn at times, but he wasn't always like that. The accident changed him. I don't think he'll ever get over it."

"I can see why. He lost his whole family."

Ethan sighed. "It's not just the grief. He's consumed by guilt."

I looked around anxiously. "I'm not sure we should be talking about this."

"You're wrong, Amelia. You're the one person who needs to hear it."

"He could come back."

Ethan turned facing the path. "I'll see him if he does."

"Even so, this feels intrusive to me."

"It makes me uncomfortable, too. Whatever is going on between you and John is none of my business. You're both adults and maybe I should leave it at that. But you seem like a nice person and John is like family."

I glanced at him in surprise. "I had no idea the two of you were that close."

"We're not anymore," Ethan said. "After the accident, he cut most of his friends out of his life. I think he wanted to rid himself of all the reminders. But there was a time when he, Mariama and I were inseparable. I was Shani's godfather."

"I…didn't know. I'm sorry."

He nodded, his eyes bleak. "I was with John when he got the call about the accident. We'd all been together earlier that day at their house. Mariama had planned a barbecue. She'd been looking forward to it all week and then John got called into work unexpectedly. They'd been bickering on and off all day, but that phone call was the trigger."

"A trigger for what?"

He hesitated. "Mariama was a passionate, impulsive woman. Her unpredictability was part of her charm, and I think it was one of the reasons John fell for her so hard.

She was so different from him. But she could also be jealous, vindictive and possessive, even about his career. She knew how to push his buttons and she came to enjoy it. She said some things that day, nasty things that she knew would set him off."

"And did they?"

He ran a hand through his hair and glanced away. "Yes. The argument got pretty ugly. Nothing physical, of course, just words spoken in anger that could never be taken back. The worst part was that Shani heard everything. I remember the way she kept tapping on John's leg to get his attention. I think she was trying to console him, but he was too angry…too caught up in the moment to notice. He stormed out of the house, and when he drove off, Shani was standing at the window waving goodbye. That was the last time he saw her alive."

I thought of the way the little ghost clung to Devlin's legs now and I wanted to weep.

"I can't even imagine," I said softly.

"Who can? I'm sure John would give his own life to go back to that one moment. If he could just hold Shani in his arms one last time…"

This was too much. I didn't want him to go on and yet I was in too deep. I had to hear the rest.

"After he got off work, he called me and we had drinks. He needed an ear. At some point, Mariama tried to reach him on his cell phone. He saw her name on the display and ignored it. He later learned that she'd placed the call within seconds of reaching a 911 operator. Her car had gone off a bridge and she was trapped in her seat. Trapped in a sinking car, she and Shani. Maybe Mariama knew help would arrive too late. Maybe she called to give John a chance to say goodbye. And he didn't pick up."

I wrapped my arms around my middle, shivering.

"This is what he lives with," Ethan said. "This is what he carries with him, always. There isn't much room in his life for anything else, I'm afraid."

"For me, you mean."

Ethan's gaze was gentle. "I just thought you should know."

Ethan's disclosure had upset me badly and for the rest of the day, I'd avoided Devlin. I just couldn't face him yet. Not after all that. I couldn't imagine what he'd been through. I didn't want to imagine it. And yet it was all there in his eyes and on his face and in the ghosts that clung to him.

By the time I got home, I decided it might be good for my mental well-being to immerse myself in the mundane for a change, like laundry and grocery shopping. When I returned from the store, I fixed myself a glass of iced tea and carried it out to the patio where I could sit and enjoy the garden.

The morning glories had long since wilted, but the pink four o'clocks by the house were open and swarming with honeybees and hummingbirds. I meandered out to the edge of the garden, sat for a moment in the swing where I'd seen Shani's ghost and then bent to examine the little mound where I'd buried her ring. I didn't know what I expected to find, but the ground was undisturbed, the heart exactly as I'd left it.

Mariama's visit had been even more disturbing than Shani's, so I shut out the image of those ghostly eyes peering at me through the darkness and tried to concentrate on the glorious scent drifting up from the peonies.

As I bent to pick one of the blooms, I noticed that the outside door to the basement was ajar.

That was odd.

That door was always kept locked even though nothing of value was stored there. The inside basement entrance had been bolted shut—along with the door at the top of the staircase in the entrance hall—when the space was divided into apartments.

The idea of an intruder, even in broad daylight, frightened me, especially with everything else that had happened lately. I'd left my phone inside. I'd have to go in the house to call the police, but I didn't want to be too hasty. It was possible the lock hadn't caught and the wind had blown open the door.

I approached just close enough to peer down the steps. I saw a light on inside and heard a series of thuds and thumps as storage boxes were shuffled around.

Then the door opened and I retreated back into the garden.

A moment later, Macon Dawes strode up the steps with a black suitcase in his hand. When he saw me standing in the yard, he stopped and waved.

"Hey."

"Hey." I pressed a palm to my heart. "You scared me half to death. I thought someone broke in."

"No, just me looking for this." He held up the bag. "Sorry to startle you. I guess you wouldn't be expecting to see me around this time of day. Or anytime. I've been a phantom these past few weeks."

"Busy schedule at the hospital?"

"Killer," he said with a grimace. "I'm just coming off a seventy-two-hour shift."

"I don't know how you do it."

"Caffeine and desperation. I've amassed too much debt to turn back now."

I nodded toward the suitcase. "Are you going somewhere?"

"Yep. I have two whole weeks off and a buddy of mine is letting me stay at his family's place on Sullivan's Island. I don't plan to do anything but sleep and eat. And drink. And sleep."

"Sounds like just what you need." The small talk was awkward seeing how we barely knew each other. I'd always found Macon Dawes a little intimidating, though I had no idea why. I hardly knew anything about him other than he was a hardworking medical student and a quiet neighbor. A phantom, like he said.

"Do you think you could keep an eye on my place while I'm gone? Not that I expect any trouble," he added with a grin. "This neighborhood's mind-numbingly quiet."

"Sure. No problem."

"Thanks. Remind me to buy you a drink when I get back."

He bounded up the outside stairs as I stood there ruminating on this latest turn of events. A drink with Macon Dawes?

I wondered if the universe was trying to tell me something.

By nine-thirty that night, the dishes were done, the laundry was folded, furniture dusted, hardwood floors swept, and still the night stretched before me as endless as the tunnels beneath Oak Grove Cemetery.

Loneliness was an old friend, but tonight that friendship was strained. I didn't want to be alone and I hadn't a single soul I could call. Temple was my closest friend, but our relationship was still more superior-subordinate than equals. And other than the occasional offhand remark at dinner or over drinks, I really knew very little about her personal life.

I was twenty-seven years old and I'd never had a best friend, never had a real confidant and had never once fallen in love. From the time I was nine years old, the dead that walk among us had isolated me from the living. With that first sighting, my life had been changed forever. Like my father, I'd learned to live with my secret, had even come to embrace the solitude, but there were times, like tonight, when I wondered if madness might not also wait for me behind the veil.

But the loneliness I lived with couldn't compare to the desolation Devlin must face every time he entered his empty house. I didn't want to dwell on his tragedy or my plight or why fate might be so cruel as to bring the one man who would always mourn another woman into my life. It had always been painfully clear that Devlin was not the man for me and yet I could imagine myself with no other.

I moved through the house like a ghost, floating from one room to another, endlessly searching. I told myself I wouldn't turn on the computer. I needed to unplug for a while. I was coming to rely more and more on the company of nameless, faceless strangers. But thirty minutes later, I was all tucked in bed with my laptop propped against my knees. I went straight to my blog and checked the comments section. Someone had posted a new entry less than an hour ago:

A quiet life, a quiet death.
Sleep now, Beloved.
Our secret is safe.

I was almost certain the lines were from an old poem, but I had also seen the verse today, carved in stone, at Oak Grove.

With a quivering hand, I picked up the phone and called Devlin.

THIRTY-TWO

It was late and the graveyard was quiet. The army of cops had retreated from the tunnels and pathways, leaving behind two sentries at the front gate. The uniforms followed us inside and I led the way through the somber labyrinth of headstones and monuments to the north side of the cemetery, where the seven slot-and-tab box tombs gleamed in the moonlight.

Playing my flashlight over the center tomb, I highlighted the epitaph and imagery carved into the lid. Above the name and year of birth and death was a single tulip—love and passion—and a butterfly, the soul in flight.

"He's setting them free," I said softly.

Devlin's head came up and he stared at me across the tomb.

"The imagery is all the same—the feather, the winged effigy and now a butterfly. The soul in flight. But he isn't just releasing their souls—he's freeing them from their earthly shackles." I glanced back down at the stone.

"Hannah Fischer's mother said that her daughter had a history of abusive relationships, starting with her father. She kept the identity of her latest boyfriend a secret because she knew her mother would try to save her. Do you remember the epitaph on the headstone of the grave where she was buried? 'The midnight stars weep upon her silent grave. Dead but dreaming, this child we could not save.'"

Devlin eyed me silently.

"The remains that were excavated yesterday... Ethan said she'd been in a terrible accident before she died. Her injuries were so severe she probably had chronic pain and months if not years of physical therapy ahead of her. 'How soon fades this gentle rose, Freed from earthly woes, She lies in eternal repose.' Earthly woes. Physical pain. And now we have this one."

The four of us stared down at the tomb. Devlin and I were on either side and the officers stood at each end.

I read the epitaph aloud. "'A quiet life, a quiet death. Sleep now, Beloved. Our secret is safe.'"

"Damn, that's creepy," one of the officers muttered.

I drew a long breath, my gaze still on the symbol. "The lid will have to be lifted straight up off the tabs."

"Don't we need a court order for that sort of thing?" the other officer asked nervously.

"Box tombs were built to fool grave robbers. The body, at least the one first interred here, is buried deep in the ground. The remains won't be disturbed by removing the lid."

"I'll take responsibility," Devlin said, and I fancied I saw the flash of his silver medallion in the moonlight. "Let's lift it up."

The top was only a few inches up when the smell came rolling out. I stifled a gag and pulled my shirt over my nose and mouth. The officers groaned, from the weight of the cover and the putrid odor.

"A little higher," Devlin instructed as he knelt and shined his light inside. He pressed the back of his other hand against his mouth and nose. "Jesus."

As the lid slowly inched up the tabs, I caught sight of the pale face inside. It was Camille Ashby.

The swirl of police lights painted the darkness as Devlin walked me back to my car. He told me that he would have someone follow me home and make sure my house was watched all night. I thanked him and then we fell silent as we made our way to the road.

Once again, it appeared that the entire Charleston Police Department had descended on Oak Grove. We must have met at least half a dozen officers trudging through the tall weeds. As we emerged onto the road, the Charleston County coroner's van pulled up to the curb and Regina Sparks got out. She walked right past us in the dark.

"What's going to happen now?" There would have to be another search, which meant more graves and tombs would likely be defiled. I hated the thought of a mass desecration, but the sanctity of Oak Grove had been tainted a long time ago. Evil had lurked in this graveyard for years. "Why do I have the awful feeling this place will be torn apart before all is said and done?"

"We'll do what we can to protect the graves," Devlin said. "But my guess is we're going to find more bodies."

More bodies. More epitaphs. I was filled with the worst kind of dread.

Devlin stared down at me thoughtfully. "I don't think you should come back out here tomorrow. Go home and get some rest. Put this behind you for a while."

"Put it behind me? How would that even be possible? The killer is communicating through me. If he posts another epitaph to my blog, am I supposed to ignore it?"

"Of course not. I want you to call me. But call *me*. No one else."

The glint of his eyes in the moonlight made me shiver. I couldn't see the silver chain around his neck, but I knew it was there, along with the medallion. The symbol that protected him and set him above the law, at least in Charleston.

"This is a messy investigation," he said. "A lot of politics, a lot of finger-pointing. And it's only going to get worse with Camille's murder. Her people have a lot of influence. They'll want answers."

"Good. Maybe this time there won't be a cover-up."

"It's not that simple. I told you before the interest in this case goes all the way to the top. You don't want to mess with these people. You don't even want them to know your name."

"Who are *these* people?"

"The power brokers. The wealthy and the privileged. The people who run things in this city."

Does that include you? I wanted to ask.

My mouth went suddenly dry. "They wouldn't try to implicate me, would they?"

"That won't happen." He sounded dead certain. "But I still think you need to lay low for a while. Get some distance from all this."

I started to ask how I was supposed to distance myself when for all I knew that black sedan might be waiting for me around the next corner. But then I wondered if he was even still talking about the investigation. Maybe he meant I should get some distance…from him.

"If that's what you want."

"It's not that I don't appreciate all your help." He reached around me to open my door.

Being so near him was doing something to me. I didn't go weak like I did when he slept in my house. It was a different feeling. A more subtle exchange of energy. I moved closer, until I could smell his cologne and that powerful essence that was his alone.

Pheromones, Regina Sparks had called it. Whatever it was, I was completely captivated.

And I had just left Camille Ashby's tomb. What did that say about me? About my control?

Devlin drew a breath. When he spoke, I thought he sounded a little strained and I wondered what that said about *his* control. "Go home, Amelia. Get some rest."

I loved the sound of my name on his lips. That drawl did things to me, too. I wanted him to say it again, in a whisper this time, right against my ear.

I closed my eyes and let myself fantasize about that and more.

"Call me if you need me," he said. I felt his breath in my hair and a little thrill went through me. I looked up into his face and his eyes took me in. "Good night... Amelia."

Not a whisper and not in my ear, but pretty darn close.

I let out a sigh. "Good night."

It wasn't until I was well away from the cemetery that I realized something. Where were his ghosts?

THIRTY-THREE

Was it possible they were gone?

I thought about it all the way home. I'd never known anyone else who was haunted—though I had seen plenty of strangers trailed by ghosts—so I had no idea if anyone was ever released. Papa had always said that once an entity latched on to someone, that person's life would never again be their own. But it seemed to me that a ghost could move on, perhaps to another host or even to another realm.

If Devlin's guilt had kept Mariama's and Shani's ghosts tied to him, what would happen if that guilt started to fade? What would happen if *he* moved on?

I remembered what Essie had told me. Someday soon Devlin would have to make a choice between the living and the dead. What if he had already made that choice?

Then again, maybe all of this was just wishful thinking.

I tried to put it out of my mind, told myself I wouldn't dwell on it. Camille Ashby had been murdered and her killer had sent me to that tomb. For whatever reason, he'd decided to communicate through me, and the idea that I was a madman's conduit was very unsettling.

Devlin had made it clear that he no longer wanted me involved in the case, but the killer might have other ideas. I was brooding about all that when the doorbell rang a little while later. I glanced out the side window, shocked to see Devlin on my front porch. I'd assumed he would be busy at the cemetery for hours.

I led him back to my office because I didn't know what else to do with him. Like me, he'd showered and changed since our parting at Oak Grove, no doubt trying to scrub away the putrid odor particular to human decay that lingered in the nostrils. As he followed me through the darkened house, I could smell nothing but the fresh mint of his soap and the spicier notes of his cologne. I drew it in on a sigh.

We took our usual places—I plopped down behind my desk and he sat on the chaise. I could tell something was on his mind, but he seemed in no hurry to speak. Since I'd developed an aversion to long silences in his company and could think of no other topic, I asked about Camille. "Could you tell much about her wounds?"

"She was stabbed, but the wounds were different from the others. It was a fast kill. No ligature marks, either. From the cuts on her hands, it looks like she put up a good fight."

"Why didn't he string her up like the others?"

"Maybe he was interrupted or ran out of time," Devlin said. "Or maybe he's toying with us. He establishes a pattern and then deliberately breaks it. Afton Delacourt was murdered fifteen years ago. We uncover remains in a grave that have been there five to ten years. And now two murders within days of each other."

"And the skeleton in the chamber that was shackled at the wrists," I said.

"Right." Devlin ran a hand through his hair. "This guy is really starting to piss me off."

I shared his frustration. "I wonder when he got to Camille. The last time I saw her was in the archives room at Emerson."

"The best way to calculate time of death is to find the person who last saw her alive. It may have been you." He looked exhausted in the lamplight. "Camille had been dead at least twenty-four hours when we found her. We'll have a better estimate after the autopsy."

"I remember something about that day we saw her at Oak Grove. She received a text message and left abruptly. Maybe it was from the killer. If you can find her phone, you could trace that message back to the sender."

"We don't even need the phone. We can check the records."

"Of course you would have already thought of that," I murmured.

"What I didn't think of was the significance of those epitaphs. The symbols, yes. Once you explained the soul-in-flight imagery, it seemed pretty obvious. But he hand-picked those inscriptions for each of his victims. That was all you."

"I'm not sure where that gets us, though."

"It's helpful. Those epitaphs and symbols are both important elements to figuring out his motivation."

"Does he have a motive? That device we found in the chamber and the way he tortured those women..." I trailed off on a shudder. "It seems to me he kills for pleasure."

"I don't think he's strictly a thrill killer, but he undoubtedly derives a certain amount of pleasure from taking lives. Considering the symbolism and epitaphs, I think it more likely that he's devised a persona for himself as a liberator or an angel of mercy in order to neutralize actions that he knows are wrong."

"Aren't mercy-killers usually women?"

"Usually, but not always. And it doesn't explain the way Camille was killed."

"Did you know that she was a lesbian?"

He shrugged. "I've heard that rumor for years, but never thought much about it one way or the other."

"According to Temple, Camille never came out because her sexual orientation would have caused a lot of problems for her, both at Emerson and with her family."

He gave me a pensive frown. "What's your point? You think a female lover killed her?"

"That epitaph just seems so personal. 'A quiet life, a quiet death. Rest now, beloved. Our secret is safe.'"

We had our moments. Wasn't that what Temple had told me about her fling with Camille?

"But the inscription wasn't written for Camille," Devlin reminded me. "That tomb is over a hundred and fifty years old. Not to say the killer didn't somehow find out about her personal life. He could have chosen the epitaph for its dual meaning. Maybe he considered Camille's death liberation from the burden of her secret."

"You seem convinced the killer is male," I said.

"Like I said before, most predatory killers are. Just because he's convinced himself the kills are justified doesn't mean he's not tracking his victims."

Shadowy images crept through my head. "So how do we figure out who his next target is?"

"We try to connect the kills. The greater the time lapse between murders, the harder it is to find a connection, so the logical place to start is with the two most recent victims—Camille and Hannah Fischer."

I toyed with a paper clip, not certain I wanted to give voice to a terrible suspicion. "Do you think Camille could have been somewhere in those tunnels when we were down there?" I lifted my gaze to his. "We never found out where those flies went."

I could tell by the look on his face that he'd thought the same thing. "We had personnel all over that cemetery and in those tunnels in less than an hour. There's no way he could have gotten her out of there and into that tomb without someone spotting him."

"Unless there's another way out that hasn't been found yet. An opening in another mausoleum, maybe. He could have waited until everyone was gone and then brought her up. The guards at the gate wouldn't have seen him if he was already inside the walls."

"Even if he'd managed to get the body up to the surface alone, he would have needed help with the lid of that tomb."

"Wouldn't he have needed help regardless of when he put her in there?"

"Not necessarily. He seems to have some knowledge of pulleys. With a reasonable amount of time, he could have accomplished it with a rope and a tree branch."

"But that chair we found in the chamber…"

"Yes," he said quietly. "That chair."

The implication of two killers—one a voyeur—was a little too much to take in. I stood abruptly. "I'll make some tea." As if a little chamomile or Darjeeling could soothe away the monstrous images our conversation had evoked.

I took my time putting the kettle on, getting cups down and steeping the tea bags. I was still in a quandary as to why Devlin had come here tonight after insisting I needed to distance myself from the investigation and possibly from him. Just when I'd managed to convince myself that he might be right...there he was at my door. How many of my father's rules had I broken by simply letting him into my house?

Did I dare hope it had something to do with the absence of his ghosts?

When I finally carried the tea out to my office, I almost expected to find him asleep on the chaise. Instead, he stood at the windows, staring out into the night. He seemed so lost in thought, I didn't want to break his concentration, so I set the tea on my desk and slipped up silently beside him.

The veil of wispy clouds covering the moon gradually peeled away to reveal the luster of a white garden. A moonlight garden, it was called. I'd been utterly enchanted when I discovered it by accident one night. By day, it lay hidden within the larger, more colorful plantings, but by the glow of the moon, the silvery foliage intensified. Once upon a time—before Devlin, before the murders—I would sit out there alone for hours, eyes closed, drinking in the mingled perfumes of flowers with names as romantic as the garden itself: bleeding hearts, forget-me-nots, moonflowers, thyme and white oleander.

It was the perfect setting for Devlin's ghosts, but the garden was empty tonight. Not so much as a shadow stirred.

Devlin looked exhausted and drained, but when he turned to face me, I saw a spark of what I thought might be longing in his eyes.

"Why did you come here tonight?" I asked softly. "Earlier, you said I need to distance myself from the investigation."

"And I meant it."

"Then why are you here?"

"Because I can't stay away."

It hit me then, for the first time, that I wasn't alone in this. Devlin felt my pull as surely as I felt his.

The knowledge that he found me alluring should have given my confidence a boost, but instead it made me feel more vulnerable. What would he expect from me? I was not an exotic temptress. I was just a cemetery restorer with callused hands and the ability to see ghosts.

He reached up and trailed his knuckles down the side of my face. "You really have no idea, do you?"

I closed my eyes briefly, savoring the warmth of his skin against mine. "I have a lot of ideas. Maybe even some that might surprise you."

"I'm intrigued," he said and I could see the shadow of a smile in the lamplight. His hand moved to my hair, curling a loose tendril around one finger. "Do you always wear your hair up?"

I grew a little breathless at the question. It was so unexpected—so intimate. "I like it out of my way when I'm working."

"You aren't working now."

Mariama had had long, glorious hair. I pictured the way the dark curls swayed against her back in my dream and I shivered. Was that why Devlin wanted me to take down my hair? To compare us?

I had to stop thinking that way, reading too much into his every word. He'd come here tonight of his own free will. To see *me*. Not his dead wife's ghost.

"I like it up," I said. "and it *is* my hair."

"Yes, it is. And in this light, it shimmers like pure gold," he said. "It smells good, too."

"How can you smell it from there?"

"Exactly."

He took my hand and pulled me gently to him. I didn't resist even for a moment, but closed my eyes and tilted my face toward his.

I felt him shudder. Then he bent his head to meet mine and our lips touched. A surge of energy plowed through me. I staggered against him and he drew me close. My arms draped around his neck as he deepened the kiss, and it went on and on, like nothing I'd ever experienced. I could feel an electric charge flowing between us. It rose and fell like the tides of an ocean, heightening my senses even as it weakened my resistance.

I didn't ever want that kiss to end, but I knew it had to because my strength was waning by the moment. Devlin was literally breathing me in.

He pulled back suddenly, looking shaken. "I don't know what's happening."

"What do you mean?" My voice quivered. I was pretty shaken, too.

He laid his forehead against mine. "It's strange, but when I'm with you, I can sometimes feel their presence as strongly as if they're right here beside me. And yet... when I'm with you, I feel them slipping away from me. It makes no sense. It's like that tug-of-war in your dreams." He didn't have to explain. I knew he was talking about the ghosts. But for him, they were memories.

He pulled me close and I laid my cheek against his chest so that I could see out into the garden.

They were still there after all, his ghosts. Or else Devlin had summoned them back. Hardly more than shimmering transparencies, they floated out of the shadows.

Shani went straight to the swing, gliding gently back

and forth, and I fancied I could hear some ethereal song emanating from her ghostly lips.

Mariama watched me with the blazing eyes of a phantom. Even through the window, I could feel the power of that gaze—cold, devious and seductive.

The room had grown frigid, though I was still warm in Devlin's arms. Tiny lines striated the frost that had crept over the windows. I watched in fascination as more and more appeared, realizing almost too late that the fissures were not in the frost but in the glass itself. As if someone—or something—had a hand on the other side of the window, pressing inward. Pressing it in on us.

Even when I heard the cracking sound, I was slow to react. I tried to pull away, but Devlin held me fast, as if he couldn't bear to let me go. As if he *couldn't* let me go.

I put my hands against his chest and shoved him away with such force, he stumbled back. Somehow, he clung to my hand, pulling me with him as the window shattered over us. I felt the sting of a thousand pinpricks in my back as I crashed to the floor on top of him.

THIRTY-FOUR

A dead tree limb had broken off and smashed through my window. Even though there had been no wind that night. Even though I'd seen the cracks before the glass shattered.

But it was the only logical explanation.

The freak accident had apparently been a wake-up call for Devlin. After helping me to drag a piece of plywood up from the basement and nail it over the opening, he couldn't get away from me fast enough. And in the nearly two weeks since that night, I hadn't seen or heard from him.

I told myself it was just as well. The accident had also been a warning for me, a grim reminder of the dire consequences for breaking my father's rules. Devlin and I could have been seriously injured or even killed by flying shards of glass. I considered myself lucky for having escaped with only those tiny splinters in my back.

The timing of the accident chilled me, but perhaps I was giving Mariama too much credit in thinking she could have somehow engineered that falling tree limb. In all my ghostly sightings, I'd never before experienced a physical manifestation of an otherworldly presence, with the one exception being the garnet ring Shani may or may not have left behind in my garden.

But...this was the ghost of Mariama Goodwine Devlin. A woman who had known things. Dark things. Witch things. A woman who believed that one's power was not diminished in death. That a spirit angered by a violent passing could use that force to interfere with the lives of the living. *Even enslave them, in some cases.*

After my talk with Essie, I'd been certain that Shani's spirit couldn't move on because she didn't want to leave her father. But now it seemed clear that Mariama was the one who lingered, caught between her daughter and the husband she didn't want to leave behind. Maybe Temple had been right. Devlin and Mariama's connection was such that nothing—not time, not distance, not even death—could keep them apart.

I'd gone home that night after my dinner with Temple and dreamed about Devlin and Mariama. And lately, I'd been dreaming about them again. The visions always started the same way: Temple imploring me to join her at that open doorway. Inside, the swirling mist, the flickering candlelight, the primitive drumbeats that drove the couple's frantic rhythm. And then Mariama would look over her shoulder and sometimes I would find myself staring back into my own eyes.

I wasn't possessed, but I very much feared I was on the verge of obsession.

It was a good thing that real life decided to run interference. With the Oak Grove restoration put off indefinitely, financial circumstances dictated that I take on a new project. As much as I had enjoyed dabbling in the investigation—and yes, I freely admitted that now—I could no longer ignore my dwindling bank account.

I kept track of any new developments online and through the newspapers and knew that the remains excavated from the second grave had been identified. Her name was Jane Rice and she'd been an emergency-room nurse at MUSC. She was single, lived alone and by all accounts had been a caring young woman who disappeared nine years ago on her way to work one night and never been heard from again.

I filed this information away in my Oak Grove folder.

Now that I was well away from the investigation—and from Devlin—everything that had happened seemed a little surreal. The killer was still out there somewhere, but I'd found no more suspicious postings to my blog nor had I spotted a black sedan lurking in my neighborhood. As the days passed, I began to breathe a little easier because I really had no choice. The police couldn't watch my house twenty-four hours a day and I couldn't hibernate indefinitely.

So I had to move on.

For the past several days, I'd been working in a small cemetery about forty miles north of Charleston. It was a plain country graveyard with simple headstones and fenced-in plots. The trees had already been thinned to allow for plenty of sunlight, and I found the personal mementos and family keepsakes—dolls, toys, framed photographs and bits of cheap jewelry—that decorated the graves touching and rather charming.

The dolls reminded me of the one Devlin had placed on Shani's grave.

I was thinking about that doll—and Devlin—late one afternoon when I felt a chill at my back and knew that someone watched me.

Twilight had not yet fallen, but I searched the landscape fearfully with my peripheral vision. When I saw no movement, no slithering dark shape at the edge of the woods, I lifted my head and scoured the countryside.

I finally spotted him beneath a live oak, in the deepest part of the shade. Gripped by an icy trepidation, I stared at him across the headstones.

Then I put away my brush, peeled off my gloves and started toward him.

He looked exactly the same as the last time we'd met. Handsome and guarded, with sunglasses shielding his eyes.

I was uneasy but not really frightened even though we were completely alone and the nearest house was at least a mile away. Devlin seemed convinced that Tom Gerrity wasn't the murderer and I trusted his judgment. But I did not trust Tom Gerrity. There was something about him that made my stomach clench and the hair at the back of my neck lift. He wanted something. And I had a feeling it would be some time before I discovered his true motive.

I walked up to him, scowling. "What are you doing here?"

"I came to see you."

I glanced around. "I don't see a car anywhere. How did you get here?"

"I walked up from the main road. The sign on the gate says no vehicles allowed in here. Being an ex-cop, I wouldn't want to break the law."

Why didn't I believe him?

Shading my eyes with my hand, I gazed down the road. Just past the gate, I saw the glint of sunlight on chrome. I glanced back at Gerrity. "How did you know where to find me?"

"You posted pictures on your blog. I recognized this place. I know someone who's buried here."

I started to ask him about that, then something else struck me. How long had he been going to my blog? Did he have a membership, a screen name?

His gaze swept the cemetery. "About time they cleaned this place up."

"You say you know someone who's buried here?"

"A cop. He was killed in the line of duty. His murder was never solved."

I remembered what Devlin had said about another cop dying because of Gerrity.

"If you'll give me a name, I'll take special care of the grave."

"Fremont," he said. "Robert Fremont."

The name sent a shiver through me, a faint ripple of déjà vu that made me wonder if I might have heard about his death on the news.

I sensed Gerrity's eyes on me, sensed that something had shifted between us. I couldn't explain it, but it was like a wall had toppled and I wasn't so sure that was a good thing.

"What do you want from me?" I asked softly.

"Your help."

"Why me?"

"There's no one else, Amelia."

I shivered again and looked away. "If this is about Devlin—"

"It's not. It's about Ethan Shaw."

My brows rose in surprise. "Ethan?"

"I need to find out what he knows about the skeleton you found in the chamber below Oak Grove."

"Then why not go talk to him yourself?"

"He won't see me."

I folded my arms. "Don't tell me. There's bad blood between the two of you."

He shrugged. "Not bad blood. I just don't have the right credentials anymore."

"I don't have any credentials. What makes you think he'll tell me anything?"

"What makes you think he won't?"

I gave an exasperated sigh. "This is ridiculous. Why do you even care about that skeleton? I thought you were working for Hannah Fischer's mother. Now that her body has been recovered, what's your interest in this case?"

"I'm interested in justice," he said. "And I mean to have it. One way or another."

An alarm went off inside me. "What are you talking about?"

"Just go see Ethan Shaw. It's all there."

"What is? Hey!"

A million questions flashed through my head, but I didn't call Gerrity back when he walked off. Mostly, I just wanted him to go away and take his vague premonitions with him.

But the pall he'd cast remained long after I watched him disappear through the gate.

THIRTY-FIVE

I couldn't have gone to see Ethan that afternoon even if I'd wanted to. On my way home, Aunt Lynrose called to tell me that my mother had been admitted to the hospital at MUSC—where Jane Rice, one of the victims, had worked. She'd been on her way there when she disappeared nine years ago.

Not that one event had anything to do with the other, but the coincidence merely served to feed the panic that was already starting to fester.

After a quick stop at my house for a shower and change of clothes, I headed straight up Rutledge Avenue, located a parking garage and then made my way over to the mammoth brick-and-glass building that housed the main hospital.

When I finally found the right wing and floor, a doctor was in with my mother and I had to wait out in the hall with my aunt, who maddeningly refused to tell me anything.

"She's going to be fine," Lynrose assured me as we

perched on the edge of a bench. "But it's her place to tell you."

By the time we were finally allowed in, I'd worked myself up into quite a state, imagining the worst. But my mother actually looked better than she had the last time I'd seen her. Her color was good and she seemed strong and alert. I went over to give her a hug and a kiss before settling myself on the edge of the bed. Lynrose pulled up a chair beside the bed and the three of us sat for a moment in loaded silence.

I didn't want to press for answers, but I could stand the silence no longer.

"Mama—"

"I have cancer," she said and instantly my eyes welled with tears.

I took her hand in mine and squeezed.

"It's breast cancer," she said. "The lump showed up in my last mammogram."

"The doctor said it's perfectly treatable," Lynrose put in. "He said there's every reason to be optimistic for a full recovery."

"That's not exactly what he said," Mama corrected her. "He said the prognosis is favorable, but the tumor is in an advanced stage and is the kind that can spread rapidly. So we have to be aggressive with the treatment and realistic about my chances."

I felt as if someone had rammed a hand inside my chest and clamped a vise grip around my heart. I swallowed hard and tried to control my emotions. "What do we do? What's the next step?"

"I'm scheduled for surgery first thing in the morning."

"So soon?"

She patted my hand. "It's not that soon. I've known for a while."

"How long?" Then it hit me. "That's why you came to Charleston for your birthday. You knew then. Why didn't you tell me?"

"We were having such a wonderful time, I didn't want to spoil it. And afterward...I didn't want you to know until you absolutely had to."

"Why? I could have been here for you." I felt a little betrayed by her silence.

"I've had Lyn with me. She's taken good care of me."

"*I* should have been here."

"There was nothing you could do. And you had your work."

"But still—"

"Amelia." Aunt Lynrose shook her head and I fell silent, staring almost fiercely out the window where the sunset over the Ashley River seemed unbearably symbolic.

"I expect to be home in a couple days," my mother said briskly. "There'll be tubes and drains...a lot of unpleasantness. I don't want you to have to deal with any of that. And, of course, chemo..."

I couldn't believe how calmly she could talk about all this. I'd always thought of my mother as fragile, but her pragmatism in the face of a devastating diagnosis astounded me. She was facing major surgery, weeks of chemo, and her main concern was that I not have to deal with tubes and drains.

Lynrose had put up a good front, but now she began to weep quietly into a linen hankie.

"Lyn, for God's sake," my mother scolded.

"I know, I know, steel magnolias and all that. But your hair, Etta. You're going to lose all that beautiful hair."

"It's just hair," my mother said crisply. "Perhaps it'll

come back in curly. Wouldn't that be something after all the money I've spent on perms over the years?"

Holding back my own tears, I fluffed her pillows, poured her a glass of water, and then with nothing else to do, I had to ask the obvious.

"Where's Papa?"

"He is a man, and therefore, worthless in a situation like this," said my aunt who, so far as I knew, had never had a serious relationship with a man in her life, much less been married to one.

"He was here earlier," my mother said. "I sent him out for some air. He never could abide closed in places."

"Really? I didn't know that."

"There are a lot of things you don't know about your father," she said, with a hint of something in her voice that made me glance up and study her face.

"Etta, I don't think now is the time—"

"Hush, Lyn. This is between my daughter and me. There's a chance I may not wake up from that surgery." She put up a hand when my aunt and I both protested. "A *slim* chance, but nevertheless…there's something you need to know about Caleb…"

Lynrose pursed her lips and took out her knitting. She bowed her head over her work, but I knew she watched us through her lashes. And I could feel the tension rolling off her in waves.

"Mama, what is it?" I asked softly. Did she know about the ghosts? I wondered. Did she know about me?

She hesitated, and for the first time since I arrived, I saw a chink in her steel, a hint of the delicate, melancholy woman who had adopted me, nurtured me and loved me. But who had never really let me know her.

My aunt's knitting needles clicked together in the silence. I wondered if she was actually making loops or merely pretending.

"Your father…"

I leaned in. I think my aunt did, too. "Yes?"

"Your father…" My mother's eyes flickered. Her gaze went past me and I glanced over my shoulder to see Papa in the doorway. He stood there for a moment, his face weathered and weary, and then without a word he backed away and retreated into the hallway.

I whirled around to my mother. "Why won't he come in?"

"I expect he's giving us our time together."

"Don't make it sound so final," I pleaded, thinking of Devlin and his missed goodbyes.

"I didn't mean it that way."

"Mama, tell me about Papa."

She exchanged a glance with my aunt.

"Your papa is a complicated man with a complicated past," Lynrose said. "Perhaps it's best to just leave it at that."

"A complicated past?" I turned back to my mother. "What does that mean?"

I could see the struggle on my mother's face, the internal battle she waged within herself on how much she was willing to share with me. She closed her eyes and sighed. "All you really need to know is that he loves you. More than anything in this world, and that includes me."

That wasn't what she'd meant to say at all. I knew her well enough to figure that out.

"Mama—"

"I'm tired now. I think I'll sleep for a while."

"It's for the best," Lynrose muttered.

I didn't want to risk upsetting my mother on the eve of her surgery, so I let the matter drop. After a while, I got up and slipped out of the room, leaving my mother and my aunt whispering together the way they once had on our front porch.

When I went out into the hallway, Papa was nowhere in sight.

My mother was dismissed from the hospital two days later, and I went home with her to Trinity to stay until she and my aunt cajoled me into returning to Charleston.

"You have a business to run and there is no reason in the world for you to put yourself in a financial bind when I have nothing except time on my hands," Lynrose insisted and my mother backed her up.

On my last night there, Papa had left the house right after dinner, and I walked down to Rosehill to say good-bye. I inhaled the roses as I made my way along the walkway. He was at the angels waiting for their cold faces to come alive in the warm glow of the setting sun.

After the fleeting animation, he turned, his gaze going past me to the gate. I knew he was looking for the ghost. His dread was tangible as dusk drew near.

"Have you seen him again, Papa?"

"I've been seeing him more and more lately."

The revelation made my blood go cold. "What does he want?"

Papa turned and the glitter of tears on his face shocked me into silence. I'd never known him to show emotion. Like me, he mostly lived inside his own head.

And then it came to me. I put a hand to my mouth. "Papa…do you think he's come back for Mama?"

He closed his eyes and shuddered. "I wish I knew, child. I wish I knew."

It was a long, lonely drive back home to Charleston. On the way, I checked my messages. One from Ethan Shaw, one from Temple and none from Devlin.

Ethan had invited me to a small gathering at the Charleston Institute for Parapsychology Studies on Friday to celebrate his father's seventieth birthday.

As I let myself into the darkened house, I couldn't help wondering if my mother would still be with us for her next birthday.

THIRTY-SIX

On the morning of Dr. Shaw's party, I woke up lethargic and out of sorts. I wondered if I was coming down with something or if all that worry over my mother had taken a physical toll. A few hours of hard labor at the cemetery left me weak-kneed and shivering.

By midafternoon, I called it a day and came home to soak in a hot bath and sip tea, which did nothing to help. Grabbing bottles of vitamin C and ibuprofen from the medicine cupboard, I noticed in the back the packet of Essie's Life Everlasting.

Good for what ails you, she'd said. According to Dr. Shaw, it was harvested from a plant in the daisy family and had the same effect as a vitamin shot. Just what the doctor ordered. I didn't expect the herb to work miracles, but I did believe in the medicinal value of natural remedies that had been around for ages.

I brewed the leaves and carried a cup with me to bed. Propped against the headboard, I sipped tentatively. The tea had both a sweet and acrid taste. Not at all unpleasant. I finished half a cup, set it aside and slid down under the covers, where I promptly fell asleep.

When I woke up, I felt much better. Either the Life Everlasting had done its job or a long, dreamless nap was all I'd needed in the first place.

Outside, dusk had fallen and the air had cooled. I lay for a few moments, luxuriating in my newfound well-being, as I finished the now tepid tea. Then I crawled out of bed, slipped into a black dress and arrived at the Charleston Institute for Parapsychology Studies fashionably late.

The house was all lit up, the doors thrown open to the mild night, giving me a glimpse of what the grand old antebellum must have looked like in her glory days. If I closed my eyes, I could almost hear the faint strains of a fiddle and the swish of hoopskirts gliding across the dance floor.

The same blonde let me in through the side entrance, then disappeared down the hallway with my gift—a replica deck of fifteenth-century Visconti-Sforza hand-painted tarot cards. As I stepped into a roomful of people I'd never set eyes on, my first inclination was to turn around and go back out the same way I'd come in. But then I spotted Temple conversing with someone across the room and she waved me over.

"I didn't know you'd be here," I said as I made my way through the crowd. "Did you drive all the way down here for the party?"

"I had business in Charleston, anyway." She grabbed a glass of champagne from a nearby tray and handed it to me. I hadn't seen her since the day of the exhumation. She looked very different tonight, in a slinky silver dress that shimmered like liquid mercury in the light.

Her companion turned then and I recognized Daniel
Meakin.

"You remember Daniel?" Temple said, barely suppressing her disdain.

"Yes, of course. It's good to see you again."

"You, as well," he said with a warm smile. "I haven't
seen you around in the archives lately."

"There's no need now that Oak Grove has been put
on hold. I've moved on to another cemetery."

He frowned. "That's a shame. I had such high hopes
for that restoration. Do you have any idea when you'll
be able to return?"

Before I could respond, Temple squeezed my arm.
"Have you seen Rupert yet?"

"I…just got here." She knew that because she'd seen
me walk in.

Looping her arm through mine, she pulled me gently
away. "We really should find him and offer our best
wishes. I think I saw him go into his office. Will you
excuse us, Daniel?"

"Oh…of course." He looked a little forlorn as we
walked off.

"I thought I'd never get away from him," Temple muttered. "He latched on to me as soon as I walked in."

"Shush. He'll hear you."

"I don't care. He gives me the creeps."

"So you've mentioned." I glanced over my shoulder.
"I think he's kind of sweet. Have you ever noticed the
way he holds his left arm? His scars must bother him
constantly."

"Scars?" She looked at me meaningfully. "As in more
than one?"

"I saw them one day in the archives room when his
shirtsleeve slipped up. They crisscross back and forth

over the vein, like he's tried many times but never gone quite deep enough to succeed. It's really sad when you think about it. Has he no family?"

"I don't know a lot about his background. I seem to recall someone mentioning once that he was at Emerson by the kindness of some well-to-do relative. I really didn't pay that much attention to Daniel. He was one of those people that just faded into the woodwork."

Like me, I thought.

"How is it that you didn't know Mariama at Emerson?" I asked. "I can't imagine her fading into the woodwork. Devlin, either, for that matter."

"Devlin was at Emerson? He must have been behind me. I didn't mingle a lot with underclassmen. By my junior year, I pretty much kept to the same circle of people with mutual interests."

"Like Camille?"

She closed her eyes briefly. "I still can't believe it. We had our differences, but I never would have wished something like that on her."

"When was the last time you saw her?"

She gave me an annoyed look. "Oh, no, you don't. We're not doing the inquisition thing tonight. This is a party. And if you don't mind, I'd just as soon not think about what happened to poor Camille. Because if it happened to her..." She broke off on a shudder.

We paused at the end of the hallway where Dr. Shaw's office was located. The sounds of a bitter quarrel emanated through a crack in the pocket doors, and Temple and I exchanged glances. Before we could retreat, the doors slid open and Ethan strode through. He stopped cold when he saw us.

"I didn't know anyone was out here."

"We just came up," Temple said smoothly.

Relief flashed across his face. It was obvious he and his father had been arguing and just as apparent that he hadn't wanted to be overheard.

"We've come to wish Rupert a happy birthday," Temple added.

Ethan waved us in. "Perhaps you can persuade him to come out and join the festivities," he said on a note of irritation. "He's being as petulant as a child about this whole thing."

"I'll do my best."

While Temple went in to find Dr. Shaw, I remained in the hallway to have a word with Ethan.

"Is everything okay?" I asked.

He looked annoyed. "He's been in a state for weeks now. One of his former assistants is publishing a book using Father's research without giving him credit."

"That would be upsetting, particularly if this assistant stole the material."

"How did you know about that?" Ethan asked in surprise.

"Last time I saw your father, he said someone had been slowly leeching his life's work."

"Yes, well, as I said, he's got himself all worked up about it. He wants to sue, but lawsuits are expensive. Father's never had to worry about money so he doesn't have a clue. But enough about that." His smile seemed to take a bit of effort. "How's your mother?"

"Her treatment is going well and she's in good spirits. Much better than I've been, actually. I'm trying to remedy that, though. I thought an outing might do me good."

"You do look more rested than the last time I saw you."

I tried to remember when that was. At Oak Grove, hours before we'd discovered Camille's body. He'd told me about the day Mariama and Shani had died. And later Devlin had come to my house and kissed me, but I tried not to think about that.

Now that the office doors were open, a steady stream of people filed in to see Dr. Shaw. "I should go say hello."

Ethan nodded. "Like I said, he's in a mood, but I'm sure he'll be happy to see you."

But Dr. Shaw seemed fine to me. I saw nothing of the disheveled, suspicious man who'd been convinced someone was stealing his life's work. I wanted to ask him about that, but a celebration was hardly the place to bring up something so obviously distressing.

He watched me with keen eyes as he swirled brandy in a glass. "How have you been, Amelia? Any more events that I should know about?"

"Thankfully, no. No more shadow beings, no more psychic vampires. My life is pretty uneventful at the moment, paranormally speaking."

Someone had come up beside him, and when Dr. Shaw turned to shake hands, I saw the silver spark of his ring. I'd never been able to make it out before, but after seeing Daniel Meakin's drawing, it was so clearly a snake coiled around a talon.

The same symbol that Devlin wore around his neck.

I tore my focus from the ring and studied the faces of those gathered around Dr. Shaw. They were of all ages, well-dressed, educated, intellectuals. Emerson's finest. I wondered how many of them secretly wore that same symbol somewhere on his or her person.

Murmuring my excuses, I slipped out of the office and wandered down the hallway, feeling strangely claustrophobic in that house and inexplicably paranoid. No one there had any reason to want to harm me, but I couldn't help remembering what Dr. Shaw had said about the

killer that day. He could be someone in our midst. Someone we least expect—

A hand fell on my shoulder and I whirled, hand to my
heart. "Ethan! You startled me."

"Sorry," he said contritely. "You're not trying to sneak
away already, are you?"

"I'm afraid so. Unfortunately, I have to be up at the
crack of dawn so I can beat the heat."

"Well, that's too bad. But I do understand. I have an
early day, as well."

I glanced at him with interest. "Are you working on a
new case?"

"Yes. Some remains were uncovered just today."

"At Oak Grove?" I asked anxiously.

"No, not Oak Grove. Nothing new on that front, thankfully."

"I've been wondering…have you been able to identify
the skeleton Devlin and I found in the chamber? I've read
nothing about it in the paper."

"We don't have a name, but I have identified some
interesting characteristics."

"Can you tell me what they are?"

He leaned a shoulder against the wall. "I can do better
than that depending on how squeamish you are."

I made a face. "As long as it doesn't involve spiders,
I should be okay."

"No spiders, I promise. Drop by the morgue at MUSC
tomorrow afternoon and I'll show you what I've found."

The morgue. Maybe I was just a tad squeamish after
all.

"Is that allowed?"

"You're a consultant on the Oak Grove case, right? It
said so in the paper."

"That's a very loose interpretation."

"It should suffice. Call me when you get there and I'll come out and let you in. In the meantime…" He straightened. "If you're set on leaving so early, let me at least walk you to your car. There's something I'd like to talk to you about."

I went off to say good-night to Temple and then met back up with Ethan at the door. He seemed preoccupied as we walked around to the parking area, and I wondered if he was still upset by the argument with his father.

"You wanted to talk to me?"

"It's about John."

That was unexpected. And the very mention of Devlin's name took the wind right out of me. "What about him?"

Ethan propped a hand on the car door. "Have you seen him lately?"

"No, not in days." He hadn't called me and I hadn't called him. I was still trying to convince myself it was for the best.

"He looks terrible, Amelia. I think the investigation is taking a toll. And this time of year is difficult for him, anyway. It's coming up on the anniversary."

I felt a little catch in my throat. "I didn't know."

"That's probably why you haven't heard from him. The guilt…" He made a helpless gesture with his hand. "He spends far too much time in his own gloomy company. I worry about him. He needs to get out more."

I thought about the feminine voice I'd heard in the background that night on the phone and wondered if Devlin got out more than Ethan realized. Still, I didn't want to minimize his concern, especially now that I knew the guilt Devlin carried with him.

"I tried to get him to come here tonight," Ethan said. "But this is the last place he'd want to be."

"He doesn't seem to have much regard for the work done here," I said carefully.

"It's not just that. This is where he met Mariama."

"At the Institute?"

"It wasn't the Institute then. It was just our home. Mariama lived with us for a while. And John was my father's protégé."

"Protégé?" I stared at him in shock. "As in...*protégé?* But he doesn't even believe in your father's work."

"Not now, maybe. But there was a time when he was an avid investigator."

I couldn't even wrap my head around that notion. "We are talking about the same man."

Ethan smiled. "We are."

"What happened? He's so dismissive now."

Ethan shrugged. "He gradually grew away from it, as most of us did back then. We had graduate school and careers to think of. It really did begin to seem like a game we were playing. Except to my father, of course." I heard a shade of bitterness in his voice that made me wonder again about that argument. "On the night of the accident, John came here to see Father. He wanted help contacting Mariama's and Shani's spirits. He pleaded with Father to help him open a door so that he could cross over and see them one last time."

I could barely comprehend that level of desperation. It hurt me to even think about it. "That's..."

"I know. I think by that point he was very nearly mad with grief. He became violent and uncontrollable. Called Father a fraud and worse. Father thought he would have to call someone for help, but John finally left of his own accord. That's when he disappeared. No one knew where he'd gone off to. I think we all feared the worst. Then we began hearing those rumors that he'd been admitted to a private sanitarium. It was probably just talk. People love to embellish. But John did come back a changed man. He got better after a time, but when I saw him yesterday…" Ethan trailed off worriedly. "I think it's that house."

"What house?"

"Mariama's house. Ever since the accident, he's been renting a place on Sullivan's Island, but he never got rid of her house. It's a gorgeous old Queen Anne right off Beaufain. Mariama was crazy about it. I went by there the other day. The garden was well tended, the porch had a fresh coat of blue paint. I think he's moved back in."

"Maybe he was just ready to go back home."

"Maybe," Ethan said, but he didn't sound at all convinced.

"Why are you telling me all this?"

"I don't quite know. I just thought…here." He pressed a piece of paper into my palm. "It's the address. Just in case you're so inclined."

I was not so inclined. I told myself I was going straight home, maybe have another cup of Essie's Life Everlasting and go straight to bed. I had a long day at the cemetery ahead of me tomorrow and I needed to rest up.

And I think I would have done exactly that had I not seen Devlin coming out of the palmist's house across the street.

THIRTY-SEVEN

I had just driven around the Institute and was about to pull onto the street when I saw him on Madam Know-It-All's front porch.

They had just come out of the house, Devlin and a woman—the palmist, I presumed—and though I couldn't see her features as clearly as his underneath the porch light, I knew she was attractive. I could tell by the way she carried herself. Really gorgeous women have an air about them. Temple and Camille both had it. Mariama's ghost still had it.

Devlin appeared to be in the process of leaving, but then the woman touched his shoulder and he spun back around. There was nothing particularly sexual about the interaction, but I did sense some intimacy in the way he peered down into her upturned face and a measure of urgency when he took her by the arms. My window was open, but I couldn't hear a word of their conversation, no matter how hard I strained.

I wasn't proud of myself for trying to eavesdrop, nor

for easing onto the street behind Devlin's car when he drove off a few minutes later. I didn't know what had come over me. I hadn't been raised like this. Discretion and decorum went hand in hand in our household, and I had a sudden vision of how appalled my mother would be at my behavior. Listening in on private conversations. Following a man home without his knowledge or permission. Her imagined censure made me wince, but it didn't stop me.

I had no idea how to tail someone—much less a cop—without being spotted, but instinct told me to hang back. Traffic was light so I allowed a good half block between us. But with such a wide gap, I was afraid I might lose him if he made too many turns.

Thanks to Ethan, I had some idea of where Devlin was headed. From Rutledge he turned right on Beaufain, then left onto a side street. I drove past the intersection and circled back, giving him time to park and get inside.

Switching on the interior light, I checked Ethan's note as I drove slowly down the street, searching for a lovely Queen Anne with a blue porch and a well-tended garden. When I spotted the address, the windows were all dark and I didn't see Devlin's car. He must have parked around back, I decided. Or else he'd spotted me in the mirror and driven on by.

I checked my own mirror just to make sure he hadn't doubled back and come up behind me.

No one was there. Coast all clear.

Now what?

Pulling to the curb, I shut off the engine, cut the lights and just sat there, my thoughts in turmoil. Why had I come here? I wanted to blame the impulse on Essie's tea or the few sips of champagne I'd had at Dr. Shaw's party. I wasn't behaving like a woman who had always lived her life by a strict set of rules. I could see my reflection in the car window and thought, *that's not me. She has my eyes, my nose, my mouth, but inside she's morphed into some strange, reckless creature I don't know anymore.*

"Go home, Amelia." I said it aloud because I thought the words might have more power. Home to my safe, pleasant, empty sanctuary where I was guarded from ghosts and governed by my father's warnings.

But I didn't start the engine, didn't turn around, didn't drive off into the night. Instead I sat there for a while longer and then finally I got out.

Crossing the street, I stood at the bottom of the veranda steps, my face upturned to the sky. Clouds drifted across the moon and I could feel something in the air. A storm was coming. The drop in pressure tickled my scalp and I felt almost giddy with excitement as I lifted my arms and let the wind sweep over me.

It was a very liberating moment, a casting off, but then I turned toward the house—her house—and something darker coursed through my veins. Someone stood in the front window. A shadow that darted away when I saw it.

Shivering, I knocked on the front door. It swung open and I took a cautious step inside. "Devlin?"

I took a moment to acclimate my eyes to the gloom. Directly in front of me, an elegant staircase curved up and around to a wide second-story gallery. Beyond the stairwell, a long hallway led back into the house and to my right was a murky parlor.

Moving to the arched doorway, I allowed my gaze to travel over the old-fashioned furniture, which surely had not been Devlin's choice, and the imposing portrait of Mariama over the mantel, which surely was. The air smelled faintly of sage and lemon verbena—like Essie's house—with a musty undercurrent of dust, abandonment and unspeakable despair.

Veiled moonlight shone through the large front window, and for a moment I saw Shani standing there staring out. *Watching for Devlin. Waiting for him to come back and say goodbye.*

She was tiny and luminescent, and as I stood there observing her, she faded into nothingness.

The fresh coat of blue paint on the porch had not kept out the ghosts. The chill of their presence surrounded me. Not just Shani and Mariama, but the ghosts of another life. The ghosts of a happy family. The ghost of the man Devlin had once been.

As I backed into the foyer, my gaze lifted to a flickering light beyond the gallery. I could hear music up there now, something exotic and tribal. A drumming that stirred primitive instincts.

Slowly, I climbed the stairs, calling out Devlin's name. Something cold swept against me, the merest brush of a silk dress, and I knew it was her. A mirror hung on the wall, and as I passed by, I caught a glimpse of my reflection. Only this time...I didn't see my eyes, my nose, my mouth. For a moment, I could have sworn I saw Mariama staring back at me, but the illusion was fleeting. Once again it was me in the mirror. Wide eyes, freckled skin, bedraggled ponytail. Hardly the vision of a temptress.

And yet as I neared the top of the stairs, I grew bolder, freer. When I reached the landing, I paused to remove the band from my ponytail and shake out my hair. My head fell back, swaying in abandon as the rhythm of the music seemed to crawl inside my skin.

The sound came from the room down the hallway. The door was open and the beat seemed to intensify as I approached.

Inside, everything was hazy and candlelit. It was like stepping into someone else's dream. The breeze that blew in through the balcony doors stirred the flames and rippled like waves through the silky fabric that cocooned the bed. An eerie audience of African masks hung from the walls, and the hollow eyes seemed to watch me as I walked across the room to Devlin.

He stood on the veranda looking down on the garden. His shirt was open and the wind blew it back. As he turned, something cold floated between us. I felt her touch, her icy breath, and shivered. But I wasn't afraid. Which was strange because here in her house she would be at her strongest. I had already seen what she could do and yet...I wasn't afraid.

My gaze locked with Devlin's and a current of heat surged through me. He felt it, too. His eyes flared and his body went very still.

The moment stretched on and on.

And then he closed the distance between us and I heard him mutter, "I knew you'd come," but I didn't know if he meant me.

I reached up and traced the silver medallion with my fingertip. A symbol of his mysterious past, a talisman of all his secrets. The metal was cold, but I could feel the heat of his skin drawing me to him as surely as his warmth enthralled his ghosts.

Rising on tiptoes, I offered him my mouth. He took it with a groan, crushing me to him in an embrace that seemed at once familiar and foreign, desperate and devastatingly controlled.

He tasted of whiskey and temptation and my darkest fantasies. I wanted to hear him say my name in that seductive, decadent drawl. I wanted to skim my tongue along his hot skin, press my mouth to the throbbing pulse in his neck, wrap myself around him until nothing could come between us. *Not time, not distance, not even death.*

Backing me up against the wall, he tore aside my clothes right there on the balcony while a voice inside my head warned: *This is not you, Amelia. This is* not *you.*

But it was me. It was my hands that flung his shirt aside. My mouth that opened so readily beneath his.

My decision to discard the rules by which I'd lived my whole life.

He lifted my legs around him and, half drunk with desire, I let my head fall back against the wall, exposing my neck. He devoured me hungrily, his teeth nipping and tugging the tender skin at my throat, his tongue laving and soothing the pleasurable sting.

Through slitted eyes, I caught the barest hint of movement down in the garden. When I looked again, I saw only the flutter of leaves in the wind.

And then I saw nothing at all as Devlin whisked me into the bedroom. The charged air came with us, tingling over bare skin, feathering along aroused nerve-endings.

From where we stood, I had a view of Mariama's dressing mirror, oval and ornate. In the candlelight, I could see the ridges of muscle in Devlin's back as he bent over me. I had the strangest sensation of being outside my body, of watching something forbidden, something dangerously taboo.

I slipped from his embrace and when he turned, I pressed him against the wall, trailing my lips down his chest as I fumbled with his belt buckle and opened his zipper. Smiling up at him, I slid to my knees and then I did things to him I never knew I was capable of. He shuddered as I encircled him, and when I felt he was on the verge, I turned again to glance over my shoulder at the mirror. My smile now was sly, wanton. A temptress's invitation.

Rising, I put my lips against his ear. "I will never leave you," I whispered, and where those words came from, I had no idea.

Devlin's eyes smoldered and before I could move away, his hand shot out to grip my chin. He tilted my head back, searching my face.

"Amelia." It was almost a question.

The sound of it made me tremble. "Yes, yes, yes," I breathed and wound my arms around his neck, pulling him down for my kiss.

The breeze through the open doorway whipped the candle flames as the silky curtains billowed and beckoned.

Devlin pulled away and stared into my eyes for the longest moment, and then with a muttered oath he swept me up and carried me to the bed. The fabric parted in the breeze, and before I could catch my breath, we were falling through that shimmering fabric into another world, dark and lush. Devlin's world.

Mariama's world.

I heard nothing of the music now but the drumbeats. The primitive sound thundered in my ears as he rose over me.

Trapping my wrists, he lifted my arms over my head, kissing me again and again and again. Long, hot, out-of-control kisses that left me thrumming. That left me begging. I closed my eyes tightly as his lips slid over my stomach.

My arms were still over my head, but the fingers around my wrists had turned cold. I tried to move, but I couldn't. Something held me in place as I felt Devlin's tongue skim the inside of my thigh.

I squirmed and tried to free myself. Tried to say his name.

He lifted my hips to meet his mouth, and as a white-hot pleasure filled me, I heard her laugh.

Slowly, I opened my eyes.

A ghost hovered over the bed. Eyes burning into mine. Mouth twisted in a ghastly grin.

I tried not to react, but how could I not?

Tearing my hands free from whatever held me, I tried to push Devlin away. He looked up, eyes heavy with desire. "What's the matter?"

They were all around us. Drawn by the heat and energy of our lovemaking. Drawn to the most elemental act of life…of what they could never experience again.

Hungry and covetous, they watched us. Leering from the darkest corners. Crouching like gargoyles atop bedposts. Touching diaphanous body parts in grotesque parody.

A scream rose in my throat as Devlin moved up beside me. "Amelia? What's wrong? Did I hurt you? Scare you…?"

He didn't have a clue they were there. How could he not feel the cold dankness that surrounded us? The evil that had blown in with the breeze?

Across the room, the entity I'd seen in the garden at Rapture sat slumped in a chair. He wore shackles, one clamped around his wrist, the other dangling free. Lifting the loose end to his face, he sneered knowingly at me through the hole.

Devlin touched my shoulder and I flinched away. "I… have to go."

"What is it? What did I do?"

I slid out of bed and grabbed my clothes. "I'm…" *Haunted.* "I have to go!"

I ran blindly from that room, Devlin's voice calling after me. "Amelia!"

Later when I looked back on that night, I never remembered dressing or leaving the house. Had I not been so traumatized, I might have noticed the shadow that lurked at the corner of the veranda. I might even have recognized the troubled visage that tracked me.

As it was, I barely had any recollection of how I got home. I knew that I must have driven like a bat out of hell, though, because I was already inside my house, locked in my own little sanctuary, by the time Devlin caught up with me.

He beat on my front door, called out my name, but I didn't let him in. I slid to the floor, arms wrapped tightly around my legs, shaking uncontrollably as my father's warning pounded through my head.

...*take care you don't let them in. Once that door has opened...it cannot be closed.*

"Papa," I whispered. "What have I done?"

THIRTY-EIGHT

I woke up the next day to sunlight and a ringing telephone. I was in my bedroom, but I had no idea how I'd gotten there. The details of last evening were cloudy. Something told me I was better off that way.

Drawing the covers over my head, I waited for the caller to give up. I wasn't up to dealing with real life. I wanted to drift a little while longer, but little by little, everything came back to me and I felt very alone and afraid. I had no one to talk to, no one to turn to. I couldn't tell Papa. I couldn't bear to see the look in his eyes. I couldn't tell Devlin, either, because he would never understand, no matter how hard he tried.

He'd spent the night on my front porch, only inches from where I lay curled on the floor in the foyer. But he may as well have been a million miles away for all that it mattered. I couldn't open the door to him. I imagined them out there, circling like vultures. As long as I remained in my sanctuary, they couldn't touch me. As long as I stayed away from Devlin, they wouldn't want me.

Or so I told myself. But I wouldn't know for sure until dusk.

He'd finally left at sunup and taken his ghosts with him. I'd pulled myself up off the floor and staggered into the bedroom to collapse fully dressed on top of the covers. I didn't remember nodding off, but I must have slept deeply because now I had that sluggish, hungover feeling of daytime slumber.

I wished I could doze off again, but I couldn't afford to sleep the day away. I had work, things to take care of. Life went on for me and for Devlin...just not together. Unless I could find a way to shut out the ghosts. But even here in my sanctuary I wasn't safe. Not from Devlin.

The phone started ringing again. This time I picked it up, thinking it might be him, though I hadn't a clue what I would say to him. I wasn't ready to face him. That much I did know.

"Hello?"

"Amelia? It's Ethan. Did you forget our date?"

I sat up. "Our date?"

"You were going to come by the morgue today. Unless you changed your mind."

I pressed my fingertips into my temple. "We talked about this last night, right? At your father's party?"

"Yes. Are you all right?"

"Just a little groggy. I guess I overslept."

A pause. "Overslept? It's almost two o'clock in the afternoon."

My gaze flew to the clock. "That's impossible." But there it was in bright, neon blue.

"Are you sure you're okay?" Ethan asked worriedly.

"I just need a minute to pull myself together." Of course, I needed a whole lot more than that, but it was a relief to have something to think about other than the

ghosts. Other than Devlin. Suddenly, I had an overpow-
ering urge to be out among the living. A morgue would
not have been my first choice, but the appointment had
already been set with Ethan and I was curious about the
skeletal remains we'd found in the chamber. "I'll be there
in twenty minutes."

"Call when you arrive so I can walk you in. And,
Amelia?"

"Yes?"

Another pause. "Nothing. I'll see you soon."

I hung up the phone with one thought uppermost in
my mind. How many hours did I have until twilight?

Ethan came out to greet me at MUSC. As we rode the
elevator down to the morgue, I could feel his inquisi-
tive gaze on me. He must have wondered about my appearance, but was too much of a gentleman to ask. One
glance in the mirror after my shower had confirmed a
cold suspicion. My eyes were sunken, my cheeks hollow.
Already I had assumed the gaunt visage of the haunted.

"Are you sure you're up for this?" Ethan asked as we
walked down a short hallway.

I offered him the first excuse I could think of. "I'm
just feeling a little under the weather today. It's nothing
serious."

"If you have a weak stomach, this probably isn't the
place for you," he warned.

"No, I'm okay."

Famous last words.

He pulled open a door and we were met with a swoosh
of cold air and the pungent aroma of antiseptic layered
over the putrid, slightly sweet scent of death. My stomach recoiled as he led me into the locker room of the
autopsy suites. He handed me a set of scrubs and then

disappeared while I changed out of my street clothes. After a few minutes, he came back to collect me and we went into one of the rooms where the skeletal remains had been placed on a stainless-steel table.

"He's just a number right now," Ethan said. "No name, no face, but we actually know quite a bit about him."

"Him?"

"The shape of the hip bone tells us the remains are those of a male."

The other victims were female. The pattern had changed yet again. If there was a pattern. "Does Devlin know?"

Ethan nodded.

"What did he say?"

"You know John. He doesn't give a lot away."

I thought it odd that even here, Devlin's presence was with us.

Ethan walked around the table as we talked, but I stood in one place, not wanting to jostle my stomach, though there wasn't much smell in here and the bones looked scrubbed and disinfected. Still, we were dealing with human remains.

"The skull indicates that he was Caucasoid. Around five-ten, stocky build. He was young—between eighteen and twenty-five. His bones were still growing." Ethan traced a finger along the collarbone. "The raised ridges indicate a young adult. You can feel them if you like."

"No, that's okay. I'll take your word for it."

He flashed a grin. "Some of the teeth are still in their sockets, but in poor condition. We can't identify him that way."

"How long was he in that chamber?"

"Going by the lack of articulation and the gnawing—"

"The what?"

"Rats," he said. "Over time, they can do a lot of damage. I've noted tooth marks on the ribs, pelvis, carpals and metacarpal bases..." He gestured toward the skeleton. "There's also a hole in the skull, probably made by rodents or insects, and a good amount of bone and cartilage rot. He had to have been down there at least a decade."

"That long?"

"Maybe longer."

I went over the kills in my head. Afton Delacourt was murdered fifteen years ago, this unknown male at least ten years ago, Jane Rice nine years ago, and Hannah Fischer and Camille Ashby mere weeks ago. There seemed to be no rhyme or reason to the timeline. No continuity to the killer's victims or methods, although such a large gap might indicate he'd been out of commission for whatever reason until recently. It might also mean all the bodies had yet to be discovered.

"Do you think more bodies will turn up?"

"John seems to think so."

"How do we find them?" I murmured. "A combination of electrical resistivity and terrain conductivity? Ground penetrating radar? It would take forever to check every grave."

"I imagine the simplest way is to find the killer," Ethan said.

My gaze dropped to the skeleton. "He must have family, friends. Someone who's been missing him all this time."

"One would think."

I studied the remains, a tightness in my chest. He'd been left in that chamber to be forgotten. "You said last night you'd identified some interesting characteristics."

"Yes. I can't tell you who he is, but I can tell you how

he died. The breastbone is punctured and cuts in the ribs indicate wounds to both sides of the front chest and two more in the upper back. Seven major wounds altogether. And more could have penetrated the soft tissue without touching bone. It was a vicious kill." He noticed my grimace and said, "Let's move on to something a little less gruesome."

I nodded.

He opened a black plastic bag and displayed the contents. "Interestingly enough, the clothing that was found with the remains may be our best hope of identification."

"Really? I only saw bits of fabric. Hardly anything."

"On the body, yes, but some other items were found nearby. Shoes, belt and, more important, a leather letterman jacket. The rats didn't leave us much—"

"Wait a minute." The room started to spin. I put a hand on the wall to steady myself. "Did you say a letterman jacket?"

"Maroon with a gold letter, possibly a *V* or *W*." He glanced at me in concern, then closed the bag. "Come on, let's get you out of here. You've gone as white as that sheet."

It was a gold *W,* in fact. I knew because I'd seen that jacket on a ghost lurking in the garden at Rapture and again last night as he'd leered at me through the shackle that dangled from his wrist.

THIRTY-NINE

A simple Google search led me to the library at West-bury High School, located north of the Crosstown, in an area that had languished for years but was now on the upswing. A pretty librarian named Emery Snow showed me to a room where all the yearbooks were stored.

"They go all the way back to 1975," she said, running a finger along the maroon-and-gold volumes. "That's when Westbury opened."

Since Ethan estimated the skeleton had been in the chamber for at least ten years, I used that as my reference point and worked back. It was a tedious task. After a few books, all those bright, shiny smiles melded together. I started to wonder if I would even recognize the face of that ghost.

And then I found him.

His name was Clayton Masterson and I experienced the blackest mood as I stared down at his picture. His mouth curled in that same sneer I'd seen last night, his eyes gleamed with the same cunning cruelty. Shivering,

I glanced over my shoulder to see if someone—some-
thing—had crept up behind me.

No one was there, thank goodness. I could hear Emery
humming behind the desk. I took comfort at her nearness, her normalcy.

I glanced back down at the photo and tried to muster
up something akin to pity. As a young man, he'd been
viciously murdered, his body hidden away all these years.
I should feel *something.* But I did not. I could see only
hate in his eyes, an emotion that seemed to ooze from
his very soul. Little wonder that he'd met a violent end.

Suppressing a shudder, I carried the yearbook out
to Emery's desk. Since it was summer, the library was
mostly empty and eerily silent. I resisted the urge to
glance over my shoulder yet again as I spread the pages
open before her.

"Did you find who you were looking for?" she asked.
I'd told her very little about my search, only that I was
trying to locate a former Westbury student who had disappeared over ten years ago.

"I think so. Now I'm wondering if anyone might still
be around who was here when he attended."

"I graduated from Westbury. So depending on the
year…" She turned the yearbook over and glanced at the
front. "I was a freshman. The student body was pretty
small back then so it's possible I can help you. I have
to say, though, that I don't remember hearing anything
about a missing student."

I pointed to Clayton Masterson's photograph. "Do you
remember him?"

She seemed to recoil exactly the same way that I had.
"Vaguely. He was a few years ahead of me, but I seem
to recall some scandal. My aunt mentioned something

once. An arrest maybe. He and his mother lived in her neighborhood."

"Do you think your aunt would be willing to talk to me?"

Emery smiled. "Oh, Tula will talk to just about anyone. The trick is getting her to shut up."

Tula Mackey waited for me on the front porch of her tiny Craftsman-style cottage on Huger. As her niece predicted, the woman started talking the minute I walked up and didn't stop to draw a breath as she led me into the house and down a small hallway to a sunny, yellow kitchen, where she offered me sweet tea and cookies. I accepted the tea because it was rather warm in her house and holding the glass gave me something to do with my hands.

Finally, she sat down across from me at the dinette, her eyes bird-bright and avid as she watched me sip the tea. "Emery says you're looking for that Masterson boy."

"I'm not looking for him so much as I'm trying to find out what happened to him," I explained. "I can't say much more than that, but anything you can tell me about him would be a big help."

She tucked her gray hair behind both ears. "He and his mama lived a few houses down from me in that blue two-story on the corner. So I have a lot of memories of that boy, none of them good."

"Can you elaborate?"

"He was a bully," she said. "The meanest one I ever saw. I'm not talking malicious in the way kids can be to one another, but so cruel and sadistic his own mama was afraid of him."

"Can you describe his physical appearance?"

"Average height, I would say, with a stout build. Not

fat, mind you, but solid muscle. Wide shoulders, big arms.
Hands the size of hams. He looked liked he could pick up
a car if he had a mind to. He played football for a time,
but he was too vicious even for that. Hurt another boy
so bad they had to kick him off the team. I reckon that
set him off. Sports was about the only thing he ever took
any pride in. You never saw him without that jacket, even
when the weather was warm."

"You say he was a bully. What kind of things did he
do?"

"He murdered my poor little Isabelle." She picked at
the neck of her blue-flowered housedress. "Prettiest white
Persian you ever laid eyes on, with a real sweet disposi-
tion. She was a house cat, but she got out one day and I
must have walked the neighborhood a dozen times over
until I finally found her hanging from a tree in my own
backyard. He'd strung her up like a deer waiting to be
gutted."

My stomach churned at the picture. Strung her up...
like Hannah Fischer and Afton Delacourt. But at the time
of Hannah's murder, Clayton Masterson had already been
dead for years, viciously murdered, his body left to rot
down in that chamber.

"The way he tortured that poor creature..." Tula broke
off, tears pooling in her eyes as she touched a napkin to
her nose. "I never got over it. I still can't go out in the
backyard without seeing that sweet little kitty hanging
from that tree."

I murmured my sympathies and gave her a moment
while I mulled everything over. The more I learned, the
more confused I became. Who had carried on Clayton's
legacy? "How did you know he was responsible?"

"He had the nerve to brag about it," Tula said angrily.
"He killed Myrtle Wilson's little Pekingese, too. She

found him just like poor Isabelle. And there were other animals. Squirrels, rabbits, even possums. It got so you hated to go outside because you didn't know what you might find hanging from the trees."

The grotesque imagery made me shudder. "Did anyone ever call the police?"

"That boy was far too clever for the law. Even when he was little he knew how to hide his tracks. And by the time he was grown, people around here were too afraid to call the authorities, afraid he'd burn their houses down around them while they slept. Then that little girl on Halstead went missing. A couple of detectives showed up and took him in for questioning. They never could prove he had anything to do with her disappearance, but I think they must have found something on him. They sent him to one of those detention halls for juvenile delinquents. Or maybe it was a mental hospital. His mama moved away while he was gone. I never saw her or the boy again. Or the other one, either, come to think of it."

"The other one?"

Her face softened. "He was a quiet, scrawny little thing. He and his mama lived in a rental house a few blocks over. From everything I heard, she wasn't much of a mother. A drinker, they said. Always bringing strange men home with her. Some example she set for her boy. He never stood a chance. I used to see him out wandering the streets at all hours. Or just sitting alone on the front porch. I guess that's why he took up with Clayton Masterson. Poor kid was lonely. The two of them were inseparable for a while, but I don't think he had anything to do with killing those animals. Not by choice, anyway."

"What do you mean, not by choice?"

She leaned forward, her eyes clouded. "Used to be a vacant lot by the river. A lot of kids played over there.

One of the neighborhood boys claimed he saw Clayton and the other kid back up in the woods one day. Clayton had strung up an old mangy dog and he tried to get the other boy to kill it. When the little one refused, Clayton bound their wrists together and forced the knife into the kid's hand. Forced him to plunge the blade into that poor dog's heart." She leaned back, hand clasped to her throat. "Can you even imagine such a thing? You know what I call somebody like that? A natural-born killer, is what."

I was afraid she might be right. "What was the other boy's name?"

"I don't think I ever knew. He and his mama kept mostly to themselves. I did hear rumors that she was from a well-to-do family and they'd disowned her years ago." Tula paused with a pensive frown. "They said she was a Delacourt. But you know how people love to talk."

As I drove away from Tula Mackey's house, my first instinct was to call Devlin. I'd made an important discovery, but revealing it could be tricky. How could I explain that Clayton Masterson's ghost—and that letterman's jacket—had led me to him?

I'd have to give the matter careful consideration, and in the meantime, I decided to go see Tom Gerrity. He was the one who had sent me to Ethan Shaw in the first place, and it was apparent to me now that he'd known all along what I would find there.

I used my phone to look up the address of Gerrity Investigations. The office was located north of Calhoun not far from where I found myself now. The area had once been residential, but most of the original houses had long since been converted into apartments and offices or torn down to make room for ugly brick commercial buildings that housed a variety of businesses.

Pulling to the curb, I scoped out the immediate vicinity. Gerrity's was in one of the shabbier buildings on the
block, an old Charlestonian-style clapboard with drooping porches and peeling paint. No gardens here, only a
tangle of scrubby brush and weeds that hadn't seen a
mower in months.

As I headed up the cracked sidewalk, I took another
look around. Since my conversation with Tula Mackey,
I couldn't shake a sense of foreboding—that no matter
what I did or where I went, my destiny was on a collision
course with a killer.

The outer door was unlocked, and I stepped through
into what had once been an elegant foyer. Now the
grungy space and its threadbare accoutrements—gold
velvet armchair, moth-eaten rug and sagging Venetian
blinds—served as a lobby for a handful of shady endeav-
ors. After checking the row of mailboxes for a name and
number, I climbed the creaky stairs to the second floor
and found Gerrity Investigations all the way at the end
of a long, dim hallway.

The door stood open, but the office looked deserted.
I paused on the threshold to glance around. Like the rest
of the building, the space had seen better days. An old
metal desk faced the doorway. The only other furniture
was an equally battered filing cabinet and a couple of
plastic chairs.

There were no other doors. The one room apparently
comprised the whole of Gerrity Investigations.

Bending backward to glance down the hallway, I
walked over to the desk and glanced at the items littered
across the surface. Pens, broken pencils, yellow legal
pad, stapler, paper clips—nothing out of the ordinary.

I heard the squeak of footsteps outside and hurried
back over to the door. A man strode down the hallway,

but he wasn't Gerrity. They were probably around the same age, but the newcomer was white, a few inches shorter and a few pounds heavier than Gerrity.

Darting back to the desk, I resumed my inventory. The only personal item in the whole space was a framed photograph of police cadets on graduation day. As I scanned the faces, a thrill of discovery raced through me. I recognized Tom Gerrity and Devlin. And too late…the man I'd seen in the hallway.

Sensing his presence, I turned to find him in the doorway, one hand beneath his khaki jacket as if reaching for a weapon. "What do you think you're doing?" he growled.

Quickly, I set the frame back on the desk and backed away with my hands in front of me in a manner I hoped was nonthreatening. "I'm looking for Tom Gerrity. I have some information for him."

His brows rose at that. "And what information would that be?"

I was pretty nervous by that point, but if anyone knew how to conceal fear, it was me. "Are you a colleague of his?"

"You might say that." He let his arm drop to his side as he walked slowly into the office.

Now that he'd apparently decided not to pull a gun on me, I breathed a little easier. "Do you happen to know where I can find Mr. Gerrity?"

"You're looking right at him."

I stared at him in bewilderment. "I'm sorry. I'm looking for *Tom* Gerrity."

"I'm Tom Gerrity. Leastways, last time I looked."

I didn't see the slightest resemblance between this man and the Tom Gerrity I knew. Could there be two private investigators in Charleston with the same name?

Then I glanced back at the photograph and felt a strange sense of destiny again.

"Were you hired by Hannah Fischer's mother to find her?" I asked slowly.

"That's privileged information," he said. "Unless you want to tell me why you're really here, I think we're done."

"I've been working with John Devlin on Hannah's case." My gaze dropped briefly to the photograph. "I assume you know him."

His contemptuous smirk made my skin crawl. "Oh, I know him all right. What's he to you?"

I didn't like the way he looked at me. Nor the way he spoke about Devlin, but I was careful to keep my disgust concealed. I didn't want to upset him. Not yet at least.

"I told you, Detective Devlin and I have been working together."

"You're not a cop."

"No. I'm a consultant."

His gaze flicked over me in a manner that told me just what he thought of that revelation. "So what is this information you have for me?"

"I'm afraid there's been a miscommunication. This is the man I'm looking for." I picked up the photograph and pointed to the man who'd been masquerading as Gerrity.

His eyes flared and he took a menacing step toward me. "What is this…some kind of sick joke?"

I held my ground. "No, not at all. As I said, there appears to be some sort of miscommunication—"

He grabbed the picture from my hand and laid it facedown on the desk, as if my having seen it, let alone touched it, was some kind of affront to him. "I don't know who you are or what you're after, but you tell Devlin the next time he sends someone to snoop around in my office, he'd better watch his back. I won't bother filing a complaint. I'll handle the problem myself. And as for you..." His eyes narrowed menacingly. "You want to find Robert Fremont? Then I suggest you try Bridge Creek Cemetery in Berkeley County."

"Robert Fremont?" Where had I heard that name? Then I remembered. Robert Fremont was the name of the cop killed in the line of duty. The one whose grave I had promised Gerrity—rather, the man pretending to be Gerrity—I would pay special attention to.

Cold fingers curled around my spine.

How could I not have known? It seemed so obvious to me now.

Fremont was dead and I was his conduit...between this world and the next.

FORTY

I sat in my car for the longest time before I dared start the engine and drive off. My hands shook so badly I didn't trust myself behind the wheel.

How could I not have known he was a ghost?

How could I not have felt the cold breath of death down my collar? The chill of his otherworldly presence?

A ghost masquerading as a man had entered my world and I had no rules to deal with such an entity.

I glanced at the sky. The sun was still shining, but that slow westward glide had already begun. Dusk would fall in a matter of hours. The light would fade, the veil would thin and the ghosts would slip back through. I had no protection at all now except for the walls of my home.

When I got there, I locked myself inside. Not that a bolt would keep them out, but I also had to worry about a killer.

How had my life come to this?

Trying to control my jitters, I made a cup of tea and walked through the silent house, alone and more lonely than I had been in years. Was this the way it would be from now on? Just me, here, locked away from the ghosts?

I thought of Devlin and wondered where he was. He hadn't tried to contact me all day, but then…who could blame him? All he knew was that I'd pushed him away and run out of his house like a madwoman. He'd followed me home, begging for an explanation, and all I could do was keep him locked out, too.

As I allowed myself a wallow in self-pity, Clayton Masterson slipped from my mind entirely. And that proved to be a very grave mistake.

I'd gone to the front window to glance out, and as I turned, a dizzy spell struck me. I stumbled and spilled my tea. The house was completely still so I don't know what made me look up. Daniel Meakin was there at the top of the stairs, a timid, wary shadow staring down at me. Behind him, the bolted door that separated my apartment from the second story stood wide open.

Something came back to me then—Macon Dawes in the garden telling me he'd just come off a seventy-two-hour shift when I'd heard footsteps in his apartment two nights before. Someone had been up there walking around that night. Someone else had loosened those bolts, opened that door, and now I blinked to bring that someone into focus.

The room started to spin and I clutched the wall for support. "What are you doing here?"

He didn't rush me, but eased down the stairs in a half crouch.

I knew I should turn and try to make it to the front door. Escape was only a few steps away. But I couldn't walk without holding on to the wall. Now my gaze fixated on the spilled tea. Had I been drugged?

With an effort, I lifted my head. "What—"

"It's just a sedative and a muscle relaxant. Nothing that will harm you," Daniel Meakin offered helpfully. "Perhaps you should sit down."

I didn't want to obey him, but I had no choice. My knees folded and I collapsed to the floor.

"Oh, dear," he murmured, hurrying to my side. "That was much faster than I expected." I tried to get up but he placed his hands on my shoulders and pressed me back. "Lie still now. You'll hurt yourself if you try to move around. I suspect that's impossible right now, anyway."

He was right. My arms and legs had gone numb.

I lay back against the floor, trying to still the rotating ceiling.

"Here," he said. "Let me make you more comfortable." He bustled about, cleaning up the spilled tea and fetching a pillow from the parlor, which he carefully placed beneath my head. "Better?"

"Why?" I tried to whisper, but the sound came out thick and garbled.

He seemed to understand what I meant. He sank to the floor with a deep sigh, cradling his legs against his chest and resting his chin on his knees. "You have no idea how much I hate this," he said. "You were one of the few people who ever saw me…really saw me, but you saw him, too, didn't you?"

I shook my head helplessly and tried to speak.

"Shush," he soothed. "It's okay. I know about you. I know about your ability."

How was that possible? Unless…

I thought of Tula Mackey's description of the other boy:

…quiet, scrawny little thing. I used to see him out wandering the streets at all hours. Or just sitting alone

on the front porch. I reckon that's why he took up with Clayton Masterson. Poor kid was lonely.

My gaze moved to Daniel's wrist. His shirtsleeve hid the scars, but I could still see them in my mind, a jagged crisscross of agony.

Clayton bound their wrists together and forced the knife into the kid's hand. Forced him to plunge the blade into that poor dog's heart.

The ghost of Clayton Masterson had worn shackles last night. One end fastened about his wrist, the other end dangling free…because Daniel had been waiting for him in the front yard. The silhouette I saw at the end of the porch…

Still clutching his legs, Daniel began to rock back and forth, humming beneath his breath. He laid his cheek on his knees and watched me. "Do you know why this house is safe for you?" he finally asked.

I shook my head again.

"There used to be an orphanage on the property. This is where the chapel was located. Eventually, there were so many orphans, they had to relocate to another facility out of the city. That place burned down in 1907 and a lot of the children died."

The angels, I thought. Papa's angels had a connection to this house. No wonder I felt so safe here. Until now…

He lifted his head and glanced around. "I knew this place was special the moment I first set foot inside. You're lucky to have found it. Though I'm not sure luck had much to do with it. Everything happens for a reason. Why else were you sent to Oak Grove if not to free me?"

"How…long…?"

"Have I been watching you? Since that night at Rapture. I came here to keep track of you. I needed to know your weaknesses, your routine. How best to approach you. It was easy because your neighbor's schedule is so erratic. But then when he left on vacation, I got the idea that I could stay here. That I might be safe here, too. But it was only a temporary reprieve. There is only one way I can truly be free of him."

He reached over and very gently checked the dilation of my pupils. "I saw your face that night at Rapture, you know. You spotted Clayton's ghost in the garden. No one else would have noticed that look in your eyes, but I knew. I *knew*."

He went back to rocking.

"All these years, no one else could ever see him. You have no idea how lonely that was for me."

"You're...wrong..."

He put a hand on my arm in remorse. "Forgive me. I spoke out of turn. You're the only one, perhaps in the whole world, who can understand what I've had to live with."

I heard both wonder and sorrow in his voice.

Then his eyes filled with tears. "You can't get rid of them, you know."

"I...know."

"No matter how deeply I sliced, I couldn't cut him loose. And then I saw you at Rapture and I thought maybe there was hope after all. I went home that very night and began to plan how it would end. It took some time and I had to be careful that Clayton didn't catch on. I knew he would try to find a way to stop me, but this time I was too clever for him. I finished my last book, put all my affairs in order and then I sent you clues so the bodies could be found. I couldn't go with that on my conscience. I tried to give most of them a decent burial with the proper respect but it wasn't always possible..."

"How...many?"

He closed his eyes and shuddered. "I don't know. I've lost count. I tried to be judicious with the selection... choose only those poor souls that needed freeing. The rest was Clayton. The shackles, the torture..." He said the last word on a whisper. "I was once foolish enough to think that I could stop him, back when we were young. I was so happy when the police took him away that time—like I'd been reborn—but eventually he got out of that place and showed up at Emerson. When he told me what he had done to my cousin Afton...that he had been plotting her death for years to taunt me, to spite me...I knew I would have to find a way to end it. He would never leave me alone."

"You..."

"Yes, I killed him. And his ghost has been bound to me all these years. Still making me kill." He stared at me through tormented eyes. Haunted eyes. "You have no idea the things he's forced me to do. Those poor women..."

He rocked now with his eyes closed. "Time and again I tried to end it...take my own life, but he always found a way to stop me. And then one day I realized that even if I managed to kill myself, he would have been waiting on the other side...binding me to him for all eternity..." His breath caught on a little sob, and in spite of everything, I felt a rush of pity because I knew he spoke the truth. He had been driven to the very brink of madness by Clayton's ghost.

He sniffed and wiped his eyes. "But it's all right now because I know now how to finally end it. Every last obstacle has been removed."

"Camille...?"

He drew a shaky breath. "I didn't want that. If there'd been any other way..."

He had killed Camille. Not Clayton. Whether he

wanted to believe it or not, there was a bit of that monster inside him.

"I thought you'd caught something with your camera
that day, but you were never a threat. It was Camille. She
saw me on the path one night coming back from Oak
Grove. I told her I was researching my book, but she was
too smart for her own good and started asking questions.
If she could have just left well enough alone for a little
while longer, it wouldn't have mattered. She could have
gone to the police, told them what she suspected and I
would have still been free of Clayton forever."

"How...?"

"By allowing him to come to you, Amelia."

An icy shiver went through me.

"After tonight it wouldn't have mattered," he repeated
sadly.

And then I understood. The moment Clayton's ghost
latched on to me, Daniel planned to kill himself. It was
the only way he could be free of his ghost. For all eternity.

"Sleep now," he said softly. "It'll soon be over."

FORTY-ONE

I woke up with the taste of vomit in my mouth and the smell of decay in my nostrils. The surface beneath me was cold and rough, and something cut into my cheek so I tried to lift my head. A wave of nausea rolled over me and I retched violently.

Collapsing back to the floor, I lay perfectly still until my head began to clear. Bits and pieces came back to me. Daniel Meakin had been in my house. He'd confessed to killing Clayton Masterson. What was it Ethan had said about the murder? At least seven major stab wounds. It was a vicious kill.

He'd tried to free himself of his tormentor, only to find he was still bound to Clayton's ghost. Now he meant to lure Clayton to me.

Stumbling to my feet, I shuffled forward until I felt the wall. It was damp and slimy, like the walls in the chamber below Oak Grove.

I reached down and patted my pocket, surprised to find he'd left my cell phone on me. Why wouldn't he?

There was no signal down here, no way of calling for help. At least the display offered some illumination and maybe that was his intention. I'd gotten the impression he wanted me to think kindly of him. It was important to him that I understand his motivation.

I did understand. But I couldn't condone or forgive.

Holding the light up, I inspected my prison. Ancient, brick walls. Thick, drapey cobwebs. I had a feeling I was deep, deep underground, in an undiscovered part of the tunnel, but unlike before, I saw no opening, no door, no way out. Nothing but solid brick.

How could that be? He'd put me in here. There had to be a way out.

Unless the wall had been sealed behind me...

A scream welled in my throat, but I pushed it back down. I couldn't panic. I couldn't lose my focus or I would be doomed.

I walked the room again and again, tearing through the sticky webs and prying at bricks until my fingers were raw and bleeding.

Exhausted, I sank to the floor and buried my head in my hands. How would anyone know to look for me here behind a solid wall?

As I sat there, I felt a cold presence. Something stirred my hair, skimmed the back of my neck. Tugged at my hand...

My head came up in panic and I lifted the cell phone, but I could see nothing in the gloom.

Was Clayton already here? Terror washed over me and I scooted back against the wall, my eyes wide and searching.

After a moment, the coldness faded and I told myself I'd imagined it. I was still suffering some of the aftereffects of the drugs he'd put in my tea. He must have been

observing me for some time to know my habits well
enough to predict I would have a cup when I came home.
Maybe he had peepholes in Macon's apartment through
which he'd been watching me.

I shivered and wrapped my arms around my middle. I
was cold, scared and so very lost. I thought about Mama
and Papa and Devlin. All the people I cared about. Would
I ever see any of them again?

At some point, I must have dozed off, because I saw
myself fleeing down an endless tunnel where hands
reached through walls to grab me. I ran through rooms of
hanging corpses, ghosts floating at my heels, and somewhere in the distance, always just beyond me, I could
hear Devlin's voice calling out to me. *This way! Hurry!*

But it wasn't Devlin who guided me. It was Shani.

She tugged on my hand, urging me forward. Then,
just ahead of us, I saw the ghost of Robert Fremont. He
hovered beyond the hanging corpses, waiting for us. As
we made our way to him, he turned and disappeared
through the wall.

I could hear footsteps behind us and the sound of dragging chains. Tearing my way through the cobwebs, I
closed my eyes and followed Fremont through the wall.
I looked down at my hand. Shani was gone. For some
reason, she hadn't come through the wall with me. I
wanted to go back for her, but the wall was solid now.
I'd lost her....

With a start, I lifted my head and gazed around. I was
alone in the chamber, but for a moment, I'd felt their presence so strongly...

Struggling to my feet, I walked over to the wall where
I had seen Fremont disappear in my dream. I held up the
cell phone and scrutinized every inch of the wall, finding nothing but badly crumbling mortar.

And then I saw it. My way out.

If a fly had led Devlin and me to that first hidden chamber, another would show me the way out of this one.

I would never have noticed the crack in the wall if not for the iridescent glint of a fly slipping through a tiny hole in the mortar. I traced the fracture with my fingertip.

It was a door of sorts, cut so that the bricks matched up perfectly when fitted into place. Setting aside the phone, I pressed with my hands, then leaned a shoulder against the bricks. Finally, I dropped to the floor and kicked as hard as I could until the panel fell away, revealing another chamber.

The smell of putrefaction rolled out of that opening, along with a black cloud of buzzing flies.

They lit on my arms, my face, my lips. I swatted them away and, pulling my shirt up over my mouth and nose, inched up to the hole with the light. The smell was definitely coming from inside. I gagged and rocked back on my heels, shuddering at what must lie beyond.

Bodies. The ones Daniel hadn't had time to bury.

How many? I wondered.

I've lost count. I tried to be judicious with the selection...chosen only those poor souls that needed freeing...

Ignoring the crawl of tiny legs in my hair, I swung the cell phone light into the opening. More brick walls. More cobwebs. The silhouette of what I feared might be a hanging body.

And that smell. It was everywhere, permeating every crack and crevice, clinging to my clothes, my skin, the inside of my nostrils...

I pulled my shirt tighter against my nose.

As I stepped through the opening, water sloshed over my boots. The smell rose again, stronger than ever, and I wondered about that liquid beneath my feet.

I wouldn't think about it...*couldn't* think about it now....

My feet slipped from under me and I landed with a horrible splash. Water splattered into my face and I screamed. I pulled myself up, gasping and gagging.

Careful of my footing, I eased along in the darkness.

The drone of flies filled my head, making me thankful I couldn't see beyond the anemic illumination of my cell phone.

I walked in a straight line as best I could until I came to another wall, and then I searched and searched until I finally stumbled upon a second opening. Wet and shivering, I crawled through only to find myself in a similar room.

Just when I despaired of ever getting out of that maze of chambers, I crept through yet another hole into a long, narrow tunnel. The air was fresher here and the fetid odor faded. I hoped that meant I was near an outside entrance.

I stood for the longest moment in an agony of indecision. Which way to go? Then I heard footsteps coming up hard behind me, and I didn't wait to see who would emerge from those shadows. Who else could it be but Meakin?

Turning, I fled down the tunnel, the cell phone barely lighting my way.

Scurrying through yet another hole, I found myself in a round, well-like enclosure and I knew exactly where I was. I glanced up and saw the soft lavender of a twilight sky and felt like weeping for joy.

I began to climb. I was almost all the way to the top when I heard footsteps, the scramble of a body through the hole and the clang of the metal ladder as my pursuer came up after me.

He said my name. Just that. *Amelia.* In that soft drawl

I loved so much and I glanced down into Devlin's up-turned face a split second before a hand clamped around my wrist.

I would never have thought Daniel Meakin so strong, but he dragged me through the opening, slammed the cover shut and shot home a bolt that had not been there when Devlin and I had come up through the well weeks before.

Devlin pounded on the door and I tried to get to him, but Daniel grabbed me and I went at him like a demon, clawing, kicking, pounding him with my fists.

He cowered away, then whirled with a knife, slashing the blade across my upper arm. I felt searing pain and a gush of blood as I staggered back and fell to the ground.

He stood over me, but he was no longer alone. Now that twilight had fallen, the ghost of Clayton Masterson had slipped through the veil.

His right hand bound to Meakin's left.

It was Clayton who had slashed my arm…

Daniel whimpered. "You can see him. I know you can. All you have to do is acknowledge him and it will all be over. Please…please…let it be over."

It would be over for him, but not for me. So I did not acknowledge the ghost. I lay with my gaze fixed on Daniel. As blood gushed through my fingers.

He fell to his knees, face crumpling, and for a moment, he and the ghost were caught in a terrible struggle. I saw my chance and lunged for the well. My fingers closed over the bolt and I shot it back just as Daniel rose with the knife. I knew what he meant to do, but Devlin did not. As he flung open the door and came up out of the well, he saw Daniel standing over me with a bloody blade. He couldn't see Clayton. He couldn't know the battle that waged between them.

He called Daniel's name once, twice, and then he fired.

* * *

I lay sprawled on the ground, head spinning.

The paramedics had arrived on the scene. One of them applied pressure to my arm while the others worked on Daniel, but they were too late. I knew the second he died. I saw his spirit drift away, still bound to the ghost of Clayton Masterson. For all eternity.

And then from the corner of my eye, I caught a glimpse of a dark silhouette emerging from the edge of the woods. Then another and another, until they surrounded and engulfed the two ghosts.

The shadow men had not come for me after all. They had come for Daniel Meakin.

My arm would need stitching, but for now the bleeding was under control. I sat at the back of the EMT van, my gaze riveted on Devlin, until I spotted a familiar face lurking in the background. It was odd to me that no one paid him any attention, but then I remembered why.

I walked toward him, a little unsteady from the painkillers. "You were down there with me, weren't you? You showed me the way out." He and Shani had saved me. "Why?"

I could feel his icy gaze on me through his dark glasses. "Because I mean to have justice," said the murdered cop. "And you're the only one who can help me."

"Amelia?"

I turned as Devlin walked up beside me. He stared at me with a strange look on his face. "Who were you talking to?"

I glanced around. No one was there.

He put a hand on my shoulder. "Are you all right?"

"No," I said with a shiver. "But I will be."

I wanted to ask how he'd found me tonight, but at

the moment, it seemed too much trouble. I had a feeling Robert Fremont had played some role. I shuddered to think what his ghost wanted from me, but that was a worry for another day. Right now, I wanted to savor my moment with Devlin.

I laid my head against his chest and he held me so tenderly I wanted to weep.

But the moment was fleeting. Twilight was upon us and his ghosts were waiting.

EPILOGUE

Days later, I still didn't understand how Devlin had found me that night. He said they'd tracked my cell phone signal to the mausoleum, but I didn't see how that was possible when I'd been so far underground. I couldn't shake the notion that Robert Fremont had somehow been instrumental in leading Devlin to me, just as he and Shani had guided me out of the chamber. I was indebted to him, but the thought of what he would require of me made my blood run cold.

So many questions…so many mysteries…

I left it all behind to recuperate in Trinity with my parents. I was there for a week and on my first day back home, I dug up the tiny ring I'd buried in the garden and drove down to Chedathy Cemetery, where I placed it in the center of the cockleshell heart. I suppose I meant it as some sort of thank you or maybe even a farewell, but I had a feeling I would be seeing the ghost child again.

Devlin drove up as I was leaving. If he thought it strange to find me there, he didn't say so. I waited for him at the edge of the cemetery and he caught my hand as he walked by. We stood there for a long moment—I on my way out, he on his way in. I tried to pull away, but he held on to me.

"Are you ever going to tell me what happened that night?" His gaze burned into mine. "Why did you run away from me?"

I shivered and glanced away. "Someday I'll explain. But not now. It's not our time."

He didn't question me because I think he knew it, too. He had his ghosts and I had my demons.

I slid my fingers from his and walked back to the car.

Glancing in the rearview mirror, I saw him standing at the edge of the cemetery looking forlorn, but not alone. Mariama and Shani were on either side of him, their ghosts as intrinsic to him as my loneliness was to me.

But this was not to be a final goodbye. Our story was not yet finished.

I couldn't know at that moment, but somewhere out there, a hidden grave awaited my discovery and I would soon become more determined than ever to uncover my father's secrets.

Directing my gaze to the road, I drove off into the twilight.

* * * * *

ACKNOWLEDGMENTS

It takes a lot of people to bring the germ of an idea to fruition. I'm deeply grateful to the whole MIRA team for helping nurture my vision. A very special thanks to my editor, Denise Zaza, for her tireless advocacy and endless patience. To Lisa Wray and Alana Burke for their enthusiasm and expertise. And to the Art Department for their stunning visual interpretation of my story.

My admiration and appreciation goes to Funhouse—Leanne Amann, Lucas Amann and David Warner—for bringing so much creativity and originality to the Graveyard Queen vision.

Thanks to Mary Talbot for answering all my cemetery questions and to Kathy D. and Lucas A. for sharing their ghost stories.

Many thanks also to all the book bloggers who have helped get the word out. You know who you are—you've made all the difference.

And finally, I'm so grateful to my agent, Lisa Erbach Vance, for taking a chance, keeping the faith and always having my back.